LETHAL AGENT

Hasan struggled to stay conscious. The boot of a tall man was planted on his chest, and he looked up at the two 9mm automatics pointed at his head. The man standing on his chest shifted his other foot onto Hasan's right wrist, forcing the dagger out of his hand, while a second, heavyset man maintained his aim on his head. The heavier man was wearing an enormous diamond ring on his hairy ring finger—and Hasan recognized him with a shock. *Who is this man who killed Kemal and will now kill me?* he thought. *Mafia? Government?* His gaze drifted to the man's mouth, where a sinister smile had begun to f⋯⋯⋯⋯⋯⋯⋯⋯⋯ned. Hasan knew what ⋯⋯⋯

And ther⋯⋯⋯⋯⋯⋯⋯⋯⋯⋯⋯ould-be killers disappe⋯⋯⋯⋯⋯⋯⋯⋯⋯⋯san initially couldn't gr⋯⋯⋯⋯⋯⋯⋯⋯ *dead now,* he thought ⋯⋯⋯⋯⋯⋯⋯? Only then did he hear ⋯⋯⋯⋯⋯⋯⋯⋯ gun. Aaron had let loose a continuous cannonade of fire, as many as fifty rounds in all, fired on the run. As a result, Hasan's assailants were hurled into the air and flung against the nearby wall.

They were dead before impact.

Also by Stan Johnson

ONCE A RANGER

Published by Signet

LETHAL AGENT

Stan Johnson

A SIGNET BOOK

SIGNET
Published by New American Library, a division of
Penguin Group (USA) Inc., 375 Hudson Street,
New York, New York 10014, USA
Penguin Group (Canada), 10 Alcorn Avenue, Toronto,
Ontario M4V 3B2, Canada (a division of Pearson Penguin Canada Inc.)
Penguin Books Ltd., 80 Strand, London WC2R 0RL, England
Penguin Ireland, 25 St. Stephen's Green, Dublin 2,
Ireland (a division of Penguin Books Ltd.)
Penguin Group (Australia), 250 Camberwell Road, Camberwell, Victoria 3124,
Australia (a division of Pearson Australia Group Pty. Ltd.)
Penguin Books India Pvt. Ltd., 11 Community Centre, Panchsheel Park,
New Delhi - 110 017, India
Penguin Group (NZ), cnr Airborne and Rosedale Roads, Albany,
Auckland 1310, New Zealand (a division of Pearson New Zealand Ltd.)
Penguin Books (South Africa) (Pty.) Ltd., 24 Sturdee Avenue,
Rosebank, Johannesburg 2196, South Africa

Penguin Books Ltd., Registered Offices:
80 Strand, London WC2R 0RL, England

First published by Signet, an imprint of New American Library,
a division of Penguin Group (USA) Inc.

First Printing, February 2005
10 9 8 7 6 5 4 3 2 1

Copyright © Stanley M. Johnson, 2005
All rights reserved

 REGISTERED TRADEMARK—MARCA REGISTRADA

Printed in the United States of America

PUBLISHER'S NOTE
This is a work of fiction. Names, characters, places, and incidents either are
the product of the author's imagination or are used fictitiously, and any resemblance to actual persons, living or dead, business establishments, events, or
locales is entirely coincidental.

To Ken and Mary,
my parents,
and
Al and Jessie,
my wife's parents

ACKNOWLEDGMENTS

Once again, I find myself totally indebted to Nora, my wife, for her great editing and rewriting skills. An author in her own right, she nonetheless took a great deal of time away from her screenwriting to edit *Lethal Agent* before it went to my official editor, Doug Grad at New American Library. I could not have done this without her.

Thanks to doctors Carl Schiff and Eric Weiselberg for their advice and input on the medical and pharmacological aspects of this work; to Doug Grad at New American Library for all of his valuable input and advice; and to Leily Lashkari and Lili Taheri, colleagues at my law firm, for their help with Farsi.

Special thanks to a bunch of very impressive people: the Delta Force operators, Night Stalkers, Rangers, SEALs, and others of the U.S. Special Operations Command (SOCOM) who are out there doing incredible things at great risk to themselves with no publicity or fanfare to keep us safe from the terrorists. We owe them much more than most of us realize, and we need more of them.

As always, thanks to my three children for being patient (well, relatively so) with me and my wife as we wrote this book.

ONE

"Get in closer," the Turkish Army captain urged his lieutenant, his voice barely audible, eyes adjusting to the darkness. "All I can make out is the sound of machinery in the building. Can you hear what they're saying?"

Lieutenant Hasan Ertugrul shook his head. "Four men . . . I think they're the Iranians who got off the truck, two from the cab, two from the rear. They're in fatigues, but it looks like they have no rank insignia or name tags. The ones in back have submachine guns. I couldn't tell if the men in front are armed," the lieutenant whispered. "There must be at least ten local Georgians inside the warehouse, maybe more from the sound of it. They're wearing civvies."

Captain Bulot was about to respond, but stopped abruptly when he saw a bright yellow forklift approach the truck that the four men in fatigues had just driven into the large bay doors of the plant. Bulot and Ertugrul, temporarily assigned from the Turk First Commando Brigade to the Turkish National Intelligence Organization, better known by its Turkish initials, MIT, stood on the Central Pier between two rows of shipping containers piled four high. Their position was safe for the moment, but from the confines of the container stacks they could see only a part of what was going on in Building 15.

The southern harbor of the Black Sea port of Poti was deceptively quiet. It would not officially come alive for another four hours, when workers showed up for the seven o'clock shift. The lights in the warehouse were bright; no one bothered to close the two huge doors behind the heroin-filled truck after it entered. Inside, workers were pulling back the canvas that covered the bed of the vehicle, permitting the forklift operator to slide the prongs under the pallets of heroin bricks and remove them to a part of the building that Captain Bulot and Lieutenant Ertugrul could not see from their present position. The Georgians in civvies milled about with AK-47 assault rifles strapped casually over their shoulders, the weapons bouncing sloppily against their backs as they walked. The men believed to be Iranians watched protectively as the cache was transferred to the depot.

Even at a distance of forty meters, Captain Kemal Bulot observed that the men in fatigues appeared tired. Three leaned heavily against a loaded pallet. One, who Bulot thought to be the leader, barely kept himself upright, his shoulders hunched, a cigarette dangling from his lips. Bulot noted that no one in or near the building seemed to have any fear of being detected, and guessed that the right Georgian officials had been sufficiently bribed. The Turkish officers took stock of their enemy. There were four men in fatigues—thought to be Iranians. At least two were heavily armed. He assumed that all four were professionals and would fight well if confronted, no matter how tired they appeared. The local Georgians were paid thugs who would most likely panic if the two Turk commandos were to open fire. Still, there were many of them, and Bulot's mission was not to make contact but to find out what they and the Iranians were doing in the narcotics business.

"Hasan," Captain Bulot whispered, "I'm going to work my way around that grain elevator over there"—he indicated with a wave of his handgun to his left—"and come up behind Building 15 on the side opposite the pier. We need to know what's going on inside. You pull back behind these containers and move west twenty or thirty meters so you can see more directly into the warehouse and the freighter tied to the pier. If our intelligence is right, the Italian Mafia is purchasing the heroin from the Iranians. The Italians run the ship. Watch out. They're no doubt heavily armed."

Captain Bulot patted his good friend on the shoulder. Their eyes locked on each other, aware of the danger. Crouching low, his 9 mm automatic clutched firmly in his hand, Bulot clung to the shadows of the shipping containers until he reached the end of the stacks next to the intersection of two narrow gravel lanes. A half-moon appeared intermittently between passing clouds that only an hour before had dumped an inch of rain on the port. The grain elevator was forty-five meters away. Careful not to splash in the deep puddles, Bulot darted across the intersection. Ducking into the shadows at the base of the grain elevator, he paused to see if anyone had spotted him. The concrete structure was comprised of ten cylindrical silos, two rows side by side, each six stories high. Silence. He breathed a sigh of relief, exhaling softly. So cautiously did he proceed that it took him a full ten minutes to reach the south side of Building 15. He was sweating now despite the cool, early October air. His right hand was slick on the pistol grip. He switched the weapon to his left hand and wiped the palm of his right hand on his pants leg, checked to see that his Glock was in the fire mode and inched his way forward.

As Captain Bulot approached, he saw three small windows spaced evenly on the side of Building 15, each barely a half-meter square. The nearest one was closed but the next was open, pushed outward at the bottom. Years of accumulated soot on the windowpane obscured the view, but what he saw through the opening confirmed MIT's intelligence reports. Men in clean white smocks worked at conveyor belts, first removing what appeared to be bags of heroin from trays stacked at each workstation, and then, as half-liter cans bearing labels marked TOMATO PUREE in English and Italian moved down the belt, placing the bags inside the cans. Bulot estimated that about one-third of the cans were equipped with hidden compartments for the contraband. After the hidden compartment was sealed, the can rounded to the next workstation, where it was filled with tomato puree and sealed. Farther down the assembly line, each can was stamped with a bar code. Rounding yet another curve on the belt, the cans were loaded into cardboard boxes that were also bar coded. Bulot couldn't see what was happening on the other side of the building, but he was sure the boxes were piled on pallets, shrink-wrapped and then loaded onto the Italian ship that he and Lieutenant Ertugrul had spotted earlier.

The sophistication of the operations surprised Bulot, but the heroin traffic was not what his superiors at the MIT were primarily interested in. Heroin trafficking was out of character for the hard-line mullahs who ruled Iran. In fact, they would readily mete out the death sentence to their countrymen who dealt in the addictive drug. No, the Iranians had another agenda, and he was determined to find out what that was. He inched forward along the side of the building, nearer to where the soldiers had been sitting just moments before. The northernmost window was only five meters from the front of the building, close to the gravel road that led to the entrance, and it was open. His back would be exposed, but a midsize Dumpster would offer him some measure of protection from an approaching vehicle.

The pane was as grimy as the one he had just peered through, but the acoustics were better. Two of the men he had presumed to be Iranians were seated just two meters from the open window, and though they spoke in hushed tones, he could hear them clearly. What Bulot overheard stunned him. The men in fatigues were currently speaking in Arabic, not Farsi. Yet prior intelligence indicated they spoke in Farsi and carried Iranian passports. Captain Bulot was fluent in Farsi, having first studied it in high school in Turkey and then later as an exchange cadet at West Point, where he had excelled. As he watched and listened, one of the men rose from the overturned plastic tub on which he sat, stretched and began to walk toward the huge open doors through which he had previously driven the truck. It was the opportunity Captain Bulot had hoped for. If the man ventured far enough away from the building, they would knock him out and somehow get him back to Turkey, where they could extract from him the details of their operation and find out who they really were.

Bulot stepped back from the window, crouched low and inched his way toward the corner of Building 15. Sweat streamed down the back of his neck. He was no more than a meter from the corner of the building when a late model Mercedes with Georgian government license plates careened down the gravel lane behind him, splashing noisily as its tires hit the huge rain-filled puddles. Bulot leapt back into the shadows, seeking refuge behind the Dumpster, and landing with a horrific clatter on several empty paint cans. He gripped his Glock tighter.

Bulot hoped that the approaching vehicle would enter Building 15 like the truck before it, but instead the Mercedes pulled in front, its headlights illuminating the side of the warehouse. He thrust himself against the Dumpster, away from the beam, but he was too late. The bodyguard in the front passenger's seat and the man in the left rear had already spotted him, their attention having been drawn to the sound of the falling paint cans. With a resolve born of equal parts desperation and military training, Bulot rose from his failed hiding site, gripped his right wrist with his left hand and fired twice at the bodyguard who had just jumped out of the left rear door, his submachine gun at the ready. The first shot hit the man square in the sternum, plowed a tunnel through his heart and lodged against his spinal column. The second bullet hit him in the throat and exited behind his ear. He stumbled backward, the base of his spine against the black car, and slid slowly to a seated position on the gravel. Death came to him before he could fire a shot. In an instant, Bulot turned his attention to the guard who had been sitting in the front passenger's seat and who was now standing on the opposite side of the car from Bulot. The Georgian was uncharacteristically tall and made an easy target as he raised his Russian-made submachine gun toward the Turkish captain. Bulot swiveled slightly and fired three times. The first bullet hit the man in the stomach, the second penetrated precisely two inches above the first and the third another two inches above the second, each bullet climbing up the man's torso, the result of the violent kick of the powerful weapon despite Bulot's effort to steady the Glock in his hands.

Five shots fired, five bullets remaining in his clip before he would have to reload. The enemy was engaged, and he and his lieutenant were terribly outnumbered. Bulot turned to his right and raced with all his speed toward the grain elevator. As he crossed the opening between the buildings, he prayed that Lieutenant Ertugrul would follow his prior orders and stay out of sight. To engage in battle against so many would be useless and only get both of them killed. The only valid strategy was to flee.

Captain Bulot had run no more than ten meters when he saw the flash of light. That it came from the direction of the grain elevator surprised him. He had not anticipated that the enemy could assemble there so quickly. He had expected to hear the bullets whiz by him from the back, from Building 15, but instead they hit him in the front of his left thigh, hip, ribs and shoulder, spinning him around, tossing him to the ground. Bulot landed in a puddle, immediately rolling from his back to his belly and readying his automatic, searching for a target in the faint moonlight. He saw men running. Two, maybe three, from the direction of the bullets that had just hit him. Several more could be heard in the darkness next to the outer wall of the warehouse, near the northeast corner. Captain Bulot fired five times at the men approaching from the grain elevator, hitting one fatally and wounding another. The third grabbed his wounded comrade and together they retreated, giving Bulot a chance to put a fresh magazine in the Glock. He fired off a few more rounds, then held his fire, looking for targets in the dark.

From his position northwest of Building 15, Lieutenant Ertugrul heard the gunfire but could not see what was happening. The distinctive sounds of a Glock 9 mm and AK-47 assault rifles told him that the news was bad. His instinct told him to run to his captain's aid, to save his friend. But those were not his orders. He was under strict instructions from Captain Bulot to escape and get back to Turkey. The lieutenant chose to get closer to the scene of the fighting to see if a diversion was possible. He ran along the wall formed by the stacked shipping containers, and dropped to the ground when he could get no closer. The headlights of the Mercedes were still on, and the driver was repositioning the vehicle so that its lights would shine directly on Captain Bulot, who was now taking fire from the directions of the warehouse and the grain elevator.

Captain Bulot, a friend and mentor to Lieutenant Ertugrul, lay unprotected, wounded but still returning fire. Bulot could not see the lieutenant but sensed he was somewhere near the towering stacks of containers. *Run, Hasan, run,* he wanted to cry out. Willing himself to his feet, with five rounds left, he got off three shots in the direction of the enemy to cover Ertugrul's escape.

Despite his military training, Lieutenant Ertugrul was in a near panic. He had the ability to kill a few of the men who would kill Bulot, but he knew that if he did so, his position would be revealed and he, too, would die. He also understood that his friend's fate was sealed either way. He shivered involuntarily as he watched Bulot take several shots to his chest and fall backward. As the predators advanced toward their stricken prey, Lieutenant Ertugrul finally retreated into the shadows in the narrow passageway between the containers, shaking with anger and frustration.

A heavyset man wearing a suit opened the right rear door of the Mercedes and stepped out, motioning to one of the others to hand him an AK-47. He approached Captain Bulot slowly, methodically, as if he were enjoying himself. Several soldiers in fatigues followed him, assault rifles positioned. Lieutenant Ertugrul could not hear what was said, but the man in the suit stood over Bulot and appeared to be talking to him. For a moment, the lieutenant held out some hope that Bulot would be taken prisoner, but as he watched in horror, the man slowly raised the assault rifle, pointed the barrel directly at the captain's forehead and fired.

Lieutenant Ertugrul retreated farther into the maze of containers, cautiously making his way from the South Pier, where Building 15 stood, toward the Central Pier, where a change of clothing and passports for both him and Captain Bulot had been stashed. It took him two full days to get back to Turkey, days during which he spent every minute plotting his revenge against the heroin traffickers he still believed to be led by Iranians.

Like his older brother, who called himself Faramaz ben Sarah, Yaakov claimed to be an Iranian Jew who had escaped from the Islamic Revolution. With the American authorities profiling Arabs, it had been worth the effort to learn Farsi, the language of Iran, and Jewish culture, thus gaining the cover that being a Jewish refugee provided. Like his brother and mentor, the young man was of formidable intellect, courage and determination. His résumé was impressive: Ph.D. in neurobiology from Washington University in St. Louis, where he had also received his master's degree, with honors, and where he conducted postdoctoral research in neuromuscular disorders. During his years in St. Louis, he had taken a wife, who called herself Gita, a brilliant and dedicated woman. Yaakov and Gita had a daughter, Dinah, now seven.

While studying in St. Louis, Yaakov made contact with another couple, Ramin and Sheri ben Peeran, both biochemistry graduate students at St. Louis University and recruited by Faramaz. They too had presented themselves to the U.S. Immigration and Naturalization Service as Jewish escapees from the ayatollahs and had gained acceptance within the university community, so effective in their language and cultural skills that they were convincing even to real Iranian Jews.

In late 1998, Yaakov completed his postgraduate work and moved his family across the river to Belleville, Illinois, close enough to Washington University but physically and psychologically separated enough by the Mississippi River to be somewhat isolated from his former professors and postgraduate students. The couple from St. Louis University also moved to Belleville and joined Yaakov in forming a new business, NMS Biologics, Inc., a biotechnology company specializing in the therapeutic use of the *Clostridium botulinum* bacterium, or rather the toxin produced by it, to treat neuromuscular spasms and contractions associated with cerebral palsy, Huntington's disease, multiple sclerosis, Parkinson's disease and other disorders. Soon, they began to raise money from disease-specific charitable foundations and from government grants.

The Chamber of Commerce of Belleville was thrilled to see Ph.D.s from across the river establish a biotechnology company in the community. Local politicians and the state officials in Springfield, encouraged by the promise of high-end jobs on the east side and the prospect of finding a treatment, if not a cure, for some of mankind's most debilitating and heart-wrenching diseases, arranged for research grants. The company obtained a lease, subsidized in part by the state, in a nondescript building behind a popular catering hall, near Illinois Highway 159 and Interstate 64, a centrally located transportation hub.

Yaakov's family rented a modest but relatively new three-bedroom clapboard ranch on Village Drive, while their friends and business partners, Ramin and Shari, settled into a renovated farmhouse on Old Caseyville Road. Both homes were in the Wolf Branch school district, the best in the area, as would be expected of parents who were themselves highly educated. While the fathers showed little interest in school functions, the mothers eagerly participated in the PTA and frequently volunteered to help out the class mothers with school trips and fund-raising. The two families fit right in.

The process took longer and cost more than initially planned, but by early winter 2003, NMS Biologics was up and running with a U.S. Food and Drug Administration–approved Biosafety Level-4 laboratory, in which they produced *Clostridium botulinum* toxin for legitimate research purposes, and in which, on weekends, Yaakov and his cohorts manufactured up to five grams a week of an enhanced form of botulinum-A, the most deadly toxin known to man.

TWO

Aaron Korda embraced General Bulot warmly and then hugged Kemal Bulot's mother, tears streaming down her cheeks. The funeral for his good friend would have been extremely difficult under any circumstances. It was all the more so because Captain Bulot's body remained somewhere in Poti, Georgia, not in Bebek, an affluent suburb north of Istanbul where Lieutenant General Bulot and his wife lived in retirement, or on the nearby army base where the services took place. Their son, Aaron's roommate at West Point for two years, left behind a beautiful wife and two children.

"Kemal was a brother to me," Aaron said in fluent Turkish to General Bulot. "He taught me your language and so much more. He was a great soldier. I would have been proud to serve with him in combat."

The soldier within Bulot fought to maintain composure, but the father in him won out. The general, former commander of the Turkish tank corps, broke down and cried quietly upon hearing Aaron's words. His son had loved this brash American, whom he, as an exchange cadet from the Turkish Military Academy, had first met at West Point. General Bulot embraced Aaron. "My son had great respect for you. He told me that you served with honor in Iraq during the first war and also in Mogadishu. He was so proud of you. He thought that you would have ultimately become a general, had you stayed in. I'd like to think that Kemal would have, too."

Aaron stepped away from the general and Mrs. Bulot,

ostensibly to give the general a moment to collect himself and to allow the throngs of family and army officers to pay their respects. But once standing apart, Aaron wasted no time, anxiously scanning the crowd, searching for the name tag belonging to Lieutenant Hasan Ertugrul. He approached several younger officers, asking if they knew the whereabouts of Lieutenant Ertugrul. After a series of suspicious shrugs, a captain wearing a First Commando patch nodded knowingly and pointed to a young man in uniform who stood with a woman and a small boy on the far side of the officers' club. Even from across the room, Aaron could see that his eyes were puffy, his complexion ashen. As he neared, Aaron was sure that the lieutenant had not slept in days.

"Lieutenant Ertugrul? My name is Aaron Korda. Kemal and I were roommates at West Point," Aaron said softly as he extended his hand, surprising Ertugrul and his wife with his easy command of Turkish. "May I speak with you for a moment?" His demeanor and tone signaled to the wife that he needed to speak privately with her husband but that no disrespect was intended. She nodded to Aaron and then to Hasan, hoping the American could somehow console her husband. Aaron noted that she was pregnant. Seven months, he guessed.

Aaron led the lieutenant out of the officers' club and down a long series of steps. They walked a short distance to the street and stopped near a truck that blocked them from view of anyone who might have followed. "You witnessed Kemal's murder?" Aaron whispered, wasting no time with idle talk.

"Yes, but I did what Kemal ordered me to do," the lieutenant began, momentarily looking away from Aaron as he felt his eyes well with tears. "He was my friend. He was my captain and I . . ."

Aaron read the uncertainty and proceeded cautiously. "I don't doubt that you did everything you could, Lieutenant," Aaron continued, his tone softer but still businesslike. "Kemal was an excellent soldier, an excellent commander. He would not have chosen you if you were not worthy of the First Commando Brigade." Hasan said nothing, as he thought of Kemal's last moments and how helpless he had been to save him. "I assume you could find your way back to that warehouse in Poti?" The lieutenant nodded slowly, wondering what the American really wanted and whether he could trust him. "Would you recognize the men who killed Kemal?"

"I think so," Lieutenant Ertugrul said, still tentative but starting to feel stronger than he had since witnessing his friend's death.

"I understand from my sources that your government has chosen not to pursue the investigation that led you and Kemal to Poti. . . . A shift in priorities or something." Ertugrul nodded, trying not to appear bitter but still reeling from the news that he, too, had heard earlier that morning. Aaron smiled tightly and continued. "The MIT and the Turkish government will pretend this did not happen, and they will do nothing. That's how it works. But I'm not bound by their rules. Can you recruit two or three of your and Kemal's men . . . soldiers we can trust from the First Commando? Can you take a few days' leave and come with me to Poti?"

"What do you have in mind?" Lieutenant Ertugrul asked, his voice more firm, intrigued by the American's direct approach and inspired by the resolve he saw in his eyes.

"We will do what your government cannot . . . or will not do. We're going to find the men who murdered Kemal and bring them to justice." Lieutenant Ertugrul stared into Aaron's eyes, seeking clarification. "We are going to kill them."

"This is Dark Eagle. Repeat, this is Dark Eagle. Do you copy?"

"Copy, Dark Eagle. This is Spider One. We're approaching Syrian air space."

"Spider Three copies. I read you five-by-five." The chopper pilot's voice signaled confidence and controlled excitement. Like the other Night Stalkers, she thrived on the rush of a nighttime covert mission. Aside from her family, a husband and a three-year-old boy back in Kentucky, this is what Lieutenant Pamela Toll lived for.

"Spider Two copies," the chopper pilot responded. "I need one of Harry Potter's invisibility cloaks," he added with a laugh.

"Roger that. You got it," the pilot of the U.S. Air Force EA-6B Prowler said to the pilots of the three Army UH-60K Black Hawk helicopters nearing the remote northeast sector of Syria. The choppers, code named Spiders One, Two and Three, were piloted and crewed by members of the 160th Special Operations Aviation Regiment (Airborne), the Night Stalkers, as they called themselves. They were a long way from their homes at Fort Campbell, Kentucky, but each pilot, copilot and crew chief had eagerly volunteered for the assignment. They, like their "customers," the Delta Force operators each chopper carried, were trained for nighttime operations. This was their third run deep into Syrian territory in two weeks.

The Prowler was equipped with the world's most powerful airborne electronic jamming devices. Its mission tonight was to circle above the Black Hawks at fifteen thousand feet and jam all Syrian antiaircraft radar so the choppers could not be seen electronically. The cloud cover was thick at two thousand feet, the moon a slender crescent in the night sky. The Black Hawks would be safe as long as they remained at their current 4,100 feet. When they dropped to treetop level, the Prowler could not help them against machine gun fire or rocket-propelled grenades.

Lieutenant Colonel Martin Korda sat on the floor in the rear of the Black Hawk, shifting his weight to ease the throbbing in his left hip, his carbine/grenade launcher in hand. He surveyed the cabin. Staff Sergeant Chris Shafter sat on the floor, his legs outstretched, cradling his M-60 machine gun on his lap, stroking it like he would his golden retriever back home. The other Deltas onboard held their respective weapons as gingerly and as fondly as Shafter did his. Sergeant First Class Brown, a pious Catholic from Providence, Rhode Island, fingering a rosary, praying that the mission would succeed and all would return safely to Turkey, sat on an ammo crate next to Sergeant First Class Ross Joyner. Staff Sergeant Juarez of the 160th SOAR(A), a crew chief manning the six-barreled Gatling gun on the right mount, rubbed gunsmith's oil on the barrel of the weapon. It didn't need the lubricant, but it was Juarez's way of steeling his nerves. At the left gunner's mount, Sergeant McCarthy, also a Night Stalker from the 160th and the lowest-ranking soldier present, gently ran his fingers along the link-belt that fed ammo into the voraciously hungry Gatling gun. Sergeant First Class Pawhuska, a direct descendant of a chief of the Big Osage Indians, nicknamed Red Eagle after another Osage chief from his native Missouri, sharpened his Gerber Mark II commando knife, as was his custom in the lull before a mission. The blade was already razor sharp, but he honed it, anyway. Master Sergeant Crocker, the electronics and communications specialist and an avid guitar player, sat lotus style with his legs folded in front of him, tapping the palm of his hand gently against his knee, keeping the beat with music only he could hear. Staff Sergeant Galante stared at nothing in particular, the heel of his boot padding rhythmically on the aluminum floor, his M-60 held against his chest, the barrel pointed upward. First Sergeant Trippe slept, a skill that never ceased to baffle his fellow commandos. Staff Sergeant Gonzales, Chalk One's medic, reexamined his kit and the extras onboard that would be dropped to him if the supply of IV bags, Corlex, morphine, syringes, antibiotics and other supplies he carried with him were to run out. All commo gear was checked and rechecked; the microphones and receivers in each of the nine operators' helmets were working fine. Chalk One, Delta Force, was ready.

Martin Korda closed his eyes and listened to the hum of the twin turbines and the staccato *pop-pop-pop* of the rotors. It was their third mission into Syria. He had personally conceived of the plan as part of his annual lecture series given at the Army War College, not really expecting it to be carried out. Titled "Special Operations Theory, Out-of-the-Box Solutions," his two-week seminar and workshop for senior army officers was the most popular course each summer. Consisting of a series of extremely difficult situations fraught with seemingly insurmountable obstacles, the task for the breakout groups after each lecture was to find an answer, any answer, as long as it worked. Conventional thinking, army doctrine, even the law were to be discarded. The only thing that mattered for purposes of the seminar was to solve the problem and win.

One particular lecture and problem-solving session caught the attention of General Gus Hall, commander of the combined Special Operations Command, or SOCOM. How, Lieutenant Colonel Korda had asked, can the United States assure itself that Iraqis had not moved biochemical laboratories and weapons to Syria before or after the U.S.-led invasion? Some evidence existed that these labs were at some point in time operating in the Iraqi cities of Samarra, Al-Ramadi, An Najaf and Al-Fallujah, yet after the invasion no hard proof of Saddam's biochemical weapons program could be found. There were some indications that Iraqis had set up facilities in the Syrian cities of Hassake, Raqqa, Deir ez-Zur and Aleppo. But world opinion would not sanction, let alone join, yet another full-scale invasion of an Arab country by the United States.

As the instructor, Korda had called for those attending his seminar to come up with solutions as to how the army should address the problem. Some of the attending officers argued that the answer lay within the UN. Others countered that America should go it alone and invade Syria with forces currently in Iraq, perhaps in conjunction with an Israeli attack from the west. Korda had a different solution: nighttime raids on the suspected Syrian facilities by helicopter-borne Delta

Force teams of eight to ten operators per chopper, who would attack targets known to be innocuous while at the same time planting eavesdropping devices on nearby buildings that were really suspected of housing the bio-chemical facilities.

He had given the example of Deir ez-Zur. Intelligence reports indicated that the hospital might have a bio-chemical lab in its basement. Iraqis were known to hide such facilities in schools and hospitals in Iraq because they believed the Americans would never bomb them. It was believed that they were doing the same in Syria. Delta Force would deliberately go after the wrong target, which in the case of Deir ez-Zur was a school, and search it, purposely leaving traces of their having been in the building. While files and documents in the school were being rifled and the building defended, if necessary, another Delta Force squad would secretly plant listening devices on the basement windows and foundation of the nearby mosque. One or more receivers/transmitters would be placed on the roof to pick up the signals from the bugs below, amplify them and transmit them to NSA satellites circling above in space. If the plan worked, the recorded conversations, it was hoped, would provide the evidence the United States needed to prove to its allies that the Iraqi exiles were continuing to produce bio-chemical weapons.

That very evening, General Hall had pulled Lieutenant Colonel Korda aside and discussed the operation with him well into the night. Ten days later, Operation Shell Game was given the go-ahead. One month later, Lieutenant Colonel Korda and his handpicked team of elite Delta Force operators, along with helicopters, crew and maintenance personnel from the 160th, were air-lifted under the tightest security to Incirlik Air Base in southern Turkey. Although the air force pilots and crew who manned the Prowlers, and Air Force Brigadier General Richard Davies, commander of the Thirty-ninth Wing, Sixteenth Air Division at Incirlik, knew that the Delta operators were making incursions into Syria, even they had not been briefed as to the true objectives of the top secret mission.

As the Black Hawks approached Deir ez-Zur, the hypnotic staccato beating of the rotors above him, Martin folded his arms against the cool October winds that rushed through the open side panels to conserve body heat. It reminded him of the cold winds back at Fort Drum when he was growing up as an army brat, and his thoughts turned to his younger brother. In many ways, Aaron had been the better soldier. His grades had been higher at West Point than Martin's. Aaron had a gift for languages. He had also shown exceptional bravery and skill in both Desert Storm and Somalia. Yet Aaron had found the army lifestyle too limiting, and had longed for greater riches. Breaking with three generations of Korda family tradition, Aaron had resigned his commission when his mandatory five-year stint was up. Martin recalled how hard he had been on Aaron then. It had put a strain on everyone and had frayed the bond that held the brothers together. Now, years later, as he prepared for the raid on Deir ez-Zur, Martin wondered what his brother was doing at this very moment. Within the Korda family, only Martin knew that Aaron was a special consultant to the CIA.

The Black Hawk suddenly jinked right and upward as the pilot and copilot instinctively pulled away from the bright trail of a Syrian SAM streaking through the night sky three kilometers to the east.

"Bastards are shooting blind," Eulas Cole, Spider One's pilot, said evenly into his speaker to the Night Stalkers and Deltas onboard and to Spiders Two and Three behind and to either side of him, the formation of helos forming a V. "The Prowler's got 'em jammed good." Another surface-to-air missile burned skyward a few miles in front of them. "Their radar ain't for shit. They're launching in the dark, hoping to hit something."

"In seven minutes, we're going to take this bird over to the river and shoot south a few feet above the surface. The Prowler's electronic jamming equipment won't do us any good at that level. McCarthy, you got enough good luck charms to get us all through this?"

"Roger that," Sergeant McCarthy, one of the two crew chiefs onboard, responded into his mouthpiece. He looked to Staff Sergeant Orlando Juarez, the other crew chief, who nodded and checked his shoulder harness and seat belt. Like synchronized swimmers, McCarthy and Juarez swiveled their Gatling guns, flipping off their safety features at the same time, ready for business. Crew chiefs in Spiders Two and Three did the same.

"Spiders Two and Three. Do you copy?" Eulas Cole asked.

"Spider Three copies five-by-five."

"This is Spider Two. That's a rog."

"This is Aaron Korda," Lieutenant Hasan Ertugrul said as he introduced the former American Ranger to his fellow First Commandos. "He was Kemal's roommate at West Point and they were like brothers." Aaron smiled and held out his hand. "Be careful," Ertugrul warned the commandos, "he speaks Turkish fluently." Aaron laughed heartily and the two shook hands with him enthusiastically. It wasn't often that an American would go to the trouble to speak their language.

Aaron approvingly studied the two men, both of whom wore the First Commando unit patch and beret. The mission would be challenging, and Ertugrul appeared to have chosen well. The first, a master sergeant, looked as if he might be able to kick a hole in an armored personnel carrier. He stood only five feet seven inches tall, but his shoulders and chest were enormous, and his legs, although short for his physique, looked powerful. The second soldier, a staff sergeant, was taller and leaner, conveying none of the physical strength of the first. Yet there was something about the steady gaze of his coal black eyes that signaled calm demeanor under fire, something that seemed even more lethal than his physically stronger counterpart.

"Kemal Bulot was my very good friend," Aaron said.

"He was my commander and a very good officer," Staff Sergeant Yusuf Ciller said simply. Master Sergeant Naim Sukur nodded.

Aaron smiled. *Men of few words,* he thought. *Men of action.* "Sergeant Ciller, Lieutenant Ertugrul tells me that you're from Trabzon," Aaron said, "and that you're an expert in explosives." Am I correct that Trabzon is a Black Sea port town, of a couple hundred thousand people, close to Turkey's border with Georgia?" Ciller nodded, his expression revealing nothing. "Think you can get us enough C4 to blow up that building that Kemal had under surveillance?" Ciller nodded again, this time a hint of a grin forming on his lips. Aaron paused, his eyes moving from one man to the other. "Are you in?"

"Yes, sir," the two recruits said simultaneously.

"Three or four kilos of C4 should do the trick. . . . Less if we can add gasoline," Aaron said, focusing on Ciller. "According to Lieutenant Ertugrul, who was there and saw the warehouse, it's only made of corrugated sheet metal on a frame of steel beams. We don't need to flatten the support columns—just take off the roof, sides and wipe out everything inside." Yusuf listened intently. "We'll need weapons. Submachine guns, assault rifles, handguns. Use your judgment. Go to Trabzon and get them. This should cover it," Aaron said, handing Ciller a wad of one-hundred-dollar bills the size of a fist.

"Yes, sir," Yusuf responded, nodding decisively.

Aaron continued. "The rest of us will meet you in Trabzon in two days. We'll steal a car and head to Georgia. I hear the border is porous at night on the backcountry roads; we shouldn't have any trouble getting through. I'll bring enough one-hundred-dollar bills to grease the palms of any border guard who needs encouragement. We'll take out the warehouse in the dead of night, find a boat and head back to Trabzon by water. Any questions?"

The two sergeants shook their heads solemnly, without taking their eyes off Aaron's. Aaron turned to Lieutenant Ertugrul and asked if he had anything to add. The Turkish officer stared at the American for a moment, saluted and said, *"Çok teşekkuaur ederim."* (Thank you very much.)

THREE

"This woman here is Russian, but speaks Polish perfectly and uses it to hide the fact that she's working for the Russian Mob. Her boyfriend is Leonid Lenozofsky, a wealthy businessman who lives primarily in Geneva. We believe she was connected with the Mafia's effort to import bootleg over-the-counter painkillers throughout the European Union." Gerhard Schmidt, a division head within Abteilung Eins, the Operations Directorate of the German CIA, or Bundesnachrichtendienst, paused to take a sip of water, and then continued. "When the Americans brought down that operation, there was not enough proof against her so she was not prosecuted. Right after that, she went into hiding. She was spotted in Geneva two weeks ago, and in Istanbul this past Monday. Bäcker, you and Kerschner will track her, shifting teams as per standard procedures with Ostettler and Mencken. Any questions?"

The two male-female teams of field agents singled out by Schmidt nodded to each other, but had no questions. The skies over northern Germany were unusually clear and the air crisp and dry. The BND agents were ready for some down time on the fashionable streets of Berlin, as opposed to the more far-flung and less hospitable locales around the world where they were often stationed.

"Do you need all of us to stay?" Michelle Bäcker asked. "If not, I'm going to do some shopping." She looked at Schmidt and shrugged with a smile.

"I suppose there's no need for you to stick around,"

Schmidt said, looking over his notes. "Buy me something nice," he said with a laugh.

"This guy," he continued, clicking to the next frame, "is American. We think he works under some sort of special arrangement for the CIA, but we have no proof." He pressed the button in his left hand and directed his laser marker to the PowerPoint slide that appeared behind him. A red dot showed brightly on the American's face. "His name is Aaron Korda. He's a vice president with the prominent New York consulting firm of Heller and Clarke, specializing in advising pharmaceutical, biotech and petrochemical companies. Korda speaks German fluently. We believe he has engaged in industrial espionage and reconnaissance against our pharmaceutical enterprises."

Schmidt continued his briefing on Aaron Korda to the eighteen remaining field agents, but his words were lost on Kristina Sturm. She was in shock, but tried not to show it. Krissi, as she was still known to her friends, hadn't seen or heard from Aaron since they graduated from high school in Wiesbaden seventeen years before. Now here he was, on the screen, staring at her. One of the BND agents would be assigned to follow him, make contact and spy on him.

"Krissi . . . Krissi? Are you with us?" Schmidt asked, snapping her out of her reverie.

"Ich bin hier." She flashed her dazzling smile at him, hoping it would divert him from her obvious inattention.

"You have a background in chemistry and have worked a little with pharmaceutical companies before. You up to this?"

"Sure, I can handle it. When do I start?" she asked, trying to control her breathing.

"Your cover is that you're a vice president for sales at Westfalen Pharma Gruppe. You'll be given the appropriate company ID, credit and business cards. Korda may know some of the sales and marketing people at Westfalen, so you'll have to become acquainted with their names in case that comes up." Gerhard handed her a four-inch-thick folder. "In here you'll find the names of Westfalen's drugs already on the market, research programs and drug candidates in clinical trials in Europe and in the U.S. You must familiarize yourself with all of them, their prices, their side effects, competing products, and so forth. We have an expert lined up to coach you. You have five days to get up to speed before you reach San Diego."

"Why San Diego?"

"The International Federation of Pharmaceutical Companies, the IFPC, is holding its annual convention at La Costa, a golf resort and spa north of San Diego. Aaron Korda is scheduled to attend on behalf of Heller and Clarke. We've worked out an arrangement with Westfalen so that you'll be representing the company at the next few conferences. International pharmaceutical companies are big on industry-wide research, sales and marketing symposia, which usually take place at the most attractive resorts, with the best beaches and golf courses." The agents in the room laughed. "Anyway, we'll synchronize your attendance with Korda's, so that your contact can be ongoing." She nodded, hoping that no one noticed her hands shaking.

Krissi perused the background dossier briefly, immediately wanting to know more about the man who had been her high school boyfriend back in Wiesbaden. Her school had initiated an informal student exchange with the American high school on the military base. Those students who wished to got together to practice each other's languages. Krissi and Aaron were immediately drawn to each other during the first meeting and soon started seeing each other, still honing their language skills, but as boyfriend and girlfriend. She read further, momentarily ignoring her boss.

"Is everything okay?" Gerhard asked, puzzled by her strange behavior. Kristina Sturm was known for her implacable demeanor. He had never seen her appear preoccupied before.

"*Alles in ordnung*. I'm okay. I was just curious. So

this is the guy who brought down Offenbach Chemie Werke over the sarin gas mess with Libya?"

"Yes. Why?"

"Well, I never knew the name of the American who did that, but I understand that it was an amazing piece of espionage within Libya, and that several Libyans were killed in hand-to-hand combat. Is he the man?"

"Yeah, that's right. It was damn good work on his part. He apparently tricked—he's reported to be very clever—the Libyans into thinking he was an officer of Offenbach. We think that when he got too close to the sarin gas manufacturing facility, poking around with too many questions, the Libyans tried to kill him. Instead, he wiped them out. The rumors are that he killed five of them, but that may be exaggerated. Still, he is perhaps one of the CIA's most lethal agents. So be careful."

With his brother's lab in Belleville, virtually identical with the one in Mechelen, Belgium, finally up and running, Faramaz ben Sarah counted his blessings and thanked Allah as he rose from his prayer rug in his bedroom. While most of his recruits had failed to get jobs at the targeted pharmaceutical companies, two, Nasreen and Saba, had penetrated National Pharma Corp.'s facility in Trenton, New Jersey, the largest insulin manufacturing facility in the United States. One woman landed a position in the production department, and the other a key spot in the quality-control group. With stockpiles of liquid botulinum-A growing at NMS Biologics, Nasreen and Saba began making the long drive from New Jersey to southern Illinois and returning with the lethal toxin.

Faramaz rolled the small carpet and placed it under his bed, smiling to himself. The simplicity of the plan was also its beauty. Nasreen would add the liquid botulinum-A toxin at the point in the production process just before a large batch was mixed and the individual vials of insulin were filled. Saba in quality control would spot-check the various production runs and falsify the results, thus clearing the product for shipment into the stream of commerce, with pharmaceutical companies unwittingly distributing the lethal biological agent throughout the country.

Despite some delays in production, botulinum-A produced at the Mechelen, Belgium, lab was similarly delivered to Midlands Chemicals in England and to Westfalen Pharma Gruppe in Germany, where Faramaz's operatives had infiltrated the production and quality-control departments, and to the Nederlanden Pharmacie Groep's facility in Holland, where Faramaz himself had landed a job as the director of production. Like scientists in other countries, Faramaz had learned many years before back in the lab in An Najaf that such weapons were fickle instruments of warfare. The difficulty was not in manufacturing, but in delivery. Small quantities of toxins and nerve agents could be exploded in artillery shells over the enemy's head, but nothing would stop the wind from shifting and blowing the poisons back on one's own troops. For this and other reasons, biochemical weapons were of little practical value on the traditional fields of battle. Faramaz, however, had devised the ultimate delivery system: The pharmaceutical companies themselves would deliver the lethal prescriptions, and penetrate deep into enemy territory.

Sitting on the edge of his bed, Faramaz allowed himself a moment of satisfaction, reflecting on his jihad before showering and going to work at one of Nederlanden's production facilities a few miles away in Sliedrecht, near the Dutch port of Rotterdam. Nasreen had been his first recruit, and remained his most trusted operative. Both schooled in England, they had become friends afterward in Lebanon during several visits they had made as part of a relief mission to the Shatila refugee camp near Beirut. There, where thousands of Palestinians were crowded together in unsanitary conditions, he, Abia, as Nasreen was called in Iraq, and others had arrived with what they thought were ample medical supplies, only to find that the quantity was not sufficient and was quickly exhausted. Without antibiotics, they watched children die from simple infections that became deadly in the squalor of the camp. For this he blamed the Israelis and the Americans, as well as their Western allies.

At first he wanted to devote his life to improving the conditions at the camp, but the problems were insurmountable and the amount of food, potable water and medicine he could deliver made little difference. Always a devout Muslim, at the same time he saw the goings-on at Shatila he began worshipping at a new mosque led by an ultraconservative imam who despised the West. Seemingly overnight, he began to think that his countrymen who preached violence as the only method of change were right.

Faramaz—Fauad Al-Metar in Arabic before he adopted his Iranian-Jewish name—had formulated the plan after the fourth trip, during the long, dusty bus ride home through the deserts of Syria and Iraq. He presented his idea to Nasreen, and she had readily signed up, which gave him the confidence to bring it to the national intelligence directorate, the Iraqi Mukhabarat. The officials had been impressed with the concept, his dedication and willingness to sacrifice his life, his thoroughness, and most of all the numbers of deaths it would inflict. Faramaz's delivery system for the botulinum-A toxin was ingenious. The concept of sabotaging Western medical supplies and using the pharmaceutical companies themselves to disseminate the lethal biological agent, bringing terror into the homes of the infidels, was brilliant. Hiding Iraq's biochem labs in the heartland of America and in a nondescript town in Belgium was so clever it provided the intelligence officers a rare occasion to laugh. Long before the American invasion, the officials had refined and tweaked the project, coming up with the idea of funding what they began to dub Operation Lethal Agent with the cash proceeds of the heroin trade based in Poti, so that no money could be traced back to them.

Faramaz was given full responsibility for the project,

and he and Nasreen had recruited carefully. Many volunteered, but only seventeen made the final cut. In the end, only eight, all pretending to be Iranian Jews, succeeded in landing key positions inside major pharmaceutical companies. The others became runners, messengers who would travel under multiple passports to deliver cash from the heroin profits, give instructions and gather status reports that could never be discussed over phones or the Internet, or transmitted by mail or fax.

Faramaz and his cell had devoted years to researching the most toxic substances in the hidden facilities throughout Iraq, enhancing *Clostridium botulinum* in the labs in Samarra, Al-Ramadi, An Najaf and Al-Fallujah to make it even more deadly, dismantling the labs in Iraq and reconstituting them in Belleville, Illinois, and Mechelen, Belgium. They had spent a great deal of time making contact with the Afghans, who grew the poppies and processed the heroin, establishing their heroin-packing facility in Poti and breaking into the heroin trade, setting up the money flows from dealing in drugs, and making sure no cash could be traced to Saddam's government. Then the American invasion came, crushing the Iraqi army. The occupation of his country infuriated Faramaz, but apart from inspiring him to speed up his own attack on the United States and its allies, the war did not affect Operation Lethal Agent. The researchers at the secret facilities in Iraq had already shut down their operations. Years before, Faramaz had moved his botulinum-A facilities so deep inside enemy territory that no weapons inspectors would ever think of looking there.

Deir ez-Zur straddles the Euphrates River, which heads west to east in the desert of eastern Syria, but the small market town was not centered on the river itself, but rather on a tributary canal half a kilometer south. The lead helicopter on this raid, Spider Three, Lieutenant Pamela Toll at the stick, raced along the north bank, rising a few feet to clear an earthen dike at the juncture of the Euphrates and the canal, and then skimmed over the waters, following the canal east. The town of Deir ez-Zur lay before her in the eerie green light of her night-vision goggles and the FLIR display screen on her instrument panel. Spider One was holding steady one hundred meters behind her; Spider Two another one hundred meters behind Spider One. Pamela Toll crossed the central bridge leading from the marketplace to the train station and headed to her drop zone, a soccer field immediately west of the Deltas' ostensible target, an elementary school, and 250 meters away from the real objective, a small, run-down mosque on the canal and situated at the south footing of the central bridge Lieutenant Toll had just flown over. At three o'clock in the morning, the soccer field was still; no signs of life except for a dog that scampered away from the noise of the Black Hawk's rotors. Toll slowed Spider Three to a stop, hovering fifteen meters above the four-story school, ChemLites attached to the ends of the helicopter's rappelling ropes glowing eerily. "Ropes out," Master Sergeant Beecher, the designated fast-rope master, reported into his mouthpiece. Without hesitation or a word said, Staff Sergeant Ryle, sniper rifle strapped to his back, carbine/grenade launcher belted to his chest, slid down one starboard rope, while Staff Sergeant Metz, SAW tied to his chest, rappelled down a port-side line, each immediately removing his gloves upon impact and readying weapons.

"Ropers away," shouted the fast-rope master, who would remain on Spider Three. "Ropes clear. Move right." Lieutenant Toll and Chief Warrant Officer 3 Kopinsky, her copilot, eased the Black Hawk to the right twenty meters to clear the building and descended ten meters to allow all four ropes to touch the ground. Sergeants Ravirez and Stang went down the two port-side ropes while Sergeant First Class Burns and Chief Warrant Officer Rainer rappelled down the starboard side. "Ropers away." Beecher released a cotter pin on each hook and let the heavy ropes fall to the ground. "Move right and back," he reported to Lieuteant Toll, who glanced at the clock on her instrument panel. *Thirty-two seconds,* she thought. It wasn't her personal best, but six operators on the ground deep inside enemy territory in thirty-two seconds wasn't bad by any Night Stalker's standards. Lieutenant Toll retreated back to the wide expanse of water where the Euphrates meets the canal, the point where she had just traversed the river, ready to return at any moment to exfiltrate her "customers" or to provide covering fire if the operation turned sour. Thirty-five seconds later, Spider One had successfully inserted Chalk One and was following Spider Three back to the juncture of the river and the canal.

Spider Two, with Chief Warrant Officer 4 Carl Foreman as pilot and Lieutenant Laura Alvarez as his copilot, Major Lewis Kinloch in command, assumed position at two thousand feet above the area of operations, surveying any and all movement on the FLIR screen on the instrument panel. Sergeants Knight and Rodriguez pointed their Gatling guns downward to either side of the chopper, ready to strafe the Syrians if the Delta operators on the ground ran into trouble.

The eight Deltas comprising Chalk One silently traversed the short expanse of the soccer field to a lane that separated the field from the mosque. This particular mission was made all the more difficult by the fact that the local police station was located next to the mosque, between the Deltas and their goal. They made their way down a narrow alley behind the station so silently that the dog, asleep inside the building, like the three officers on duty at this late hour, did not hear them. Nor did they hear Sergeant First Class Brown, Spider Man, shimmy up the telephone pole behind the station, cut the line and silently return to his team. Galante, Gonzales and Trippe took the point and led Chalk One down the alleyway, crouching low, moving quickly, peering through their NVGs for any sign of life. Red Eagle and Spider Man followed several meters behind, weapons ready, stepping carefully to avoid the rubble littering the narrow lane. Korda, Shafter and Joyner followed, alternating the direction of their weapons from their front to their rear. So far, so good.

Trippe, Galante and Gonzales reached their position behind the mosque at the juncture of two alleyways. Galante hefted the heavy and very powerful M-60, the "pig," as the Deltas called it. Gonzales, a medic, carried the lighter CAR-15, while Trippe, the first sergeant, toted his M4 carbine/grenade launcher. Any Syrian soldiers or police would have to go through them to get to the rest of Chalk One, although if things went as planned, no one in Chalk One would engage. Its mission was to plant its tiny, extremely powerful listening devices and transmitters and get out of Dodge before the Iraqis who had fled the American invasion and who were suspected of having set up shop in Deir ez-Zur could detect that they were anywhere near the mosque, and before any Syrian troops could detect the presence of the Deltas.

Those few residents who heard the helicopters near the soccer field assumed that Syrian army troops were moving under the cover of darkness to suppress whatever resistance movement might have been formed to oppose the Assad regime. Not one dared even crack open their heavy curtains, fearful of being caught gazing upon soldiers moving in the night. Like the other Deltas on the ground, Trippe's, Galante's and Gonzales's faces and hands were covered with black-and-green greasepaint, and their uniforms were camouflaged for nighttime operations. As they huddled in the narrow alleyway, they were virtually invisible to the naked eye. Their NVGs, however, gave them ample light to see the large doors of the garrison headquarters swing open. Syrian soldiers were assembling hastily in the large courtyard. A siren began to wail. Trippe looked at Galante and Gonzales as if to say *Oh, shit*. Gonzales stepped across the alley and situated himself in the cover of a bend in the wall opposite Galante and Trippe. Galante merely grinned and raised his machine gun into position, almost hoping the Syrians would be foolish enough to come running their way.

The siren continued to scream. Shafter, who was already attaching his eavesdropping equipment on the window and foundation of the north side of the mosque, heard it, but continued at his rapid yet businesslike pace. Korda and Joyner heard it, too, and were also unfazed. They had already planted two instruments on the east wall, and were working their way around to the other side of the building. The listening device planted on each basement window was no larger than a thick nickel.

While the other operators in Chalk One were doing their work on the ground, Spider Man and Red Eagle each shot to the roof a grappling hook on a rope, tugged hard to secure it and began their ascent. An electronics expert, Brown had risen fast in the Third Special Forces Group before he applied to Delta Force three years earlier. At twenty-eight years old, he was already a sergeant first class and recognized by those around him as a man to be reckoned with. He stood five feet eleven inches tall but weighed only 150 pounds, all sinew, muscle and brains. Shafter watched him scale the brick wall of the hospital. Aptly nicknamed Spider Man, it was Brown who had given the code name *spider* to each of the three Black Hawks on the mission. To each Black Hawk was assigned a "chalk," or team: Spider One carried Chalk One; Spider Two, Chalk Two; and Spider Three, Chalk Three. Sergeant First Class Pawhuska, Red Eagle, ascended as effortlessly as Spider Man, reaching the roof a few seconds after him.

Spider Man and Red Eagle worked separately but in unison. For the ascent, each removed the CAR-15 strapped to his chest and the rucksack from his back, and surveyed the roof through his NVG. All clear. Unlike many mosques, this house of worship, being in a poorer market village, lacked a dome. Its roof was flat, the poured concrete now covered with a thin layer of desert sand and dust. Red Eagle moved silently toward the west wall, while Spider Man remained near the east wall, where they had ascended. Kneeling, each retrieved from his rucksack an aluminum device designed to look like the mushroom-shape exhaust fans that dotted the top of the structure. They secured with studs the fanlike receivers/transmitters to the surface of the roof, where they could pick up the electronic signals from the coin-like bugs planted on the windows and foundation four floors below. After securing the third one, Red Eagle paused for a few seconds to study his handiwork. The receivers/transmitters looked almost identical to the real exhaust fans on the mosque. It would take an expert to notice the difference, and he would have to be looking for it. Red Eagle removed a Ping-Pong paddle that he had borrowed from the rec room back at Incirlik and fanned the sand on the roof as he retraced his steps, covering his tracks, back to Spider Man.

Spider Man and Red Eagle each removed the rope and grappling hook from his rucksack, detached the hook and stored it in his now almost empty bag. Each strapped his CAR-15 tightly to his chest, placed the sack on his back, threaded the long rope around the base of sturdy-looking, four-inch-thick, two-foot-high exhaust pipes that protruded from the roof and began his descent, holding on to the doubled rope and rappelling silently down the wall. Red Eagle, kneeling on the parapet, his boots dangling precariously over the side, once again fanned the sand with the Ping-Pong paddle, masking the traces he and Spider Man had left. When Red Eagle reached the bottom, he released one end of the rope and pulled the other until the line dropped into his arms. Brown did the same and checked his watch; the entire process had taken a little more than four minutes. Each operator stored his rope in his rucksack, gripped his weapon and looked over to Lieutenant Colonel Korda, who nodded silently in the affirmative. *Job done. Time to boogie.*

From the roof of the school several hundred meters away from the mosque, Ryle and Metz saw the Syrian soldiers step out into the street in front of the garrison. They had obviously heard the helicopters and were investigating, the senior soldier pointing toward Sharia Khaled ibn al-Walid Street, in the direction of the mosque. The two Deltas did not so much as even glance at each other. Their mission was clear. The Syrian NCO was leading his men toward the mosque. The Deltas on and near the school were to draw the Syrians away from the mosque and toward them. Ryle was the first to fire. The 7.62 mm bullet left the muzzle of his sniper rifle at 2,550 feet per second and tore through the chest of a senior noncommissioned officer four hundred meters away. As the man fell, Ryle was already chambering another round in the bolt action M40A1. The Syrian never knew what hit him, and by the time his comrades realized that their first sergeant was dead, Ryle had taken down two more of them with clean torso shots. Meanwhile, Metz cut loose with a withering salvo from his SAW, spraying the Syrian squad of twenty men with nearly half of his two-hundred-round magazine. Eleven more went down, five dead and six badly wounded. When Metz paused to take stock and steady his aim, Stang, who had positioned himself on the ground behind a stone wall about ten meters from the school, began to fire his M-60 machine gun at the enemy. Instead of a steady stream of lead, he fired in short bursts of fifteen to twenty rounds each, pulverizing those Syrians brazen enough to be in the open. Six more fell, either dead or wounded. The others temporarily retreated to the safety of the courtyard, protected by the garrison's northern wall.

While Ryle and Metz engaged the Syrians from the rooftop of the school, Rainer and Ravirez focused on the task of ransacking the basement of the school, in order to make the Iraqis and Syrians think the Americans believed that the biochemical facility was in its basement, not in the mosque. Once all files were emptied and the floor strewn with the rifled papers, the two

Deltas moved to the first floor, disturbed yet more files and prepared to exit.

Into his mouthpiece from his position at the west wall of the mosque, Shafter whispered, "We're green."

"This is Chalk One leader. We're also green," Martin Korda responded on the other side of the building, as he and Joyner concealed the last coinlike device. "Move out."

"Roger that," Trippe whispered from the darkness of the still-quiet alleyway next to the mosque. "Let's roll," he added as he began to back away. "Fuckin' rag heads been pissin' in this alleyway for centuries. The ammonia's about ready to burn an extra hole in my nose." Galante and Gonzales kept their thoughts to themselves as they backed out of the narrow confines and with Trippe headed west toward the others, turning frequently to cover their rear and flanks.

From his perch on the roof, Ryle saw them first. As many as forty Syrian troops had left the garrison—not through the large gates that led north from the courtyard into the withering fire of Metz's SAW on the roof and Stang's M-60 on the ground, but from the east. Between the school and the garrison building were two single-story cinder block buildings. The area immediately south of the school was empty, except for a rusted-out skeleton of a playground. "One, possibly two, squads approaching behind the cinder block hootches," Ryle reported in a businesslike tone into his mouthpiece. Ryle said nothing more, but the Deltas heard his sniper rifle fire, which told them that targets of opportunity were presenting themselves.

On the ground, Ravirez and Stang were heating up the Syrians who had regrouped in the garrison and who were now making their way down the street south of the school, using parked vehicles and a Dumpster as cover. Ryle and Metz were taking heavy fire on the roof, as were Ravirez and Stang on the ground, misdirected bullets pocking the sides of the school, chipping off its stucco facade.

"I'm going to get a better angle so I can hit the bastards behind the Dumpster," Ravirez shouted to Stang, who nodded but did not take his eyes off the narrow lane in front of him, continuing to fire his M-60 at the approaching enemy. Bullets whizzed past him and chipped away at his stone redoubt, decreasing his opportunity to fire in response. Meanwhile, Ravirez bolted across the lane toward a parked van, but did not make it. Hit by an AK-47 round in the leg, he went down with a thud, the wind knocked from him. Despite the pain in his leg, immediately after slamming to the rock-hard dirt he rolled to his side and tried to position himself to fire his carbine. He belly crawled as best he could back to the stone wall while Stang, who saw his predicament, let loose with the remainder of his ammo belt as cover, reloading the instant the last round on the link-belt fed into the chamber.

Still shooting and under fire, Stang stepped two paces away from the relative safety of the stone wall and reached for Ravirez's outstretched hand. Their hands met and locked, and Stang pulled with all his force. Ravirez tried to project himself forward with his legs, but his right femur was broken, the enemy round having splintered the bone several inches above his knee. Stang continued to pull with his left arm, still firing the M-60 at the approaching forces, holding the heavy "pig" in his powerful right arm but shooting inaccurately. The first bullet to hit him struck him in the chest and propelled him backward. Although it was not a lethal shot, having rebounded off his Kevlar vest, it threw him off balance long enough for a Republican Guard to aim and empty the entire magazine of his AK-47. One bullet hit Stang in the leg, followed by several more to his chest, pounding him hard. As the burst of automatic rifle fire climbed up Stang's torso, one bullet tore through his throat, killing him instantly. Emboldened by the sight of Stang's body collapsing to the ground, the Syrians stepped out from behind a truck sixty meters from the stone wall, where Ravirez now lay exposed, and emptied their magazines in his direction. Most of the bullets went wildly high and chipped harmlessly into the wall of the school behind Ravirez, but with more than seventy shots fired, enough lead found the target and killed him.

"Chalk One leader," Major Kinloch reported from Spider Two, circling above. "The southern flank of Chalk Three's position has collapsed. Ravirez and Stang are down. I say again. Ravirez and Stang are down. Chalk One, you must fill the breach immediately south of the school. Eastern flank also under heavy fire. We are moving to provide suppressing fire."

"Spider Two, this is Chalk One leader. We copy," Lieutenant Colonel Korda responded in his mouthpiece as he and his team reached the south side of the soccer field. Running at full speed, the eight operators who had come from the mosque quickly reached the stone wall. Under a withering cannonade of covering fire from the others in Chalk One and from the Gatling guns of Spider Two circling above, Joyner and Shafter dragged Ravirez's and Stang's bodies back behind the redoubt. Butler, Chalk Three's medic, and Gonzales, Chalk One's medic, immediately checked for vital signs. Looking up to Lieutenant Colonel Korda, their eyes said it all. Delta Force had lost two operators.

"Ladder exfiltration for Chalk Three not possible," Korda reported solemnly into his mouthpiece. "Spider Three will land at the far end of the soccer field and lift off immediately. Chalk One will remain on the ground until Spider Three is airborne, and then ladder exfiltrate."

The pilots onboard Spider Two saw on the FLIR screen the thermal images of the Syrian soldiers moving en masse to the south side of the school, continuing to be sucked into Chalk Three's decoy and ignoring the mosque. Swooping around to the enemy's east, Chief Warrant Officer 4 Carl Foreman positioned his Black Hawk so that Sergeant Frank Knight, right-side crew chief, had a clear field of fire. In less than ten seconds, Knight's Gatling gun, spinning like a fan, began to shower the approaching Syrian troops with nine hundred rounds of white-hot lead. Swinging the chopper 180 degrees, Foreman gave Sergeant Rodriguez, the left-side crew chief, an open field of fire, and he repeated Knight's action.

"Spider Three, this is Chalk One leader. I want you on the ground now. Far west side of the soccer field. Chalk Three withdraw. I say again. Withdraw and link up with Spider Three. Ryle and Metz—get off that roof. Chalk One will provide covering fire while Chalk Three gets Stang, Ravirez and the rest of Chalk Three on the helo. Move it *now*," he ordered. "Trippe. How much more ammo do you have?"

"Not much. A couple more minutes, max."

"Rappelling down," Ryle said from the roof a second before he and Metz came down the ropes on the side of the school. A moment later, Metz and Ryle were on the ground and running toward Spider Three, whose wheels were just touching down on the dirt field, sending up clouds of dust from its rotor wash. They joined Rainer and Burns, who, along with Butler and Gonzales, were carrying Ravirez and Stang. Burns was limping, the result of a bullet that grazed his thigh. He was having a hard time supporting Stang's lifeless body. Ryle relieved Burns, and Metz assisted Butler and Gonzales as they loaded the fallen Deltas into Spider Three and climbed in after them.

Spider One moved in, hovering fifty feet above the soccer field, two rope ladders dangling from either side, side gunners firing with their Gatling guns for effect at the approaching Syrians.

Shafter was the first to reach his rope. He immediately slid his left leg between two rungs, wrapping his left arm around a higher rung of the ladder and clamping a snap link on his extraction harness to a rung, his muscular right arm holding the M-60, ready to fire. The other operators of Chalk One repeated the maneuver. "Clear," shouted the rope master and the chopper rose, following Spider Three back to the area where the canal joined

the Euphrates and across the river, Deltas dangling
above the wide waterway. Spider Two provided cover,
firing its Gatling guns as it turned, following Spider One
west across the ancient river, heavy machine gun fire
whizzing past it, tracer rounds lighting the night sky.

Spider One gently eased the Delta operators clinging
to the exfiltration ladders below the Black Hawk to the
ground in the middle of a field two miles north of the
Euphrates, while Spiders Two and Three provided air
cover. As Spider One had crossed the river, Lieutenant
Colonel Korda, still dangling from his rope ladder, heard
through his earpiece the conversations between the med-
ics. Beecher had lost two fingers and half of his palm
from an enemy bullet that hit the forestock of his carbine as he was firing. Trendler, also in Chalk Three,
had taken a round that shattered his elbow. Both would
require extensive medical treatment and physical ther-
apy. They would remain in Delta Force, but only in administrative positions. Burns and Galante had both
suffered superficial wounds. But Stang and Ravirez were
dead. Korda cursed himself. He had known that the mission would be dangerous, but he had not fully anticipated the numbers and the tenacity of the Syrian troops.
They had pushed ahead toward the fallen Deltas, boxing
them in, despite the hail of lead thrown at them. *Damn
it. Damn it,* he cursed inwardly, while at the same time
pushing away the thoughts, compartmentalizing them for
later. He would revisit his self-recriminations at the post-
mission debriefing. Now, however, it was time to get
back onboard the Black Hawk and get as far away from
Deir ez-Zur as possible.

FOUR

He wore a hat to conceal his sandy brown hair, sunglasses to hide his hazel eyes and a midpriced Turkish business suit to blend in with his two colleagues as they deplaned from the forty-six-passenger turboprop and made their way with the other passengers across the tarmac toward the small terminal. Aaron Korda was surprised at the newness and cleanliness of Trabzon Airport. He had half expected a chopped-up runway and a dilapidated terminal building with reeking restrooms. Instead, the tarmac was recently paved, the terminal building modernized, and the men's room comparable to those in northern Europe, though overly scented with cheap deodorizers.

Lieutenant Ertugrul, dressed in civvies, along with Master Sergeant Naim Sukur, also in civilian attire, waited for him outside the lavatory. When Aaron rejoined them, he and Naim followed Hasan past the parking lot and onto the main road. Each held only lightweight carry-on bags and appeared no different from other travelers heading toward the bus station to go into town. A few meters before reaching the crowded station, Hasan flipped open his cell phone, pressed the speed dial and paused for an instant. "We're here. See you in a couple of minutes." He closed the cell phone and replaced it in his pocket, and without anyone saying a word, the three men were on their way. They turned down a dusty street and after a brisk twenty-minute

walk, came to a house surrounded by an eight-foot-high
cinder block wall interrupted only by a thick wooden
gate painted cobalt blue like the well-maintained tile
roof. Sergeant Yusuf Ciller, who was waiting for them,
opened the gate. Once inside, Aaron, Hasan and Naim
greeted Yusuf warmly.

"Is this the car?" Hasan asked Yusuf, looking at the
beat-up Volkswagen Gulf. Yusuf nodded. "When did
you take it? We can't afford for the police to be looking
for it."

"Allah korusun," Aaron said, sizing up the nearly bald
left front tire. The other men laughed at Aaron's reference to the popular Turkish bumper sticker "God protect me."

"We put that sticker on all our cars that are over a
year old," Yusuf laughed.

"I know that. But this one needs it," Aaron said, only
half joking. "Look at this tire." He kicked the hubcap
and then walked around to the front end of the vehicle.
The doors were corroded nearly through at the bottom.
Rust blisters pocked the hood, roof and truck.

"Okay. Okay. And the spare in the trunk is worse. . . .
Or about the same," Yusuf said, holding up his hands
in mock apology. "But the tire in the garage is good,"
he told them. "And we can put the new one on after
we have eaten, or maybe we can call AAA. They may
take some time to get here, but we don't need to leave
for a while." Yusuf laughed heartily. He was proud of
his knowledge of American culture gleaned from watching American shows on TV.

"The people of Trabzon are famous for their practical
jokes," Lieutenant Ertugrul, rolling his eyes, explained
to the American. Aaron smiled, relieved that they had
a decent spare. "But you didn't answer my question.
When was this junker stolen?" Hasan was from Istanbul,
and not as prone to the countryside humor as those
from Trabzon.

"Well, you see, it belongs to my friend, so it's not
really stolen. He just wants it to be stolen. So we'll take

it to Georgia, and he'll collect some insurance money. He won't report it for a day or two, so the police won't be looking for it until then."

Lieutenant Ertugrul nodded approvingly. "The engine?"

"It's good," Yusuf responded. "Surprisingly good. My buddy took care of it. It's just the salt air from the sea that was too much for the body. Come inside. I'll show you the weapons that I bought. I do believe that Allah has been very good to us."

Aaron sat silently in the back of the Volkswagen Gulf, gazing at the tea plantations that covered the hills to his right along the two-lane highway leading east from Trabzon to the Georgian border. To his left, the Black Sea was growing darker in the heavy rain and low clouds. Naim sat in the passenger's seat, with Aaron directly behind him, next to Lieutenant Ertugrul. Yusuf drove, frustrated with the slow pace of the eighteen-wheeler in front of him. "It's always raining like this in the fall," he said to no one in particular as he strained to see through the smears left by the worn windshield wipers.

The combination of rain and the sharp mountain curves made the traffic flow slowly. Although there were more commercial vehicles here, the terrain reminded Aaron of the California coast. The right front window was open a couple of inches. He found the cool air and occasional splash of raindrops refreshing. It kept him awake and clearheaded. He absentmindedly slid his right hand into his leather jacket and removed his Makarov 9 mm automatic and reached for the cleaning kit resting on the floor between his feet.

Lieutenant Ertugrul nodded knowingly to Aaron. Instinct had told him he could trust Aaron from the beginning, and he had grown very fond of him in the short time he had known him. As he watched Aaron clean the Russian weapons that Yusuf had procured on the black market, he knew he could trust Aaron in combat.

On the other hand, he was also impressed with the humanity of the former U.S. Ranger, the way his eyes moistened in Yusuf's home when they had toasted Kemal with a glass of raki, and the kindness Aaron showed to Yusuf's five-year-old daughter. Aaron had rolled up a ten-dollar bill into a type of origami ring and had placed it on her finger, earning a bright smile from the child enchanted by the foreigner who spoke her language and who could make jewelry from paper money. Yes, he could very much understand the strong friendship that had existed between Kemal and the American.

"How much farther to the border?" Aaron asked as they left the town of Rize and continued east along the highway toward Georgia.

"We've come about a third of the way," Yusuf answered, his eyes fixed on the intersection in front of him to make sure he didn't take the wrong road. "We're better off detouring up into the mountains and crossing the border there. No need for us to stand out by driving to the harbor directly on the coastal highway. We'll be less conspicuous if we approach the port from the other side of town. I know a small village about ten kilometers away from the main road. For a couple hundred dollars, the border guard will let us pass." The silence in the car told Yusuf his passengers were worried about the timing. "Don't worry," he said reassuringly. "We'll get there on time."

Moments later, the jolt yanked Aaron out of his reverie as the small Volkswagen braked hard and swerved to avoid a deep pothole only a few minutes after the turn off the coastal highway. The drive up on the mountain road to the small border crossing was a short run as the crow flies, but the crater that would have dented a wheel rim and caused a flat tire portended more to come.

For a pleasant moment, Aaron had been drifting in a daydream, one that he had frequently. Since he graduated from West Point, he had been with women, many of whose faces and bodies, but not their names, he could recall. He had briefly flirted with the idea of marriage once. Others had been lovers or just friends or just forgotten. Over the years, though, his thoughts went back to one woman, his high school love. He supposed many men were like that. Aaron had once confided this to his brother and Martin had laughed when Aaron said how often he still thought of her, telling Aaron every man remembers his first lay. Aaron had let it go at that, embarrassed to tell his older brother that he and Krissi had never had sex. Some heavy petting in the car before taking her home after a movie, yes, but that was it.

Aaron and Krissi had met during an informal exchange between the local German high school in Wiesbaden and the American school on base, when his father was stationed there in the mid-eighties. Aaron and Krissi had become friends quickly and dated, not unlike high school kids back in the States. Movies. Burgers after a basketball or soccer game. A make-out session in the backseat of his parents' car. Both of them enjoyed the outdoors, and they took long walks around the army base and hikes in the nearby forests. They had a lot in common and there was, they thought, nothing they couldn't talk about with each other. Then Margaret died, and their world changed.

Maggie had burst into the Korda family and left so fast that it was hard for Aaron to remember his little sister completely. Even that pained him. He looked out the window into the darkness so Lieutenant Ertugrul could not see the glistening in his eyes. After all these years, half a lifetime ago, he still could not bear it. She was only five when she died. After becoming very ill for a few days, Maggie was diagnosed with bacterial pneumonia and the doctor had prescribed amoxicillin, which she had taken before. To everyone's surprise, however, Maggie became allergic to the antibiotic, developing a life-threatening serum sickness. Martin, then in his third year at West Point, was flown to Germany to be with his family. Intravenous Benadryl given in the emergency room reversed the allergic response, but the penicillin substitute didn't faze the pneumonia and Maggie's condition worsened. Finally, the doctor decided to try vancomycin, then the antibiotic of last resort, even though it was known to run the risk of causing harmful side effects—and was later found to be contaminated. But the vancomycin either didn't work or it didn't kick in fast enough, and the side effects of the powerful drug ravaged her already frail body. Two days later, Maggie died in the hospital in her mother and father's arms, with Martin and Aaron looking on.

In a way, Aaron took it the hardest, and never fully recovered. Clinically depressed for the balance of his senior year of high school, he became moody and aggressive. He fought often, badly hurting one classmate. Krissi tried to comfort him, but he rejected her many efforts and avoided her after the funeral. Later, much later, he realized that during that terrible period he didn't want Krissi's or anyone else's help because he didn't want to feel better. As he then saw it, resuming the charmed life after Maggie's death would have been denying how important she had been to him, and that was unacceptable. Better to cut himself off and grieve privately.

Aaron pointedly did not say good-bye to Krissi when he left for West Point. He knew even then that he had wounded her badly, broken her heart, but he wasn't ready to let go of his grieving and couldn't look into her eyes without breaking down. It was all very confusing at the time, and for a while he thought he was going mad. He wasn't, and when he went back to the States time and the change of scenery were powerful healers. He still missed Maggie terribly, and Krissi for that matter, but he allowed himself to be absorbed into life at the Point and went on.

Yusuf slowed the car. Aaron straightened up and reached for his false German passport to give to the Georgian border guard at the crossing. As the Volkswagen pulled away from the checkpoint, Aaron wondered what had ever become of Krissi.

*   *   *

No one needed to be told that the continuing rain worked to their advantage, especially when the wind off the Black Sea drove the drops into pellets, crashing against the sheet metal roof of Building 15 and the tops of the shipping containers. They had abandoned the Volkswagen near the northern wharf, making their way on foot to the south pier, concealing their weapons under their raingear and in duffle bags that were discarded once they reached the stacks of shipping containers. There were mountains of them. It was the same maze Lieutenant Ertugrul had used to conceal himself while he witnessed the murder of Captain Bulot. Aaron pressed the illuminator button on his Ironman watch—02:53. The cloud cover was low, the ceiling at only a few hundred feet, permitting only streaks of moonlight to break through to the wharf below.

Naim stepped closer in the darkness toward his agreed-upon rendezvous point with Hasan, Aaron and Yusuf. He had just returned from inspecting Building 15 and was eager to brief them. "Kemal," Naim whispered from the blackness, using the code word for the night and making it clear he was not an enemy to be shot.

"Bulot," Lieutenant Ertugrul responded with the agreed-upon countersign. After taking in all that Naim had to report, the commandos edged closer to the front of Building 15.

The garagelike double doors and the windowed entryway next to them on the front of Building 15 were closed, but inside the lights shone brightly. Naim reported that there was a door in the rear of the building, but no opening on the east side of the structure other than three half-meter-square windows. By looking through a window, Naim had observed that two men in fatigues, armed with Kalashnikovs, stood guard inside the open front gates, while their comrades slept in plain view and Georgian workers tended to their packing operations. On the west side of the building, the only openings were two small windows and a narrow cargo door large enough for a conveyor belt that ran the short expanse of the wharf to a freighter tied to the pier.

Once the plan was finalized, Naim saluted and hefted his heavy machine gun in his right hand, picked up his duffel bag containing six drum-shape magazines, each filled with seventy-five rounds, with his left and disappeared in the darkness.

Yusuf's initial mission was to ignite enough C4 to blast a hole through one of the corrugated sheet metal bay doors. The blast would, it was hoped, shock and disorient the enemy long enough for Lieutenant Ertugrul and Aaron to dash through the opening and take the drug traffickers by surprise. Yusuf left the others and made his way to the front of the building. He planted some of the C4 he had brought with him and then quickly picked his way across the gravel lot away from Building 15 and back to Hasan and Aaron. "Fifty-two seconds," he whispered to them.

Suddenly, the door next to the bay gates opened and a man stepped out. Although he appeared to be unarmed, the three attackers instinctively retreated a couple of paces into the canyon formed by the stacks of containers on either side of them. As they watched, the man unzipped his fly, turned away from the doorway and relieved himself. He bounced twice on the balls of his feet and zipped his pants. Three seconds later, his life ended as the exploding C4 drove fragments of metal through him at several hundred feet per second.

The instant the metal shards stopped flying, Yusuf darted out from their hide site between the stacks of containers and ran into position near the Dumpster, while Hasan and Aaron, crouching low, ran toward Building 15. As expected, the charge of plastic explosive tore off a large portion of one of the bay doors, the opening framed by snarled, razor-sharp metal. Surprisingly, the lights hadn't been blown away by the blast, and two men were visible lying on the concrete floor. One, the closest to the explosions, was not moving. The other, bloody and clothes tattered, was struggling to reach his assault rifle. His efforts were put to an end by a burst of fire from Hasan's machine gun. In one fluid motion, Hasan turned and sprayed the large room with 7.62 mm rounds, wreaking havoc on those inside who had survived the blast and who were scattering toward the rear of the building.

The Georgians were ill prepared. The combination of the explosion, shrapnel and machine gun fire sent them into a frenzy as they stumbled over cans, boxes and each other to reach the rear of the plant. Hasan and Aaron knew at once that Naim could handle them when they fled out the back door. It was clear, however, that the men the attackers took for Iranians, readily identifiable by their fatigue uniforms, were well-trained soldiers. They reacted quickly, retreating behind the truck and then into the recesses of the canning plant, directing fire at Hasan and Aaron, who were forced to seek cover behind several pallets loaded with heavy drums of pureed tomatoes. The men in fatigues rapidly consolidated their position near the cargo door where the conveyor belt ran through the west wall and out toward the moored freighter. They used AK-47s with thirty-shot magazines, and they carried extra ammunition in magazines clipped to their ammo belts. Several of them had already emptied their weapons in controlled bursts of fire at the attackers and were reloading, while others covered for them with suppressing fire, peppering Hasan and Aaron's position.

Using his Russian RPK-74, a powerful machine gun with a seventy-five-round drum magazine, Aaron fired a twenty-round burst under the truck, attempting to force those behind it to flee from the lead ricocheting off the smooth concrete floor. A man screamed as the heavy 7.62 mm rounds tore through his foot and threw him off balance. The man closest to him took a bullet in the shin and collapsed to the pavement next to his fallen comrade. A second twenty-five-round burst fired under the truck struck both men in their upper bodies, instantly putting an end to their misery.

"Let's get out of here," Aaron heard one man farther to the rear of the building shout. Several rounds were fired in Aaron's direction, but he was able to duck behind the heavy drums and was not hit. He managed to squeeze off the remaining thirty rounds in his magazine in the direction of the enemy. He hit no one, but the hail of bullets pinned down the men wearing fatigues long enough for him to sprint to a new position from which he had a better angle of attack. He quickly reloaded and let off a torrent of bullets in the direction of the fleeing enemy, killing two and wounding one badly. "I'm hit," one man screamed to his comrades. "For the love of God! Help me." His plea went unanswered. Even if his comrades had been inclined to come to his aid, the suppressing field of fire that Aaron sent in their direction made it impossible to do so. The wounded man turned to shoot Aaron, but Aaron fired first, making it unnecessary for the other men in uniform to rescue him.

Naim's job was to prevent those fleeing from the rear exit from circling around to the front of the building, where they could fire on Hasan and Aaron, whose backs were unprotected. He performed it well. Hasan, Aaron and everyone else inside Building 15 heard Naim's machine gun barking at the Georgians as they tried to escape. He held his fire as the first man emerged, biding his time until several men were in his line of fire, cutting most of them down. Those who survived the first stream of bullets were forced back inside as Naim shot through the doorway. He then turned his fire on the walls surrounding the door. The bullets from his Russian RPK-74 punched through the thin metal sheeting with ease, striking men inside, forcing those still able to run back into the canning plant from which they had just fled.

By this time, Aaron estimated that about two-thirds of the enemy were down. But the survivors—three Iranians and seven Georgians—were trapped in the warehouse, and left with no choice but to fight, began shooting at Hasan and Aaron with everything they had. Aaron watched with growing anxiety as his operation bogged down in a protracted exchange of fire, rather than being the lightning-swift knockout blow he had planned. There were many more men in fatigue uniforms than he had anticipated. To make matters worse, Aaron could hear Yusuf's machine gun and the enemy's returning fire coming from outside near the freighter, and that told him that Yusuf had met stiff resistance from the Italians upon boarding the vessel. The impasse had to be broken.

"Cover me," he yelled to Hasan in English, the stress of the moment such that he forgot to speak in Turkish. "I'm going to rush the conveyor belt near . . ." He stopped and repeated himself in Turkish, though Hasan spoke passable English. "I'll rush the door where the belt goes through the wall and then sweep to the center. Swing to your left and circle around to that side." Hasan gave him the thumbs-up and emptied his magazine in the direction of the men in uniform.

Under the cover of Hasan's fusillade, Aaron ran a few meters to a full pallet of boxes. Seeing the partially exposed shoulder of a man in uniform kneeling behind a stack of drums, he took careful aim with his machine gun and squeezed gently. He was rewarded with the sight of the enemy hurling backward against a stack of boxes, fully exposed. One quick burst from the weapon sent the man to his maker. The two remaining men in uniform followed Aaron's strategy, and while one sprinted toward the conveyor belt that exited the building, the other provided cover. Their weapons were ineffective against Aaron's heavy machine gun. He fired from the hip, pulling forcefully against the trigger, taking down both men while he struggled to keep the weapon from kicking upward. Wasting no time, he released the empty magazine and let it fall noisily to the concrete floor. Six seconds later a full replacement magazine was locked in place. Two seconds after that a round was chambered, and the powerful weapon was back in business.

Aaron was trying to decide how to deal with the Georgians who were still firing in his direction when he saw through the snarled opening in the bay door a dark-colored Mercedes slowly pulling up behind Hasan, its lights off. Between the relentless rain pounding on the roof and the roar of machine gun fire, Aaron doubted that Hasan could hear the sedan's tires crunching on the gravel roadway as it approached. A man from inside the car leaned out the window and began to take aim on Hasan, who was fully exposed. "Hasan, behind you," Aaron shouted with all his might. Years of training saved the young lieutenant, who without hesitation sprang to his right, evading the three rounds of 9 mm bullets that would have riddled his back.

Undeterred, the men in the Mercedes continued to fire in Hasan's direction, and taking advantage of the diversion, three Georgians still inside the building made a run for it. Aaron directed a burst of machine gun fire in their general direction, but his attention was now rightfully on Hasan. He missed and was himself hit. One bullet grazed his left forearm, another slammed into a four-by-four just inches from his head. A chip of wood cut Aaron's cheek. His forearm was white-hot for a moment, but he forced himself to ignore the pain.

Hasan was in real danger and Aaron had to act fast. Silently, and under cover of a high pallet, Aaron lowered himself to the concrete floor and low-crawled as fast as he could, first around the perimeter of the large room. Then, angling off forty-five degrees, he quietly but quickly worked his way toward the Georgians until he was behind them. They were in the open. One was re-loading his 9 mm automatic while the other three poked their heads above and around the chest-high pallets, looking for signs of the intruders. Firing on full automatic, Aaron did not stop until the four men were dead on the floor.

The three Georgians who had taken flight made it out of the building through the hole in the bay door, narrowly escaping Hasan's efforts to take them down with his automatic, having set down the heavy machine gun on the floor near him. They were tough street thugs from

Tbilisi, the capital of Georgia, and had held their own in the firefight with Aaron, but they had had enough of what they thought was an attack by rival heroin traffickers and were ready to flee. The sight of the black Mercedes, and fear that its prominent passenger might see them fleeing, served to renew their courage. They regrouped behind the car.

Inside the limousine, one bodyguard signaled to the other by tilting his head slightly. The first man opened one door and ran quickly to cover, and was out of Hasan's line of sight. The second bodyguard dove through an open window, rolled away from the car, and belly crawled to the protection of a stack of fifty-five-gallon drums, holding his 9 mm, ready to fire. But he wasn't fast enough, and Hasan got off several shots, striking him in the hip. The man screamed out in pain, but recovered quickly and slithered behind the drums, still presenting a threat to Hasan, who was no more than fifteen meters away.

Instinct told Hasan that something was coming. He turned his attention away from the injured bodyguard and swiveled to his left, turning his weapon rapidly in the direction of the perceived threat. At that instant, the first bodyguard charged Hasan, who managed to fire once, grazing the attacker's leg, but only slowing him down slightly before the Georgian slammed into him.

Hasan fought for his life. The bodyguard was burly, at least thirty pounds heavier than the young lieutenant. Hasan's special-forces training in hand-to-hand combat helped him anticipate the big man's moves, leveling the playing field somewhat. Panting and cursing, the bodyguard attempted to slam the butt of his handgun into Hasan's head, but Hasan evaded the maneuver with a jerk of his head in the opposite direction, momentarily throwing his attacker off balance and giving him the opening he so desperately needed. Hasan's special-forces dagger, which had been strapped to his right calf, entered the bodyguard's abdomen slightly left of center and slid upward toward the man's heart, the sharp blade cutting through cloth and flesh like butter. A guttural sound followed, the guard involuntarily spat blood onto Hasan's face and then died on top of him. It was both horrifying and satisfying to Hasan. He had avenged Kemal Bulot's murder the old-fashioned way, by hand with his commando dagger rather than with a firearm.

Hasan shifted and pushed out from under the lifeless body, trying to ignore the blood and gore now covering him. It was not over yet. Still holding the knife, he rolled rapidly toward the machine gun he had set aside and rose to a kneeling position and reached for the RPK-74, only to be knocked to his back by the wallop of a large automatic weapon being slammed into his forehead. He struggled to stay conscious. The boot of a tall man was planted on his chest, preventing him from moving. He looked up at the muzzles of two 9 mm automatics pointed at his head. The man standing on Hasan's chest shifted to place his other foot on Hasan's right wrist, forcing the dagger to drop from his hand, while the second heavily built man maintained his aim on Hasan's head. The heavier Georgian was dressed in a dark blue suit, with a lighter blue silk shirt and red tie. An enormous diamond shimmered on his hairy ring finger. Hasan recognized him immediately. When anticipating this moment, Hasan had thought he would look away. Oddly, now that he was here, he wanted to watch. *Who is this man who had killed Kemal and will now kill me?* he thought. *Mafia? Government?* His gaze drifted to the man's mouth, where a sinister smile had begun to form. The man's right arm stiffened. Hasan knew what that meant.

And then everything changed, and both would-be killers disappeared. It was so fast that Hasan initially couldn't grasp what had happened. *I must be dead now,* he thought. *Is this how it is on the other side?* Only then did he hear the thunder of Aaron's machine gun. Aaron had let loose a continuous cannonade of fire, as many as fifty rounds in all, fired on the run. As a result, Hasan's assailants were hurled into the air and flung against the nearby wall, dying before impact.

Aaron reached Hasan almost instantly. Twenty meters away, men huddled behind the Mercedes saw an opening and made a run for it. Yusuf, who appeared from the side of the building, dropped one of them with a burst from his assault rifle, but the two others got away, disappearing into the darkness. Naim motioned to let the men go. They were no longer a threat and it was time to move on. "Hasan! Aaron! Are you all right?" he called out. "The freighter is secured. We have to get out of here."

"We're okay," Aaron responded for both of them. Naim and Yusuf approached cautiously. Yusuf was limping, the result of a minor leg wound. He and Naim gasped when they saw that Hasan was covered with gore and blood. Still shaky, he assured them that he was okay, thanks to Aaron, who smiled modestly. Each one of them had fought courageously, but as Aaron reminded them, there was more to be done.

Reduced to a drizzle, the rain no longer pelted the aluminum roof. Building 15 was eerily quiet. A foghorn sounded as a vessel approached the harbor. "Aaron, Naim's right. Let's get out of here," the lieutenant said soberly, rising to his feet with some difficulty as his boots slid on the blood-covered floor.

"Torch the place," Aaron said quickly. "But first check for documents. We should complete Kemal's work." The others nodded in agreement. While Naim emptied five-liter drums of gasoline, Yusuf planted charges of plastic explosives. Aaron, meanwhile, searched an office in the corner of the plant. He rifled through the drawers, finding only bills of lading, invoices and shipping schedules. Disappointed, he considered searching the surrounding buildings for documents, but they had very little time and insufficient manpower, so he dismissed the idea.

Hasan examined a small office downstairs but found nothing of use. Unwilling to give up, he began to search the dead, rifling through their wallets, taking what documents he could, and helping himself to two expensive-looking Rolex watches. He was about to move his search to the back of the building when he heard the high-low pulsating sirens of police vehicles approaching the port, growing louder as they neared. "Head for the boat. Head for the boat," he shouted. The others had heard the sirens, too, and the four of them grabbed their weapons and ran to the pier.

Yusuf had had his hands full but finally took possession of the freighter, dispatching four of the Italian sailors with his powerful machine gun, and the last, who tried to hide in the engine room, with his special-forces dagger. After assuring himself that there were no other traffickers hiding on the boat, he had rejoined his comrades. He was the first to reach the *Roman Goddess*. He ran up the gangway and climbed the steps to the bridge. Having worked for his uncle, who owned a small fleet of trawlers, he had experience with the steerage of vessels of this type and would skipper the crew back to Trabzon. Naim, Hasan and Aaron hurriedly untied the fore, middle and aft lines and boarded. The fifty-meter-long freighter roared noisily as Yusuf gave it full throttle and it began to inch away from the wharf into the drizzle and fog. The freighter was completely dark, as Yusuf feared turning on even the running lights.

The Southern Harbor was still, the water like glass, protected from the stormy waves beyond by a towering stone breakwater recently rebuilt and strengthened by the Georgian government. The stevedores and long-shoremen who worked the graveyard shift along the docks of the Southern Harbor had fled for home or to the nearby brothels upon the first shots of machine gun fire coming from the direction of Building 15. Other heroin traffickers in two nearby buildings stayed put as ordered, on the hope that the attackers would think

Building 15 was the only center of operations. The only sounds were those of the ship's engines and the police sirens.

Through gaps between the buildings on the Central Pier, only fifty meters from his position on the deck, Aaron and the others onboard saw the reflection of the flashing lights of the police cars against the low-lying clouds. The sirens came closer and they all understood that they had to get past the Central Pier and into the channel before the headlights of the squad cars exposed them.

At first, Yusuf was surprised by how rapidly the decrepit-looking freighter responded, but then reminded himself that the vessel was used to run heroin. It was designed to look slow, but its diesels were new and powerful. He checked the knot meter. Twelve knots and they were just clearing the corner of the Southern Pier. He cut it close to save time, coming within ten meters of the concrete wharf. Within a few seconds they entered the Northern Harbor. It, too, was totally dark, except for a few lights barely visible in the rain on the Northern Pier at Yusuf's one o'clock. Dead ahead, due north, lay the mouth of the harbor. A flashing green light and a flashing red light. Yusuf timed them. Three seconds each, just like he had studied on the navigational chart. Yusuf prayed to Allah for more speed.

The sirens were louder now. The Poti police cars were racing down the main road leading to the Central Pier. The freighter picked up speed and was now approaching twenty knots. Yusuf again looked at his watch—03:24. The ship steamed north-northwest across the Northern Harbor to the channel. He looked at his watch again— 03:27. The police cars had not yet reached Building 15.

At 03:29, the calm of the Southern Harbor was shattered by the eruption of Building 15. The combination of several pounds of C4 and five hundred liters of gasoline was spectacular, the explosion sending the sheet metal roof and walls of the heroin-packing plant several hundred meters in all directions. Shards of molten metal rained down on the approaching police cars, forcing the drivers to slam on the brakes. The officers stared in shock at the flames only two hundred meters from where they stopped. Pieces of metal fell in the water near the freighter. Aaron, Naim and Hasan, exposed on the deck, sought cover as the vessel, too, was showered with fragments. From the bridge, Yusuf saw his cabin and bow momentarily brighten from the detonation behind him, but he kept his eyes on the flashing harbor lights ahead.

Several minutes later, the freighter steamed past the red and green lights. They had escaped, and they had avenged Kemal Bulot's death. Aaron stood on the deck, ignoring the drizzle and cold wind, watching the fire grow smaller.

Once past the harbor lights, Yusuf turned the freighter into the wind and headed west for five nautical miles, directly into the storm, which had regained its fury after a brief lull. He then steered southwest in a direct line toward his hometown of Trabzon, while the others onboard began dumping cases of tomatoes and heroin overboard into the swirling waters. Powerful winds buffeted them from the west, on the starboard side of the craft. At times the waves towered above the deck, the sea threatening to swallow the small vessel. Still, Aaron, Hasan and Naim worked continuously for two more hours, ridding the vessel of its contraband. They were not on an official mission, and the last thing they needed was to be arrested by the Turkish police for trafficking in heroin. When finally done, they joined Yusuf, happy to get off the frigid deck and into the warmth of the enclosed and heated wheelhouse.

"Yusuf, where is the package I gave you?" Hasan asked after several moments. Without taking his eyes off the bow, barely visible in the souplike fog, Yusuf motioned toward a cardboard box on a ledge to his right.

"These are the papers I found on the truck and the dead Iranians," Hasan explained as he opened the plastic bag that he had used to keep the papers dry. "And these are the spoils of war." He held up a clear plastic bag by its corner to show Aaron the massive gold-and-diamond ring and cufflinks the Georgian official had worn, as well as two Rolex watches he had liberated. Yusuf cast a quick glance and nodded with approval. "I want you to have the man's ring and cufflinks," Hasan offered, raising the bag closer to Aaron so that he could get a better look at its contents. The diamonds sparkled impressively, even in the dim red light of the bridge.

"Thank you," Aaron said and smiled warmly. The two men embraced briefly, and Aaron kissed his friend on both cheeks. Although war trophies had never been his style, he was touched by Hasan's gesture and put the bauble on his ring finger. Too loose, he placed it on his middle finger, where it fit snugly. He then put the cufflinks in his pocket, winking at Hasan as if to say he'd wear them another day. After a moment, Aaron added, "Let's take a look at the papers."

Hasan and Aaron stepped into the chart room next to the bridge to examine the documents. The first thing that struck Aaron about them was that most of them were in English, though the bad grammar and spelling mistakes indicated that they were written by someone whose native tongue was anything but English.

"Everything here looks like routine customs papers, bills of lading, invoices and receipts," Aaron announced after about twenty-five minutes. "Except this. Do you remember where you found it?" Aaron handed Lieutenant Ertugrul a folded, worn sheet of paper from a yellow ruled pad, with what appeared to be notes handwritten in a mix of Farsi and English.

"Yes, it was in the jacket pocket of one of the Iranians. I think he was one of the leaders. He seemed to be the one giving the orders, at least from what I was able to see. What do you make of it, my friend?" Hasan handed the paper back to Aaron, who shrugged and shook his head. "I only know a few words and expressions in Farsi. I can't read it, but I'll have someone take a look at it back home."

FIVE

Syria Claims U.S. Attacked with Ground Forces, Reuters, Damascus

Senior Syrian officials claim that American commandos attacked deep in Syria this morning, damaging an elementary school and killing "many" Syrian soldiers in Deir ez-Zur, a small market town astride the Euphrates River, approximately one hundred kilometers from the Iraqi border.

"This is yet another example of the American and Israeli imperialists slaughtering Arab peoples," Tariq Al-Saif, spokesman for the Foreign Ministry, said at a hastily called press conference in Damascus. "Is it not enough that they invade Iraq, threatening our eastern border, and push ever toward us to our west with the Israeli settlements? Is it now necessary that they butcher us in our sleep?

"Deir ez-Zur was until this morning a peaceful town. There was no danger to the imperialists there. Now the aggressors have brought the war to yet another Arab village, and yet more Arabs know the pain of holding their deceased loved ones in their arms."

Syrian army officers in Deir ez-Zur pointed out to the foreign press corps that the ground floor and basement of the school had been ransacked and that hundreds of bullet holes pockmarked nearby buildings and vehicles as well as the school itself. These officers would not say how many Syrian soldiers were killed and wounded, but they said that casualties were heavy. "They came early in the morning, killing like devils," said an army captain who had removed his nametag and refused to disclose his identity. "See these shell casings?" the captain told the press, giving each member of the foreign press several spent cartridges to take with them. "These are American shells. Syrians have been butchered by American commandos sent here by the Zionists."

Kate Brind, National Security Adviser, put down the article that had just come across the wires and that her deputy had put in front of her and took a seat opposite him. It was 4:15 in the morning and they were pulling the graveyard shift, working the crisis.

"Shit," Kate hissed through clenched teeth. "The Syrians are going to raise holy hell in the UN." She looked at her watch. "Either way, this is big. We have to decide how to spin this. Let's assume we're going to deny it. We'd better get ready before the president wakes up."

"Well, that's not all," her deputy said. "The Georgians announced that someone killed their minister of the interior in Poti—someone heard to be speaking in American English and Turkish," he added as he handed her an *Agence France-Presse* wire in French. Kate read the article and slumped in her chair. There was only one person she could think of offhand who spoke American English and Turkish, though she couldn't imagine why he would have been in Poti.

"Son of a bitch, Korda. What in the hell were you thinking? What a ridiculous fucking stunt to pull. I'm not going to mince words with you," Stanton Clarke said as he walked around his well-appointed corner office at Heller & Clarke Consulting and kicked his waste can. He wished he were going to lunch at the Racquet Club instead of dealing with this mess. "You killed the goddamn interior minister of a country we're trying to enlist to help us go after the terrorists. Shit," the older man railed, his West Virginia twang now quite apparent despite his having left the Allegheny Valley many years before. "The fucking minister of the interior," he continued, shaking his head. "The CIA is furious. You were on a rogue mission in bum-fuck Pee-oh-tee. A goddamn personal vendetta. Hey, I don't give a shit if you knocked off a few heroin traffickers. The client doesn't give a damn about drug dealers. But the CIA's trying to infiltrate the Georgian government, not kill the bastards." Clarke took a deep breath and sat behind his desk. He looked at Aaron on the other side. "Aw, ferchrissake. At least take off that goddamn bandage before our client gets here," he added, referring to the gauze covering the two-day-old cut on Aaron's cheek. Clarke looked at his watch. "They'll be here at noon. What do you propose we tell them?"

Aaron, very much jet-lagged, started to shrug and say he didn't give a damn what Cold Spring Biologics, a front for the CIA based on Long Island, and what the suits from Langley thought about his "stunt," but he held back. Outwardly, Clarke was calming down, but Aaron knew he was still upset, and the truth was that he had a right to be. As right as his personal adventure in Poti felt to him, it hadn't been authorized by Langley, and Aaron was in serious danger of losing his biggest client, and possibly his job altogether. That was the problem on Aaron's mind. He enjoyed his consulting job. Heller & Clarke's clients were a diverse group of large and small companies in a variety of industries, although Aaron focused mostly on pharmaceutical, biotechnology and petrochemical accounts, having developed a highly regarded expertise in these industries. In addition to the intellectual aspects of the work, he liked the travel, and especially enjoyed the $325,000 he made last year. Before the current flap over the incident in Poti, he had been told and thoroughly expected that this year would be even better. Now there might be nothing at all.

Cold Spring Biologics had been the first client Aaron

personally had brought to Heller & Clarke, and it was by far still his biggest. The CIA had sought him out. Chemistry major from West Point, former Airborne Ranger, MBA from the University of Chicago, single, no kids. Good cover. Made to order. The agents who had scouted him had carefully checked out his security clearance and psychological profile. Bravo Company, First Battalion/Seventy-fifth Rangers. During Desert Storm, then Second Lieutenant Aaron Korda had led his squad on a raid to destroy an Iraqi radio broadcast tower near the Jordanian border. The team's mission was a success. Aaron had conducted himself well under heavy enemy fire, and was slightly wounded in the process. The CIA background check indicated that after being reassigned to the Second/Fourteenth, Tenth Mountain Division, he was promoted to first lieutenant, and had gone on to serve with distinction in Mogadishu. He was a student of languages. He spoke fluent German to the point of having no accent, and his Turkish was almost as good. His Arabic was passable, although he wasn't fluent. The scouts' reports were unqualified and enthusiastically sent up the chain of command within the CIA. RECOMMEND IMMEDIATE RECRUITMENT AND TRAINING. The deputy director for operations, the DDO, had personally given the go-ahead. Cold Spring Biologics would engage Heller & Clarke, pay its full fare for Aaron's hourly rates, and move him in and out of Europe and the Middle East.

"What do you propose we tell them?" Clarke repeated, detecting some hesitancy on Aaron's part. The gray-haired man folded his arms impatiently, a gesture with which Aaron was fully familiar.

Hold your tongue, Aaron told himself as he searched for an answer. "I'll tell them that nothing in Poti can trace the incident back to me, let alone Cold Spring Biologics or the CIA. We left nothing behind. The weapons were Russian. . . . Off the black market in Trabzon. All shell casings left behind were Russian. I'll also tell them that we wiped out an important quantity of heroin, destroyed a drug-packing plant and disrupted a major supply line for the importation of narcotics into Europe. I know . . . I know," Aaron acknowledged, holding both hands up as if to surrender when he saw Clarke about to pounce, "they don't give a shit about heroin in Europe, but our NATO allies do. That should count for something," he said, his voice sounding less convinced than he intended. "And . . . well, I guess I'll point out my record. I've got an ass-kicking, shit-stomping track record, Stanton. You and the CIA know that."

Aaron was playing to Clarke's penchant for locker room language. The older man knew it, but said nothing as he removed his glasses and placed them on one of the many stacks of paper on his desk. Aaron saw that he was scoring points and decided to press onward. "When Offenbach Chemie Werke of Germany was selling sarin gas compounds to the Libyans, I fingered them. How many CIA agents can speak Turkish as well as I do, and have the cover that I have?"

"You don't have to persuade me, Aaron. Heller and Clarke loves you. We really do. You've made us a lot of money. You broke up the Russian mob's effort to sell counterfeit over-the-counter painkillers in Europe, and that saved our clients a bundle. We know you're good." Stanton folded his hands behind his head and leaned into the high-back chair. He paused to study the handsome younger man seated across from him. In his thirty-five years in the business of consulting for international companies, Clarke had seen few consultants who were better than Aaron. He was extremely bright, creative and confident, known for thinking out of the box and getting the job done. Although he was impulsive and a bit of a hothead, his clients rarely, if ever, saw this side of him unless he wanted them to. Aaron always came off as being in command of himself and the situation. *Until now,* thought Clarke. "But the problem with you, Aaron, is that you're out of control. Do you realize—" he began, but was interrupted by his secretary. He picked up the phone and replaced it in its cradle without

saying a word. "Okay, they're waiting. In Twenty-six A.
Let's go see if we can pull your . . . er, our nuts out of
this fire."

Clarke entered the interior conference room first, with
Aaron right behind him. The chill was palpable. The two
men from Cold Spring Biologics, CIA agents known to
Aaron, sat on one side of the long, highly polished table.
No one stood when he and Clarke entered. After Korda
and Clarke seated themselves, the latter's secretary connected Kate Brind by video conference.

"Okay, let's get on with it," Donald Prebish, the senior of the two agents, said curtly. "This is Kate Brind,
who I'm sure you know is the president's national security adviser." He motioned to the younger agent to turn
on the tape recorder that sat in the middle of the table.

"Mr. Korda," Kate began, "we've never spoken, but
I have followed your work for this country quite closely.
You have served the nation well so you start out with
the benefit of the doubt, but let's cut to the chase. We're
here to learn what you were doing in Poti, Georgia, and
why you killed the interior minister. You understand
that we have a first-rate diplomatic mess on our hands.
The Georgians are furious. We have denied involvement. We said a rival drug gang must have carried out
the killings. However, two, and only two, locals got out
of that building alive. Unfortunately, they heard someone call out in English. One of them used to live in
England and he recognized that the accent was American. He also heard that same person speak in Turkish.
The Georgians don't know this, and we're not about to
tell them, but there aren't many Americans roughly fitting your description who speak Turkish. So you see,
Aaron, you've put us in a bit of a box."

Aaron liked her. She made her point without shoving
it in your face, and at least so far she seemed pretty
reasonable. "Okay. I'll start from the beginning. Kemal
Bulot was my roommate at West Point and my very
good friend. . . ." A few minutes later, Aaron finished
by telling them that the official who arrived in the Mer-

cedes was about to kill Lieutenant Ertugrul, and that he had shot the man out of necessity, sparing the details of how many bullets riddled the interior minister, and leaving out the part about the ring and cufflinks. As he spoke, he admitted that while avenging Kemal's death had been satisfying, he and the others had also embarked on the mission to find out why and by whom he was killed, knowing that the Turkish government had decided not to pursue it, and feeling that he owed Kemal, who was like a brother, at least that much. Prebish interrupted several times, quite angry, although not with the fact that the interior minister of Georgia was dead, nor that the State Department and White House had to deal with the diplomatic fallout, but rather with Aaron's insubordination. Aaron practically ignored him, convinced his best shot was with Kate Brind, and believing correctly that Prebish would never approve.

". . . So after we set the C4 explosives, we got the hell outta Dodge. Fortunately, we were far enough away when the blast went off. Then when we were out to sea, we dumped the cartons of canned tomatoes and heroin overboard and headed back to Trabzon."

"But why didn't you keep them as evidence?" Prebish asked sarcastically.

"That's easy. We weren't on official business, either for the U.S. or Turkish governments. There was no way we were going to import heroin into Turkey and risk ending up in jail."

"You could have turned the contraband over to the local police, or to the army," the younger agent suggested, speaking up for the first time. For the first time in the meeting, Prebish noticed the large gold-and-diamond ring on Aaron's middle finger and the matching cufflinks. Aaron had never worn jewelry before, other than a modest watch and his West Point ring, and Prebish wondered what caused him to sport such an ostentatious display now.

"I thought about it, but we weren't in the mood for publicity. And for whatever reasons, the MIT seems to have dropped the investigation after Kemal's death, which, like I said, was part of the reason I felt I had to go." Prebish rolled his eyes and chortled, which Aaron ignored. "The Turks obviously would not have wanted any press. The police would have had to make reports, and it could have hit the local papers. And by the way, if we had gone public with this and the Turkish government had been drawn in officially, you'd be hard-pressed to deny that an American was involved, wouldn't you?" Aaron sensed that he had scored a point with Kate Brind, who nodded, although Prebish remained unmoved.

"Thank you, Mr. Korda," Kate Brind said. "I'll say this for you. This is one of the most honest and straightforward testimonies I've heard in a long time." Aaron did not know that Brind had also had similar blunt conversations with his brother, Martin, and that Brind admired, was even refreshed by, the Kordas' straightforwardness. "However, that doesn't solve our problem, and we'll have to take this under advisement."

Aaron smiled in appreciation. He considered mentioning the notes in Farsi that Lieutenant Ertugrul had taken off the dead man in Poti, but something told him to hold back. It still hadn't been translated, he had no idea of what it meant, and *What the hell,* he thought. *It might be an ace in the hole to play later.*

Faramaz ben Sarah stood in the doorway of the shipping container that served as the office of his chief deputy in Poti, Mohammed al-Mistani, who had had the good fortune to not be in Poti at the time of the attack. Instead, he had been on a vessel in the Caspian Sea, shepherding a large delivery of heroin from Turkmenbashi, Turkmenistan, where the heroin had been processed and refined, to Baku, Azerbaijan, for transshipment by truck over the Caucasus to Poti for delivery and sale to the Italian Mafia. Mohammed's luck was such that he was not only spared death at the hands of Aaron and his friends from the Turk First Commando

Brigade, but also from Faramaz, who was in no mood for incompetence.

"Our men were taken by surprise in the dead of a cold, stormy night," al-Mistani continued in his briefing. Faramaz had his back to him and was looking out the door, surveying what had been Building 15 and his packing plant. "No one was posted outside. It was all very unfortunate and very stupid. They were trained to do better, but even if they had done their job, there is nothing to indicate that they could have prevented the massacre. Our men and the local Georgians were outmanned and outgunned. But we don't know who they were or how many men they had. As they ambushed and killed our men in the plant, they overtook the Italians on the ship and tossed their bodies into the harbor. Only two men, both Georgians, survived." Faramaz lit a cigarette and nodded. Al-Mistani paused until Faramaz gestured for him to continue, his back still to his deputy. "Of course, we questioned the survivors. Both heard men speaking Turkish. One of them is certain that he heard an American yell out to the others. The American also spoke in Turkish. We questioned the Georgian extensively on this. He lived in England for a few years and claims to be able to distinguish between the American and English accents."

"Your guards in Buildings 11 and 13—did they go to the assistance of our men under attack in Building 15?"

"No, sir. As per my standing orders, they are not to do anything to draw attention to Buildings 11 and 13 unless they are attacked directly. We've discussed this before, Fauad. All of the documents, the computer files . . . we cannot let anyone know that we are also working out of those buildings. "

"Do not use my Arabic name," Faramaz said sternly. He pulled deeply on the cigarette and blew the smoke out noisily between his teeth. One part of him wanted to set an example by punishing those present during the attack, another was happy to not have to kill valuable foot soldiers. After several moments, he said, "What do you think the American and Turks were doing here? What was their objective?"

"They appear to have been interested in the canning operations and disrupting them. They didn't go anywhere near Buildings 11 and 13," he added after a pause, referring to offices where al-Mistani ran the operation. "We're installing a temporary canning plant in Building 13. I'll show you the progress whenever you want. It's crowded and our production is somewhat slower, but we're making do."

"Don't bother to rebuild Building 15. Step up the pace of the canning operations in Building 13. We're nearing the end, Mohammed. Don't lose sight of that." Faramaz's stern gaze lingered, then a thoughtful expression came over his face. "So, tell me your thoughts about the attackers."

"It seems that they wanted to put us out of business, or at least slow us down. . . . Perhaps they were rival heroin traffickers. Nothing indicates that they were Turk or American intelligence agents. . . . Otherwise they would have gone for our offices and our records. They would have taken a prisoner or two to interrogate them. Instead, everyone has . . . well, mostly the bodies . . . been accounted for. And they certainly didn't try to break into this office," he added, tapping the side of the metal container.

"Have you considered moving to another city . . . to, say, Baku?"

"Yes, sir," Mohammed said. "But that would take a great deal of time, and the Azerbaijanis are too closely allied with the Americans these days and cannot be trusted. We haven't found the right person to serve as our protector. We have connected with the new Georgian minister of the interior, a cousin of our friend killed here the other night, and he has agreed to work with us on the same terms as his cousin."

Faramaz tossed his cigarette to the ground in front of him. "You may be right that the attack came from rival traffickers. We have broken into a tightly guarded network, and we have made a lot of money. But we have to be certain that the American and the Turks were not CIA and MIT. I will personally track them down and make sure that you are right about that."

Faramaz lit another cigarette and turned to his friend, who sat at a desk near the end of the twenty-foot container. "Phase three is nearing completion. The first drugs are scheduled to be on the shelves in North America and Western Europe by Wednesday, November 10. The botulinum-A manufacturing facilities in Belgium and Illinois are operating according to plan, and there are absolutely no signs that the Western intelligence or police agencies suspect anything there, which is why I think you may be right about the attack." He stepped farther into the container and took a chair near his trusted lieutenant. He was physically drained from the long, circuitous flights he had taken from Holland, where he was based, but his eyes still held his fiery determination. "You have been doing the computer modeling. What are our current kill estimates?"

"They've been revised upward somewhat," al-Mistani reported quickly, eager to give his leader some good news at last. "Our labs have been able to enhance the shelf life of the botulinum-A toxin and to make it more resistant to heat in the pharmaceutical manufacturing process. . . . Even better than our facilities in Iraq were able to do. Your brother and the others in Illinois have found a way to enhance the toxin so that with patients using nebulized albuterol, the poison enters the bloodstream and the gastrointestinal system faster and in greater amounts than we were able to achieve back in Iraq. They're brilliant, Fauad," Mohammed added, again using Faramaz's Arabic name. Faramaz was too fascinated by the report to rebuke his colleague. "They somehow managed to attain a greater dispersal of the toxin after an injection so that a vaccine shot, for example, won't just paralyze the tissue stuck with the needle, but will spread rapidly to the child's respiratory muscles, bringing asphyxiation and death within twenty-four to thirty-six hours." .

"What if the enemy has antitoxins?" Faramaz asked, his eyes riveted to his colleagues'.

"We don't believe that their current antitoxins are effective against our enhanced poison. But even if they are, there won't be nearly enough antidotes to combat mass exposure and not enough time to administer what they might have. Also, there won't be even remotely enough respirators to help ventilate the vast numbers of people with respiratory paralysis."

"What kind of numbers are we now talking about?"

"In America and Canada where we're directing the bulk of the shipments, we expect to kill as many as half a million. Perhaps as many in Europe." He smiled for the first time since Faramaz had arrived in Poti a few hours earlier.

"Mohammed, my friend, the freighter . . . the *Roman Goddess*. Do we know where it is now?"

"We've traced it to Trabzon. Our Italian friends won't touch it until they see if the Turkish government intends to do anything with it. In the meantime, it's moored in the old part of the harbor."

"That will be my next stop before I return to Holland. You stay in Poti and see to the operations here. But I'll need two of your best men."

SIX

"Hey, there. Hey, down here," a man on the dock yelled to get the attention of someone onboard the freighter tied alongside the pier. The tide was out and the deck of the vessel was only a meter higher than the pier. A sailor appeared from the bridge and acknowledged the stranger with a wave, indicating with his fingers that he would join him on the dock in five minutes.

The stranger, tall and muscular, buttoned his peacoat at the neck and pulled his Greek fisherman's cap farther down his forehead. He examined the freighter with great interest. Several dockyard workers were onboard repairing it. Welders had filled in the bullet holes and sanded the weld flush with the hull and bulkheads. The ship's name, *Roman Goddess,* had been wire-brushed off, but was still legible pending the painting that would come when the weather cleared.

A sharp gust blew, driving large pellets of rain into Faramaz's face. The water was choppy, even this far back into the harbor. Three-inch-thick lines creaked against iron cleats on the pier as the winds tried to push the freighter adrift. He shoved his hands deep into his jacket pockets, growing impatient with the Turk who had waved to him and who had remained on deck, talking to the repairmen. Finally, the sailor stepped down the slatted wood gangway. The two dockyard workers on the deck had stopped what they were doing and kept an eye on the stranger, hands in their pockets, ready to draw their weapons and shoot him. The Turk ap-

proached warily. Strangers didn't come to his part of the
harbor often. The newer, deeper-draft commercial vessels were moored in the recently dredged part of Trabzon's port. Back here in the old port, where the piers
were rotting and the bottom was filling in with silt, only
the smaller boats came, tended by poor fishermen and
rich gunrunners.

"Hello," the stranger said simply, keeping his hands
in his pockets, his right hand firmly grasping his Walther
P88 9 mm. One of the men on the deck moved aft to
get behind him, ready to kill the stranger if his hand
were to come out of his jacket other than empty. "Is
that your vessel?" A foghorn sounded loudly at the entrance of the harbor, signaling the arrival of a large container ship, but neither man took his eyes off the other.
The Turkish seaman was in his fifties. The whites of his
deep-set eyes were laced with red and were watery, the
result of too much salt air and booze, and too little sleep.
A sparse, almost colorless ponytail protruded from the
back of his worn woolen cap. The week-old stubble on
his taut, leathery face stood up like gray porcupine
quills.

"Why do you want to know?" the sailor asked, making no effort to hide his hostility.

"I'm interested in buying it. I know this vessel, and I
know that it's faster than it looks. Hey," he added, as
he slowly removed his hands from his pockets and raised
them level with his shoulders, open palms facing the man
playing with him. "I will pay good money, cash. If it's
yours, perhaps we can have coffee and talk." He gestured in the direction of a seedy bar/tabac on the wharf
near the end of the pier.

"How do you know the *Roman Goddess*?" the Turk
asked, wondering what the stranger was really after.

"I know it from Poti, and I know that the Italians
used it to run drugs," Faramaz volunteered evenly. "I
also know that the Italians will want it back. They can
take it from you and not pay you a single lira. Why I
want it need not concern you. I heard about the shoot-

ings in Poti last week, which is not my concern. I only
want to buy this ship and go about my business."

The sailor had agreed with the boat's new owner to
take only part of his wages in cash, deferring the balance
until the vessel was sold. The idea of cashing out early
was appealing. "Unfortunately, it's not mine to sell. It
belongs to a man named Ciller. He runs a few fishing
trawlers. His wife runs a small hotel, the Trabizond,
about one hundred meters on the other side of the harbor master's building," he said, pointing to a two-story,
pale yellow stucco building across the harbor to the west.
"Ciller," he repeated and returned to the freighter and
his work.

"Mr. Ciller. How do you do? My name is Faramaz
ben Sarah," a man in a peacoat and Greek seaman's cap
said in Iranian-accented Turkish. "Your man onboard
the *Roman Goddess* directed me to you. I would like to
buy it. Cash."

Captain Ciller, as he was known around the port of
Trabzon, regarded the stranger suspiciously. Ciller's
partner had called him moments before, alerting him
that a strong-looking man of olive complexion would be
coming to negotiate the purchase of the vessel. Instead,
there were three strangers. Ciller had taken the precau-
tion of having one of his sailors with him in the room,
armed with a Makarov 9 mm. The man, who was also a
friend, stood dutifully in the corner of the brightly lit
lobby, his back against a ceramic tile wall, his right hand
in his coat pocket. As tough and cagey as he was, a chill
went up Ciller's spine as he studied Faramaz, and he
mentally began to reduce the price he would negotiate
for the freighter.

It was early afternoon, but already two prostitutes sat
near the door on French café chairs that in better
weather would be outside in front of the hotel on Iskele
Street, a steep lane leading up from the docks. The
women, Russians, or Natashas as the Turks called them,
bared their long legs from underneath their great coats.

Each overly made-up hooker, one with blond hair cut in a 1980s shag, the other a faux redhead, pulled back the lapels of her coat to advertise enough cleavage to indicate she was worth the price. The blonde, who was barely nineteen, flashed a smile at the men. The redhead, the older one at twenty-five, looked like she had been on the streets her entire life. Her lips twitched more than smiled.

The man who called himself Faramaz remained near the entrance as the other two strangers stepped deeper into the lobby. When his comrades were closer to Captain Ciller, Faramaz shut the stainless steel–framed glass door, flipped the CLOSED sign to the outside, turned the dead bolt and pulled down the shade with one hand, the other still in his jacket pocket. He then yanked the curtains on a small chest-high window, ensuring that no one from the narrow street could see in. With a jerk of his head, he motioned to the prostitutes to his right to remove themselves from the lobby through a side door leading to what looked like a small office. They did not move. He removed his Walther automatic and waved it at them and to the side door. The women understood that message and complied. Faramaz followed the Natashas to the back office, screwing a silencer onto his weapon as he proceeded.

Like her husband, Cari Ciller was in her early sixties. But whereas the captain was grizzled and paunchy, she was an attractive woman who took pride in her appearance. Her brown hair was tied back in a chignon, her blue print dress and white sweater clean and well fitting. A gold locket passed down to her by her maternal grandmother hung on a gold chain from her neck. "Who are you?" she demanded, rising from her chair behind a desk, then seeing the weapon. "What do you want from us?" she asked in disbelief. She cast a quick glance at the two women who plied their trade in her eight-room hotel to see if they understood. The teenage blonde shrugged indifferently. She had, she told herself, been in more difficult situations. The redhead had been around a lot longer and knew from the half-grin forming on the killer's lips that her time was running out.

The silenced weapon spat out two bullets, both hitting the redhead in the chest just above her cleavage line. *Plap, plap.* The impact lifted the woman off her feet, throwing her lifeless body over a table. Mrs. Ciller began to scream, but Faramaz moved forward and shoved the silencer into her open mouth, arresting any further protest. "Come with me," he ordered in heavily accented Turkish. The blond prostitute's breath of relief at having escaped her friend's fate was her last. As Faramaz removed the barrel from Cari Ciller's mouth, he pushed her toward the door leading back to the lobby. He briefly swung around and, with seemingly little effort, pointed his weapon at the teenager's head and fired.

Upon entering the room, Mrs. Ciller saw that her husband stood facing the two men, but their broad shoulders obscured her line of vision to his face. In the corner, propped up against the wall, lay what remained of their friend who had been summoned to help, blood dripping from his mouth. Despite the horror, or maybe because of it, Cari's eyes were drawn to the lines of blood trailing down the ceramic tiles caused by the bullets exiting the back of his head. Captain Ciller's eyes were fixed on the silencer now held to his wife's temple.

"Captain Ciller," Faramaz began, "we can do this the easy way, or the hard way. My comrade here," he continued, motioning to the man who had just murdered the Cillers' friend, "is very good at what he does. He will make you talk one way or the other."

"What do you want from us? I was told that you wanted to buy the *Roman Goddess*. I will give it to you. It is yours. Just leave us alone."

"I do not want your pathetic boat," Faramaz answered impatiently. "But tell me who brought it to you. I want to know the names of the men who sailed it into the harbor last week."

"I don't know who they are, only that they abandoned the vessel at the pier. The harbor master gave it to me to sell. He's my cousin. We didn't report it to the authorities. We did it for the money. We only wanted to make a few lira. But please, I beg you, the boat means nothing to us. Just spare my wife and me. We are discreet people. We will say nothing to the police about this," he pleaded, mistakenly believing that there was a chance these men would spare them.

Faramaz said nothing to the assassin who stood next to him, but the latter knew the next move. *Pssst*, the weapon spat. The bullet hit Ciller's left kneecap with a hideous *plap* of lead on bone. The captain collapsed in agony. "The names of the people who brought the ship to you," Faramaz demanded, his voice measured and calm. "The next bullet will be in your wife's knee. And, my friend, that will only be the beginning." The killer holding Mrs. Ciller gave a quick shrug, and removing the muzzle of his weapon from her temple, pushed the weapon into her pelvis. She let out a yelp.

"No. No, please," the captain sputtered. "There was an American. He spoke Turkish. I didn't hear his name. They were on the pier for only moments. . . . And left in a hurry. It was dark . . . raining. I didn't see their faces."

Cari Ciller didn't hear the bullet leave the muzzle of the silenced weapon, nor did she note the sound it made when it removed her knee, but she did see the flash. All went silent for her as she crashed to the lobby floor. The pain was so intense and the shock so great that for a moment she could not push enough air from her lungs to scream.

"I will tell you. Allah forgive me," Captain Ciller said hoarsely. "We did not wish this to be brought into our lives. My nephew, Yusuf. He's in the army . . . a sergeant. An officer . . . a Lieutenant Ertugrul . . . Hasan Ertugrul . . . yes, I think his first name is Hasan."

"Are they garrisoned here in Trabzon? Are they with the unit housed in the barracks east of town?" Faramaz asked, his demeanor steady, unchanged, but his interest clearly aroused.

"Yusuf's family lives here but he is stationed near Kayseri," Captain Ciller blurted out, praying that he would not be punished in the next world for the betrayal of his favorite nephew. "I don't know his exact unit," he lied convincingly. Even if he couldn't get to Yusuf in time to warn him, these terrible men, he believed, would meet their match if they tried to take on a trained commando. "Kayseri . . . yes, they're located in Kayseri . . . an infantry company . . . some sort of infantry, I believe."

"Why did your nephew steal a boat in Georgia and bring it here?"

"I think it was an army mission. What else could it be? For the love of Allah, that's all I know. Please leave us alone. We have done nothing."

Convinced that the old man had nothing more of use to tell him, Faramaz nodded to his gunmen, one of whom casually approached the captain, still lying on the floor, and without a word aimed his weapon at the captain's head and squeezed the trigger. He then walked over to Mrs. Ciller, careful not to slip on her blood, and executed her with one shot to the chest.

Stepping out of the hotel onto Iskele Street, Faramaz tugged at his cap and pulled the collar up on his peacoat to ward against the chilly rain. "Tell the Italians where they can find their boat," he ordered his cohorts, and his thoughts immediately returned to the matters at hand. *Kayseri. First Commando Brigade.* After the old couple, their friend and two burnt-out whores, it would be an interesting challenge to take out the two commandos, but he had no doubt that he could do it. First, though, he would find Yusuf's family in Trabzon and get his photo. But the timing worried him. He had to locate them, find out what they knew, identify the American, eliminate him and then quickly get back to Holland and back to work on the project. There was no time to waste.

*　　*　　*

"Look! On the right. The green Volvo is pulling out."

"Hey, Yusuf, my lucky day. Maybe I should play the lottery and get my wife a real birthday present," Lieutenant Ertugrul laughed as he hurried to get the space on Kizilay Street, happy to save a few Turkish lira by not parking in a lot. On his wife's birthday, they normally took the family and friends to Beyazsaray restaurant, her favorite. But she was eight months pregnant and not up to it, so the young lieutenant had volunteered to pick up dinner there and bring their friend Yusuf home for a small dinner party. The First Commando Brigade had been training hard in the mountains north of Kayseri for the past six days. The exercises had gone well, but the lieutenant and sergeant were tired, eager to have a few drinks and a decent dinner with the officer's wife and three-year-old son.

It was early, and the line at the takeout counter was short. The restaurant was popular, and in an hour the queue would snake its way outside the door and onto the sidewalk on Millet Street. Hasan ordered plenty of kabob, *ayran* and salad. "Let's get some sweet cakes. Divan's pastry shop is just up the street near the car. My wife loves Divan's *börek*."

"Great idea. Give me the bag," Yusuf volunteered, reaching for the sack of food as they left the restaurant, and in doing so brushing into a large, broad-shouldered man wearing a peacoat and Greek fisherman's cap. Yusuf immediately apologized, not noticing that the man's eyes were fixed on Yusuf's name tag sewn on his fatigue jacket.

Kayseri is high in the mountains and the snows come early. White flakes had begun to fall, tossed about by a rush of frigid air coming down from Mount Argeus, which towered over the town. Yusuf peered inside the small shop as Hasan entered. Divan's was busy and there was barely enough room for more than six or seven persons. Normally, he would have waited outside, but he had had enough of the outdoors in the past few days, and the warmth and smell of the pastries seemed very inviting. He stepped inside.

After making their purchase, the two soldiers stepped out of the shop onto Millet Street. Pedestrians made their way down narrow sidewalks, weaving in and out of the tightly packed cars, some of which encroached on the already limited walkway. The snowfall was heavier now, and the wind had picked up. "Let's go home before the kabob gets cold," Lieutenant Ertugrul said. "I could use a glass of raki or two," he added as he juggled the bag of pastries in one hand and fumbled with the keys to unlock his two-door Fiat. Once the driver's-side door was open, Hasan unlocked the passenger's door by pressing the button at the base of the driver's armrest, placed the sack of pastries he was carrying on the floor behind the seat, straightened his fatigue jacket and began to slide behind the wheel. At the same time, Yusuf put the bag containing the kabob on the floor behind the front passenger's seat and started to get into the car.

A piercing pain in the back of Yusuf's head literally took his breath away. He felt himself passing out, but rallied his strength. His right foot was still firm on the pavement, his left on the floorboard. He struggled to stand up, trying to figure out what had happened. His first thought was that he had bumped his head on the doorframe, but the unmistakable spit of a silenced weapon hissing in his ears dispelled that hope. At that instant, he understood that his short life had taken a very bad turn. He saw the splatter of his own blood on the interior of the Fiat before he realized that the bullet had torn through his right flank and exited through his abdomen. Still, he wasn't going to make it easy for his assassin. Gathering what power he could, somehow he was able to spin his torn body around and maneuver his legs between those of his attacker, his right hand knifing through the air with stunning speed. He jerked his legs and caught the assailant's jaw with his karate chop, sending the killer to the cobblestone pavement next to the car. His odds had improved, but only for a moment. Lying on his back, the attacker fired point-blank into Yusuf's right knee. The sergeant went down with a cry of pain.

On the other side of the car, Hasan fared no better. His attacker had not underestimated the abilities of a special-forces commando and had not run the risk that Yusuf's had. Faramaz shot clear through the lieutenant's knees from the back, bringing him down, his upper body in the car and his mangled legs on the pavement, straddling the open doorway. Hasan looked up, incredulous as the assailant proceeded to fire his silenced Makarov automatic into each of his elbows. The lieutenant, like his trusted sergeant and friend on the other side of the Fiat, was immobilized, unable to use any of his formidable self-defense skills.

The attack had taken no more than a few seconds, but pedestrians were already running away. The two gunmen, accompanied by a third man who had stood guard ten meters away, stuffed the two soldiers into the backseat of the vehicle. The third killer, somewhat less bulky than the others, pushed into the backseat and placed the muzzle of his weapon firmly against the lieutenant's temple, while the two larger men sat in the front. Slamming his door, the driver hurriedly started the engine and edged out of the tight parking spot. Clear of the other vehicles, he raced the car up Kizilay Street, turned onto Millet Street, and headed southwest, out of the city to an auto body garage they had appropriated earlier in the day from its now-deceased owner.

The auto body shop was a dank, greasy pit of a place, nestled into the side of a cliff near the edge of town, on a narrow road that eventually meandered south down the mountains to the town of Niğde. The mechanic and proprietor lay crumpled in the corner near drums of used oil and an air pump.

Faramaz took the lead in breaking Yusuf's joints one by one with a tire iron. As he did so, he calmly explained to Yusuf what he had done to his uncle and aunt in Trabzon. He also explained that he had found Yusuf's home address in Trabzon and had paid a visit to his wife and daughter to obtain pictures of Yusuf. Yusuf died before the torture and sodium pentothal could make him talk. Once Faramaz, who spared no detail, told him what he had done to his wife and daughter, the sergeant's desire to live evaporated. He willed himself into Allah's arms, and there was nothing more his torturers could do to him.

Lieutenant Ertugrul was less fortunate. His fingers were slowly and systematically broken, but still he held on. He refused to talk even when they squeezed his testicles with pliers. One of the killers removed a needle from his duffel bag and injected the lieutenant with sodium pentothal. But it was not until he heard Faramaz describe to his dying friend what he and his fellow assassins had done to Yusuf's family that he lost all resistance. Wracked with pain, his ability to control his thoughts weakened by the drug, he uttered the words: "Aaron Korda. The American's name is Aaron Korda."

"What was he doing in Poti?" his torturer demanded.

"Like us. He wanted to avenge Captain Bulot's murder. They were friends. They had studied together in America."

"He is a soldier?"

"No . . . no . . . no more. Stop. I don't know anything more about the American. I met him only at Kemal's memorial."

"Is he a CIA spy?"

"No. I don't know." His speech was slurred. Blood drained from him. Faramaz knew that the lieutenant would not last long.

"Your English stinks. How did you communicate with Aaron Korda?"

"He speaks our language . . . very well our language," he said, punctuating his words as he coughed up blood.

"Who killed the interior minister?" Hasan looked

confused for a moment, but that could have been delirium from pain and the drug. "The man with a suit, you idiot . . . who killed him?"

"Aaron. Aaron shot him . . . with a machine gun."

With that, Faramaz looked at his watch—7:36. Soon, the garage owner's family would come looking for him. The lieutenant's wife may have already called headquarters of First Commando in the hills not too far from where the auto body shop was located, looking for her husband. *We're running out of time.* Still, he tried one more question.

"Where does Korda live in America? He must have said where he lives. He would have invited you to his home . . . this man who speaks Turkish."

"No, no." Lieutenant Ertugrul shook his head back and forth, ignoring the pain that tore through his body. "No. Don't know where he lives. I swear. He was rude. No invitations," he lied, his last act of courage. Aaron had, in fact, given his Turkish comrades his address, phone number and e-mail address, and had made clear that they were welcome to visit him anytime. The sodium pentothal was working. Hasan would not be able to resist.

"Think, idiot. Think!" Faramaz yelled.

"New York. He said something about New York," Hasan admitted hazily, now fully under the influence of the powerful drug.

"Now you can go to Allah." Calmly, Faramaz pulled out his Walther P88, pointed it at Hasan's temple and pulled the trigger.

After removing their bloody gloves, the three killers climbed into a beat-up Nissan outside the shop, a vehicle that the mechanic had repaired moments before his death earlier in the day and was to be picked up by its owner the next morning. With Faramaz navigating in the front passenger's seat, they set out for Adana, taking a route that would pass through Niğde and other mountain villages. In Adana, they would cleanse themselves. His two henchmen would catch a plane back to Georgia, while Faramaz would return to Holland.

"So how do we find this Aaron Korda? New York. It is a big city, no?" the killer in the backseat of the car asked Faramaz, who sat quietly.

"Finding him would be the easy part," Faramaz said after a long pause. "We could probably locate him on the Internet. . . . And the stupid Americans list their numbers and addresses in their phone books."

"I will go with you. I will kill him," the man in the rear volunteered.

Faramaz was silent for several minutes, his eyes fixed on the winding mountain road ahead of him. "We are nearing the completion of our project, and I must get back to Nederlanden Groep. I have used all of my vacation days and only have a few more sick days. The more I am out of the office, the more attention I'll attract. We have to be cautious and not get sloppy as we approach the finish line. We will find the American and kill him, but if he is a CIA agent he'll have backup protection," Faramaz said, mostly to himself. "We need to isolate him from the American authorities." After several minutes of reflection, Faramaz said, "I don't believe for a moment that this American traveled all the way to Poti, risking his life, to avenge the death of his friend, the captain who was killed earlier. Revenge of that sort? A Turk, yes. An Arab, certainly, but not an American. They are weak. They lack the passion. He must be CIA . . . or from one of the other agencies. When is the next boatload of heroin coming across the Caspian?" he asked, turning to the driver.

"Tomorrow night," the driver responded without taking his eyes off the switchback in the mountain road.

"Get a message to Mohammed. Have him find out what he can about the American. In the meantime, let's also get in touch with our men on the vessel. We'll have them talk from ship to shore on an unsecured line, saying that Korda is part of the drug smuggling. We'll use his name openly." He snickered at the thought. "The conversation will take place when the vessel is in the middle of the Caspian, so that there is little other phone traffic. We don't want the NSA to miss anything." Faramaz smiled, pleased with the cleverness of his own plan. With any luck, the CIA would hunt down Korda for him.

SEVEN

Kate arrived a few minutes early for the Monday morning meeting so that she could have a word privately with the DCI. Rather than take a seat in the conference room next to the DCI's office, she stood, looking out the window through the mist at the Virginia hillside.

The DCI joined Kate in the conference room moments later. "Kate, it's good to see you," Michael Andersen said, wondering what Kate had on her agenda for this tête-à-tête.

"Same here," she responded, waving away the coffee an assistant offered. "We need to talk about Aaron Korda," she announced, leaning against the credenza. "I think you agree that the Georgians are going to let this blow over. The interior minister was obviously in on the heroin traffic. Why else would he have been in that warehouse at three in the morning?

"Your man at Cold Spring Biologics—Prebish—wants Korda's head. But I don't. We need him back in action. He speaks German and Turkish perfectly, and is pretty good in Arabic from all indications in his file. Look what he did for us in Libya. He single-handedly shut down Gadhafi's sarin gas project, and put Offenbach Chemicals out of business. That has to count for some goodwill here." She thought about Aaron's defense in the conference room back at Heller & Clarke and smiled inwardly. There was something appealing about his candor. "Sir, let me be blunt. I want a favor. Rein in Prebish and give Korda some room."

The DCI took a deep breath, collecting his thoughts. "You know this vendetta thing for the Turkish captain was stupid. Korda should have stayed out of it. We didn't have a dog in that fight."

"Water under the bridge. If the Georgians don't pursue it, there's no reason we have to. And we're convinced Korda's more than just a valuable asset. He's one of the best. If you were in the field and in trouble, wouldn't you want Korda on your side?"

"Goddamn right I would, but we can't control him, you know." He paused to reflect, sipping his coffee to buy time. "Okay . . . okay, we'll paper this thing over and get Aaron back in action. There's a medical device and instruments trade show coming up next week in Damascus. Korda is supposed to be there, but I've been rethinking whether he should go. Maybe we stick with plans and send him. Come to think of it, right after that, there's also a pharmaceutical trade show in Damascus. Maybe he should go to that one, too. The new Syrian minister of health is putting it on. We may have a way of getting into the good graces of the health minister through a French connection. God knows we need the Syrians' help in rooting out the terrorists, and if the Iraqis did move biochem labs secretly into Syria as we invaded Iraq, then we'll need to know whether or not the Syrians know where the biochem labs are. We had been planning on using Aaron for this. Christ, he's perfect for the mission. I'll have the DDO talk to Prebish."

Kate didn't press for more. She had gotten what she wanted. She grabbed her briefcase and walked down the hall with the DCI to a larger conference room for the weekly interagency briefing.

Piet Stolten, Chief of Security at Nederlanden Pharmacie Groep's production facility on the outskirts of Rotterdam, rose from the uncomfortable sofa in the reception area, stretching in an exaggerated manner, and thinking that he might, in fact, find a cozy sofa in a corner somewhere out of sight and catch some sleep.

It was the only place Stolten had ever worked since graduating from technical school thirty-nine years earlier. In his last year with Holland's foremost pharmaceutical company, he contented himself with the thought that his pension was adequate, assuring him and his wife a modestly comfortable living in their small cottage in the countryside south of Sliedrecht.

He thought back to the time when the plant was operating around the clock, the place abuzz with workers and the hum of machinery inside the clean-rooms. He recalled nights when ten trucks at a time would be backed up to the freight docks, drivers milling about, smoking, telling jokes as their vehicles were being loaded with cases of pharmaceuticals for which Nederlanden was famous. He tugged on his shirtsleeve and looked at his watch. It was 3:45 A.M., and the place was a graveyard. The union rules that had made his life so comfortable had also made it too expensive to run the plant during the night shift. *How will we ever keep up with the Americans and Japanese?* he wondered. Slowly but surely, the competition was killing Nederlanden.

From the executive offices near reception, Stolten made his way down the long corridor to the production offices on the other end, conscious of the pain in his arthritic knee and looking for a chair to rest his sixty-two-year-old frame. In one of those offices, where the quality-control officers ensured the integrity of Nederlanden's products, he would find a chair and rest.

Piet Stolten slid his company identification card though the lock, heard a buzz and pushed the door open. The corridor in front of him was dark except for three red emergency lights that remained on through the night. He proceeded to two double doors that separated the production group from the quality-control department. To his left, down yet another corridor, lay the decontamination rooms, where the technicians washed and clothed themselves in clean suits before entering the plant. Such was the need for cleanliness in the plant that several TV monitors scanned the production plant around the clock.

No one was allowed to enter the production facility without the protective clothing and hairnet, and Stolten was in no mood for that hassle. The head of quality control, a youthful first-generation Iranian, Daniel ben Malek, had a high-back chair and an úncluttered desk. Stolten figured he'd hole up in ben Malek's office, put his feet up on his desk and catch twenty minutes' sleep.

Stolten was about to let himself into Malek's office when something caught his eye and caused him to look down the hall. There was a light coming through the frosted glass on the door to Faramaz ben Sarah's office that reflected onto the opposite wall of the hallway. *That's odd,* Stolten thought. A frugal Iranian Jew, who had escaped from his home country and had joined Nederlanden a few years before, ben Sarah was not known to waste anything, not even electricity. Piet continued down the hallway, his rubber-sole shoes scrunching on the polished linoleum floor. From the outside of ben Sarah's door, he heard two men speaking in a language he didn't understand. He tapped gently on the door. "Mr. Sarah. Is that you in there?" he asked in a loud whisper. "It's Piet Stolten," he added, and opened the door with his master key.

"Piet, you surprised me," Faramaz said in his English-accented Dutch as the security chief entered. "Please come in. You know Mr. Malek," Faramaz said, gesturing to the quality-control officer whom he had recruited a few months after his own arrival at the company.

"Sure, we've met," Stolten said, offering his hand to Malek, who smiled broadly, as if on cue, extending his hand. "My, my, you folks work as hard as we Dutch used to. You're not scheduled to start until the seven A.M. shift. Have you been up all night?" Without being asked, Stolten seated himself in a chair opposite the production officer's desk. Years of experience told him that the two men were ill at ease.

"Unfortunately, you got it right. We're encountering production problems and will have to step up the manufacturing operations to meet the delivery schedules. Obviously, we can't sacrifice quality, so Daniel volunteered to work late with me," Faramaz explained. Malek nodded in agreement.

Ben Sarah's résumé indicated that he had studied in Manchester in the north of England, which was consistent with his accent and the diploma and transcript he presented when he interviewed for his position in 1999. His friend Malek had been similarly credentialed. Everything at the time had seemed in order. *But not tonight,* Stolten thought. The chief of security noticed how Faramaz's broad, powerful forearm lay over the notepad, covering the top sheet of paper on his desk. Was it his imagination or was ben Sarah trying to prevent him from seeing what was on the pad? "Have we received more orders for products than usual? I thought sales were down."

"Well, you can blame the Americans," ben Sarah said, forcing a smile. "Apparently, one of their big pharmaceutical companies hit a production snag, and we're trying to fill that gap. We already sell our DPT and MMR vaccines in North America, but this is a great opportunity to increase our market share. I'm surprised you didn't hear about it."

"No. First I've heard about it. I must be slipping in my old age. Time was when I would have known about a ramp up in production even before . . . well, almost before you gentlemen in manufacturing." The security chief's eyes veered downward to the desktop. The pad was still partially covered by ben Sarah's forearm, making it impossible to read his notes.

"Come, now, Mr. Stolten, not much misses your attention," Malek said, casually shifting his weight from one foot to the other as he remained standing, his back to a small whiteboard. He rubbed his white smock against the surface of the board, erasing something that had been written in red with a felt-tip marker. The subtle gesture did not go unnoticed by Stolten. Ben Sarah moved his arm slightly so that the pad on his desk was more concealed. He studied Stolten's lined face and blue-green eyes, as did Malek, making no eye contact with one another.

"Well, thank you, Mr. Malek. I'll take that as a compliment and bid both of you good night." He glanced at his watch. "Or should I say good morning? Anyway, back to work. And give those Americans a run for their money." Stolten rose from his chair and let himself out of the office. Only after he disappeared beyond the double doors leading from production to the QC department, did ben Sarah and Malek resume their whispered conversation.

"Did you hear what happened to Piet?" the plump cashier in the cantina asked the young security guard, who shrugged noncommittally. He was exhausted from pulling a double shift and only wanted his coffee and bread and to be left in peace. "It's such a tragedy," the cashier persisted, finally getting the guard's attention. "So you didn't hear. Piet and his wife died early this morning, after he went home from the night shift."

The security guard, who worked directly for Stolten, was visibly shaken. "What . . . what happened?" he stammered.

"There was a fire. . . . His house, it was an old farmhouse, you know. It caught fire early this morning. He and his wife died." The cashier, who had known Piet for more than eighteen years, started sobbing.

"Unbelievable," the security guard said in a whisper, unable to comprehend. He and the chief of security were friends, and Piet had been so kind as to cover for him while he dined with his wife late the night before. He had been to the Stoltens' home and had known his wife for years.

"What happened?" asked a man who had suddenly appeared in line at the register behind the security guard. The cashier repeated the story.

"You're Mr. Faramaz ben Sarah, aren't you?" the guard asked the man who stood beside him.

"Why, yes . . . I am." The production officer established eye contact with the security guard in a pleasant, nonthreatening manner. "And you are?"

"Gunnar Trent. I worked under Piet."

"Pleased to meet you," ben Sarah said, shaking the Dutch man's hand. "What a terrible, terrible loss."

"Yes, yes," Gunnar said with genuine sadness. "Funny, Piet left me a message this morning before he left that something had come up with you and Mr. Malek. He didn't say what it was about. Is there anything wrong with security in your part of the building?"

"No. Nothing that I'm aware of. I did tell Mr. Stolten that both Mr. Malek's and my ID cards are slightly off. I think some well-meaning technician in MIS input our birth dates on some of our documents based on the Iranian calendar, which is an Islamic calendar, even though we're both Jewish. Mr. Malek has the same problem. But it's so insignificant in light of this tragedy. It is such a pity that a good man like him died. And his poor wife! I understand that he was close to retirement."

Krissi Sturm returned from the lavatory on the long flight, a Boeing 757-400 direct from Berlin to San Diego, as the pilot warned of turbulence over Newfoundland and put on the FASTEN SEAT BELT sign. She sat back down, snapping the buckle shut, and continued studying the thick dossier. Aaron had excelled in languages at West Point and was an A student in chemistry. Beyond that, his academic performance was a solid B. Distinguished military service. Desert Storm. Mogadishu. Then out after five years. Chicago. MBA. Heller & Clarke. Successful international consultant. High salary. Expensive tastes. Still single.

She finished the dossier and shut her eyes. Her thoughts shifted from the facts the BND had gathered about Aaron to the younger man she had known and loved. How much had he changed after Maggie's death? He had been such an idealist when they were together in high school. All of their classmates thought they could

change the world back then, but Aaron stood out from
his peers because he was so convincing. After his little
sister, Maggie, died, he became as negative as he had
once been optimistic. He was angry and distant, with-
drawing from family and friends as if punishing himself
and them for the tragedy that no one could have prevented. Despite her youth and her own grieving, Krissi
had stood by him, struggling to hold on to him, but he
was unable to accept comfort from anyone. She thought
about that devastating period in her life as she drifted
off into a troubled sleep.

The flight attendant woke her, inquiring if she had her
seat belt on beneath her blanket. Momentarily annoyed,
she let her irritation subside and tried to go back to
sleep, wondering what he would be like now, at thirty-
four, twice the age he had been the last time she saw
him. Unable to sleep, she opened the dossier again and
withdrew his picture, glancing over her shoulder to verify that the passenger next to her was still sleeping. The
recent photo had been taken on Park Avenue from
about half a block away, the MetLife building visible in
the background. Aaron had a bandage on his right cheek
and wore an open trench coat, a dark suit underneath.
His hair was midlength, not as close cut as it had been
in high school. It appeared that he had filled out somewhat, but even with the coat on, she could tell he was
still trim and athletic. Krissi put the photo back in the
file and closed her eyes. *Seventeen years. Will he recognize me? Can I really spy on this man?* And then a stray
thought entered her consciousness. *Will he find me
attractive?*

After showering, Aaron wrapped a towel around his
waist and shaved. He wondered why he bothered to put
the towel around him. There was no one else in his
apartment. It was a habit he had learned at the Point,
he guessed. He brushed his teeth while inspecting his
new and still mostly unfurnished home. He traveled so
much that he had not previously bothered to buy a

condo or co-op, choosing instead to rent a one-bedroom apartment in Greenwich Village. But with his larger salary, his accountant had persuaded him that he was better off owning than renting. The two-bedroom on Beekman Place was an expensive investment, but the mortgage interest was deductible and, when in town, he could walk to work. *Besides,* he thought, gazing out the window to the East River and the sun coming up over Queens, *the view is incredible.* Toothpaste dripped over his lower lip, forcing him to cup the white liquid and return to the bathroom. He looked at the digital clock on the counter. *Damn. How did it get so late?* The intercom buzzed, the doorman reminding him that his car service was already downstairs waiting. He had packed the night before. Within ten minutes he was in the backseat of the Lincoln Town Car heading for Kennedy Airport.

Later, he settled into his seat and immediately opened his briefcase, pulling out his files on those attending the International Federation of Pharmaceutical Industries symposium at La Costa. High-ranking representatives of every major pharmaceutical company and many biotechnology companies would be present at the conference, giving Aaron a chance to meet with them in a relaxed environment. It was a great opportunity to catch new clients, and he was looking forward to it.

After declining the coffee offered by the flight attendant, Aaron reclined in his seat and dozed. He slept for only a few minutes, his thoughts going back to Poti and Building 15. There was something troubling him about what happened that night, but he couldn't put his finger on it. He woke repeatedly, sweating, casting wary glances at those around him in business class. Images of Kemal being killed appeared incessantly in his mind, as did the near death of Hasan. But there was something else he was missing, and the more he tried to figure it out, the farther it seemed to slip from his grasp.

"Good morning, Nasreen. How was your vacation?"

"It was wonderful, but a little too short," she said,

hoping her boss, Fred, the production manager, wouldn't be offended.

Fred sensed her embarrassment but understood. "Hey, I know how you feel, and you're right. Vacation time in this country is so limited. You plan and anticipate and plan some more, but before you know it, your week's up." She nodded in agreement. "Did you go anywhere fun and exotic? I was in England transitioning Midlands before you left and didn't get a chance to ask where you were going."

"Well, just to visit some friends of mine who are working near St. Louis. Between you and me, I would have preferred to lie on the beach in Miami, but I owed them a visit. Still, we had a good time. St. Louis is nice in the fall." Nasreen, Faramaz ben Sarah's first and most trusted recruit, wondered if she should have said she was in some other city close to St. Louis. She knew she shouldn't draw attention to her comrades in Belleville, but she also couldn't run the risk of getting caught in a lie. She had learned her lesson back in Champaign-Urbana at the University of Illinois. She had lied and said she was in Memphis over spring break when, in fact, she was helping set up the lab in Belleville. One of the girls in the dorm was from Memphis and had asked her too many questions about her stay in that city that she couldn't really answer. Since then, she had decided to play it straight and simply tell others that she was visiting friends in Belleville, and hope that no one later would retrace her tracks and discover with whom she was meeting and why.

"Jay says Saba was away, too. Did she go with you?"

"My, my. Twenty questions." She smiled teasingly. "Do you also have an interest in Saba?" she asked, knowing the answer. Fred had introduced Nasreen to Jay on her first day, even before she got to her new office. He had flirted with her and although she could have played along, it wasn't necessary since she already had the position. However, when Nasreen learned that the head of quality control was single and, moreover, was looking for a quality-control person to fill a newly budgeted position, she jumped on the opportunity and offered to introduce her friend Saba to him. Several weeks later, after the requisite interviews and references checked out, Saba got the nod and became Jay's assistant. Within a month, the young and very attractive woman, who, like Nasreen, claimed to be an Iranian Jew whose family had escaped from the Islamic Revolution, was attending religious services with Jay, a conservative Jew. Soon thereafter, they became lovers.

"No, of course not. But Jay sure does. I've known him for years, and he was always a committed bachelor. I tell you, though, I think he's going to give all that up."

"Wonderful," she lied. It would be impossible for Saba to marry her American boyfriend, and she wondered how Saba would deflect the offer. "Are we going to be busy right up to Thanksgiving?" she asked, successfully changing the subject.

"You bet. We've got a huge amount of product to push out the gate over the next month to meet our projections. Are you up for it?"

She nodded, trying to look enthusiastic and hoping he wouldn't notice the dark circles under her eyes that she had covered with makeup. The drive to and from southern Illinois had been exhausting, as usual, and she hadn't arrived back in Trenton until well after midnight. She hated all that driving, but it was just too risky to fly these days. She couldn't hide the specially sealed metal double container in her carry-on bag. It would show up on the X-ray and too many questions could be asked. Her accent was perfect, but she still looked very Middle Eastern. Checked baggage was a possibility. Only 5 percent was examined by Homeland Security. But even a 5 percent chance of discovery was too great, they had decided. Besides, everyone knew that airlines were notorious for losing luggage, and that would have presented a real problem. *Okay,* she comforted herself. *One, maybe two, more trips to Belleville, and then we're ready.*

* * *

Three days after Nasreen and Saba returned to work from their trip to southern Illinois, the two commenced a production run of insulin at National's Trenton plant, assisted by unwitting colleagues in what appeared to be a routine day's work. Working methodically in her clean suit, Nasreen assembled the compounds, which had been tested, sealed with tamper-evident tape and quarantined upon their delivery to the Biosafety Level-3 Facility. Saba scanned each canister's bar code, removed the QUARANTINE sticker, replaced it with a RELEASE sticker, and instructed her coworker to place the materials in the first stainless-steel pressurized tank in the manufacturing process.

Working in tandem, Nasreen began the blending process for the first 100-kilogram batch, calling out the type and weight of each ingredient through her face mask, with Saba, also wearing a clean suit, noting everything in the log on her laptop, which transmitted the information to a hard drive outside the clean room. After the first blending and sterilization, Saba recorded the loss of weight in the batch due to evaporation and entered the reduction in yield on her laptop, falsely understating the loss by a fraction of a percent. In a production run of 100 kilograms, a variation in yield of one half of one percent to three percent could be expected. The difference between the true loss and the falsified amount would be replaced with botulinum-A toxin at the right moment in the production process.

As the batch was moved from one sterilized tank to another through sterile tubing, the process was repeated until just before the compounds reached the Filler, the device that would fill up the individual vials and seal them. When the blended compounds were delivered to the last tank before going to the Filler, Nasreen opened the sterile sample port on the side of the stainless steel vat, inserted a large syringe and took a sample of the batch. After Nasreen capped the syringe, she set it aside on a clean table. Saba immediately stepped forward to block Nasreen from the view of the other workers and the overhead surveillance cameras, attaching a label to the sample and noting the time and date. While Saba provided cover, Nasreen quickly removed an equally large syringe, which like the first one lacked a needle, from under her gown, removed the protective cap and injected one half of a kilogram of botulinum-A toxin through the sample port. Nasreen recapped and replaced the now empty syringe in a pocket under her clean suit and paused to let the toxin blend fully with the other compounds inside the tank. When Nasreen nodded to indicate that she was satisfied with the blending, Saba instructed the computer to weigh the batch, which now was within normal yield expectations. As soon as she had entered the requisite information in her laptop, the completed batch of insulin was emptied into the Filler. She suppressed a smile as she watched the filled and sealed vials make their way down the belt and workers placed them in boxes to be shipped to pharmacies, clinics and hospitals throughout the United States and Canada. After the instruments were cleaned, dried and sterilized, Nasreen and Saba repeated the process throughout the day.

EIGHT

"Kristina Sturm. Kristina Sturm," the uniformed man with a cap yelled above the other drivers who crowded the baggage carousel. "Kristina Sturm?"

She signaled to the driver with her right index finger as she approached, pulling her wheeled black suitcase with attached briefcase behind her, a medium-size handbag slung over her shoulder. She hadn't checked any luggage and was ready to go before the throngs from economy descended on the conveyor belt.

"I'm from San Diego Limousine Service. You're Kristina Sturm from Westfalen Pharma Gruppe?" he asked, reading from a notepad and stumbling over the German name.

"Yes, I am, thank you. Do you know the way to La Costa?"

"Yes, ma'am," the chauffeur said, reaching for the handle of her suitcase. Krissi was tired from the flight, and nodded appreciatively.

As the Town Car sped away from the airport, she gazed blankly out the window, wondering what it would be like to see Aaron again and worrying about how she would handle the situation. She recalled how she and Aaron would sit in his parents' backyard on the swings, laughing and talking about all sorts of things until late in the afternoon when, more often than not, Mrs. Korda would step out on the porch and ask if she wanted to join them for dinner. And because her mother worked evenings, Kristina almost always accepted. She recalled these dinners warmly. Martin was already studying at West Point so it was Colonel and Mrs. Korda, Maggie, Krissi and Aaron around the table. The conversations often focused on current events—the Cold War, geopolitics, the military, President Reagan's big arms buildup, the Pershing missiles and the Greens' protests against them. *That was all before Maggie died,* she thought wistfully.

The driver slowed the limo to a stop in front of the main building, then turned around partway and passed a voucher to Krissi. "Just sign on the bottom."

"Sure," Krissi answered distractedly as she scribbled her signature on the voucher and handed it back to the driver. She sucked in a large gulp of air and let it out slowly through pursed lips, giving off a faint whistle. Her stomach was full of butterflies, her throat suddenly dry. She wiped her sweaty palms on her slacks, feeling very unlike the tough BND agent her colleagues respected.

"May I join you? I've been meaning to introduce myself, but time just seems to fly by. Anne Carton," she said to the new production manager, extending her hand. "How long have you been here? Has it been eight or nine months?"

"Asher ben Soraya," he responded as he put down his lunch tray on the nearest table and shook hands with the quality-control technician. "So pleased to make your acquaintance, Ms. Carton. It's actually been a little over a year already," he said, correcting her with a smile.

"My heavens. It seems like yesterday that you joined us." She sat down opposite him without being invited. After all, she had raced through her morning, hoping to run into him, and wasn't going to give up easily. She placed her large leather handbag on the seat next to her, hoping that it would deter others from joining them. "I hope you like it here. Midlands Chemicals is a great place to work. I've been here for fourteen years. Never even thought of switching jobs, although I am a tad concerned about the Americans coming in. They say they will keep up the status quo, but I don't buy it. Did you attend the meeting yesterday with the executives from National Pharma?"

"Ah, yes. I was there, but I thought it went pretty well," Soraya responded, trying to appear interested.

"Oh, come now. I hear they plan to transfer albuterol and insulin production to New Jersey. Sure, they claim they will leave the higher-end production here—even develop new products here—but can we believe them? How secure is anyone's job?" Soraya shook his head, he hoped sympathetically. In a few weeks, he would be in a safe house in Yemen and would not care a bit about National's absorption of Midlands.

"I must ask you something," she said. "In fact, I really don't know how to say this, so I'll just let it out and hope you understand. Here goes. I stepped into your office yesterday. You were out. I wanted to invite you to lunch, and when you weren't there I decided to leave you a note." Soraya stared wordlessly, finally very interested in what she had to say. Anne Carton mistook his look as encouragement and continued. "Anyway, your desk is so tidy that I couldn't find any paper, so I opened a drawer, and, well, your notes . . . you know . . . for the new product." Soraya looked at her incredulously, his heart racing. He had a searing impulse to reach across the table and strangle her, but the company cafeteria, now filling rapidly for lunch, was not the time or place. Production of the botulinum-A toxin had been slowed at the Mechelen facility due to greater-than-anticipated costs and the need to proceed cautiously, forcing Soraya to consider other ways to contaminate Midland Chemicals' pharmaceuticals. It now appeared that Carton had stumbled upon some of his preliminary ideas. It was a careless mistake on his part, and he cursed himself for it.

"At first, I couldn't figure it out," she said, relieved she had gotten this far and oblivious to the hatred fermenting in his eyes, "and I wondered what was going on. You can't mix beta agonists with methylxanthines, certainly not in those dosages!" She lowered her voice to a whisper. "Your formula for albuterol would cause cardiac arrhythmias and sudden death. Your formula for insulin would cause diabetics to go into severe hypoglycemic shock within an hour of taking it. It would kill them." He watched her in disbelief. "But then I realized that you must be working on new product lines. . . . Something altogether different that'll keep us on the map here in Coventry. I heard that someone was involved in research at this facility, but I didn't know who it was. That's why you were brought in prior to the merger. Am I right? You don't plan to use these formulae at all, do you?" He shook his head. "I didn't think so. I figured you are secretly working with the folks at R and D," she added with a self-satisfied smile, and then, catching herself, stopped. "You're not upset that I found the notes?"

"No, no. Of course not. They're nothing more than silly scribbling of random thoughts. You know how it is when you're trying to create something new. What do you call it . . . brainstorming?" She nodded. "Still, it was stupid of me to leave that scratch pad in my desk. At the direction of management, I and a few others have been tasked to do some totally out-of-the-box thinking about new products. As I think through this process of new drug development, I believe that too little research has been done on the helpful effects of what are generally considered dangerous mixes of compounds. What I've been told to do is explore our existing technologies and see if our current compounds, in differing dosages, can be used to treat other disorders, thus creating higher-end, higher-profit-margin products. I'm sure that you understand that it's confidential. Only a few people in R and D even know about it, and you, of course." She blushed. She agreed eagerly, excited to be in on the secret.

"May we sit here?" asked a young woman wearing a white laboratory smock, motioning with her head to her colleague and the two empty seats at Soraya and Carton's table. The cafeteria was full now, with employees carrying trays laden with lunch and searching for an occasional empty chair or two.

"By all means. We're done," Soraya responded before Carton could speak. He rose from his seat, placing his utensils on the tray. Anne did the same and walked toward the exit with him.

"Do you live in town?" he asked casually as they left the cafeteria and entered the main building.

"Oh, no. We live in the countryside. Do you know Bedworth?"

"Yes, I believe I do. It's north of here, isn't it?"

"Very good. You'd be surprised how many people from these parts don't even know that. We live a short drive to the east of Bedworth. It's a lovely area." She glanced at his wedding band. "You know, we'd love to have you and your family over for dinner. I'm sure my husband and children would enjoy that, too. Do you have children?"

"Not yet, but my wife is pregnant. She's due in three months," he lied. In fact, he had no wife and the ring was just a cover.

"Outstanding," Mrs. Carton gushed. "Well, then, I'll call Nigel and make sure we have no other plans before confirming, but how about dinner this Sunday?"

"Ah, we would very much enjoy that," he said, smiling.

"Wonderful. I'll send you an e-mail with the directions as soon as I get back to my desk." They had reached the central corridor. She would be turning right toward quality control, whereas he would be heading back to his office in production, closer to the factory floor. "I am so truly pleased that we finally had lunch," she said with a wink. "And don't worry. Your secret is safe with me. I won't tell a soul."

"You know, I'm sure you won't. And don't forget to send me those directions."

Asher ben Soraya returned to his office and pretended to be busy. He checked his e-mail three times before her message arrived. He printed it, put on his coat and left for the day, telling a colleague he was feeling ill.

Since the birth of her five-year-old, Nicholas, it had become Anne Carton's routine to wake up between 2:30 and 3:00 A.M., go to the loo, check on the kids, first Molly, now three, and Nicholas, and then sneak down to the kitchen for a cup of chamomile and biscuits before trying to go back to sleep. This night was no different, except the clock was flashing 12:00 when she woke, indicating that the power had gone out for some reason or another, and had been restored. She pressed the illuminator button on her digital watch—3:17 A.M. How odd. She reset the alarm on her clock radio for 6:00 A.M.

The temperature outside had plunged, unusual even for late October, and the house was chilly. She put on a heavy terry cloth bathrobe, relieved herself in the loo and headed to her daughter's room, adjusting the thermostat in the hallway. The clock on Molly's nightstand was also flashing 12:00, as were the ones in the cable box on top of the TV in the living room and the clock built into the microwave. She'd reset them in the morning. Since it was uncomfortably cold, she decided to forgo the tea and biscuits, instead pouring herself a tumbler of water and returning to bed.

Life is very comfortable, she mused. She and Nigel worked hard and together earned a good living. He recently made partner at his small accounting firm, and their income had increased significantly in the last two years. The house was quite roomy and solid as a rock. They had renovated much of it themselves: new roof, windows, kitchen, bathrooms, and a modest solarium annexed to the kitchen. This coming summer, their plan was to replace the old oil heater in the basement with a cleaner, more efficient gas appliance. Then they would begin to remodel the rest of the basement.

At 4:15 A.M., when the heater came back on, it began to leak oil onto the floor of the basement. The Carton family was sound asleep. At 4:45, an electric wire in the

basement began to spark. Asher ben Soraya, whose father had been a skilled electrician in Iraq, had worked
hard to create the appearance of faulty wiring. He knew
he was good, but just in case the sparks weren't enough
to ignite the heavy fuel, a thin plastic cigarette lighter
had been set on the floor, programmed by an inexpensive plastic watch to ignite at 5:00 A.M. An experienced
homicide arson team or insurance examiner might ultimately find the device, confirming the heinous crime, but
the gamble was that arson would not be suspected, and
even if it was, investigators would never be able to trace
it back to him, at least not before he was safely thousands of miles away. The authorities would notice that
the smoke detectors had been disabled, but they would
blame it on the Carton family, at least at first.

The flames spread through the old house like a brush
fire. Hideous red tongues of heat slithered along the
wooden beams and wide flat boards, making their way
serpentlike up through the wood lath interior of bone-
dry walls sealed when the house was built in 1923.

The Carton family barely had time to react. Anne was
the first up. She jumped out of bed with a scream that
woke Nigel, and ran out into the smoke-filled hall to
save her children. By the time she reached Molly's room,
the little girl was already unconscious, engulfed in
smoke, her burning bed a growing fireball. Anne tore
through the searing heat in a valiant but futile effort to
save her daughter. Scooping up the girl in her arms, she
tried to outrun the flames, but the fire was faster and
there was no place to run. Mother and child hit the floor
hard, the wood planks beneath them sagging, already
half eaten through by the monster now consuming their
home with astonishing speed.

Nigel did not make it to Nicholas's room. The flames
shot through a cast iron vent in the hall, near where the
boy slept, igniting Nigel's pajamas. He struggled out of
them as he shouted to Nicholas to wake up. Overcome
by smoke, his last thought was that he had failed to save
his children.

No one was there to see a white van parked on the street in front of a florist in the small village. The lights were out in the store, as they were in the four other shops in the hamlet. Behind the wheel, Asher ben Soraya looked down the sloping country lane to the glen where the Carton residence was located. The bright glow of the fire was visible through the windows, which would soon shatter from the pressure of the walls collapsing above them. The flames had reached the roof and were beginning to gnaw their way through as the fire made its inexorable climb toward the sky and more oxygen.

Asher ben Soraya glanced at his colleague, who sat next to him in the passenger's seat. The other man nodded silently. It was time to leave. Soraya shifted into first gear and pulled away.

"Thank you for coming so quickly. When are you returning to Holland?"

"This morning at 9:15, on the ferry. Faramaz was delayed in Georgia. I don't know the details, but he followed up on the attack on our facilities in Poti and just returned a few days ago. He's sending the cash with one of the runners, instead of bringing it himself. How much do you need?"

"Forty-one thousand, five hundred pounds sterling."

"Why so much?" the man who was called Daniel Malek asked.

"It turns out to be more expensive than we thought to bring in the toxin from the lab in Mechelen. And we can't use the phones or e-mail. We must travel constantly and that costs real money. I have been working on alternative formulae in case we can't produce enough botulinum toxin."

"Anything that will work?"

"Yes, well, maybe. But let's be realistic. Botulinum-A toxin is still the best and most reliable method. We know that from our studies back home and from what our people in Illinois have done to make it better. It's perfect. Nothing in the manufacturing process—even boiling for extended periods—kills or even attenuates our enhanced bacteria. If we can keep the labs running for a couple more weeks, we'll have enough. If things take longer, we'll have to consider different ways to poison the infidels."

"Faramaz will see that you get your money. Praise Allah. The infidels who destroyed our plant in Poti failed to damage the other buildings. We are still up and running, and the cash from the heroin trade continues to flow, just more slowly."

The van approached the small town of Bedworth. Soraya turned down a side street to avoid the center of town. "Ahmed," his passenger said somberly, surprising him by using his real name, "we must move quickly. We've killed the head of security at Nederlanden Pharmacie Groep, and now this. The two fires and deaths are too remote to be linked by the Dutch and English police, but still, the risks are great. You should also know that Faramaz is very concerned about an American who was involved in the attack on the Poti facility. We have to step up the pace."

NINE

"Could you tell me what room Mr. Korda is in?"

"Sorry, we're not allowed to give out that information," the young woman behind the desk answered.

"Oh, that's okay. I'll wait. We're old friends, if you know what I mean, and I was hoping to surprise him with a bottle of champagne," Krissi responded with an exaggerated wink.

"Well, you can certainly have a bottle sent to his room," the clerk said while tapping on her keyboard and squinting at the screen, which Krissi could not see, giving the BND agent the information she needed: Aaron had already checked in.

"You know, that's all right. I'll surprise him at the reception this evening."

After unpacking, Krissi stood at the window of her room overlooking the golf course, watching a foursome play through the fourteenth hole. She enjoyed golf, but she had no expectation of playing. A natural athlete, she was a better-than-average golfer and a formidable tennis player, though she had not brought her racquet, either.

Her thoughts shifted. Was it possible that Aaron Korda was guilty of what the BND suspected? Could a person change so much? Would she even like the man he had become? Her pulse raced; she could feel it pounding in her chest and temples. She wanted to go, even needed to go, for a run to help her unwind.

She checked the evening's schedule. Six o'clock cocktails and reception in the Poinsettia Foyer, dinner at seven in the Poinsettia Room, welcoming remarks from this year's president of the federation. She looked at her watch—5:10. *Damn. Not enough time.* She flipped on the TV. The local news bored her. CNN wasn't much better. A *Three's Company* rerun—ugh. She looked at her watch again. She figured it would take only two to three minutes to get from her room to the Poinsettia Foyer in the conference center. *Okay, I can do it.* She jumped into her running shorts, bra and top, laced up her running shoes, grabbed her sunglasses and baseball cap, and was out the door in less than two minutes. Avoiding the area near the main building—she was determined not to run into Aaron before she was ready—Krissi took a service exit out to the road leading west toward the ocean.

It was worth the effort. Twenty-five minutes and, she estimated, three and a half miles later, Krissi was back in her room, sweating but refreshed. She allowed herself a few minutes to cool down and then showered. As the water cascaded down her tall, lithe body, she wondered if Aaron would find her attractive after all these years.

After blow-drying her hair, she returned to the bedroom. She briefly regretted not bringing her black cocktail dress. The conference brochure had said the dress code was "California casual," whatever the hell that meant, and she thought the dress was too formal. The last thing she wanted was to look like she was trying too hard. Krissi decided on the dark blue slacks and printed silk camisole. Standing fully clothed in front of the mirror, she twisted around and looked at herself from the back. *Not bad at all.* She put on an off-white, medium-weight cashmere cardigan, leaving it unbuttoned. She then slid into her sandals with two-inch-high heels. Looking in the mirror one last time, she brushed her hair away from her face. She didn't wear much makeup, just a touch of lipstick and eye shadow, but that was the way she liked it. Five minutes to showtime. *I can do this. I can do this.*

* * *

The reception was in the Poinsettia Foyer, a grand open space one hundred feet long and forty feet wide. She entered through the Gardenia Foyer, arriving at precisely 6:00. No one was there yet, except the La Costa staff, who had prepared three bars, one near where she entered, another midway down the long hall and a third at the very end near a terrace that overlooked the golf course. She pinned on the name tag that the receptionist gave her. For a moment, she felt uncomfortable arriving so early, but dismissed the thought. She had wanted to find a seat where she could observe Aaron entering the reception so that she could see him before he spotted her.

Krissi accepted a club soda from the bartender and staked out her observation post, a cushioned banquette against the wall opposite the bar, and stood next to it. Removing the conference brochure from her handbag, she unfolded the paper and pretended to read, her eyes scanning the entrance. In all her years as a BND agent, including a mission gone bad in Rio, she had never felt like this. *Maybe I was wrong to take this on.* She took small sips of the ice-cold soda to soothe herself, and waited.

Soon, the reception area began to fill with attendees eager to see acquaintances from last year's conference. Everyone seemed to know each other. Not knowing anyone except for Aaron, she stood alone for a few minutes until the president of the International Federation of Pharmaceutical Industries came over to greet her. An aging man with a bald head and paunchy belly, he was eager to be seen in the company of the beautiful woman who had replaced the previous representative of Westfalen Pharma Gruppe. Within minutes, Krissi was surrounded by representatives, mostly male, of several companies who were more than pleased to have been introduced to her by the organization's new president.

A tall, heavyset official from a Canadian company, the name of which Krissi did not catch, shifted his weight from one foot to another, momentarily blocking her view of the entrance. She sidestepped to her right to reestablish a line of sight with those few still entering the now crowded gathering. She didn't want to look at her own watch, but was able to read the Canadian's—6:20. Still no sign of Aaron. *Maybe he doesn't come to this sort of thing. Maybe he's still playing golf. Perhaps he hasn't really checked in yet.*

"Can I get you another drink?" the president asked solicitously.

"Yes, please. Club soda." She glanced to her left and almost dropped the glass before she could hand it to the older man. She felt as if her heart froze. Aaron was no more than ten feet away, staring at her.

He had entered the Poinsettia Foyer at the far end of the room, from the clubhouse, and had come from behind her. As he dutifully worked the crowd, greeting existing clients and introducing himself to prospective ones, he was distracted by the shapely form of a woman, standing next to the federation's president, he noted out of the corner of his eye. Not one to pass on an opportunity, he stopped scanning the room and focused on the woman. He started with her legs and worked his way up, appreciating her hips and trim waist, then her firm breasts and slender neck. Then he saw her face. There was no mistaking it. She was older, yes. More mature-looking—that, too. But, he thought, no less beautiful than she had been seventeen years before. Yes, the woman standing no more than a few feet from him was Krissi.

She had wanted to be on the offensive, to walk up to him and say a simple "Is that you?" as if seeing him again here was a pleasant coincidence and nothing more. She had anticipated the moment many times over on the plane and had practiced her delivery in her room in front of the mirror just before coming to the reception. Instead, not knowing about the rear staircase, she found herself unprepared. Her lips trembled. Her breathing quickened.

"Krissi?" Aaron whispered loudly, still standing where

he was when he first laid eyes on her. She could barely hear him over the din of the crowd.

"Yes," she responded, not actually uttering a sound, but moving her lips. She took a few steps in Aaron's direction.

It was as if she had parachuted into his world from nowhere. The glass in his hand became heavier than the barbells he had used in the health club before rushing to the gathering. He wanted to say something but his mouth was suddenly so parched that he couldn't form the words. He wanted to move but his feet wouldn't budge. The woman about whom he had thought so often since leaving Wiesbaden seventeen years earlier was now standing in front of him. He extended his arm, not to shake her hand, but to touch her. He needed to touch her to see if she was real.

"Aaron . . . Aaron. I can't believe it. It's really you," Krissi whispered, not knowing if he could hear her. She had traveled nearly seven thousand miles expressly to see him, but still could not believe her eyes. Krissi fought back the emotions, trying to live up to her reputation as a tough BND agent.

Somehow, Aaron found enough strength to step toward her, still wanting to but now not knowing whether he should touch her. He didn't have the presence of mind to see if she wore a wedding or engagement ring. His eyes were glued to hers, and her eyes were exactly as he had remembered. Deep blue, hypnotic, more compelling than any he had ever seen before or since he had left her. He reached out with his hand, trancelike, for her elbow, sending shivers up and down her back. A waiter offering champagne and wine asked if they wanted more refreshments. Aaron placed his half-full glass on the tray without taking his eyes off Krissi's.

"Oh, my God, it's you. You're here," he said, still holding her elbow. They continued to stare at each other, oblivious to their surroundings. The president of the federation was watching Krissi when she spotted

Aaron, and he continued to look on, as did the others with whom Krissi had been talking. "Can we sit down?" Aaron mumbled. "My knees are going to give way."

Somehow, weaving in and out of the crowd, they made their way to the less populated space near the back stairs. Spotting an unoccupied banquette, they headed for it without saying a word, Aaron unaware that he was still holding her arm. Sitting down, they faced each other expectantly, each unsure of the other's reaction but at the same time sensing the waves of emotion. He studied her face, upward to her hair and down to the small scar on her chin, the result of a fall when she was a little girl. Unable to control himself, he brushed her cheek gently with the back of his fingers. He smiled nervously, wanting to say he was sorry, but no words came.

"You look good," she said softly, breaking the silence after several moments. "The years have been good to you."

"You're beautiful. Absolutely beautiful," he said, almost incredulously. "I can't believe it. What are you doing here?"

"I work for Westfalen Pharma Gruppe," she lied, pointing to her name tag. It felt wrong to deceive him, but she dismissed her guilt. Maybe, just maybe, the BND had it wrong and the investigation part of their encounter would come up empty. "You're with Heller and Clarke?" she asked, reading Aaron's name tag and feeling another pang of guilt.

"Yeah . . . yeah. I've been with them for five years now. How long have you been with Westfalen? I've never seen you at the conferences. God, it's great to see you, Krissi," he blurted out, not letting her answer his question. He took her hands in his, hoping he wasn't being too presumptuous and praying she wouldn't pull away. She saw his uncertainty and smiled. His hands felt good.

"I've been with Westfalen for only a few months. Before that I worked with the government," she said. "This

is my first conference, so I'm afraid I don't know anyone here."

"I do. I could introduce you. . . . But I'd rather not.
At least not tonight." He grinned and pressed her hands
in his with a playful pat. She recognized the Korda grin,
an irresistible mix of intelligence and boyish mischief.

"Me, too," she said, not too eagerly, she hoped. Her
lips quivered and her eyes began to well with tears. "Did
you think about me over the years?" she asked, immediately angry at herself for showing her vulnerability.

"Oh, Krissi, not a week has gone by—not one—that
I didn't think of you a lot. Seeing you here tonight is a
dream come true." Hearing those words, earnestly and
simply said, she relaxed a bit and smiled. "Is it important
for you, this reception . . . dinner?" he asked, gesturing
to the crowd now being ushered into the dining room
by white-gloved waiters. She shook her head without any
hesitation. "Shall we take a walk?"

The sun was setting and the lights around the golf
course were already on. A gentle breeze blew through
the palm and California oak trees carefully planted along
the fairways. They walked slowly down a steep embankment from the conference center, crossed the putting
green and wandered toward the pond. Just beyond the
fifteenth hole, they sat down on the thick grass near a
grouping of pine trees. Ducks and geese paddled noiselessly across the water. On the other side of the pond,
water cascaded down a wall of boulders carefully land-
scaped to appear natural. Neither had said anything
since leaving the reception. Aaron had taken her hand
when they went down the first hill, and she hadn't let it
go until they sat down.

"Are your mother and father well?" Krissi asked, her
knees tucked under her chin, her arms around her shins.
She did not look at him, but stared at the waterfall
across the pond.

"My dad died fourteen months ago. Heart attack. It

was very sudden. He was, you know, retired from the army. He was teaching political science part time at a community college. Enjoying himself, too—fishing, hunting. Then one day . . . he just didn't come home."

"I'm sorry, Aaron. I always liked him." Once again, she felt tears welling up. They had missed such a big piece of each other's lives.

"Thanks. He was always crazy about you, you know."

"Yeah. I remember." She tried to smile. "How's your mom?"

"She lives in North Carolina, not too far from where my brother is stationed. She's actually doing pretty well, considering . . ."

"Your brother. My God. How is Martin?" Her tone revealed her pain. She had spent so much time with the Korda family during those years at Wiesbaden. Martin had treated her like a sister when he came home from West Point on leave for Christmas and other holidays.

"He's good. Married. Two kids . . . a six-year-old son, Joey, and a four-year-old daughter, Susie. Still in the army. He's a lieutenant colonel, but he's up for full colonel, and I'm pretty sure he'll make it. In fact, no one doubts that he'll be a general someday, just like our dad, and our grandfather."

"Since you're here . . . working for Heller and Clarke," she said, gesturing to his name tag, "I guess you decided not to stay in?" she asked, knowing the answer from the extensive dossier she had read.

"I got out after five years. It was a big decision. . . . And it put a real strain on Martin and me. He, of course, wanted me to stay in. God, country, family . . . and all that. Frankly, I was tired of the military and I wanted more control over my destiny." She gave him her amused, slightly skeptical, what-are-you-not-telling-me look, which he recognized immediately and still, after seventeen years, found irresistible. "Yeah," he said with a short laugh, "I wanted to make more money." She nodded knowingly. "So I got out, went to business school and became a consultant. But enough about me. I want to know about you. How are your parents?"

"They're both gone. My mother passed away in ninety-three, and my dad died four years later. They both smoked like chimneys, you remember. It eventually killed them." There was a long silence. Aaron leaned back against the thick base of a pine tree, and Krissi, right next to him, did the same. Only their shoulders touched, and they spoke without looking at each other. "I went to Tübingen. Well, I think you knew I was going there. I graduated in eighty-nine. I guess that's the year you graduated from West Point." He nodded in the affirmative, although she didn't look at him for verification. "I majored in international affairs, studied Spanish and Portuguese, went to work at the Ministry of Foreign Affairs in Bonn . . . later in Berlin . . . and became a specialist on South America. I minored in chemistry . . . which helped me get my current job. A few months ago, I quit the government and went to work for Westfalen. I guess pretty much for the same reasons you left the army." It was all true, except for the last part. She had, in fact, briefly worked for the foreign ministry, and was quickly recruited by the BND.

"You're not wearing a ring. You're not married?" He tried to keep his voice neutral. He knew he had hurt her terribly after Maggie died, and almost felt that he didn't have the right to ask the question after so many years.

"No. Well, almost. Twice. But neither time worked out. I broke off one engagement. The second guy broke it off for me. I have no regrets about either," she added truthfully. "And you . . . are you single? Married? Divorced?" She already knew the answers to those questions, but she had to keep up pretenses. Besides, she wanted to know why.

"No. No. I'm not . . . and never really came close."

Krissi was silent for several minutes. Large tears streaked down her cheeks. "Damn it, Aaron," was all she said, all she could say. She leaned forward and placed her face in her palms. "Goddamn you, Aaron," she sobbed softly. "I loved you. We loved each other, and you didn't even say good-bye. Not a word. All these years and you didn't even write. Do you know . . . do you know what that did to me?"

"Krissi . . . Krissi. I'm so sorry. So sorry. I just couldn't handle losing Maggie. It was crazy, but somehow I blamed myself. . . . Like I could have fixed it or something . . . willed her to recover. I couldn't talk about it . . . not even to you. I know . . . I know I should have reached out to you. Part of me wanted to. You were great. I remember that. But I was too confused, I guess. And too immature." Tears were flowing freely down his face. He said nothing, nor did she, for several minutes, but the mood had been lifted. He continued. "When I saw you back there—at the reception—I thought I was in a dream. I mean it, Krissi. God, I've missed you. You're the only woman I ever really loved. You're not going to get away from me now. I won't be a fool twice."

She turned slowly to him, establishing eye contact for the first time since they sat down on the grass. His cheeks were wet and he made no effort to dry them. She didn't know what to say, but she knew what she wanted to do. She reached to him, placing her hand behind his head and pulling him to her, kissing him on the lips at first softly and then more passionately. She met no resistance. The force of their kisses pressed his back against the tree, their tongues exploring each other. They broke away momentarily to look at each other, to verify that this was real. They came back together. He eased their entwined bodies away from the tree and slowly back onto the grass, with Krissi on top, pressing herself against him.

After a few minutes, she put her hands on his shoulders, pinning him to the ground and raising herself an arm's length above his face. She pressed herself against his groin, arousing both of them. "I've missed you, Aaron," she said, kicking her off her sandals.

He caressed her, slowly at first, then more firmly, their

eyes interlocked. "I love you, Krissi. I will never hurt you again. Never. I promise. Make love to me, please."

She began to open the buttons of his shirt when suddenly the water sprinklers came on. Within seconds, they were drenched. "Where's your room?" she asked, laughing and gathering her sandals.

"All the way at the end. Room 299." He stood, holding her hand, laughing at their predicament. For a moment they were two teenagers back in Germany, their frolicking in the grass interrupted by forces beyond their control. "This reminds me of the time the MPs caught us making out in the grove behind the bowling alley," he said, still laughing.

"My room's closer—234." Krissi's water-soaked camisole and slacks clung tightly to her body. "Hey, Korda, I bet I can still run your ass into the ground," she said as she broke into a sprint, getting the jump on him. He ran as quickly as he could, but she was faster, darting barefoot between the sprinklers, purse and sandals in hand. She waited for him at the top of the hill, near the outside stairs that led to her second-floor room.

Aaron and Krissi took the steps three at a time, holding hands. Soon they were inside her room, their bodies pressed together, caressing and undressing each other all at the same time. Their wet clothes dropped to the floor and stayed wherever they landed in a path toward the king-size bed. Within seconds, they were between the sheets, on fire, making love to each other for the first time.

As the moment approached, he slowed his pace, raising himself above her with his arms. In doing so, his erection pressed more firmly against her, and she loved the way it felt. She radiated pleasure. He looked into her eyes, and then he stroked one of her nipples with the back of his fingers, the way he had brushed her cheek at the reception. His eyes came up, slowly, rose and made contact with hers. "Krissi," he whispered, trying to find the words. There were none. No way to make up for the pain caused, impossible to bring back the lost years.

Instead, he lowered his lips to hers and they made love slowly, each enjoying every inch of the other's flesh. They woke during the night and made love again.

* * *

Aaron and Krissi woke at 9:30, having missed breakfast and the first session of the symposium. They lay in bed as they brought each other up to date with the details of each other's lives over the past seventeen years, leaving out only a lover or two, the BND and the CIA.

They showered together. Aaron washed her back with a washcloth in one hand and a bar of soap in the other. He pulled her to him, her back against his chest, and softly ran the warm cloth along her neck and breasts. "This is great, but I'm starving."

"American men," she teased. "Always thinking about your big stomachs." She pinched the skin on her flat belly. "Not that I should talk. I'm famished, too."

"Whoa," he exclaimed. "You don't need to lose any weight." He shifted gears. "Here's an idea. Let's blow off the conference today. I have a rented car . . . a convertible. There's a diner down the road. We can eat there and take a ride up in the mountains. Mount Palomar isn't far from here."

"Well, I'm supposed to be here for Westfalen," she lied, feeling guilty again.

"Screw them," he said, caressing a breast with his soapy right hand. "Trust me. Your bosses won't even know you're not in the meetings." He slid his hand downward, over her stomach to her pubic mound, and lathered her up in more ways than one.

"My God, you have a way about you," she moaned with pleasure. "Okay. Okay. Let's go eat and take a drive, but first finish what you're doing."

After she had dressed, Krissi followed Aaron to his room, where he threw on a pair of jeans, a polo shirt, running shoes, and a light brown leather jacket. Thirty minutes later they were having breakfast at the diner. They ate voraciously, and took refills on the coffee each time the waitress offered. "You didn't bring your cell phone, did you? Just your wallet and keys?" she asked, noting the lack of interruptions. He nodded. "I thought senior consultants at places like Heller and Clarke would have had phones stuck to their ears round the clock," she said playfully after finishing her omelet, hash browns and a good portion of the pancakes.

"Who said I was *senior* at H and C?" he asked matter-of-factly, taking another long sip of his third cup of coffee.

"Would H and C really send a junior person to a great place like this? Besides, I can't picture you as anything less," she recovered, cursing herself for revealing what she had learned about him from his dossier.

Aaron paused for a moment, then smiled. "You're right, but no phones today. No laptops, no BlackBerry, no e-mail. Just you and seventeen years to make up."

"Can we really do that, Aaron? Can we make up for lost years?"

"Who knows?" he answered truthfully. He paused, his lips pressed together tightly, his brow showing his pain. His expression relaxed and he said, "But I'm sure as hell going to try." From across the table, he took her hands in his and brought them to his lips. She knew that he really meant it. "Here's an even better idea. Let's blow off this conference altogether. We'll take a few days and tour around. . . . Go up to the mountains, see the Palomar Observatory, stay in a B and B . . . go to the desert, maybe take in the Salton Sea. I've never been there. Have you?" he asked, his mind and words racing. Krissi shook her head, smiling.

"Damn," Aaron said suddenly. "I'm supposed to go to the Middle East for a client, leaving New York on Monday night." He was silent for a moment. "Oh, let them send someone else." He flashed the grin she remembered so well. "Yeah, screw 'em," he said, convinced.

"I don't think I can do that," Krissi responded seriously. "Well, maybe I can figure out a way," she added with a sly smile. In fact, her current assignment was to be with him, and this fit perfectly into both her job responsibilities and her personal desires.

"Deal." He leaned over and kissed her on the lips. "Let's go back to La Costa and get our gear."

Aaron and Krissi put the top down on his rented Mustang. The sun was shining brightly, with only traces of clouds in the azure sky. They took in Mount Palomar and its famous observatory, and then headed to the Anza-Borrego Desert. Aaron had been in the Yuma desert and in the Sinai on training exercises, and later in Iraq during Desert Storm, but he had never been to the Anza-Borrego. Krissi had never been to any desert, other than a drive from Las Vegas to L.A. a number of years before.

Late in the afternoon, they stopped at Happy Jack's Jump School to inquire about an airplane ride over the desert and mountains the next day. Aaron had read about Happy Jack in the papers a couple of years before and had seen him on television, and wanted to meet the legendary figure.

Aaron opened the door to the corrugated sheet metal building near the runway. The sun beat down on the roof, but inside it was cool, the air conditioner humming away. Jack Heed sat with his feet up on his desk, chatting with a group of students to whom he had just finished giving a preliminary gliding lesson.

"What can I do for you?" Heed asked when the students left the office. He removed his ball cap and finger combed the hair on either side of what was otherwise a bald head, and replaced the hat.

"Hi. I'm Aaron and this is my friend Krissi. We were hoping you could take us flying tomorrow over the desert and mountains. We obviously don't have reservations, but we're flexible. We could do it whenever you have time. . . . If you have time."

"This here's a jump school and glider school. Name your passion, or poison, as the case might be," Jack said, using his hand for emphasis. He studied Krissi approvingly, then turned to Aaron. "Either of you ever wonder why anyone would want to jump from a perfectly good airplane?"

"It's the pilot I'd be worried about," Aaron shot back, ready to match Jack's playfulness.

"You army or marines?"

"Army. I've jumped a lot, and I remember the joke," Aaron laughed.

"Well, well." Jack hesitated, regrouping and thinking of another barb. "What unit?"

"Seventy-fifth Rangers, then the Tenth Mountain Division. I got out in ninety-four."

"What unit in the Tenth Mountain?" Jack was probing, studying the fit-looking couple.

"Second Battalion, Fourteenth Regiment."

"Mogadishu?"

"Yes, sir."

"The Seventy-fifth Rangers were in Desert Storm. Did you see action there?"

"Yes, sir. And you, my friend, know your military history well. I'm impressed." As was Jack, who had learned all that he needed to know about Aaron and decided that the young man was perfectly capable of jumping from Jack's plane without additional training, and would be unlikely to sue if he broke his ankle. Now it was Krissi's turn.

"Ever jump from a plane? Damn, what's a pretty woman like you doing with a beat-up veteran like this guy? Ever think about dumping him and going for a . . . well, more experienced man, say, like . . . well, me, for example?"

"No," she lied in response to the first question. She had, in fact, learned to jump as part of her BND training, though she had never jumped on a mission. "And no. I like younger men," she added, giving the older man a radiant smile and a wink.

"Ferchrisake!" Jack muttered, returning to his chair. "Must be losing my touch. Sit down, sit down." He motioned for them to take the seats opposite his desk. "Where you staying tonight? You got a room nearby?" Aaron shook his head. "Hot damn! You'll stay at my wife's B and B in Julian. Stone's throw from here. A twofer—she and I both make money off you. That's the way we like it," he added, rubbing his palms together. "Ma'am, your handsome man here and I will teach you how to jump from my beautiful plane. Let's do it now." Aaron looked at Krissi for approval. She rarely passed up an athletic challenge and nodded with a smile. "I'm game."

"Great. We've got an hour and a half of daylight left. We'll do some training out back and then fly over the desert and mountains like you want for forty-five minutes, then we'll circle back here and you can make your first jump. Afterward, you can follow me back to my place. My wife and I are having dinner with friends tonight. Otherwise, I'd invite you. Always like talking to soldiers. By the way," he said, turning to Krissi. "You German, ma'am?" Jack asked, raising one eyebrow, as if sizing her up. She nodded again. "Hot damn! They do nice work in Germany."

After settling in at Happy Jack's B&B, Krissi and Aaron walked to a nearby Italian restaurant, where they continued catching up on the years they had missed, holding hands across the table when they were not eating, their eyes fixed on each other's. She looked beautiful in the warm glow of the candlelight. He hadn't shaved that morning. To her, his day-old beard made him even sexier.

"You handled that chute like a pro. Sure you never jumped before?" he asked between forkfuls of salad.

She swallowed hard. As much as she had tried to appear like a novice, when the chute approached the ground she couldn't force herself to land clumsily and risk a broken ankle. Instead, she instinctively hit the ground, the balls of her feet planted firmly, and rolled like she had been taught. "Thanks. Was I really that good? I just followed the instructions you and Jack gave me. I guess you guys are pretty good teachers," she responded, trying not to sound defensive. After all, Aaron was only trying to give her a compliment. *Relax,* she told herself. *Relax.*

He was impressed at her level of fitness and coordination. Somehow, he had forgotten just how athletic she had been in high school. "Hey, it has nothing to do with me and Jack. Face it. You were always a jock." He looked at her lovingly. "And that's just one of the many reasons you're so great." She winced, as if wounded, and he asked, "What did I say wrong?"

"Nothing. Nothing. It's just that over the years the tomboy thing has been a sore point with me. . . . An insecurity, if you will." This wasn't really a lie, but it wasn't the thing that was bothering her. Of course, she couldn't talk about that, so she continued. "I hated playing with dolls. I liked playing soldiers, cops and robbers. In high school, when the other girls wanted to talk about makeup and fashion, I was happy to talk to you and your family about politics and the military. Maybe it's silly, but it has always made me feel a little . . . well, like I wasn't quite feminine enough."

It was Aaron's turn to wince. "Not feminine enough? You're kidding, right? You're gorgeous and sexy. . . . And believe me, the fact that you can take a few simple instructions, jump out of a plane at three thousand feet without hesitation and parachute to the ground, landing like a pro, doesn't take away from your femininity. Just the opposite."

She squeezed his hand and gave a wan smile, but her look was still pained. As Aaron made a mental note to be more sensitive about this issue, even though he thought it was crazy, she wondered what he would think if she told him the truth about being a BND agent.

TEN

The mechanic's wife entered the garage at 8:45, disturbed that her husband had not come home for dinner. Flicking on the lights, she first saw the mutilated bodies of the two soldiers, then that of her husband, almost unrecognizable, in the corner, strewn across a pile of old tires like a heap of garbage. She fainted, hitting her head on the fender of a car parked inside. She came to sometime later with a splitting headache and struggled to the telephone.

The Kayseri Police arrived quickly, and were appalled by the brutality of the murders. No wallets were missing, and no effort had been made to remove the name tags from the two commandos' field jackets. The mechanic's wife could think of no apparent motive—her husband had no enemies that she knew of—and the police could offer no assistance.

The commander of headquarters company, First Commando, was notified. He, four MPs and Master Sergeant Naim Sukur arrived within a half hour. It was clear that Lieutenant Ertugrul and Sergeant Ciller had been tortured, which meant that the murderers were trying to extract information. In fact, the following morning the autopsy revealed that Hasan and Yusuf had been given sodium pentathol, confirming that theory. Only Naim guessed accurately what the assassins wanted, but he kept his suspicions to himself. For safety reasons, he decided to stay on First Commando's compound until he could piece together more information and determine if he, too, was a target. Later that day, he learned of the hideous murders of Yusuf's wife and daughter in Trabzon, and then of the five killings in Yusuf's uncle's hotel. For Naim, the trail was clear. It all led back to Poti. He knew at that moment there would be more bloodshed. That afternoon, he dashed off an e-mail to Aaron informing him of what happened and warning him to be careful.

"What do you mean, you're sick? You can't be sick. You just can't tell them that you've got a bug or something. Don't you realize what's at stake? It's not like I can send just anyone on this assignment," Stanton Clarke shouted into the speakerphone on his desk. "How many consultants do you think we have with your language skills? Christ."

Aaron held the cell phone at arm's length, but still heard Clarke well enough. He had stepped away for a moment to check his voice messages and to make the difficult call to his boss, giving him the news that he had caught a terrible stomach flu and was laid up in a hotel in Southern California. He had taken a walk up the hill behind the B&B, leaving Krissi to explore the shops along the main street in Julian.

"What can I do, Stanton?" Aaron said weakly, trying to sound as if he were in pain. "This is not just something I ate. I've spent half the night on the can. I've got chills, muscle aches and a 102.5-degree fever." Strange, he didn't feel the least bit guilty lying to Clarke. *Screw the CIA,* he thought. *Let them send a real agent, not a part-timer like me.* "Look, I'm not on a secure line here, so I'm going to be a bit cryptic. After the device and instrument trade show this week, there's a pharmaceutical trade show at the beginning of next week. I'm already scheduled to attend it. That's seven days from now. There's no real need to attend both. I'll be recovered, and that gig's a lot more important from our client's point of view than this one. Work your magic, Stanton. They'll listen to you. Tell 'em that it makes no sense for me to travel that far only to be holed up in my room, sitting on the can. Tell them whatever you want to keep 'em happy, but listen, I'm not moving from here until I feel better."

"Shit," Clarke sighed. "All right, but get your sorry ass back here as fast as possible. What's the number of the hotel there?"

"Call me on my cell phone."

"You turn the goddamn thing off half the time."

Aaron suppressed a laugh. *That's exactly the plan, Boss.*

"Sir, can I talk to you for a moment?" the analyst asked, knocking on the glass door of the assistant deputy director's office. "Satellite eight picked up a cell phone conversation while passing over the Caspian Sea, and . . . well, sir, it might concern one of our CIA agents. I know it's unusual, but the message, which apparently came off a vessel called *Krasno Star,* came through loud and clear. I . . . er, thought I'd better bring it to your attention." She handed the transcript, verbatim except for bracketed notations by the analyst/translator, to her boss, who read it immediately.

National Security Agency Situation Report

TO: Assistant Deputy Director

Classification: Top Secret

Satellite: INMARSAT

Location: above the Caspian Sea, 51.6° latitude, 41.8° longitude

Time: (Local) 0317 hours; (Zulu) 2317 hours; (EST) 1917 hours

Time elapsed: 2 minutes, 4 seconds

Means of communication: Nokia cell phone sending; Ericsson cell phone receiving

Language: Farsi, accent is that of western Iran, possibly close to the Iraqi border

Translated by: Specialist Rima Safavieh

Baku, Baku, can you hear me? [We believe *Baku* refers to the capital city of Azerbaijan on the west coast of the Caspian.]

Yes, Krasno Star. You sound like you're down the street. Are you making good time? [We believe the *Krasno Star* is named after Krasnovodsk (now known as Turkmenbashi), the city in Turkmenistan from which the ship departed.]

Perfect weather, and we have the goods that we want. Is all in order on your side?

In Azerbaijan, yes, but in Georgia we have the same problem. The new interior minister is as greedy as the last. His payments for safe passage will cut into our profits substantially, but we can live with it, I guess. [The reference to the prior interior minister is believed to be to the man who was assassinated in Poti on October 11. You will recall that there were rumors of American involvement.]

Don't worry about the new minister. We'll have our Yankee friend, Korda, take care of him the way he did the other pig. Have you met him?

No, but I have heard he's with the CIA and the toughest there is.

Yeah, must have learned his ruthlessness from the Turks. He speaks their language fluently and thinks like them. He is expensive . . . 5 percent of our profits, but that is less than we were paying the minister. Once Korda takes care of the new interior minister, let's hope whoever they appoint gets the message. [laughter]

Okay, this is a good plan. When do you expect to dock?

Later today at about 1400 hours.

Good sailing. We'll have a nice hot lunch for you.

[Aaron Korda shows up in our data files in connection with the efforts of the Libyan government to produce sarin gas, aided by a German chemical company subsequently put out of business. Mr. Korda works for an international consulting firm based in New York City named Heller & Clarke Consulting. This firm has been engaged by the CIA to provide Mr. Korda's services. A copy of his bio is attached. Also attached is the bio of his older brother, Martin Korda, Lt. Col., U.S. Army, Delta Force.]

The assistant deputy director carefully read the translated report and attachments, taking his time to absorb all the facts, neglecting to offer his subordinate a seat. "You did good bringing this to my attention." The senior official dismissed the analyst, asking her to close the door behind her. Once the woman had departed, the assistant deputy director punched in the deputy director's four-digit extension, and to his relief, his boss was in on Saturday. "Sir," he began, "we have a situation here that requires the director's immediate attention. You'll want to be in the loop on this."

"Come to my office. I'll call the director. You can brief me on the way to his office."

Twenty-five minutes later, the director of the National Security Agency was fully briefed, prepared to raise the topic at the regularly scheduled Monday morning meeting with the director of the CIA.

*	*	*

"Mr. Clarke, if this is some sort of joke, I'm not laughing."

"I would not joke about this, Mr. Prebish. And neither would Aaron," Stanton Clarke added, hoping what he had just said was true. "You know how dedicated Korda is to Cold Spring Biologics and its projects. He would not take the time off if he was not seriously ill. Look, you've got him on both trade shows in Damascus and the pharma convention in Istanbul. I suggest that the second show in Damascus is more important, anyway. He can attend that one, and then go directly to Istanbul."

Prebish was silent. Clarke's explanation was weak, and the CIA man, Aaron's handler, was furious. He dreaded taking the news of this turn of events to the Deputy Director of Central Intelligence, who in turn would likely make him explain it to the DCI himself and the national security adviser.

"All right," Prebish said, without a hint of resignation in his tone. He'd deal with Korda later. "We'll keep him booked and cleared for the second trade fair. In the meantime, he's got to be in Vienna at the end of this week for a meeting of the Association of Pharmaceutical Scientists. We've been tracking a Dr. François Maraud, and we've just learned that he'll attend. Aaron's assignment is to get close to him. He's the founder of France Biologiques, France's up-and-coming biopharma company. We know that he's a friend of the minister of health of Syria. This could prove to be an extremely valuable connection. Korda needs to spend as much time as possible with this Frenchman. The bond will be their knowledge of Turkey. Maraud's a history buff . . . an expert on the Ottomans. Only Aaron can pull that off. We have no other asset with that capability."

"I understand. He'll be there. You have my word."

"Good. But let me tell you something, Clarke. I've got to explain Korda's absence from the first show this week in Damascus to some really high-ranking folks in

D.C., so why don't you patch him in. I want to be able to tell the people at Langley that I got Korda's personal assurances that he'll be onboard for the second. That he's not just yanking our chain. Okay?"

Clarke cursed under his breath. *Damn you, Aaron.* The fact that he wasn't surprised by Prebish's request didn't mean that he was prepared for it. He had tried repeatedly to reach Aaron on the latter's cell phone and there had been no response. Apparently, Aaron had turned it off, and worse yet, Clarke had no idea where his hotel was. "I can't do that. I've tried to reach him myself, because I figured you'd want to speak with him directly. He must be sleeping, because he's not answering."

"Then call the goddamn front desk and wake him up."

"Uh, well, that's not possible at the moment. We haven't confirmed where he's staying."

"What? What the hell kind of operation are you running there? I've got to explain this situation to the highest levels in the intelligence community, and you don't know where your goddamn employee is?"

"I'll find him, Don," Stanton Clarke promised. He could almost see Prebish's ruddy skin turning a deeper shade of red, almost feel the vein pulsating at the highstrung man's temples. "If you'd like, I could give you his cell number."

"I have it, and I'll find him." Prebish slammed down the phone without signing off. He paused for ten seconds to calm himself as his doctor had advised, and then called in his assistant. "I want the NSA to put a watch on Korda's cell phone," he ordered, turning to his computer and pulling up Korda's information on Lotus Notes. "Tell them to monitor everything between L.A. and Tijuana, but to concentrate on the area between Carlsbad and San Diego. If he uses it, we'll find him. They are to alert me immediately."

"Is that all, sir?" The young assistant stood in front of his desk, hopeful that it was. Even in a good mood, Don Prebish was not a pleasant man to be around.

"Yes, yes," he said after a period of silence, impatiently waving away the assistant. He was determined not to let Korda get under his skin. "Get me the FBI field office in San Diego."

After a six-mile, early morning run, Aaron and Krissi had breakfast with Happy Jack and his wife, Claudia, at the B&B, said their good-byes and headed east. They spent a glorious day together, driving through the mountains toward the desert and the Salton Sea, stopping several times along the way to enjoy the scenery. Aaron found himself being more open with Krissi than he ever had been with any other woman he'd been with. At 2:00 P.M., they found a beautiful trail skirting a small inlet of the Salton Sea. They parked the Mustang at the side of the road, grabbed the bread, cheese and wine they had purchased a few miles back, and took off hand in hand. Neither spoke for several minutes.

After walking a little farther, they found a small clearing right off the trail and decided to stop, open the wine, and eat. After a few moments, Krissi said, "You know, my friends used to tease me that you were more like my brother than boyfriend, and that Maggie was my little sister." It was true. Maggie had been like a little sister to Krissi, too. She felt her eyes well up and tried to turn away.

"I know," Aaron said, putting his arm around her and pulling her close to him. "You know, I was twelve when Maggie was born, old enough to share my parents' excitement when they learned Mom was pregnant, and aware enough to pick up on the fact that she had been an accident. That's why there was such a big gap between her and me. I remember the day she was born. All of a sudden, there she was. Martin and I got to hold her at the hospital. The years went so fast. . . . Watching her get big, laughing at her baby talk. You know, she called me *Ah-am* until she was three." Krissi smiled but said nothing, not trusting her voice to remain steady. "She had the sweetest little smile. Then one day . . .

in the blink of an eye, she was . . ." Aaron choked, holding back.

"Tell me what happened then," Krissi said gingerly. "I don't mean how she died. I mean what happened to you?"

"Depression. I didn't know it then, but I learned later—quite a bit later—that I was clinically depressed. For the life of me, I couldn't understand why she was gone and the rest of us were still here. For a while, I even thought about taking my own life, just to sort of get it over with, but something stopped me. At least I knew that much."

"Oh, my God, Aaron. I didn't know."

"How could you? I couldn't talk to you, or anyone else for that matter. I think doctors, even your average parent, knows a lot more about depression today. But back then, it was like . . . as long as he's not talking about killing himself, he must be okay." Krissi looked at Aaron and slowly nodded her head knowingly, encouraging him to continue. "I'm so sorry, Krissi. I couldn't share it with anyone then. Not you, not my parents . . . and not even with myself. It seemed at the time that if I told someone what I was thinking . . . well, I might . . . lose it. I guess you were the person closest to me, since I pushed you away the hardest. By the time I was ready, and believe me it took a long time, you were an ocean away."

Krissi wasn't surprised by the depth of his reaction to Maggie's death, but hearing him describe the pain that she remembered so well confirmed what she had come to understand over the years about why he left. "I feel happy—well, maybe *happy* is the wrong word, but it feels good that you're talking to me now, that we can finally share it. You do know we're lucky." They held each other for a while. Whatever hurt she had felt, they had the rest of their lives to sort things out, to work this through together. *But do we?* she asked herself, her thoughts coming back to her job, a BND agent assigned to spy on this man, not fall in love with him.

It was getting late, and arm in arm, they made their way back to the car. Later, he pulled into a gas station to fill up.

"I'm going to the ladies' room for a moment, but first I've got to call back to Westfalen and tell them why I missed my plane."

"What are you going to tell them?"

"That some guy was at the conference with a terrible flu. We kissed a lot and I caught it, too." They both laughed. She shrugged and raised her eyebrows. "Hey, it's possible." She tried to power up her Motorola, but the battery was dead.

"Use mine." Before she could answer, he reached into his pocket, turned on his phone and handed it to her.

Krissi panicked for a moment. She was calling her office, the BND, not Westfalen, and if she used the phone, the number would be stored on his cell and could be redialed. *Calm down,* she told herself. *He's probably not going to notice. He hardly uses it, and if he does see the number, well, maybe I'll just come clean and tell him the truth.* "I still can't get over how little you use this thing," she said. "I've only seen you on it once since Friday night."

"Hey, I don't want to be interrupted when I'm in love. It doesn't happen very often," he deadpanned, and headed toward the men's room. Krissi wandered off to the edge of the asphalt where the scrub brush and desert take over, talking to her boss, telling him that all had gone well, but keeping it brief. She explained that she and Aaron had gotten together and were doing some sightseeing. Schmidt seemed pleased with the progress and urged her to keep at it, which was exactly what she intended to do.

That night in Palm Springs they continued their conversation over dinner, retreating to their room to make love. He fell asleep first, on his back with her head resting on his shoulder, his muscular arm wrapped protectively around her. She lay awake for more than an hour, wondering where things were going with them, perplexed as to how and when she would give up the dual role she was playing.

"Anything new?" Prebish asked his assistant, taking off his wet trench coat and hanging it on the hook behind the door to his office at Cold Spring Biologics. Long Island's north shore was being hammered by a nor'easter, and Prebish was drenched from the short run from his car to the office.

"We have word on Korda, sir. NSA picked up a cell phone conversation on his phone out in the desert south of Palm Springs. The conversation was in German. . . . Some woman on Korda's phone and, get this, some guy in Berlin. She explained that she had met Korda, that the two of them were shacking up for a few days, traveling in California. It didn't bother him; in fact, he seemed pleased. Go figure. We're trying to track the number, but there was a glitch, so we may have to wait to see if she calls it again. She used the same phone again a little later to call the Hilton in Palm Springs to make a reservation. So the FBI sent a couple of agents out there to tail them. Korda and the woman registered at six forty-five, had dinner and spent the night. It's early there, so the FBI thinks they're still asleep. Anything further you want them to do?"

"Yeah, follow them . . . and find out who she is and what the hell is going on."

"So, where did you learn so much about the pharmaceutical industry?"

"Well, I guess it's like anything. . . . You have to know it for your job, so you make yourself learn it. And I've been at it for almost six years now. You'll see, there's no magic to it. At first there's data overload, and then later it all starts to make sense. For example, you just joined Westfalen. So I've got a leg up on you. I probably know more people at your company than you do, and I almost certainly know more about the new CEO's business plans than you. I've studied Westfalen for a long time. Hey, it's the largest manufacturer of over-the-counter and prescription drugs in Germany, and one of the biggest pharmaceutical companies in the world. Do you know that it accounts for more than twenty-five percent of the sales of birth control pills in the United States? About the same percentage in Europe as a whole. And I'm confident that it's an excellent product. Doesn't seem to reduce the sex drive at all."

"Whoa—have you been snooping in my toiletries?"

"No, but you left them on the counter near the bathroom sink. . . ."

Krissi thought about that as she poured skim milk on her granola, and decided to drop it. They had had a nice workout in the gym, followed by lovemaking and a shower, and were now enjoying breakfast on the terrace at the Hilton. At 9:15 A.M., the breeze off the desert was warm, but a cheerful blue-and-white awning, and the fashionable sunglasses each wore, protected them from the already strong sun.

"Come on, Krissi. I can't help but check out which brands of pharma products people use," he said, lowering his sunglasses on the bridge of his nose so she could see his eyes.

"You're forgiven. But tell me, what do you know about the new CEO's plans?" she asked.

"A lot, actually. I read his working papers and know a bit about the way he thinks."

"How did you get his working papers?" She tried her best to sound nonchalant, which was difficult, since she was dreading what his answer might be.

"I wrote a good part of his business plan."

"Really. How so?"

"This is confidential, so keep this to yourself." He didn't wait for her response. "When he was negotiating his employment contract with Westfalen, part of his deal with the chairman was that Heller and Clarke be engaged to help him prepare a business plan. All very hush-hush, you understand. I spent a few weeks in and out of your headquarters and visited many of the manu-

facturing sites. That's how I know so much about Westfalen. I wrote part of your business plan. If I had known
you'd be working there, I'd have created a new position
for you with a higher salary." He laughed and kissed
her on the cheek.

"Do you do that a lot for German companies?"

Aaron heard, but was distracted for a moment. A man
seated on the other side of the patio ostensibly reading
his newspaper was watching him and Krissi too closely.
Another person, a woman on the other side of the pool,
nursed a cup of coffee, her open purse lying on the table
with a tiny camcorder pointed at them. He pretended to
look for their waiter, and waved at a busboy instead.
"Could you ask our waiter for more coffee and then the
check, please?"

"Yes, sir. Right away," the young man answered, hur-
rying to fulfill the request. The gesture to the busboy
had been quick enough so that the two FBI agents monitoring them did not notice that Aaron saw them.

"Sorry. To answer your question, more than they
would like to admit. As you probably know, your new
CEO was president of Offenbach for a brief period, but
left that company when he uncovered a scandal and resigned." He wanted to tell her about Offenbach and how
he had discovered its sale of sarin gas compounds to the
Libyans, but some things were still classified, at least at
the present, and he kept it to himself. "By the way, he
was clean as a whistle . . . your new boss. When he
started negotiations with Westfalen, he brought me back
in to help him formulate the new business plan."

Krissi took a long sip of her iced coffee and wondered
if the BND had it wrong about Aaron. Perhaps they
didn't know that German executives discreetly engaged
American consulting firms to help with their new strate-
gies. Those executives wouldn't want to advertise that
their plans for the future of their companies, so boldly
presented to the press and investors as the product of
their own business prowess, were, in fact, conceived by
persons outside the company. Maybe he didn't spy on

German companies at all; they just gave him their secrets.

"Come on. Let's check out and hit the road. Maybe we'll drive up to Fort Irwin and see an old army buddy of mine." She didn't realize that the fort was far to the north in the desert, nor that he had made the comment for the benefit of the two people trailing them. His intention was not to drive up north, but rather to lose them in the traffic leading to Los Angeles.

"When is your flight?" he asked in a low voice once they left the restaurant and were walking down a long corridor toward their room.

"Well, given that I missed my scheduled plane two days ago," she said with a laugh, "I'll take whatever plane you do to New York and go on to Germany from there. I have to be in Vienna Friday night, and have tons of stuff to clean up on my desk before I leave," she added. She sensed a slight change in his demeanor.

"Good. Let's pack fast and hit the road. I'm pretty much ready, but I should check my e-mails and voice messages." He hadn't turned on his laptop since they met at La Costa.

While Krissi packed her bags, Aaron checked his e-mail, fearing scores of irate messages from Stanton Clarke and his handlers at Cold Spring Biologics. Skimming over the spam e-mail, deleting them as he scrolled down the screen, he was surprised at how few e-mails he actually had from Clarke, who sounded downright sympathetic. *Okay. I'll go to the pharmaceuticals trade show,* Aaron thought. Another e-mail informed him that he was to attend the Association of Pharmaceutical Scientists conference in Vienna later that week. His heart leapt. Krissi would be there, too. *Too good to be true.* He scrolled farther down the sea of red, unopened e-mails, clicking and pressing the DELETE button on 80 percent of what he saw. Then it caught him. Naim's message. He hurriedly opened it, then read and reread it several times. Hasan and Yusuf both dead in Kayseri, tortured and drugged with sodium pentothal. Yusuf's wife and daughter brutally murdered in Trabzon. His uncle and aunt, along with three others, murdered in their hotel in Trabzon. It all traced back to Poti, Naim said. Aaron agreed with the conclusion and the warning.

"What's wrong?" Krissi asked, putting her workout clothes in a plastic bag to be washed later. "You look upset."

"Nah . . . nah. It's nothing," he said unconvincingly. "Just that my boss is pissed at me for being out of touch. I expected it, and I don't regret it." He tried to smile, but couldn't, as the horror sunk in. Hasan and Yusuf dead. Yusuf's wife and his daughter, the little girl for whom Aaron had made a ring out of a ten-dollar bill. It was almost too terrible to think about right now. *But damn it. What about the two spooks at the restaurant? How did they find me? Christ. No weapon. Nothing. Not even the peashooter,* he thought, referring to the small-bore, 6.35 mm Walther PPK he sometimes carried when he needed a smaller, more concealed automatic. *If they followed me here, then maybe the car is bugged. It looks like they know every move I make.* He looked at Krissi, who was now watching him, concerned and worried. *What have I gotten her into?* He grabbed the phone on the night table and called the local Hertz office. "Hello, this is Aaron Korda. I'm a Gold Card member. Yes, here's the number," he instructed the clerk, who then put him on hold and came back. "Listen, I'm having trouble with my Mustang and need another car run over to the Hilton immediately. Yes. Yes. No, I'm late. Yeah, fine. A Taurus is okay, but I need it immediately."

"I didn't know there is anything wrong with the car," Krissi commented after Aaron hung up, wanting to know more.

"It's fine, but the convertible is noisy in L.A. traffic, and . . . what the hell," he hesitated, searching for something plausible. "I'd like us to be able to talk and not compete with the sounds of the highway."

She shrugged. "Makes sense." Ironically, if she didn't

have her own secrets, she would have been more aggressive in pursuing his.

"By the way," he said, pausing for effect, "do you know anyone attending the pharmaceutical scientists' meeting in Vienna?"

"As a matter of fact, I am," she said.

"Me, too. I just read an e-mail from my office telling me that it's now on my agenda. Hey, I'm stalking you," he said with a laugh, though she could tell he was only half thinking about Vienna at the moment.

"Sir, they just checked out of the hotel, but we've got a problem," the field agent reported to his office in San Diego. "He must have seen us near the pool. He switched cars. We could follow, but we're driving a standard-issue navy blue, four-door Crown Victoria. We'd stand out like a sore thumb. Might as well wear FBI jackets."

"Great! I guess you two didn't pay too much attention in the training session. Come on back. Anyway, we know what flight they've booked and we can wire their seats." The senior agent put down the phone and looked for Prebish's phone number.

ELEVEN

Delta Airlines employees in blue jumpsuits pushed the heavy airfreight containers from the cargo bay to the awaiting forklift, sliding them on rollers welded to the floor of the Boeing 747-400 cargo hold. The aluminum container shimmered in the bright Atlanta sunlight as the operator of the forklift extracted it from the side door of the big bird and slowly set it into a green-and-yellow eighteen-wheeler. The tractor-trailer was owned by National Pharma Distributors, Inc., a subsidiary of National Pharma Corp., engaged in the distribution of National's products, including those imported by it from its soon-to-be subsidiary in England, Midlands Chemicals PLC, along the East Coast to pharmacies and hospitals.

The forklift operator took his time in offloading the plane and filling up the trailer, not wanting to risk dropping a container. Besides, he got paid by the hour. *What's the rush?* he thought. The trucker had a different agenda. He had been up at 4:00 A.M. and reached National's motor pool by 4:45, hoping to get an early start on the road. The 747's late arrival at Hartsfield International Airport pissed him off. He had planned to get on the road by eight o'clock and shoot up I-85 to Raleigh, where the bulk of his cargo would be unloaded at the distribution center of the largest pharmacy chain in North Carolina. After that stop, he would loop south to Fayetteville and deliver the balance of the pharmaceuticals to Womack Hospital on Fort Bragg. With a little bit of luck, he could hit the honky-tonks and massage parlors by 6:00 or 6:30. He got his paycheck on Friday afternoon and had been careful not to spend it over the weekend, saving it for this trip. Now on Monday morning, his thoughts alternated between frustration at the cargo handler's pace and fantasies of getting it on at his favorite massage parlor with a twenty-year-old brunette who called herself Ashley.

When the eighteen-wheeler was fully loaded at 8:25, the driver hastily signed the bills of lading and other transfer documents, acknowledging that Delta Airlines had duly delivered the shipment to National Pharma. He made good time on I-85, pushing the powerful Mack ten miles per hour faster than the speed limit. By 6:15 that evening, he stood on the loading dock in the rear of Womack Hospital, chatting with the receiving clerk, a good ol' boy from the Smokies whom the driver had known since he started on this route nine months earlier. One by one, the man put a line through each item on the computer printout that served as the shipping manifest, and simultaneously placed an *X* with his marker on the corresponding case of pharmaceuticals. "You guys go through a lot of albuterol," the driver observed.

"Yup, sure do," said the clerk. "Seems to be an outbreak of asthma. Army here at Bragg, air force over at Pope Air Force Base. Lots of kids. Military families have lots of kids."

The vice president, accompanied by his national security adviser and an assistant, joined the White House chief of staff in the Situation Room. Others present included the assistant secretary of state for Middle Eastern affairs (sitting in for the secretary, who was traveling), the secretary of defense, the director of Central Intelligence, the chief of staff of the Army, the chairman of the Joint Chiefs, and the respective heads of the NSA and NRO. Connected to the video conference by secure phone lines were the respective four-star generals in charge of SOCOM and CENTCOM, both in Tampa, and

Colonel Brice Whitman, Delta Force commander, at
Fort Bragg. Lieutenant Colonel Martin Korda and his
second-in-command, Major Lewis Kinloch, were patched
in by secure satellite uplink from Incirlik Air Base in
Turkey. Everyone knew each other from prior teleconfer-
ences and were spared introductions. The vice president led the meeting.

"General Owen," the veep began, "I believe your
group has the status report."

"Yes, sir," the CENTCOM commander responded
crisply. "Thank you. To date, neither the Syrians nor the
Iraqis who we think have set up operations in Deir ez-
Zur, Raqqa and Hassake have found the sensors or
transmitters placed on their facilities. The devices at
Deir ez-Zur and Raqqa are fully operational, but we
are having continuing problems at Hassake, the apparent
result of damage from a sandstorm that hit the area a
few days ago. Information compiled thus far indicates
that there is activity under the mosque in Deir ez-Zur,
but to date we have nothing conclusive. So far, Raqqa
is quiet. We're monitoring them day and night. It will
take time, patience and, I'm afraid, a bit of luck. Now,
with respect to Aleppo . . ."

"Whoa, before anyone moves on to Aleppo, let's take
stock of what we have already learned. . . . Or rather,
what we have not learned," the vice president interrupted. "From what you have said thus far, we have
learned nothing from Operation Shell Game. Is that
right?"

"Affirmative, sir," General Owen responded.

"So we're conducting a highly dangerous and costly
clandestine operation that if detected could explode like
a diplomatic—and political—hydrogen bomb, and so far
we have zero results."

"As I said, sir, we need to be patient. If I may address
the situation in Aleppo, intelligence on the ground indicates that several Iraqi scientists may have fled to
Aleppo. It's a city of just over three million people, and
it would be relatively easy for the Iraqis to blend in with

the local populace. We have intel from good sources that they are working in the basements and subbasements of the Al-Fustaq Mosque in the old part of Aleppo. We propose to install our devices on the Al-Fustaq Mosque while a decoy team draws attention to the Great Mosque a few hundred meters away."

"And just how do you intend to indicate that we were only interested in the Great Mosque—ransack the basement like you did in the school in Deir ez-Zur? Christ, that's all we need is the whole Muslim world up in arms at our having committed a sacrilege in one of Islam's oldest and most beautiful mosques. Don't we have a diversion less sensitive?"

Martin Korda, six thousand miles away in eastern Turkey, sat up, listening very carefully. The vice president had not axed the raid on Aleppo altogether. He appeared to approve the plan, but wanted damage control. "Gentlemen, if I may say a word, there is a madrassa due west of the plaza surrounding the Great Mosque. It's a religious school, but nowhere near as sacred to the Muslims as the Great Mosque itself. We could create an adequate diversion there."

"Well, that's a step in the right direction," the vice president conceded.

"The military branches concur in this proposal, as modified," the Chairman of the Joint Chiefs said. "We have to know what Saddam's ex-scientists are up to, and we see no alternative but to continue with Operation Shell Game until we find out or we come up with a better program."

"For the record, the State Department is opposed to Aleppo," the deputy secretary of state said.

"State has been opposed to Operation Shell Game from the beginning, so what's new?" the secretary of defense hissed. "Defense agrees with the CIA on this. There are no other options."

"Colonel Korda, what is your confidence level of pulling this off without further casualties?" the vice president asked solemnly.

"Zero, sir," Martin responded without a second's hesitation. "We have to assume that we'll suffer injuries. We may lose operators on the ground. But if you ask me if I think we can install our bugs and transmitters on the Al-Fustaq Mosque without being detected, the answer is yes."

After a long pause, the vice president, overcoming his doubts, said, "Then we go with it. But understand this, Colonel. If the mission goes bad, we never heard of you."

"They're really pissed, Aaron. You've got to understand this. It's bad enough when a regular client is unhappy, but this is the goddamn CIA." Stanton Clarke spoke slowly, using his West Virginia accent to full effect. "First, this fucking stunt in Poti, and then you call in sick and miss the trip to the first show in Damascus. You just can't get away with that." He paced his paper-strewn office, tipping over an eight-inch-high stack of documents with his foot. "Aaron, you are the best. I'll give you that. You're fucking A-one good, but don't let it go to your head."

"Look, I had the flu. . . . Felt like crap, and took a few days off. I'm sorry if you had to take some heat, but I'm back and ready for Vienna."

"Oh, don't give me that. It's insulting. You're too goddamn suntanned to have been sitting on the toilet for three days. Where did you shit, in a fucking solarium?"

Aaron laughed. Clarke was in his stride now, and Aaron knew that his ire had already subsided. "Stanton, I have to hustle to get things in order here before I jump on the plane tonight. . . . Time sheets, expense vouchers, phone and e-mail messages—all that stuff. I have a stack of invoices to send out. And I have a conference call with Prebish in twenty-five minutes. I'll try to smooth things over, assure him that I'll be in Vienna and get close to Maraud. I've got some ideas about Maraud. Also, just so you know, I'm going to tell Prebish that I want my pistol and several extra magazines to carry onboard. I'll need special clearance to get on the plane at Kennedy and to deplane in Vienna. Prebish will flip. It'll get back to you, so I'm just giving you a heads-up."

"Why do you need a weapon? You don't normally carry one to the conferences. Is there something I should know about?"

Aaron considered telling his boss about Naim's e-mail and what had happened to Hasan and Yusuf, but decided not to. Poti was already a sore point. "No. Nothing. Maybe I'm just becoming more cautious."

"Do you want to talk about Poti?"

"Not right now, Stanton. Thanks. Really." Aaron rose from the chair facing Clarke's desk and walked out of the room, deliberately not looking back at the worried look on his mentor's face.

The director of Central Intelligence stared at the video-conferencing screen in his office, listening to Donald Prebish, president and CEO of Cold Spring Biologics and Aaron Korda's handler, brief him on the latest involving one of the CIA's most valuable spies. After Prebish concluded his preliminary report, the DCI looked to see what his two deputy directors had to say.

"Well," the DDO began, "we're seeing erratic behavior on Korda's part. First, this antic in Poti . . . at a time when we need the Georgians to help us fight the terrorists. Now he blows off a mission to Damascus for a woman in Southern California."

"Mr. Prebish, what do we know about the German woman?" the deputy director for intelligence asked.

"Nothing yet, but we're still checking her out. The number she called in Berlin is not Westfalen's local office, and for the moment can't be tracked. We had their seats bugged on the flight from L.A. to JFK, but it didn't help us much."

"What do you make of it?"

"Well, sir. It's all too coincidental. She pops up out of nowhere at a pharmaceutical conference, drop-dead beauty, sharp as a whip, a jock . . . oh, I forgot, sir . . .

sorry, they laughed about her running him into the ground on their morning jogs . . . that's not easy to do with Korda . . . uh, where was I? . . . oh yeah, she knows a lot about sports, international affairs and military matters. She's a real man's woman. Sir, if you know Aaron . . . well, she's perfect for him. Something's wrong here."

The DCI paused for a few minutes. "Find out who she is, and do it fast." With that instruction, the video conference ended. Once the screen went black, the director turned to his two deputies. "Watch him like a hawk. We may have a compromised agent."

TWELVE

"Dr. Maraud, I'm very pleased to meet you. I won't deny that I have taken the liberty of requesting to sit at your table this evening." Aaron shook the Frenchman's hand and nodded in appreciation to the director general of the Association of Pharmaceutical Scientists, who had made the arrangements. "And this is my friend Kristina Sturm. She's with Westfalen." Krissi smiled and extended her hand, greeting the director of research of France Biologiques in French and then addressing the director general in his native tongue, Spanish. Both the Frenchman and the Spaniard were dazzled by Krissi, and made no secret of it. Krissi's hair was pulled back simply with a large tortoiseshell barrette, accentuating her long, graceful neck and the diamond-and-ruby necklace the BND had procured for her, on loan from a Viennese jeweler. She wore a burgundy satin gown, also borrowed for the occasion, that was somewhat more fitted and lower cut than she was accustomed to, although Aaron seemed to be enjoying it. Her diamond watch, also borrowed, was a far cry from the fifty-nine-dollar Timex Ironman she usually wore. Aaron offered her the seat next to the Frenchman, and took the one next to her.

"Dr. Maraud, one of the reasons that I asked the director general to arrange for us to sit at your table is that I understand that you are interested in Turkish history and are quite an expert on the Ottomans." Dr. Maraud, who half expected to hear a marketing pitch from the industry consultant, lit up.

"Oui, en fait, je suis. . . . Excusez-moi. Parlez-vous français?"

Aaron shook his head. "No, sorry. English, German and Turkish, but no French." Aaron did not mention his rather good command of Arabic, preferring to keep that in his pocket for the time being. Krissi took note of the omission.

"Turkish? How interesting. I am indeed very interested in the Ottomans and all things Turkish, but I must decline the title of expert. And you are interested in the Ottomans?"

"Oh yes, very much. I have read a good number of books on their history, literature and architecture, and I have visited many of the major palaces and mosques. However, I'm afraid I don't get much of an opportunity to converse with people who are knowledgeable about their rich history."

Earlier in the afternoon, Aaron had mentioned to Krissi that they would be sitting at Dr. Maraud's table that evening, but had said nothing about the man's affinity with the Turks. Krissi noted the ease with which Aaron pulled the Frenchman into his confidence. She wondered what Aaron was after. As she watched him ingratiate himself with Dr. Maraud, even she couldn't tell whether he really was interested in Ottoman architecture of the sixteenth and seventeenth centuries or whether this was just part of his cover. *If it's the latter,* she thought, *then he's good. Damn good.*

"You know, Dr. Maraud, some of the finest examples of Ottoman palace architecture are in Syria. I haven't been there in a while, but I'm on my way there two days from now." Maraud looked interested. "When I travel on business, I always try to sneak away for a few hours to check out the local architecture. I don't put *that* on my time sheets." He laughed, as did Krissi and the doctor.

"I'm intrigued by your interest in Syria. I, too, find it irresistible," Maraud said, pleased to share two common interests with the younger man.

"You know, Mr. Korda, since you're going to Damascus, I'll try to arrange for you to meet a dear friend of mine, who also is very interested in Ottoman architecture. He's the minister of health. . . . And very close to President Assad," the Frenchman added with a wink, as if he was letting Aaron in on an important secret. "I do think the two of you would hit it off quite well."

Bingo. This guy is too much. Krissi was amazed. Within minutes, Aaron had maneuvered an introduction to a minister-level official in the Syrian government who happened to be a confidant of the president.

Soon, a swarm of white-gloved waiters descended on the table to remove the appetizer plates, and Maraud was called to meet others in the assembly. "Let's get out of here," Aaron whispered to Krissi. "The director general's speech will put us to sleep. I know. I've done these boring presentations myself," he said, anticipating some resistance. "Come on. There's a restaurant on the other side of the river, with good food and wine, live music and dancing, and a great view of the Danube. Do you have your cell phone in that tiny purse?" She nodded. He had left his upstairs, his Walther PPK occupying the breast pocket where he would normally keep his phone. "When the entrée comes, just pick at it. We'll eat later. I'll excuse myself to go to the men's room and arrange for one of the waiters to call you after I get back to the table. Just pretend that something important came up and we'll split."

Aboard Spider One, Lieutenant Colonel Martin Korda had plenty on his mind. One look around the Black Hawk and the faces of the other Delta operators told him that they, too, understood that Aleppo, while not as deep into Syrian territory as the other missions, would be more difficult. The prior raids had put the Syrians on edge. Elements of the Syrian Fourteenth Special Forces Division were reported to be garrisoned north of the city and could be called upon to counter the helicopter-borne American strike force.

Spider Three was the first of the three choppers to fly over the ruins of Deir Samaan, northwest of Aleppo, approaching the outlying villages that rimmed the crowded city. Through her FLIR screen, Lieutenant Toll saw the skeletons of two ancient monasteries. She glanced at her GPS indicator and then down at a stone arch partway up the hills near the remains of the former Christian community and verified that her position was within meters of her intended course. Ahead, she saw the scattered lights of Aleppo, which even at 3:15 A.M. showed some signs of activity. Several minutes later, Spider One overflew what reconnaissance photos had previously identified as a sanitation department motor pool on the outer side of the ring road circling most of the city, and truck drivers were beginning to organize themselves for their morning run. Inside the ring road, Lieutenant Toll checked the next GPS waypoint on the instrument panel and visually spotted the University of Aleppo on the FLIR screen. She glanced at her compass reading of one hundred degrees. Satisfied, she turned to her copilot, Chief Warrant Officer 3 Bruce Kopinsky, and asked, "Do you have a visual on the hotel?"

"Affirmative," Kopinsky responded. "At our one o'clock. Looks like some of the lights on the top-floor restaurant are still on. You can make out the Citadel behind it."

"Got it," she responded, focusing her eyes on the tall hotel. "Listen up, customers," she said into her mouthpiece. All persons aboard the three Black Hawks became alert to her instructions. "Four minutes from insertion. We're circling around the Amir Palace Hotel. The madrassa is six hundred meters beyond the hotel, and the Al-Fustaq Mosque is another three hundred meters past the school."

The plan that had been rehearsed on the mock-up in Hangar C back at Incirlik Air Base called for Spider Three to insert its team of Deltas, Chalk Three, in a clearing in front of the Al-Fustaq Mosque, while Spider One, Chief Warrant Officer 4 Eulas Cole at the stick, inserted Lieutenant Colonel Korda and his squad, Chalk One, on top of and around the madrassa. Spider Two, piloted by Chief Warrant Officer 4 Carl Foreman and copiloted by Lieutenant Laura Alvarez, would circle above to provide covering fire if the need arose. Inside Spider Two, Major Kinloch served as command and control, since Lieutenant Colonel Korda, as per orders from Washington, would be on the ground to personally monitor the installation of the listening devices.

Korda and the other Deltas and Night Stalkers expected that the three American Black Hawks would be noticed by the Syrians' ground and air defense forces. The prior raids on Deir ez-Zur, Raqqa and Hassake had put them fully on alert, and Aleppo was heavily defended with Russian-made antiaircraft guns. The plan for Aleppo was not to wait for detection and then respond, but rather to take the initiative by attacking known AA sites, creating confusion and diversion away from the madrassa. Satellite and aerial reconnaissance photos taken a few hours earlier indicated that a mobile ZPU-quad and crew had taken a position in an empty lot near the Belgian consulate only four hundred meters from the Al-Fustaq Mosque. No one onboard the three Black Hawks took the ZPU's four 14.5 mm KPV machine gun barrels lightly.

"I have a visual," Lieutenant Toll said, her voice calm and businesslike. "Repeat, I have a visual. Ground crew is preparing to fire. Crew chiefs at the ready."

"Roger that," said Sergeant Jimmy Cho into his mouthpiece. The crew chief manning the starboard Gatling gun leaned out the right side door of the chopper, the pressure of his shoulder harness reassuring against his chest as he strained to see the gun emplacement.

"We have to wipe out the quad on the first run. Pour on the fire."

"That's a rog," Cho responded.

Lieutenant Toll saw the flash of light out of the corner of her eye, and then the tracer bullets streaked left to right in front of the cockpit. She immediately jinked hard

to her left, lifting the chopper up in one smooth motion.
Behind her, Curtis Dorne was dangling out the side
door, held in by the harness that dug into his shoulders
and crotch. On the floor of the cabin, seven Deltas clung
to each other and the helo to prevent them all from
falling out as they slid toward the open side panel.
"There's another gunner on the roof of the Amir Palace
Hotel! On the roof!" Toll yelled into her mike. "They've
got a fucking cannon on the roof! Carl, you got it?"

"It's a zoo-twenty-three dual," Foreman shouted from
Spider Two, his voice rising with excitement. "We're
going in." He had also jinked left when he saw the tracer
rounds streaming from the hotel toward Spider Three,
and climbed to seven hundred feet. Below and in front
of him he saw the four-man crew of the Russian-made
ZU 23-2. He knew the particular weapon and feared it.
It was small, no bigger than a wheeled hot dog cart, yet
it was lethal, having caused American chopper pilots
grief from Grenada to the war in Iraq. One man could
operate it by sitting in the gunner's seat and blasting
away, though a four-man crew was optimal. The double-
barreled 23 mm cannons could fire up to one thousand
rounds per minute. At that rate of fire, the barrels would
soon overheat and melt, but the weapon system could
easily sustain two hundred to four hundred rounds per
minute until the ammo ran out. Chief Warrant Officer
4 Foreman, and his copilot, Lieutenant Laura Alvarez,
saw the four Syrian gunners scurrying to dislodge a
jammed ammo belt and swivel the ZU 23-2 toward Spider Two.

"Bastards got night-vision goggles. They can see us!"
Alvarez shouted.

In theory, the Black Hawks were armed to withstand
23 mm rounds, but Foreman knew that it would take
only a few well-placed rounds to put his chopper down
on the crowded streets and marketplace below. Behind
him, eleven soldiers heard the pilots and braced themselves for the roller-coaster ride they knew was coming.

Foreman jinked hard up to the left, then right, keeping

the side gunners pointed toward the roof of the hotel. Foreman wanted to jettison the two external fuel tanks to reduce the risk of their being hit and to give him more speed and mobility, but he needed them for the long trip home. "Fire," he commanded, but Sergeant Knight's Gatling gun was already spitting out a torrent of lead. At the same moment, the rooftop gunners began shooting. Though only every fourth round was a tracer, the fire from the ZU 23-2 was so fast that it appeared as if one continuous stream of white light was headed toward the Black Hawk, now at 1,600 feet, still well within range of the antiaircraft guns. Staff Sergeant Rodriguez maintained a steady barrage of lead on the Syrians, the Gatling gun spinning furiously, firing seven hundred rounds in a few seconds with a deafening roar that blocked out the staccato *pop-pop-pop* of the rotors and the whine of the jet engines. As the Black Hawk jinked left, the right door gunner, Sergeant Knight, fired his Gatling gun, sending an additional thousand rounds down on the Iraqi gun crew.

The two enemy squads faced off amid a brilliant white stream of cannon fire ascending from the roof of the hotel into the dark in search of the Black Hawk, and the white flash of the Gatling guns raining down hell on the Syrian position. More than two thousand rounds of 7.62 mm bullets hit the roof near the antiaircraft gun emplacement, destroying its crew. Later, Syrian soldiers assigned to cleanup would not even try to figure out which body parts belonged to which soldier, but would scoop up with flat shovels whatever could be placed into body bags and buried as is. As for the ZU 23, the steel barrels and encasement were perforated and twisted, almost unrecognizable, its rubber tires gone.

Experience and honesty made Martin Korda unwilling to guarantee the suits in Washington that no lives would be lost on the mission. But his worst-case scenario was not as devastating as what followed. As he watched from Spider One, tracer rounds headed straight toward the cockpit of Spider Two, as the pilots desperately struggled to maneuver out of their path. They were too late. Though the cockpit was designed to withstand the impact of 23 mm cannon fire, it was not equipped to handle multiple bursts hitting nearly the exact same spot on the glass. One 23 mm cannon round pierced the nose of the Black Hawk and exploded, sending large shards of razor-sharp metal through the instrument panel and into the two pilots, penetrating their body armor. Foreman and Alvarez died instantly. Three other cannon shells pounded Spider Two. One went straight through the open side panel and exploded against the ceiling of the cabin, raining shrapnel on top of the Deltas and the two Night Stalker crew chiefs. Another hit a wheel base, shooting shrapnel upward into the cabin, while the third round ignited a fuel line. Though the fuel system was designed to be self-sealing, the fire raced through the hose, retracing the flow of the volatile JP-8 aviation fuel back to the internal tank and then the external auxiliary tanks. The Black Hawk exploded in a huge ball of fire at 1,400 feet above Aleppo.

Per Andresen, a Norwegian on a bus tour of Syria along with other Europeans, was staying at the Amir Palace Hotel and had opted to upgrade his room so that he had a view of the Great Mosque and the Citadel beyond. Though he had partied hard at the penthouse restaurant and bar and had been sound asleep when the shooting commenced, he was jolted out of bed upon hearing the first burst of cannon fire from the roof on top of the panoramic restaurant three floors above him. A former member of a Norwegian artillery unit, he knew the sound of heavy antiaircraft guns. Surprised but not yet frightened, he ran to the window just in time to see the duel between the two forces. He stood there looking through the arabesque arched window, mesmerized, as the Black Hawk's bullets broke windows and pierced concrete walls above him, with hundreds of rounds ripping into the outer wall of the hotel near the roof, shattering the windows of the restaurant and penetrating the roof itself, bursting through the windows and walls on

the top two floors. But those sounds occurred too fast
and did not fully register with him as he watched the
explosion of the helicopter in the night sky. The forward
momentum of the fireball was such that it fell westward,
toward the hotel, but he realized that too late to seek
shelter away from the window. Instead, he watched as
the flaming wreck of twisted metal and burning fuel
crashed into the window at which he stood.

Other Europeans on the tour, as well as a separate
group of traveling Japanese businessmen also staying at
the hotel, had also risen at the deafening sound of the
cannonade. Some had rushed to their windows; others
sat up in bed, bewildered. Of the thirty-five Europeans
on the tour, thirteen were killed and another six were
wounded, some burned so badly that they were unrecognizable. Eight of the Japanese were killed and three
wounded.

At the first burst of cannon fire at Spider Three, Lieutenant Toll had jinked left and up to avoid the incoming
fire from the roof of the hotel, leaving the belly of the
Black Hawk exposed to fire from the four-barreled 14.5
mm ZPU positioned in the lot near the Belgian Consulate. She righted the chopper in time to see a squad of
six men removing the camouflage netting. One man was
climbing into the gunner's seat, while two others were
adjusting the ammo link-belts. She didn't need her night-
vision goggles or the FLIR screen on her instrument
panel to see the sky light up behind her, Spider Two's
explosion momentarily lighting the town below in a ra-
dius of one kilometer, including the plaza surrounding
the Great Mosque, the Al-Fustaq Mosque and as far
east as the Belgian Consulate.

Though devastated by what she knew was the loss of
everyone onboard Spider Two, Toll and Chief Warrant
Officer 3 Bruce Kopinsky, her copilot, continued their
mission as they had been trained to do. From the angle
of attack she now found herself in, her line of sight was
partially obscured by the three-story-high consulate.
However, that same building also blocked the ZPU

squad from firing on her. "Around from the right! We'll come from behind." Toll let her instincts and years of experience take over. "NSDQ," she said through clenched teeth, repeating the slogan of the 160th, "Night Stalkers Don't Quit," for the benefit of herself and everyone on Spider Three and Spider One who was listening. "Curtis," she urged the left door gunner, "you get a shot at those bastards, you take it." Sergeant Curtis Dorne, a tough former football player from Tupelo, Mississippi, nodded solemnly without uttering a word. Given the opportunity, he would send the ground crew to Allah.

"Hit 'em with a rocket if we get a shot," Toll said to Kopinsky without looking at him, her voice competing with the rotors whirling above her. Kopinsky readied a Hellfire. Toll expertly maneuvered the Black Hawk around the buildings, only a few meters above the rooftops of the tallest structures, keeping the Hellfires pointed in the direction of the consulate.

Sergeant Dorne leaned out the left door as far as his harness would permit, searching through his NVGs for an opportunity to hit the enemy with his Gatling gun. Sergeant Cho did the same on the right, angling his weapon as far to the front of the chopper as he could, his line of fire restricted more than usual by the external fuel tanks. Inside the cabin, the seven Deltas aimed their weapons out the side doors, praying for targets to send to hell.

Lieuteant Toll took the chopper over the Sharia al-Qala'a, the wide boulevard that circles the Citadel to the east of the gun emplacement, and then back west, coming in low below the rooftops through a narrow street, the tips of the Black Hawk's rotors only two meters from the buildings on either side of the lane. She came in fast from the opposite direction of her initial approach. The Syrian gunners, anticipating the maneuver, turned the ZPU on its swivel base and were a split second from firing when Kopinsky pressed the trigger. It took the Hellfire a fraction of a second to travel the five hundred meters that separated the Black Hawk from the ZPU. Designed to take out heavily armored vehicles, the rocket vaporized the fully exposed ZPU and crew before the Syrians could fire a single shot, but not before Toll pulled up hard to avoid the blast.

When Spider Two exploded and careened into the hotel, Lieutenant Colonel Korda's first thought was to abort the mission and get the two remaining choppers safely out of Aleppo, but he could not let his comrades on Spider Two die in vain. The original plan had been to send in Spider Three to the school as a diversion, while Chalk One planted sensors and transmitters on the Al-Fustaq Mosque, the real target. Between the explosion of Spider Two, the destruction of the hotel and the battle ensuing at the Belgian Consulate, there still might be enough diversion for Chalk One to carry out the mission without being detected. The decision was a very tough one, but that's what he was paid to do.

"Pam, what's your status?" he shouted, his eyes on the side door, looking for signs of danger.

"Climbing to one-five-zero-zero feet. ZPU at the consulate destroyed. Cannot, I say again, cannot, assess collateral damage, but I believe the consulate is on fire. What are my orders?"

"Continue with the mission."

"Roger that," Toll said, agreeing with the command decision. At that moment, a loud beeper and flashing red light went off in the cockpit, indicating that the enemy had locked a radar-guided missile on Spider Three. Toll immediately jinked hard to her right and down, dropping the heavy chopper seventy-five meters. A rocket streaked by, missing Spider Three by no more than a few feet, and slamming into the dome of the Great Mosque, cratering the elliptical structure inward. "Enemy choppers," Toll shouted.

In an instant, Martin Korda understood that the mission could not proceed. "Defend against enemy fire and retreat," he ordered. "Abort. I say again, abort."

Eulas Cole and his copilot had been heading toward

the insertion point near the Al-Fustaq Mosque. Upon hearing the order to counter the enemy helicopters and retreat, he spun the Black Hawk around and advanced toward the Syrian choppers and to the aid of Spider Three.

"I've got him. Fire," Lieutenant Toll roared as she pressed her thumb down hard on the triggering mechanism. An instant later, the Stinger missile acquired the Soviet-made Hind helicopter, obliterating it in a brilliant burst of red, orange and yellow, further lighting up the night sky.

"Two more! At twelve and one o'clock," Kopinsky shouted. Both Syrian choppers fired, their rockets headed directly toward Spider Three. With one hand, Toll rammed the cyclic stick as far to the left as it could go and simultaneously twisted the collective stick with the other hand, nearly rolling the Black Hawk over as she sought to avoid the bullet-fast explosive hurtling her way. The Syrian missile missed Spider Three and continued into the night above Aleppo, exploding in a residential neighborhood near the university. Toll and Kopinsky struggled hard to right the helicopter, both acutely aware that descent would be fatal.

Eulas Cole fired a Stinger at the two Syrian helicopters, but they were already retreating north toward their base and out of range. They had witnessed firsthand what Toll had done to their lead helicopter and had lost their stomach for battle.

"The mission is red. I say again, the mission is red. Abort and return to base," Korda ordered. The tone of his voice did not betray his grief, but all onboard the two surviving Black Hawks shared the agony they knew he felt. Not only was the mission scrubbed, but nine Delta operators and four Night Stalkers were gone, and contrary to all that had been ingrained in those still alive, they had to leave what remained of their dead behind.

Spider One and Spider Three raced across Aleppo at full speed, climbing as they accelerated. An Air Force EA6B Prowler flew high in the night sky, jamming Syrian radar as it had done during the earlier flight to Aleppo.

Inside the Black Hawks, the Delta operators and the Night Stalkers retreated within themselves for the flight back to Incirlik. As the commander and the "father" of Operation Shell Game, Martin Korda carried the heaviest burden. Nine Delta operators onboard Spider Two and four Night Stalkers were dead, burned to ashes in a heap now lying at the base of the still-flaming hotel back in Aleppo. They were friends. People with whom he had shared danger, hardship, laughter. He thought of what he would have to tell their loved ones.

Operation Shell Game was his project, his baby. He had conceived it, planned it, staffed it, and so far had nothing to show for it. Operation Shell Game was over, finished in a fireball. His career was probably over, too, but that was peripheral at the moment. He sat on an empty ammo canister, the pain evident on his face, reliving the moment Spider Two had exploded in midair, trying to imagine what he could have done to prevent it. Moreover, the remains of the soldiers and the Black Hawk on the ground would provide the Syrian propaganda machine with irrefutable evidence that American forces had attacked Syria and destroyed the Great Mosque and the Amir Palace Hotel. This on top of the flack America was getting from its presence in Iraq and Afghanistan. Martin had no doubt how the Muslim world would respond to the destruction of the Great Mosque of Aleppo.

THIRTEEN

Aaron tossed the blanket off and slowly sat up, planting his feet on the floor. He remained seated on the edge of his bed, contemplating the sharp pains that shot through his head and neck. *Champagne. Too much champagne. Never a good idea on an empty stomach.* He turned to see if Krissi was awake. *Good. Maybe she's sleeping it off.* He rose and went to the bathroom. After relieving himself, he fumbled through his toiletry bag looking for painkillers, anything. There were none, so he flicked his fingers through Krissi's, looking for the obvious name brands. Nothing—just lipstick, birth control pills, mascara and a toothbrush. Frustrated and hurting, he returned to the bedroom. Krissi's purse was on the desk, near the phone. He padded to the tan leather bag, stubbing his toe on the leg of a chair, cursing loudly. He held the bag in one hand, surprised by how heavy it was, and without thinking about what he was doing opened it wide, peering into its contents, searching for relief of his miserable hangover.

"What are you doing?" Krissi asked harshly.

"Jesus," Aaron exclaimed, jolted by her tone. "I thought you were asleep. I'm looking for some Advil or something. You got any?"

"Yeah . . . sorry . . . I don't know why I'm so edgy."

"Don't worry about it. You're probably just as hungover as I am," he said generously. "We should have eaten before we started drinking. That first bottle of champagne did us in."

"The second didn't help," she said in German. "I'm too old for that. Hand me the bag, please. I think there's some ibuprofen in there. Could you get some water?" she asked, relieved that he had not seen her Glock 9 mm automatic at the bottom of the purse.

Aaron brought two small bottles of chilled water from the minibar and sat next to Krissi. Each took two tablets and long gulps of water. She was naked except for the sheet that covered her from her waist to just above her knees. He wore a short robe that he had taken from the bathroom. "I guess your purse is off-limits," he commented, and finished the bottle. "The things you learn about people when they're hungover and irritable."

"Hey, I said I'm sorry. . . . And I *am* hungover and irritable. Damn it, and I have to fly to Berlin today for meetings. I'm going to be wasted all day."

"I thought you were going to Munich with me, to the conference."

"Sorry. I can't. I thought I told you that last night while we were dancing." She turned to him with a puzzled look on her face, as if to ask him if he remembered that conversation.

"I don't know. You might have. I was too drunk. What else did you tell me?" He leaned over and kissed her on the lips, indicating that her rebuke was in the past.

"I don't know," she giggled. "I might have said—or done—anything to you last night. You know what I do recall?" He raised his eyebrows as if to say *Go ahead.* "I remember you singing that Springsteen song. What is it? Yeah . . . 'I'm on Fire.' It came out in our senior year. You used to sing it before . . . well, the band played it last night, and you sang every word. Do you remember?"

"I know the song. . . . Though I'm having a short-term memory thing with my having sung it last night." He grinned sheepishly.

Krissi wanted to finish what she had started telling him the night before when he interrupted her by singing that song, but decided that now was not the right time. Instead she said, "I remember dancing in your arms, watching the barges go up and down the Danube. You were doing this thing to my neck, really turning me on. Then you said you were going to make love to me smack in the middle of the Nymphenburg Palace. . . . In the fountain, in fact." She paused. "Hey, that's when I told you I couldn't go to Munich." She backhanded him gently on his shoulder to make her point.

"Well, if we can't get it on in the fountain of the palace, what about right here, right now?" he asked, gently removing the empty bottle from her hand and placing it on the nightstand next to her. He wrapped his arms around her and lowered her back on the bed, pulling back the sheet that partially covered her and opening his robe. He pressed his body against hers. Later, when they were both fully satisfied, they lay on their sides, staring lovingly into each other's eyes.

"Do you know what time it is?" Krissi eventually asked.

"Yeah, I know . . . I know. I missed breakfast with Maraud. We blew off the better part of the morning session. Any regrets?" She shook her head. "Me neither, but my company will," he said. "Let's take a shower," he said and began to rise. "By the way, you're still going to Istanbul, aren't you?" She laughed and nodded, kissing him affectionately.

After a few minutes, Krissi finished showering and stepped out of the bathroom, wearing a robe identical to the one Aaron had been wearing. He sat on the edge of the bed, towel across his waist, staring at the TV screen with an intensity that was alarming. "What is it?" she asked.

"U.S. special forces apparently raided Syria last night. A helicopter went down in the center of Aleppo with everyone onboard killed. . . . Slammed into a hotel. Christ, that had to be Delta Force. Martin might have been on that Black Hawk."

"Martin is with Delta Force?" she asked, worried about her lover's brother, a man she had also been fond of many years before.

"Yeah," he responded, his eyes fixed to the CNN broadcast.

Krissi sat beside him and watched the news. Syrian officials were professing outrage at the "deliberate destruction" by the U.S. of the Great Mosque of Aleppo and the Amir Palace Hotel and the bombing of a residential neighborhood near Aleppo University, resulting in the death of an entire family as they slept in their home. Belgian officials, too, voiced outrage that their consulate had been destroyed by an American missile.

"It was terrible," a Danish man said, his voice cracking. "We heard machine guns firing—maybe they were cannons . . . I don't know about such things. Then there was a loud explosion and a flash of light through the curtains in my room, and the whole building shook. I went to the stairwell and ran down six flights of stairs until I found an exit. We were terrified. We found out afterward that an American helicopter had crashed into our hotel. Why this and why now? Right here in the middle of Syria? The Americans must be condemned for this," he said, crying, stopping the interview, as he was no longer able to maintain his composure.

"Fuck," Aaron snapped in frustration. He was certain it had to be Delta Force, and from what he could gather, it was the kind of operation Martin would volunteer for. He jumped up and went to the phone, tapping in a long string of numbers. "Helena?" he asked when a groggy-sounding voice at the other end of the line answered after several rings. It was 10:45 in Vienna, but only 4:45 A.M. in Fayetteville, North Carolina. "It's Aaron. Is Martin there?"

"No," she answered slowly. "Aaron, do you know what time it is? Is something wrong?"

"I'm in Europe. How can I reach him?" He tried not to alarm her, but did not succeed.

"You can't. He calls a couple of times a week, but he can't tell me where he is. You know his line of work. What's the matter, Aaron? Are you in trouble?"

"I'm fine. It's just that I was watching CNN and there's some sort of disaster in Syria involving U.S. soldiers. It looks like something . . ." He stopped, catching himself. He did not want to mention Delta Force on an open, unsecure line. "Look, why don't you put on the TV and get in touch with the command and make sure Martin is all right. I'll call back in a couple of hours." As they spoke, Aaron could hear his nephew Joey wheezing in the background.

"Okay, but I have to go now," Helena said hurriedly. "Joey needs his medicine. How can I reach you?"

"Is he okay?"

"The usual. Susie's getting over her asthma but Joey's actually a bit worse in the past few days. But don't worry, Womack Hospital isn't far. We've been there before," she added tiredly, trying to sound like a good soldier's wife.

"I'm going to be at a conference and then on the road from Vienna to Munich, but call me on my cell phone. Anytime. The number has changed. You got a pen?" He gave her the new number and hung up. Returning to the bed, he sat next to Krissi, who had been listening to both his end of the conversation and the TV at the same time.

"The public outcry and condemnation of the U.S. military incursion at Aleppo is unanimous throughout Europe," the reporter announced. "Several European and Japanese tourists have been killed or wounded, as have Syrians on the ground and in a Syrian helicopter that attempted to defend the Great Mosque. In addition, Ted, the Great Mosque has been destroyed," she added, addressing the anchor back in Atlanta. As the reporter spoke, the screen split and more footage was aired, first of victims being evacuated on gurneys from the still-smoldering Amir Palace Hotel, then of the Great

Mosque, the damage very apparent. "Behind me you can see what remains of the mosque. Ted, this is a disastrous public relations snafu for the U.S. From Saudi Arabia, Kuwait, Egypt, Jordan, Pakistan and every other Muslim country comes strong condemnation of the raid, particularly the destruction of the mosque. Riots have already been reported throughout the Islamic world."

Aaron flicked off the remote. He leaned forward and put his face in his palms, his mind on his brother's safety. Krissi sat next to him and placed her arm over his shoulder but said nothing. After a few moments, he took her hand in his, he, too, finding no words to say. He thought of Martin and the diplomatic nightmare for the U.S. A wave of depression from these events, aided by his hangover, overcame Aaron. His thoughts turned to the danger to himself and anyone close to him from the thugs who had killed Yusuf and his family and Hasan, but he said nothing to Krissi about that. His eyes lingered on his travel bag, where he kept the Walther PPK he had insisted on carrying, and he wondered how long it would be until he had to use it.

Aaron and Krissi made it to the convention in time for lunch, sitting together, keeping mostly to themselves. He visited Maraud's table and made what sounded to the Frenchman like a heartfelt apology for missing breakfast, blaming his absence on a client crisis back in the United States, something that the Frenchman, who was very diligent about his own work, understood.

Prodigious amounts of coffee revived the two hungover lovers, both of whom declined the sparkling wine offered to them by the waiters. After sitting through two numbing presentations by research scientists that afternoon, Krissi whispered to Aaron that she needed to return to their room to pack her belongings and head to the airport.

"I'll drive you. I just need to pick up the car. Let's go," he said in German, patting her thigh affectionately.

"You don't have to drive me. The airport is on the opposite side of Vienna from the autobahn to Munich. I'll get a cab."

"No way. I want to spend the time with you," he said with a tone of finality that he hoped would end the debate. What he said was true, but he was also increasingly concerned that she might be in danger. Given that he was armed, he would escort her as far as the metal detectors at the airport, hoping that airline security would take over at that point. Ironically, what she did not want Aaron to see was that her permit to carry a weapon also meant that she would not have to go through security. "I'm pretty much packed. I'll watch the news while you get ready. The car is supposed to be ready in front of the hotel."

Sky News and CNN carried almost nothing other than the carnage at Aleppo. Syrian and Belgian officials continued to express their outrage. But apart from the names and photos of the Europeans and Japanese who had been killed or injured in the hotel, the news reports added little to what Aaron already knew. Frustrated, he reached for the hotel phone and punched in the numbers to Martin and Helena's home phone on Fort Bragg.

"Helena. It's Aaron. Any word?"

"Martin called just a few minutes ago. He didn't say where he is, but he said he's okay. He's very upset about the loss of those men on the helicopter. He said he knew them all, and that they were friends. Aaron, I've never heard Martin so shaken. I told him you called. That meant a lot to him. He asked me to thank you and to tell you he misses you. He wants to have you down for Christmas. Can you make it?"

"I'd love to spend Christmas with you guys," Aaron said without hesitation, barely able to choke back tears of joy upon hearing that Martin was safe. "There might be two of us. Please tell him that I linked up with Krissi . . . from our days in Wiesbaden. He'll know who I mean. If she can make it, we'll both come." Krissi overheard Aaron's end of the conversation and could tell from his demeanor that Martin was okay, and she was pleased that she was being invited to meet Martin and his family.

"Krissi," Helena said slowly. "Isn't she the girl Martin says you never got over?"

"Shucks," he laughed, and then said in a loud voice for Krissi's benefit, "no, she's just one of several." Krissi figured out what was happening and laughed loud enough for Helena to hear her in the background.

"That's good news, Aaron. How did you find each other?"

"In California, of all places. But I'll fill you in later. We're here together in Vienna, but right now we're rushing to get her to the airport in time for her flight. How's Joey?"

"The same. The doc says to keep using the nebulizer. In fact, I was just running out to Womack to pick up his albuterol prescription. It seems like it never ends . . . but at least it looks like we're over the hump with Susie."

"I don't know how you do it. Martin couldn't do what he does without you."

"Oh, Aaron, at times like this I wish Martin wasn't doing what he does," she said, her voice breaking for a moment, and then silent as she composed herself. "Anyway, I'll tell him you called again."

After Aaron placed the phone down, Krissi sat next to him, put her arm around him and gave him a hug. "Thank God Martin is safe," she said.

"He was there, Krissi. I don't know anything else, but he was there." Despite the fact that his own and Krissi's lives might be in danger, the knowledge that Martin had been involved in the raid on Aleppo shook up his younger brother. "You heard what I said about coming with me to North Carolina for Christmas, right?" he asked, trying to lighten the tone. "Can you make it?"

"Of course I can make it. Christmas dinner at the Kordas'." Krissi smiled as she thought about it. "I wouldn't miss it for the world." She held him for a few moments. Being Aaron's lover and spying on him were difficult from the beginning, but the events surrounding Aleppo, whatever they were, made the dual role nearly impossible. In fact, Krissi had decided to tell him about the BND the night before, but when the time came Aaron began to sing and she didn't want to ruin the enchantment of the evening. *I'll tell him in Istanbul,* she promised herself.

"He must be going through hell. Helena said she had never heard him so upset," Aaron said, guilty, pulling away.

Krissi nodded supportively. "Did she tell you anything else—I mean, about what happened?"

"No," he said after an emotional pause. "Helena doesn't know, and never will. . . . At least not for years and years. She won't ask, and neither will I." He looked into his lover's eyes, searching for her understanding. "When you see him, you can't pose those kinds of questions. In fact, you know nothing about his military work. Not Delta Force, not Aleppo. Nothing. Okay?"

"Don't worry. I won't say a thing." She kissed him. "And, Aaron, I'm sorry. I shouldn't have asked."

Traffic from central Vienna to the airport southeast of the city was slow and tedious, the result of an accident in the light drizzle that had started midday. Krissi was running late for her flight, and Aaron parked illegally for the brief moment he needed to walk Krissi across the wide sidewalk to the front doors. Though he wanted a long embrace, he had to settle for a quick peck on the lips as she sprinted away into the terminal.

Depressed by the incident at Aleppo and Krissi's departure, and completely disinterested in the conference in Munich, he nevertheless made the lonely drive up the Austrian autobahn toward the German A8. Pressing the SCAN button on the radio, he found a station playing songs from the mid-eighties, music that he, Krissi and their high school friends had grown up on. The sweet memories and rhythmic beat were soothing, and as he drove his spirits lifted. Normally a fast driver, he stayed in the right lane. Cars in the left lane whizzed by him. It had only been an hour since he dropped Krissi off at the airport, and he missed her terribly. He hadn't ever felt this close to a woman. By the time he reached Salzburg, Aaron had decided that he would propose to Krissi. He would pop the question in Istanbul.

Aaron's musings were interrupted when his cell phone went off. It was inside his briefcase, which was unzipped on the passenger's seat. Reaching into the main compartment, his hand first came to rest on the Walther PPK. He fumbled for a second or two, pulled out the phone and opened it. "Hello," he answered.

"Aaron, this is Don Prebish. I'm in Munich at the Four Seasons. I need to talk to you. Where are you now?"

Aaron cleared his throat. "Sorry. I just passed the turnoff for the A12 to Innsbruck. I should be at the Vier Jahreszeiten in an hour or so." He didn't ask why Prebish was in Munich and staying at the same hotel, but he was very curious.

"Call me on the house phone when you get in. I'll meet you in your room." Before Aaron could respond, Prebish terminated the call.

"Okay, okay," Aaron cleared his throat again as he pressed the END button, put the phone back in his bag and turned up the radio. The call was troubling. *Why the hell did that weasel follow me to Munich?* he wondered. There were several possibilities, and none of them were good.

An hour and twenty-five minutes later, Aaron checked in to the Four Seasons.

"Do you need any help with your bags?" the clerk asked, eager to please.

"Nein, danke. I only have two bags," he said, pointing to his soft ballistic nylon bag that doubled as a duffel and a briefcase. It rested on the top of the suitcase that he wheeled next to him. "Are there any messages?"

She tapped on the keyboard and squinted at the

screen. "No, sir. Nothing." He tried not to show the disappointment he felt. He had hoped Krissi would leave him a message.

"Could you tell me what room Mr. Prebish is in? He's a colleague of mine, here to participate in the biotech conference."

"I can't give you that information, sir. But if you use the house phone," she offered, pointing across the ornate lobby to a black phone on a Louis XVI–style desk, "and ask for him by name, the operator will connect you."

"Don, Aaron here. I'm down in the lobby now." Aaron cleared his throat twice. "Sorry, bad sinus day. Give me ten minutes to unpack. I'm in seven oh four. Good. See you then."

Exactly ten minutes later, Aaron heard the knock, verified who was there, and let Donald Prebish and two other CIA agents in. "Do you think you need that?" Prebish asked, pointing to the automatic in Aaron's hand.

"Depends on who's at the door. Do you think you need them?" Aaron countered, gesturing to the large men in suits whom he did not know, having no doubt that each was carrying a weapon.

"No, probably not." Prebish had very little sense of humor. "But these men have something to tell you that I thought you should hear directly from them. We need to talk, Aaron. And for God's sake, put away that gun."

"Can we talk here?" Aaron asked, looking to the ceiling as an indication that the room might be bugged.

"We paid the manager to make sure this room was assigned to you. We just scanned it for bugs twenty minutes ago. It's clean." Prebish sat down and motioned to the others to be seated. Aaron noted that one agent positioned his chair so that he could see the door, unbuttoning his suit jacket for access to his shoulder holster. The other agent, jacket open, pulled up the chair from behind the desk, while Prebish took a more comfortable cushioned seat near the couch where Aaron was now seated.

"Let's get to the point, Aaron." Prebish paused for emphasis. "At La Costa you met a woman, Kristina Sturm, who purports to work for Westfalen Pharma Gruppe. You then blew off the first Damascus show and spent four days romping around Palm Springs with her when you should have been investigating what the Syrians are up to." With the mention of Krissi's name and the words *purports to work for,* Aaron went on alert, all antennae up. "How do you know this woman, Aaron? Do you know she's a BND agent?"

Aaron cleared his throat, pretending he needed to, but really stalling for time. Prebish had sucker punched him in the stomach, but he struggled not to show it. Aaron looked directly into Prebish's eyes. "Of course I know she's BND," he lied. "That's why I'm pumping her for information."

"Or maybe she's the one who's working you," the man near the desk said sarcastically. "We've checked her out. She's been with the BND for ten years. Abteilung Eins, the Operations Directorate. She's an agent of considerable talent, highly intelligent, qualified in several languages, an excellent marksman, trained for airborne deep insertion in undercover situations, and capable of working the field with little or no home office support for considerable periods of time."

"Ferchrissake, Aaron," Prebish joined in, "if you knew she was a BND agent, why in the hell didn't you tell me? You can't just go off and run an operation like this without telling us. You have a tendency to do things on your own, like that incident in Poti. You work for a client. . . . One that pays you very well, I might add. You can't just run wild on us. That's a recipe for disaster."

Aaron was relieved that Prebish seemed to be buying his story and struggled to play along. "Look, I'm sorry. I didn't think that this was such a big deal. Last I checked,

Germany was an ally." Aaron paused for a moment, trying to collect his thoughts. "I met Sturm in the Offenbach matter."

"That was never in any of your reports," the agent watching the door interrupted accusingly.

Aaron rolled his eyes. "You guys want reports to be short . . . bullet-point memos. As it was, the Offenbach report was twelve pages longer than what Don wanted. So keep your comments to yourself and let me continue. I ran into her again at the IFPI conference and decided to see what she—the BND—was up to." Prebish and the two agents looked skeptical. "Okay, I confess, I wasn't sick in California. . . . And, well, getting close to her wasn't exactly hard work. But I wanted to see what I could learn from her about the BND. That was my main objective. The opportunity was just too good to pass by."

"And I suppose she's a great lay, besides," Prebish said with a smirk.

"Not bad." Aaron forced a smile.

"Goddamn it, Aaron. You can't just take it upon yourself to blow off your mission to pursue a BND agent who may or may not reveal meaningful information. That's just not your call, at least not while you're working for us. This is a business, Aaron. A *team* business. As Vince Lombardi said, there is no *I* in the word *team*. You got that?"

Aaron nodded contritely, and the irony of the situation hit him. In a way, it was amusing. He missed the cues that Krissi was BND, and they, the fucking CIA, missed the fact that she and Aaron had been childhood sweethearts. "I hear you, Boss." The agent by the door sighed loudly. Aaron ignored him. "But hey, I'll be there for the second trade show. I leave tomorrow night, right after the biotech conference ends."

"We know your schedule. But you're missing my point. You can't make these decisions on your own. Hell, this stuff is front-burner business for the agency. Do you realize that the DDO and the DCI himself are watching what you do? Christ, we don't have any other agents right now who can do what you do in the Middle East. You are a unique asset, Korda, but the agency will drop you like a hot potato if you're not a team player."

Prebish did not tell Aaron that since the incident at Poti, a psychiatrist had been assigned to study Aaron's increasingly erratic behavior. The cancellation of the trip to Damascus, calling in sick to vacation with a beautiful woman who just happened to be a BND agent, the wearing of a very large diamond ring on his middle finger and demanding that a weapon be available for him in Vienna had not gone unnoticed. He had also switched hotels upon arriving in Vienna, thwarting the CIA's efforts to bug his room. That he had spent the evening wining and dining the BND agent rather than befriending the Frenchman as he was assigned, and paid, to do raised more red flags. Kate Brind, with all her considerable clout, had fought hard for Aaron, but some within the agency had already lost faith and wanted to terminate his consulting contract. Others, including the DDO, were concerned that Aaron was going completely rogue, requiring more than the mere termination of his contract.

"Has your girlfriend asked you anything about the agency?" Aaron was six-two and 190 pounds, and he noticed that the agent sitting near the desk, the one who asked the question, was just about the same size. Aaron just stared at him. "Has she asked you if you work for the CIA?" he repeated.

"Absolutely not," Aaron said as decisively as he could, while trying to suppress his anger and doubts. "We talked about the pharmaceutical industry. We talked about sports. It may be bullshit, but she knows a lot about baseball. We talked about traveling. . . . About all kinds of things, but she never even came close to the topic of the agency, the U.S. government, policy—none of that."

"Right. Of course. What did she tell you that's useful about the BND?" The agent near the desk was not willing to let go. Aaron continued to size him up. It dawned on Aaron that he looked like him. The resemblance wasn't perfect, but it was there. Same sandy midlength hair and style. Probably the same size suit. *Shit, he's supposed to be my double,* Aaron thought, surprised at his own paranoia but still reeling from the news about Krissi. *If things go south, they'll kill me and he'll assume my cover, check out of the hotel under my name so my disappearance will be clean.*

"Nothing so far, but we all know these things take time." Aaron stood and went to the bathroom, leaving his Walther PPK on the night table near the couch where he had been sitting.

"Let me ask you, Aaron," Prebish continued as Aaron returned and sat down on the bed, equidistant from the two agents and watching their moves. "Did you make any progress with Maraud?"

"We hit it off well. He's going to try to arrange a meeting for me with the minister of health this coming week, but the flap over Aleppo won't help. We'll just have to see. I may have to go back . . . after things calm down. The minister shares Maraud's passion, or shall I say our passion, for Ottoman architecture and furniture." Aaron looked over to Prebish to see how he was doing. Prebish's expression told him nothing. Aaron smiled confidently, which wasn't easy under the circumstances, catching the three men off guard.

"Very well. Good progress on that front," Prebish acknowledged after a long pause. "Aaron, on another topic, we—that is to say everyone all the way up to the DCI and the national security adviser—are concerned, very concerned, that this BND agent might want to pump you for intelligence about Martin . . . and Delta Force. We don't divulge the names of Delta Force operators to anyone. . . . Not even our allies. Has she asked anything about your brother . . . anything about Delta Force?"

"No. Nothing," Aaron said definitively, as he tried to calm his racing pulse.

Prebish rubbed his eyes with both hands, pushing his glasses up on his almost bald head. He reached into his pocket for a roll of Tums and threw three tablets into his mouth, chewing noisily. "I believe you, Aaron," he said when he was done. "You're a pain in the ass to manage, and you're giving me heartburn," he added, gesturing toward the roll he placed on the coffee table in front of him, "but you're one hell of an asset. Don't blow it." Aaron nodded, sensing some tension drain from the room. For now, he had been pardoned. "Learn to be part of a larger team. You did it in the army, now do it for the agency." Prebish paused to study his most valuable asset. "And this woman. Forget her. You have more important things to do."

Three hours after Prebish and the other agents left his hotel room, Aaron still lay awake in bed, unable to sleep despite his fatigue from the night before. He held back the tears that welled in his eyes, wiping them silently, grateful that Prebish and the two agents could not see him through the listening devices he had no doubt they installed in his room. Several minutes after they had left, the phone rang. Aaron assumed it was Krissi calling from Berlin, but didn't pick it up, watching the red message light go on a few seconds after the ringing had stopped. He couldn't talk to her because of the wiretap he suspected was on his phone and his state of mind, his utter sense of betrayal. She was a BND agent and he was the subject of her assignment. There was no amazing coincidence that they met in California, and probably no real feelings. At least not on her side.

Aaron wanted to shout in anger, to confront her. Instead, he lay in bed, the room lit dimly by light escaping through the partially closed bathroom door. *What had the jerk near the desk said exactly? Krissi was "trained for airborne deep insertion in undercover situations." Yeah, that's it,* Aaron remembered. *Christ, no wonder she handled the parachute jump so well at Happy Jack's. What kind of idiot am I?* Tears ran down his cheeks through his two-day-old stubble. She had used him. *Shit,* he told himself as he sat up with a start. *She asked about*

Martin. She even asked if he was at Aleppo. Fuck, she knows I'm going to Damascus. He thought long and hard about the conversation he and Krissi had had when he first saw the news of the failed mission on CNN. *Did I actually tell her that Martin is part of Delta Force?* He had trouble remembering, but then it came to him. *Christ, I did,* he admonished himself. *She knows he's a Delta Force operator . . . a lieutenant colonel. She also saw me work on Maraud to get to the Syrian minister of health. Son of a bitch,* he thought for the hundredth time that night. *The BND knows that I work for the CIA. That's why she was assigned to me. She listened to every word I said to Maraud and now the BND knows that the United States wants to get closer to the Syrians.* It mattered little that Germany was an ally. He trusted her, and in doing so jeopardized his own and Martin's safety, and on some level betrayed both his brother and his country. He could hardly believe that just hours ago he had decided to propose to her.

FOURTEEN

From all appearances, the dark blue Ford Crown Victoria heading south on the Beltway resembled hundreds of other U.S. Government vehicles in the Washington area, the weight of its armor plating and bulletproof windows being compensated for by heavy-duty springs and shock absorbers. A black Chevy Suburban led the convoy two hundred meters ahead of the Ford, while two others brought up the rear. The driver, a retired Navy SEAL who doubled as a bodyguard, eschewed the main gate to the CIA on Dolly Madison Boulevard and continued on the Georgetown Pike to the rear entrances. He pulled off the pike at the first entrance, the one normally used only for truck deliveries, and wheeled the tanklike Suburban to a set of steps leading to the freight dock. As the heavy vehicle rolled to a stop, four Secret Service agents armed with MP-5 submachine guns immediately jumped out of the car and, together with guards from the CIA's Office of Security, formed a defensive perimeter around the area. Behind the Crown Victoria, the two Suburbans tailing the convoy blocked the entrance at the security gate, backing up delivery trucks onto the Georgetown Pike as drivers waited impatiently to offload their office supplies, food and other daily deliveries to the thousands who work at Langley.

Kate Brind stepped out of the backseat of the Ford, along with two of her assistants, each carrying a heavy briefcase loaded with classified documents, and was quickly escorted up the steps and into the safety of the freight dock. Without saying a word, they made the long walk through the labyrinthine corridors of the CIA's two main buildings.

An aide to the DCI met them in the lobby of the Old Building and escorted them to the DCI's private elevator off the left side of the lobby. Getting off at the seventh floor, they immediately went to the conference room adjacent to the DCI's office. They were a few minutes early. Kate poured herself a cup of coffee and offered a cup to the assistants, who declined. She took a seat on the side of the oval conference table facing the window. It was a gray November morning, the forecast calling for rain later in the day, but still she welcomed the view. She glanced at her watch—6:56. She opened the large briefcases at her feet, pulled out her checklists, and readied herself for what promised to be a lengthy review of the nation's covert operations. First and foremost on the list was a status review of the Delta Force disaster at Aleppo.

Diane Felder, DDO, arrived at exactly 7:00, as did the director of the National Security Agency, an air force lieutenant general, the only uniformed person to attend the meeting. Within seconds, the DDI appeared. As greetings were exchanged, coffee poured and plates loaded with danish and bagels, the DCI entered, accompanied by two assistants, and took a place in the middle of the table, declining any food but accepting coffee and a notepad from one of the assistants who sat next to him.

"Okay, first item on the list is what to do about Aleppo," the DCI began. "No word from the Syrians yet, but we don't expect them to let us off the hook easily. And most of the world, not just the Middle East but also our allies in Europe, are at least publicly very unhappy with us. We have to decide what to do with Operation Shell Game and the Deltas on the ground in Turkey. Diane," he said, turning to the DDO, "what do you think?"

"Thank you, sir. The raid on Aleppo was far too risky from the beginning, and has resulted in a disaster, militarily and diplomatically. With all due respect, sir, the rest of the world is more than 'unhappy' about it. I recommend that we shut down the operation. No more raids." Kate Brind watched with disgust, but not surprise, as the DDO distanced herself from a covert operation that she had readily supported at the outset, adopting Colonel Korda's out-of-the-box proposals as her own. "Lieutenant Colonel Korda should be reprimanded." *There it is,* Kate thought. *Success has many fathers; failure is an orphan,* she thought, trying to remember who had said that. "However, we may want to leave this Delta Force contingent in Turkey for a couple more weeks. The Middle East and North Africa are inflamed by the destruction of the mosque, and we may need Delta Force operators to help the marines protect the embassies and evacuate American civilians in the region."

The committee discussed the status of the Delta operators at Incirlik, deciding in the end to recommend to the army that the contingent remain at Incirlik for a couple of weeks.

"Next is the situation on the Korean peninsula. As you all know, North and South Korean forces have exchanged gunfire. . . ."

"Wait a minute, Michael," the director of the National Security Agency said, speaking for the first time. "Before we move off Lieutenant Colonel Korda, I want to say something about his brother, Aaron." The others present tried not to show any reaction. The younger Korda brother was an asset known to only a few. The NSA, the supersecret SIGINT arm of the intelligence community, had no need to know about Aaron's covert HUMINT operations, and it was not particularly good news for the CIA to learn that the NSA was in the loop. "We have picked up communications in Farsi over the Caspian Sea, mentioning him by name. Here's a copy of the transcript of the conversation we monitored," he said, sliding copies across the highly polished table. "The conversations appear to be between the drug smugglers involved in the Poti incident, and add a twist to Korda's involvement in the killing of the Georgian interior minister." The general paused, in part to give his colleagues time to digest what they were reading, and, more importantly, to punctuate his next comments. "I'm not trying to interfere with a CIA operation, Michael, but I thought I should bring this to your attention. You may have a rogue agent on your hands."

"Thank you," the DCI said, stone-faced, unwilling to give away the fact that he'd been caught off guard. "Do you have any input on this?" he asked, turning to his DDO and DDI.

"This is news to me," the DDO answered after a pause. "We've had our problems with this asset, but we had no idea about his involvement in drug dealing."

"I know about Poti," the DCI said, hoping that this was the extent of it. "Is there more?"

"Can I speak freely?" Felder asked, motioning with her head to the air force lieutenant general who headed the NSA but addressing the director of Central Intelligence. The DCI nodded. "Well, yes, of course there is the Poti incident, which appears to tie into this conversation the NSA picked up, and . . . well . . ." The DDO briefed the small group at the table on the breach of security involving BND agent Krissi Sturm, the missed trip to Damascus, the unusually large diamond ring, and the conversation between Prebish and Aaron in Munich.

"Christ," the DCI said, fighting to maintain his composure. "One of our best assets in the Middle East may be a rogue agent who's dealing drugs and cavorting with a foreign agent. On top of that, his brother is a Delta Force officer who has just led us into one of our bigger PR debacles, at least on my watch. What a screwed-up situation." He paused to give the others the opportunity to share their thoughts. No one dared. "Okay, I'm convinced. Bring Aaron Korda in. Where is he now?"

"He turned in his weapon to someone from our Munich office and caught a plane last night, local time," Diane Felder answered. "He's in Damascus."

*   *   *

Mohammed al-Mistani pulled away from his laptop, walked over to the window of his office and looked out over the canning operations that he had hastily set up in Building 13. He stretched his back and legs, which ached from sitting at the computer throughout most of the night. Connected to the Internet through a high-speed cable, he had Googled Aaron Korda and had found much more than he had initially expected. As the last page fed out of the laser printer, he grabbed the bundle of documents and hurried to the converted shipping container that served as his and any guest's living quarters. He wanted to catch Faramaz before he returned to Holland that morning after a one-day trip to Poti to inspect the revived operations.

Mohammed knocked on the door and entered without waiting for a response. Faramaz was sitting on an army cot that served as his guest bed when he was in Poti. His bags were packed and he was fully dressed, sipping hot tea as he waited for the truck that would take him to Tbilisi, where he would catch a plane to Bucharest and then to Amsterdam. He regarded his trusted friend and colleague, eager to hear the results of Mohammed's research.

"Did you sleep well?"

"Better than you. Were you up all night?"

"Yes, but it was worth it. I did a Google search on Aaron Korda. There are a few people with that name, but I have no doubt that I narrowed it down to the one we want. His name comes up a few times since two of his presentations about the pharmaceutical industry have been published in trade magazines. It's apparent that he attends and sometimes speaks at these industry conferences. I know I have the right man because one of the publications listed a short bio. The man I zeroed in on speaks Turkish and is an ex-U.S. Army officer. I'm sure he is the right Aaron Korda. None of the others are even remotely possible." Faramaz waved his hand, indicating that Mohammed should continue.

"He graduated from the U.S. Military Academy—West Point—in 1989, which would make him about thirty-five years old now. He majored in chemistry. He speaks German and Turkish. He served in the American Army for a few years—I couldn't tell exactly how long—and then received a master's in Business Administration from the University of Chicago. He presently works for an international consulting firm called Heller and Clarke in New York. I did a search of the ten largest pharmaceutical and biotech organizations to check on the upcoming conferences. That's where I really got lucky. Two meetings just finished in Vienna and Munich. Over the next few weeks there are gatherings of scientists and business leaders in Damascus, Istanbul, Prague, San Francisco, Casablanca and Toronto. I checked the announcements for all of them. . . . They're all on the Internet. Korda is scheduled to speak at the one in Istanbul . . . at the Ceylan Intercontinental Hotel. On a hunch, I checked to see if he was attending the fair in Damascus. After several calls to the major hotels, I decided to try the Tichreen Hotel, which is very near the Damascus International Fair building. I told the concierge that I needed to leave a message for Mr. Korda, who should be arriving today or tonight, since the pharmaceutical fair starts tomorrow. After checking his computer, the man said that he would leave the message for Mr. Korda when he arrives."

"What message did you leave?"

"Simply to call his office in New York . . . without indicating who at his office called. He'll no doubt phone in. He shouldn't think anything unusual about such an ordinary message or who might have left it. Heller and Clarke is a big company. The real important piece of all this is that we know when the Damascus fair ends and when the Istanbul conference starts. They're back-to-back. So we know when he will leave Syria and when he'll arrive at Atatürk Airport."

"Do we know what he looks like? Is there any general description of him in the materials you found?"

"Nothing. But my cousin, Fauad al-Sadiqi, who I trust completely, lives in Damascus. He can attend the fair and find out what Korda looks like by asking around discreetly. We have Alima and her cell in Istanbul. She is very clever and can make the arrangements there."

"I must return to Holland immediately. I have been away too much already and run the risk of drawing attention to myself, but I'd trust Alima with my life. You must send your two best men—the same men who went with me to Trabzon and Kayseri—to Istanbul to work with Alima and her people. They must tell Alima to kill the American. They mustn't try to capture and interrogate him. Just kill him."

Krissi arrived home in Berlin later than expected, the result of weather delays in Vienna and a long wait for a gate at Tegel Airport. Worried about her job and her relationship with Aaron, she hadn't slept on the plane and was exhausted when she finally got to her apartment. Still, as soon as she put down her bags, she called Aaron at the Four Seasons Hotel in Munich and was surprised that he didn't answer. It was 2:00 A.M. For the hundredth time since she said it, she cursed herself for asking if Martin was assigned to Delta Force. Having missed an opportunity in Vienna to come clean about her being with the BND, she had resolved during the flight to Berlin to tell Aaron everything when they met in Istanbul, and she knew that the discussion about Delta Force would make it all the more difficult. She faulted herself for the indiscretion. She really had been concerned about Martin, but she knew that it would be hard to convince Aaron once she told him the truth.

Despite the sleepless night, Krissi got out of bed at her normal hour, took her coffee and did laps around the Charlottenburg Gardens near her apartment. She drove to work near the Reichstag in moderate traffic, arriving only a few minutes late. Her department had recently moved from BND headquarters outside Munich, and she had not fully unpacked. Stepping around a pile of boxes, she sat down at her still-cluttered desk and booted up the computer, typing in her security password and retrieving her e-mail messages.

"Hey, good to have you back," her boss, Gerhard Schmidt, said, standing in her open doorway. Krissi acknowledged him with a brittle smile. She had hoped to have at least an hour or so to settle in and collect her thoughts before facing any questions. "So, where were we? Oh yes, you were in Vienna with the American and you were getting close to him. So where are we now?" Gerhard took a chair in front of her desk.

"Well, we have established a close relationship. I think I have his confidence. . . . Yes, I'm pretty sure I do, but I haven't learned anything about his involvement in any type of corporate espionage. At least not yet. He's very discreet, as you would expect. We've talked about his consulting work for Heller and Clarke, but he hasn't said anything about the CIA, and I haven't picked up anything. It may be a question of time, or it may be that he's clean." Krissi kept her voice even and her expression neutral, trying to convince Schmidt that she was open to either outcome. The reality was that she had no idea what she would do if Aaron was guilty of what the BND suspected, and prayed that their suspicions were unfounded. "We're scheduled to meet again in Istanbul on Thursday. I think I'll know more after that."

"Good. Let's see how that plays out." Schmidt stood and started to walk out of her office, then stopped to turn and face her. "Don't take this the wrong way, Krissi, but I must ask. You haven't fallen for this man, have you?"

Krissi leaned back, putting her arms behind her head, adopting body language that showed openness and ease rather than the defensiveness she felt. "Gerhard, I've been with the bureau too long to let some would-be American spy take away my professionalism." She forced a laugh.

"Funny. The Italian couple at your table that night in Vienna, who by the way work for us, said that you and

Herr Korda seemed to be getting very cozy with each other."

"Since when am I under surveillance? And I thought that getting cozy, as you call it, was my assignment."

"You're not under surveillance. We just didn't know what to expect from Korda. He has a reputation of doing the unexpected. Anyway, you're right. It *is* your job. But I'm just worried about where you draw the line, or *if* you can draw the line. Our people followed you and Korda to the restaurant on the Donaustrasse. According to their report, you were so engrossed with this man— so busy dancing and drinking—that you failed to notice them. Now, that has me worried."

"Wait a minute. I'm supposed to convince Korda that I'm romantically involved, but I'm not supposed to dance with him, and leave the champagne, two hundred fifteen euros a bottle, by the way, untouched? Look, if I persuaded the Italians, maybe I'm winning over Mr. Korda as well. Of course I saw them. Stop worrying. I'll bring this to a head in Istanbul. I promise."

FIFTEEN

After attending the pharmaceuticals trade fair in Damascus, Aaron settled into the business class seat of the Turkish Airlines Damascus-Istanbul flight. He looked around the cabin cautiously. No one appeared to be following. His body hurt from lack of sleep. He had spent slightly less than sixty-six hours in the Syrian capital, but it seemed like longer. While he forced himself to think rapidly, compiling and digesting information disclosed by other salesmen and the Syrians, and fending off their efforts to pump him for information, he was nearing his limits. His efforts to meet the minister of health upon Dr. Maraud's introduction had failed, no doubt influenced in part by Syria's fury at the United States over the incident at Aleppo. Moreover, Krissi's betrayal had hit him hard, and the passage of a mere three days was not alleviating the pain. He tried to concentrate on how he would report to the CIA on the Damascus fair, but he was preoccupied with Krissi. At one point, he wondered whether she had done it for revenge, to get back at him for hurting her so many years before, but that didn't sit right. She would not have held a grudge for so many years, and would not have gone to such trouble even if she had. No, he reasoned, she, like he, was a spy, a patriot working for her government. For whatever purpose, the BND had targeted him, and had assigned her to the task, knowing of their high school romance and how it could be exploited. Professionally, he felt foolish. Personally, he had been violated.

Aaron needed sleep before his meetings in Istanbul, especially prior to confronting Krissi. His eyes burned despite generous applications of Visine. He accepted the flight attendant's offer of a beverage, took two Advil and politely requested that he not be disturbed during the short trip to Istanbul. Closing his eyes, he allowed himself to picture Krissi at the cocktail reception at La Costa, her startling beauty, the thrill of recognizing her, the pain of opening old wounds, the elation of falling back in love. He recalled how anguished she had seemed when she cursed him on the golf course for having left her without saying good-bye, and decided that she could not have been that good of an actor. Maybe she really had felt some affection toward him, despite the coldness of her deception. Not that it mattered; they were finished.

As the Boeing 727 began its descent, Aaron completed the requisite Turkish immigration and customs forms and put his shoes back on, bracing himself mentally for the face-to-face with Krissi. On one level, he wanted to confront her, to make her look at him and admit her deceit. He hoped she had some feelings for him and it wasn't all an act, because he wanted to scream at her and tell her it was over, and he wanted it to hurt. But on another level, he didn't know what to say to her or if he'd be able to say anything at all without showing how devastated he was. And he really didn't want to give her that satisfaction.

Aaron easily passed through Turkish immigration and customs and made his way through the crowds at Ata-türk International, heading toward the taxi stand for the drive east into the center of Istanbul. He pulled the wheeled suitcase behind him, his ballistic nylon duffel bag, which doubled as his briefcase, hanging on his shoulder. He was about halfway through the terminal when he realized that two men were following him. Rather than try to lose them, Aaron slowed his pace, drawing them closer. A passenger hauling a large suitcase accidentally bumped into him, which gave him the opportunity to stumble and steal a sideways glance at his pursuers, who were about twenty meters behind him. *Middle Eastern. Iranians,* he guessed. *The bastards who killed Hasan and Yusuf.* He wished he had not turned in his weapon to the office in Munich, but knew that he never would have made it in and out of Syria if he hadn't. The Ranger in Aaron told him to take the offensive, to deny the enemy the advantage of choosing when to strike, and he stepped quickly into the men's room, formulating a plan. The two men, who were part of Alima's Istanbul cell, in turn made the mistake of following him. It was one that they would never make again.

The first man, the older of the two, opened the door of the busy restroom and stood aside while a group of French students exited. As the noisy teenagers filed out, the second man passed through, his colleague holding the door. Once inside, he paused, searching for Aaron amid the men using the sinks in the anteroom. *No sign of him here,* he thought. With his comrade now at his side, he moved farther into the room, spotting what appeared to be Aaron's wheeled suitcase and briefcase on the floor near one of the urinals in the middle. Knowing that Aaron couldn't exit the long, narrow space without passing him and his partner, he queued up behind two other men, ostensibly waiting for the next available urinal, keeping a fix on Aaron out of the corner of his eye.

The younger assassin stepped into the space between the urinals and the stalls, pretending to use the stall immediately behind Aaron. Aaron was ready. He spun fast on the lead man, slamming his right elbow just below the agent's ear, breaking the man's jaw and sending him sprawling into an empty stall. The older assailant shouted a warning, but it was too late. The younger man's head crashed onto the lip of the heavy porcelain toilet with a harsh thud. Although still alive, the first man was down for the count, which would have made for considerably more favorable odds, except that the second man was now pulling a weapon from his open leather jacket.

The 9 mm automatic had cleared the assassin's jacket by no more than an inch when Aaron grabbed the man's shooting arm and punched him hard in the solar plexus. He didn't collapse as Aaron expected, but pulled hard to his right, trying to free up his hand to fire the large black 9 mm. In the struggle, the weapon discharged, fragmenting a large tile behind the toilet in the stall where the first man lay bleeding and unconscious. All hell broke loose when the gun went off, as men in varying stages of relieving themselves fled screaming from the men's room.

Aaron knew that he had only a few seconds to end the struggle and escape before airport security descended upon them. Prebish's message had been all too clear. Aaron was already in enough trouble with the agency. The last thing he needed was to be tied to another international incident. Gripping the enemy's wrist with his left hand, Aaron shot his right arm forward, his index and middle fingers stiffened knifelike, and rammed his fingers into the man's throat. The assassin's head jerked backward as his windpipe began to collapse. Despite the pain, he managed to strike one blow to Aaron's right brow, making him wince but not pause. With the speed of a trained killer, Aaron used both hands to force the 9 mm into its owner's abdomen, clasping his hand over the killer's trigger finger and firing the powerful weapon twice. This time there were no surprises. The man fell back and dropped to the floor, his life ebbing away. Aaron crouched next to him and wiped his own fingerprints from the gun, leaving it on the floor, out of reach, just in case.

Once outside, in the wide corridor leading from Arrivals to Baggage Claim, Aaron shouted excitedly for someone to call the police. "Two men are fighting in the restroom," he blurted out in German, hoping the cut on his eyebrow was not so obvious as to draw attention. "One of them has a gun," he called out as he hobbled, albeit quickly, toward the exit marked GROUND TRANSPORTATION. With any luck, police witnesses would be unable to offer any useful details about the man who emerged from the WC, except that he had a distinctive limp and spoke German. Aaron pulled a handkerchief from his hip pocket and applied it to his brow, trying to appear to be rubbing his eye. The taxi line was mercifully short.

Within minutes of the fight, and moments before airport security sealed all exits, Aaron was in a taxi heading north toward the highway to Edirne rather than east into Istanbul, seeking to shake any remaining assassins and the Turkish police. When the cab reached a large bus stop on the Istanbul-Edirne highway, Aaron instructed the driver to let him off. Getting out of the vehicle, he walked through the crowded *otogar,* mingling with the throngs of Turks rushing to catch their buses. After two trips around the premises, he took another taxi to Sirkeci Train Station in central Istanbul. He circled the sprawling station, making sure that he was not being followed. Satisfied, Aaron exited through a side door, continuing up a narrow street until he found a small, nondescript tourist hotel.

Checking in under an assumed name with a false American passport he carried with him, Aaron paid in full in Turkish lira and hurried up the three flights of stairs to his room. Locking the door behind him, he quickly proceeded to bandage the small cut on the hairline of his right eyebrow. Trained to dress his own wounds, Aaron removed from his toiletry case the flesh-colored surgical tape he carried with him and cut it lengthwise in as narrow a strip as he could while still being able to seal the wound. He shaved his fledgling mustache and one-day-old beard and changed from the suit he had been wearing into jeans, a work shirt and blue-gray running shoes. *Very American,* he thought. If the authorities at the airport were looking for a man in a suit who spoke German, the youthful American look might conceal him. A brown leather aviator jacket completed the outfit. He gathered his things, stuffed the clothes he'd worn in the airport in his suitcase, and left the room, taking the stairs to the lobby. There he observed the hotel clerk behind the counter, a young man flirting shamelessly with three English coeds who were asking about the hotel and the price for a night. He traversed the length of the small lobby at a normal gait and placed his key on the counter. "I'll be back after I deliver some of my samples," he said to the distracted clerk, gesturing to the bag over his shoulder and the suitcase he pulled behind him. The young man barely nodded as he placed the key on the hook marked 302 on the panel next to him.

Back on the ancient street, a crowded strip of open-front shops and street vendors, people were returning from work and making last-minute purchases for the night's dinner. Placing a baseball cap on his head, Aaron walked to Sirkeci Station, slouching, which was a change from his normally erect stance. After one trip around the bustling station and confident that he was not being followed, he queued up for a taxi, waiting patiently, pretending to read a tourist map he had purchased. When it was his turn, he placed his bags in the rear seat and climbed in. The driver turned to make eye contact. "The Ceylan Intercontinental Hotel, please."

Within moments of leaving Sirkeci Station, the cab was embroiled in traffic, with vehicles backed up from the ramp onto Galata Bridge, down to Reşadiye Street, inching along at five miles per hour. Employing a bio-feedback technique he had learned in the army years before, Aaron used the time to decompress, to reflect on recent events. Then it hit him. The second assailant in the men's room had warned the other by shouting "Watch out" in Arabic, not Farsi. "Christ," Aaron whispered out loud. *How could I have been so stupid?* The driver turned to apologize for the traffic, but Aaron wasn't listening.

The drug trafficker, the leader back in Poti, didn't speak in Farsi either. Like the assassins at Atatürk, he shouted "Watch out" and "Head for the exit" in Arabic. Son of a bitch. That's how I understood him. What on earth have I been thinking? Aaron wondered if he had

وسط زمین، آلبرت نفس کشید	PAAH - QCFBN
خط کشی ریاضی، جلوگیری کردن	PFAM - QCKAS
واشنگتن آب، زندان شیرین	PAS - QCFAJ
پایین شرق، نه نوزاد	PJM - QCAS
پاره بودن	PKAM/P-A3H
آروادا	P-AF/P-JAS

not been distracted with Krissi whether he would have come to this realization earlier, but decided that he could not blame her for his own stupidity. *But what the hell is going on? If the heroin traffickers at Poti spoke Arabic, like the men trailing me at the airport, why had the Turks picked up their communications in Farsi? Kemal had been sent to spy on them in Poti, in part because he spoke Farsi, and Hasan had believed that the men who killed Kemal were Iranians. Could they have been so wrong? Were certain Arab factions working together with the Iranians? Could they have put ancient hatreds and Islamic taboos against drugs aside for the right amount of money? How does the note in Farsi fit in?*

Traffic eased somewhat as the taxi finally approached the midpoint of the Galata Bridge. It was almost dark. Aaron could distinguish the lights on the ferries crossing the Bosporus, but the outlines of the ships merged with the gray-black waters and the darkening sky. He reached for the ceiling light of the taxi and flicked the switch, apologizing to the cabby, who mumbled "Okay" in English. Aaron shifted and pulled out of his hip pocket his wallet, thick with receipts, notes to himself and four

غلام بسر دائمی	£62,500
خط منحی، آبا پهلو	€110,000
خليفة المنظم	$75,000
دره آرامش	€95,000
اس ۴.۰۲/اس ۱۱۸۷	$115,000
اس ۴.۰۲/اس ۱۱۸۷	€125,000

different currencies. He spilled onto his lap the crumpled and torn taxi and meal vouchers that he would submit to Heller & Clarke for reimbursement, searching for the list that Hasan had taken from the dead man's pocket in Poti. There it was. He held the list up to the light, and tried to make sense out of the words he could see.

He'd find someone to figure that out later, he told himself, compartmentalizing. He stared out the window, looking at nothing. Among the attack at the airport, Krissi and the list, his mind was cluttered and he could not focus on the presentation he was scheduled to give the next day. The cab turned off Necatibey Street at Luna Park and headed west. Although Aaron had never been to the Intercontinental before, he had stayed at the nearby Hyatt Regency and the Istanbul Hilton and knew that he was only minutes away. His heart pounded in his throat as he thought of seeing Krissi. He hoped that he would not run into her in the lobby. He wasn't sure how he would handle the conversation and preferred a more private venue.

As he paid the taxi driver, Aaron studied the area in front of the hotel to see if he was being followed. Other than a veiled Arab woman and two small children who were getting out of a cab, he saw only a valet and a doorman, both in uniform. So far, so good. He entered the sumptuous hotel, scanning the lobby for anyone who looked out of place. He saw no one. After checking in, using his real name and passport, he headed toward the elevator. He spotted the house phone on a table not far from the concierge desk and walked over.

"Ms. Sturm, please. That's S-T-U-R-M. Thank you." No answer. He hesitated, not sure if he wanted to leave a message. The woman with the two children, the one he had seen outside, was talking to the bell captain while her children played noisily. Aaron glanced their way, and their mother shushed them with a stern hiss. He smiled, nodding to the woman appreciatively. "Krissi, this is Aaron. I'm in room eleven-oh-two. Call me . . . please." He pressed down the button with his thumb and redialed. "Dr. Nigel Corley, please." He held the phone tightly to his ear. "Doctor Corley? Hi, I'm sorry to interrupt you. This is Aaron Korda. I'm with Heller and Clarke in New York. Yes, sir, I am presenting to-morrow afternoon, but this can't wait. I know that you're the keynote speaker tonight and must be terribly busy, but I have some information that I need to discuss with you. No, I'm sorry. I can't tell you over the phone. I'm downstairs in the lobby." Corley could hear the children in the background. "I'm on my way up to my room . . . number eleven-oh-two. Please, sir, just give me fifteen minutes. I wouldn't ask if it wasn't extremely impor-tant." Dr. Corley, a renowned British researcher and businessman who was accustomed to doing things on his own schedule, was not yet convinced. "Sir, I've come across what appears to be an encrypted message. . . . An urgent message partly in Farsi. I don't read Farsi, and to tell you the truth, the letters and numbers in English don't make much sense to me, either. I know your wife is Iranian, so I thought perhaps that between the two of you . . . no, sir, please listen to me. This is *not* a joke. I have reason to believe this is a matter of concern to your government and mine, and it may be a matter of life and death." Aaron looked around the lobby again. Nothing appeared suspicious. "Yes, fifteen minutes. Okay, thank you. I'll be there at six-thirty sharp." Aaron hung up, making a mental note that the Englishman was in Room 1226 and that he had less than thirty minutes to unpack and change clothes.

He gathered his bags and walked as fast as he could to the elevator bank without drawing attention to himself. After waiting while the passengers streamed out of the full elevator, Aaron got in and pushed the button for the eleventh floor. As the doors began to close, Krissi appeared and quickly stepped inside. "You're being followed, Aaron," she whispered. "The Arab woman with the children was watching you. She signaled to two men in the gift shop across the lobby. For someone with your training, you're getting rusty," she said, very aware that she was letting him know for the first time that she knew his secret and was beginning the process of sharing hers. Not exactly the way she had pictured it, but a start nonetheless. Despite the fact that he, or now rather they, were being followed by potentially dangerous people, Krissi felt a sense of relief. She was finally going to come clean with her lover and end the duplicity.

But instead of the surprise or puzzlement that she anticipated, Aaron's expression was cold and distant, even angry. "Look," she said apologetically, "I know you're CIA. . . . Or rather part-time. It's okay. We have a lot to talk about, but it'll have to wait until we figure out who's trailing you and why." She looked into his eyes. Still nothing. "Are you armed?"

"I don't know if I should answer that, Krissi. Or should I call you Agent Sturm? Since you're the crack agent from Abteilung Eins, tell me how you know I'm being followed."

Krissi tried to absorb what Aaron was saying, wondering how he knew, dismissing the message for the moment. "I was in the gift shop buying a newspaper when I saw them." She then understood that he knew. "I was going to tell you this evening. I . . ."

"Forget it. I already know you're a BND agent, and that I'm your assignment."

"Since when?"

"The night I took you to the airport in Vienna . . . after I arrived in Munich."

"Is that why you didn't answer the phone?" she asked, holding down number 8 on the control panel and hoping the car didn't proceed directly to eleven, as currently indicated overhead.

"What are you doing?"

"My room's on the eighth floor. We can't go to yours." The doors opened, and they got off on the eighth floor and walked quickly to 836, a room with a terrace that faced the Bosporus, overlooking Luna Park. Upon entering, Krissi immediately shut the terrace doors, pulling closed the thick drapes so that no light shone through. "I wanted to tell you in Vienna, when we were dancing . . . at that place on Donaustrasse." Aaron looked at her skeptically. "Think about it, Aaron. When I told you that I couldn't go to Munich, I said that I had something to tell you. The band began playing that Springsteen song—the one you liked so much in high school—'I'm on Fire.' You cut me off and began singing it while we danced."

"So it's my goddamn fault, is it?"

"No, no, that's not what I'm saying. It's my fault. If I hadn't fallen in love with you when I was a young girl, I wouldn't have jumped at the chance to work you for the bureau. Do you have any idea what I felt back in Berlin two weeks ago when I saw your picture on the screen and my boss said, 'This is Aaron Korda. He's a consultant who we think is working for the CIA'?" He shook his head. What she was saying made sense to him, but that was exactly the kind of manipulation he had expected. She sensed she was losing him and tried harder. Whether he believed her or not, they were in danger and she had to convince him to at least trust her for now and act together. "Aaron, please listen to me. I couldn't tell you, at least not right away. And by the way, you didn't tell me you were CIA, either. Not that it's the same. I know. I really do. But please, let's talk about it later. People, very bad people, are following you. You have to tell me why."

"How do I know that you're not making this up to pump me for more information?" Their eyes locked on each other's. She looked hurt. "Don't give me that wounded look, Krissi. You're so goddamn convincing. You pushed and pushed for information about Martin. Christ, you asked me point-blank if he's with Delta Force, and in a moment of weakness, I told you. I fucking breached state secrets, and you exploited me. I'm the fool now, and you're a hero back in Berlin," he said bitterly, looking away from her.

"I told my superiors nothing. Nothing about Delta Force, Aleppo or Maraud. Nothing! The only thing I told my boss was that I'm going to bring this case to a head in Istanbul. And that's just what I've done." They were silent for a moment. She stepped toward him and put her hands on his shoulders, turning him around, their faces inches apart. His body tensed. "Damn it, I love you, Aaron. I always have. I'll quit the BND. I lost you once. I'm not going to lose you again."

He felt his eyes well with tears. What she was saying did sound genuine, and he felt himself wondering. Yet he wasn't ready to give in. He moved back a step. Krissi took a step forward, her hands still on his shoulders, their eyes still only inches away. "If what you say is true, why did I have to find out from the CIA that I was your assignment? I would have done anything for you. Quit my work for the CIA, left Heller and Clarke. Anything!"

Suddenly, Krissi started laughing. Aaron looked at her quizzically. She tried to explain. "Listen to us. Two spies ready to retire for each other." His lips involuntarily formed a thin smile, his resistance weakening. "You're as head over heels as I am," she continued. "When we get through this, I'm going to marry you. . . . Even if I have to do it at gunpoint. But in the meantime." Krissi reached for the leather shoulder bag on the night table and pulled out a Glock 9 mm, which she handed to Aaron, the ultimate act of trust between covert agents.

"Thank you," he said as he checked to see if a round was chambered. "I hope it's a spare."

"Hey, I told you I'm in love," she said with a smile.

"You're convincing me," he said, laying the weapon on the bed next to him.

Aaron looked at her cautiously, still afraid to believe what he was hearing, but hoping like never before that his gut instincts were correct and that despite everything that had happened, she meant what she promised.

"Don't comment now," she said softly, stepping forward and gently brushing his lips with the tip of her finger. "I love you, Aaron," she whispered, "but you have to tell me what is going on. I can help you."

He said nothing but slowly raised his arms around her, pulling her firmly against him. They fit together perfectly, Krissi nestled against him comfortably, her head just high enough for him to rest his against hers. The warmth of her cheek caressed his chest as his powerful hands, hands that had taken out two assassins just hours ago, wrapped around her waist reassuringly, feeling the smoothness of her skin in the gap between her sweater and jeans.

They stood like that for a few precious moments, until Aaron, reluctantly, let go and began. "Okay, let's sit down." They moved to the couch. "Four weeks ago . . . a friend of mine was brutally killed in Poti, Georgia," he said haltingly, all too aware that she was now also at risk. She sensed his reluctance and urged him to continue. "His name was Kemal Bulot, Captain Kemal Bulot. He was a Turk, my former roommate at the Point. I attended his memorial. We didn't have his body so there was no real funeral.

"Kemal was army. . . . Turk First Commando Brigade.

You understand what that means, don't you?" he asked, hoping that she understood the bond between soldiers, even those from another nation. She nodded knowingly. "At the ceremony, three of his friends—also First Commando—and I decided to go back to Poti. It was my idea," he added, his tone apologetic yet proud. "You see, from what I then knew, Kemal's last mission was to gather intel on a group of Iranian drug traffickers operating out of a warehouse in the port. The Turk MIT lost interest, but I was determined to find out what happened."

Krissi gave him a sidelong look, as if to say *What are you not telling me?* He shrugged. "You're right," he said. "We went there to kill the bastards, and we did. In fact, I took down the Georgian minister of the interior, who was somehow tied in with the traffickers. I didn't know who he was when I killed him, but that's beside the point. You may have read about that." She nodded that she had. The assassination of the Georgian official had made international headlines, although nothing had been said about his connection to the drug trade.

"Okay. Anyway, when we were in California . . . when I finally got around to checking my e-mail, I found out that two of the men who went with me to Poti were tortured and murdered." He stopped briefly to collect his thoughts. "The bastards also killed Yusuf's wife and daughter." Aaron looked away for a moment. "The little girl was only five." Krissi saw how hard this was for him and took his hands in hers. Encouraged, he continued with his story, leaving out nothing, including the list they had found back in Poti and Aaron's growing suspicion that the Iranians were really Arabs. When he got to the description of the fight earlier that day in the men's room at Atatürk Airport, Krissi interrupted.

"It's on the TV, Aaron," she said. "I saw it on Sky News when I got out of the shower. One man is dead from a gunshot wound, the other is in a coma. But I thought you didn't have a gun."

"I used his, wiped it clean, then left it with him. I would have taken it, but I wasn't sure I'd make it out of there without being stopped by airport security."

"My boss said you may be the CIA's most lethal agent. You're good, Agent Korda. You're very good at . . ."

"Killing," he finished the sentence for her.

"It *is* a talent," she said matter-of-factly. "And we may need your skills before the night is over."

"Herr Director, may I have a word with you?" the young BND analyst said, standing in Gerhard Schmidt's doorway.

Gerhard, one of the division heads of the Operations Directorate, Abteilung Eins, waved him in. The analyst couldn't help but notice that his boss looked exhausted and on edge. "What do you have?"

"Well, sir. We've been looking into the industrial espionage operations of the Americans here in Germany, and we found something surprising. . . . That is, if we can verify it . . . which I think we can."

"Yes, yes, get on with it," Gerhard said impatiently. He was running forty agents on twice as many projects with half the budget he needed. He was gaining weight from too much junk food, and was losing his hair almost as fast as his wife was losing interest in their marriage. "And I hope to God that you are solving a problem instead of creating one."

"We think they were Brits, sir. Not Americans. They pretended to be CIA, but we think they were really MI6. We probably would have caught on to this earlier, but the relocation from Munich to Berlin delayed us somewhat," the analyst said apologetically. "May I explain?" the young man asked, glancing at the chair in front of Gerhard's overflowing desk.

Schmidt gestured with his hand toward the seat. Twenty minutes later, the analyst had made his case. "So if we're right on this," Schmidt said, his mood cautiously optimistic, "it's probably a waste of our time to trail this fellow Korda, the American. We can pull Krissi off that file and get her back to Brazil, where she's supposed to be in the first place." He was still thinking it through, but this could be the break he needed.

"You know, sir. There was one funny small-world story that I picked up on during this project." Schmidt's eyebrows lifted. Nothing was ever simple. "Korda's father was U.S. military, and Aaron studied on base in Wiesbaden. But he perfected his German with students from the local German school in town. The two schools sponsored an informal get-together after regular school hours in both languages."

"I know he speaks German fluently," Gerhard said impatiently.

"Well, Krissi attended the German school. What we didn't piece together is that she participated in those get-togethers. She graduated the same year as Korda. It was a small group of particularly good students, so they must have known each other as kids."

"Are you sure?" Schmidt asked, sitting up in his seat, suddenly very interested.

"You mean she didn't tell you?"

For the first few minutes after the analyst left, Schmidt sat quietly, tapping the eraser end of his pencil on the small portion of wood visible on his desk stacked high with files. His mind raced. One of his most trusted agents, a person he had mentored, had deliberately misled him. *But why? Was she involved with this man romantically? If so, she lied to me. But maybe it's worse,* he thought. *Maybe it's worse.* Suddenly, he jumped up and raced to his assistant's cubicle. "Where is Agent Sturm?"

The assistant tapped the keyboard. "She's in Istanbul, sir, attending the . . ."

"Yes, I had forgotten," he said, cutting her off. "Find Michelle Bäcker and Lukas Kerschner. They, Ostettler and Mencken are in Istanbul tracking the Polish woman. Tell Michelle and Lukas to get their butts over to the

Intercon. I want them to contact Krissi and then go back to our office in Istanbul. As soon as Krissi's on a secure line from the office, I want her to call me."

At precisely 6:28, Aaron and Krissi pushed the freight elevator button. A few moments later, a room service waiter dressed in a starched white jacket opened the door, expecting to see one of his colleagues. "I'm sorry," he said, embarrassed. "This is the service elevator."

"We understand," Aaron said in Turkish, surprising the young man, who was unaccustomed to tourists who could speak his language. "We're going to play a trick on our friend on the twelfth floor and don't want anyone to see us. You can help. When we get to his room, you can call him, and we'll catch him with his pants down, so to speak." Laughing, ostensibly at the prank, Aaron handed the waiter, who was now smiling broadly, a twenty-dollar bill and got the response he wanted. A moment later, he and Krissi entered the Corleys' suite.

"Please do come in, Mr. Korda." Dressed in a tuxedo, the world-renowned scientist and businessman and key-note speaker for the evening's events was surprised to see Aaron in jeans, aviator jacket and running shoes, and Krissi, whom he had not expected, also casually dressed in jeans, turtleneck sweater and running shoes. Mrs. Corley, an Iranian-born scientist famous for her studies in adult-onset diabetes, was stunning in her evening gown, looking fifteen years younger than her age of fifty-eight. "By your manner of dress, I presume you don't plan to attend my speech this evening," he said with a laugh, breaking what was otherwise becoming an awkward silence.

"You'll understand once I explain, but first let me thank you, sir. I can assure you that I am . . ."

"I've checked you out, Mr. Korda," Dr. Corley said confidently, handing Aaron a glass of wine. He quickly stepped over to the wet bar of his luxurious suite and poured another glass, handing it to Krissi. "Sorry, madam, I didn't know you were joining us."

"I'm sorry. This is my colleague, Krissi Sturm," Aaron said. They shook hands.

"Very pleased to make your acquaintance." Dr. Corley turned to Aaron. "Mr. Korda, your credentials at Heller and Clarke are excellent and your presentation tomorrow on the pharmacoeconomics of new drug development should be quite interesting. What can I do for you?" Nigel Corley had not attained his position in life by wasting time. He had fifteen minutes to spare and he would keep to schedule.

Aaron understood the drill, as did Krissi. Without delay, he told the couple as much as they needed to know of Poti, including the handwritten notes, part Farsi, part English. "I don't know what to make of it," Aaron admitted as he concluded his truncated version of the events.

"May I see that list?" Mrs. Corley said. After eyeing it for several moments, she said, "It looks like a woman's handwriting, and some of it is gibberish—like Farsi is not her native language, or perhaps that some of it is the phonetic sounding of something in another language." She walked over to the desk and picked up a pad of paper and a pencil. Sitting back down, she began to translate. "This is what it looks like in English."

Together the four of them studied the notes as they passed them around. Dr. Corley was the first to speak. "Forgive me for taking things out of order, but let's start with the obvious. It appears to be some sort of payment schedule, with the third column referring, top to bottom, to pounds sterling, euros and dollars—presumably American. If you'll permit me to continue, the first four items of the second column seem to have two common elements: QC and P. QC means 'quality control'—that's the most likely meaning in the pharmaceutical industry—and P may stand for 'production.' At least those are the abbreviations generally used at my company. Perhaps the codes behind the P and the QC in the middle column refer to the initials of the people who work there. The fifth and sixth entries in that column only contain a P, so perhaps there is no QC at whatever Paderborn and Arvada are, which means that they can't be real pharmaceutical companies. Moving left on the chart and starting at the top, *Center Earth* is less clear."

"Let's think about that," Mrs. Corley said as she mulled it over. "If these notations refer to companies, *Center Earth* might mean 'Midlands.' It's just a guess," she added, shrugging her shoulders.

"Midlands is the world's largest producer of albuterol," Dr. Corley noted. "They make lots of other products, as well, but albuterol is one of their cash cows. *Albert Breathing* might have some reference to albuterol. I'm also guessing, of course," Corley added.

"And the others?" Krissi asked, excited, though increasingly she kept her eye on the door and clutched her handbag, which contained the Glock Aaron had returned to her.

"*Slide rule* is funny," Dr. Corley said, studying the translation. "That's what we call the guys at Sliedrecht in Holland, because we can never pronounce the name of that production plant of Nederlanden Pharmacie Groep. Sliedrecht isn't Nederlanden's main production

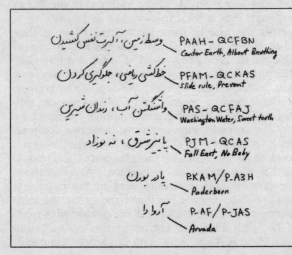

plant, but it's where they produce much of their vaccines. They're a big competitor of ours, you know." Aaron knew, and nodded. "Nederlanden is strong in many areas, but I think their most successful products are vaccines. Nederlanden makes MMR, the measles, mumps and rubella vaccine, and DTP, the vaccine to prevent diphtheria, tetanus and pertussis, usually administered to children, of course. Perhaps the reference to *Prevent* is to vaccines. Now, as for *Washington Water,* I don't have a clue," he said, looking at his wife.

She shook her head and looked at Aaron. "I think we might have to leave that to you, Mr. Korda."

"Washington's home faced the Potomac, but I'm not aware of any other body of water. . . . Oh, wait—what about his crossing of the Delaware? Caught you Brits off guard at Trenton in New Jersey," Aaron said, grinning at Dr. Corley.

"Which is the headquarters of National Pharma, your largest pharmaceutical company," the Englishman added, clearly enjoying this challenge. "It's also where National Pharma manufactures its insulin products. *Sweet tooth*

£ 62,500   غلام بسر دائمی —
    Slave Boy Heat —

€ 110,000   خط منحنی، آبا پهلو :
    Cuneiform abba side —

$ 75,000   خلیفه المنتظم —
    Caliph Al-Mutasim —

€ 95,000   دره آرامش —
    Valley of Peace —

$ 115,000   اس ۴ ۲۰۰۴/ اس ۱۱۸۷
    S1187/S2004

€ 125,000   اس ۴ ۲۰۰۴/ اس ۱۱۸۷
    S1187/S2004

might refer to insulin. Hmmm," he said as he studied the last scribbled entry on the scrap of paper. *Fall East, No Baby.* Bloody hell, I don't think I have a clue for that one."

"Maybe it should be West Fall," Krissi offered after a long silence. "Westfalen. We . . . uh, Westfalen," she added, her eyes darting to Aaron's, "makes more contraceptives than any other company. It is possible that this refers to Westfalen's birth control pills." She shrugged her shoulders modestly, as if to say *What do I know?*

"It's as good a guess as any," Mrs. Corley admitted.

"Paderborn seems an obvious reference to the German town," Dr. Corley said, "but the notation on the right is to dollars, not euros. Let's set that aside for the moment. What do you think Arvada means?"

"No idea, but do you have a laptop?" Aaron asked. Both Corleys nodded. "Are you connected to the Internet?"

"Yes, why do you ask?"

"Let's look up Arvada on the Internet and see if we can figure out what it means."

"Why not?" Dr. Corley said with a shrug, fully engaged in the intellectual pursuit. He stood and walked toward the bedroom, motioning the others to follow. Krissi stayed behind to watch the front door to the suite. It took less than two minutes to establish that Arvada was a town in Colorado, and that Mechelen, Belgium, was its sister city.

"So it looks like a payment is going to be made to . . . or received from, someone in Mechelen—otherwise, why would someone in Arvada deal in euros?" Dr. Corley asked.

"I agree. At least that's the best guess," Aaron said. "It looks like someone in Midlands' production department or quality control department is going to receive—or pay—sixty-two thousand pounds sterling, someone in Nederlanden's production or quality control is going to receive or pay one hundred ten thousand euros, and so on."

"But there is no pharma company in Mechelen," Mrs. Corley said. "I've been there. They make church bells, but not pharmaceuticals. And what about Paderborn? Shall we see what its sister city is?"

"Belleville, Illinois," Dr. Corley said after tapping on his laptop.

"I know where it is," Aaron said. "The U.S. Air Force's Air Mobility Command is headquartered at Scott Air Force Base there. But it's a small town and I'm sure there's no pharmaceutical company there. Now, what about the right-hand column? What do you make of it?"

Dr. Corley was silent. He had deliberately saved that column for last in his analysis, hoping that the information gleaned from the first three columns would shed light on the fourth. "*Slave Boy Heat* means nothing to me, I'm afraid." He looked at Mrs. Corley, who shrugged. Aaron shook his head, equally stumped. None of them could shed any more light on *Cuneiform abba side* than they could on *Slave Boy Heat. Caliph Al-Mutasim* was on its face a reference to a caliph, but there were many, many caliphs in the history of the Middle East. Dr. Corley searched the Internet and found more than one Caliph Al-Mutasim.

"*Valley of Peace,*" Aaron mumbled, deep in thought, after a long pause. "I have no idea where that would be."

"*S1187/S2004* in the fifth and sixth rows mean nothing to me," Dr. Corley said. "The reference to 2004 appears to mean the year, but the *S* and the *1187* leave me empty-handed, but I can research all of this starting tonight right after this evening's dinner. . . . Speaking of which, I really have to hurry. I can't be late for my speech, you know. . . . Though, in light of what we may be witnessing, the research is more important than the talk I plan to give."

The three of them returned to the living room, where Krissi stood behind a club chair, watching the front door. She sat with the others in silence, her eyes still fixed on the door. "So where does that leave us?" Aaron asked. His fifteen minutes were up, and he was anxious to get as much from the scientists as they could offer.

Nigel Corley took a long sip of white wine. "I would think that what you have stumbled on, Mr. Korda, is a plot on the part of someone—most likely Arabs from what we can gather, though they have gone out of their way to appear to be Iranians—to steal our trade secrets or perhaps worse. Who knows? Maybe they're scheming to somehow tamper with our drug supplies. If they have infiltrated production and quality-control departments in these companies, they would be in a position to poison our pharmaceuticals. It hasn't been done before, at least not on a grand scale. The result would be total chaos. Every one of us depends on the pharmaceutical industry. Look at the drugs implicated here. Every child in the developed world is immunized repeatedly with the DTP and MMR vaccines during the first four to six years, starting at two months old for DTP and twelve months for MMR. The boosters are generally finished by the time the child is five or six. How about asthma? It's been called an epidemic, and for good reason. How many children and adults depend on albuterol to help them breathe? And how about insulin? Unlike albuterol, which is one of several drugs for asthma, there is no substitute for insulin for diabetics. I don't have the statistics at my fingertips, but there are a lot of insulin-dependent diabetics in North America and Europe. And oral contraceptives? How many women take the pill every day? My God! If their plan is to contaminate even some of these drugs . . ."

He put down his glass and sat back on the couch, folding his arms across his chest. "If it's just theft of trade secrets, and I hope it is, well, that's a criminal matter, but nothing compared to the poisoning of our medications. But we can't assume that, not given who we might be dealing with." Aaron and Krissi looked at each other, the horror of the idea sinking in. "They may be plotting to destroy the faith that we have in the quality of our pharmaceuticals. Bloody hell," he said loudly, standing and walking to the terrace of his suite overlooking the Bosporus. "If that's the case, they might kill tens of thousands—no, hundreds of thousands—of people."

Krissi nodded grimly, knowing that she, too, took Westfalen's birth control pills. "It's pure terror. Not knowing which medications are poisoned and which are not, everyone would be afraid to take any medicine. And some, maybe many, will die from lack of treatment," Krissi said, wondering what they could do to stop the madness before it was too late.

"But if they're Arabs, why Farsi? Are the Iranians in on this somehow?"

"Maybe, Mr. Korda," Mrs. Corley responded. "Or maybe some Arabs are trying to make people think they're Iranians."

Dr. Corley shook his head and then walked over to the bar, pouring himself a second glass of wine. His wife and guests declined. "What evidence can you get us?" the dean of the European pharmaceutical industry asked, looking at Aaron. "We need proof. And we need it fast."

SIXTEEN

The woman in traditional garb who had lingered near the house phone while Aaron called Dr. Corley had changed her room, requesting a suite on the twelfth floor with a view of the water. Arriving in her suite, the woman immediately went to work with the two men who had staked out the gift shop, setting up a powerful listening device pointed at the Corleys' terrace, which was at an angle to her suite. The children were content to watch cartoons in the other room. Trained by the Iraqi secret police well before the fall of Baghdad to the Americans, Alima Abu-Saif was skilled at espionage and terrorism, and was all the more effective because she was willing to use her own children as the ultimate cover. When Aaron and Krissi bade farewell to Dr. and Mrs. Corley, she removed her earphones. She had learned all that she needed.

The conversation in the Corleys' suite had confirmed what she had feared.

The American and the German were close to uncovering Operation Lethal Agent and stood to jeopardize the entire plan.

"They're going now. The Englishman and his wife must not be allowed to leave their room or even talk on the phone. Kill them first and then go for the American and his German friend," Mme. Abu-Saif instructed. "Make it look like the American and the German woman killed them." The two men who had helped Faramaz kill the Cillers and Lieutenant Ertugrul in Trabzon and Kayseri immediately stood and walked to the door as she told them in detail what she wanted done. "Now go! *Allah Akbar!*"

"*Allah Akbar!*" Pulling the door closed behind them, the two Iraqis, now wearing latex gloves, quickly walked the few paces to the Corleys' suite and knocked on the door. They heard footsteps. "Room service. A lady and gentleman have sent you champagne and flowers."

Dr. Corley was greeted with the butt end of a 9 mm automatic in the forehead instead of the delivery he expected. He crumpled to the terra-cotta floor, his head pulsing with pain, but he did not pass out until the assailant delivered another blow to the back of his head. Mrs. Corley stepped out of the powder room and was knocked cold when the barrel of the 9 mm crashed into her nose. The force of the concussion caused her brain to hemorrhage. She died a few minutes later without regaining consciousness.

The two killers carried Dr. Corley across the room to the terrace, careful not to spill his blood on the carpet. One man grabbed two half-empty wineglasses from the coffee table in the living room and took them to the terrace, breaking them on the tile carefully, leaving large shards of glass intact. While he overturned furniture on the balcony, the other assassin created the scene of a struggle in the suite, mindful not to overdo it. When the stage was set, he joined his partner on the terrace and helped heft Nigel Corley over the railing, sending him crashing to the garden twelve floors below. They then did the same with Mrs. Corley.

They immediately exited the suite, pulling off their gloves and stuffing them in their pockets as soon as they cleared the doorway. They walked calmly to the elevator bank and went to the ground floor. In the lobby, one of them called Alima Abu-Saif on the house phone to inform her that the first part of the job had gone well. Twelve floors above, she checked on her boys, who were still mesmerized by the cartoons on TV, and called the front desk. "There is some sort of disturbance in the suite next to me. I heard shouting and then the sound of glass breaking. I saw a man and a woman on the terrace. I think they threw something over the railing. Please do something. My children are frightened," she said convincingly.

She turned off the television and told her boys that they were leaving; anyone who had to use the bathroom should do so quickly. Accustomed to their mother's sudden mood swings, they complied without argument, though they were disappointed. The room was a lot nicer than many of the places they had stayed lately, and the TV reception was better. The mother and her two young sons took the elevator to the lobby, were hailed a cab by the bellhop and headed for their safe house. Later that evening, she would link up with the two assassins and her men posted around the hotel, who by that time would have killed the American and his German friend, provided that all went as planned.

Krissi packed what she would carry in a small bag, including extra ammunition for her Glock. To her surprise, Aaron consolidated his belongings, even his small satchel, into his suitcase. "We're not going to flee with you wheeling that thing behind you?" she asked incredulously.

"There's a hidden compartment in here," he explained, patting the black suitcase and collapsing its plastic handle. "It's my bag of tricks," he added, carrying it by its leather handgrip and indicating that it wasn't at all heavy.

They walked briskly to the service elevator and took it to the kitchen, drawing attention as they made their way through the swarm of chefs and waiters preparing for the evening's events, and headed for the freight dock. Aaron recalled that the hotel was located at the intersection of two roads that crossed Luna and Taksim parks. Their goal was to make it across the intersection, traverse Luna Park to the Swissôtel Istanbul, and get themselves into a cab without being followed. Suitcase in hand, Aaron jumped off the dock, turned and offered Krissi his hand. She was as physically fit as he was, perhaps more so, and his chivalry would only slow them down, but she accepted his hand to avoid argument. Aaron leading the way, they ran up the delivery ramp toward the road, to a spot about one hundred meters west of the well-lit intersection. Partially hidden by a cluster of trees, they stopped to survey their surroundings. Traffic on the north-south road was heavy, especially near the intersection. There were fewer vehicles, and a number of pedestrians out walking, on the east-west street.

After breaking into Aaron's room, guns drawn, ready to kill him, but finding it empty, the two assassins alerted their comrades staking out the hotel exits. They then went to the hotel room that Alima had identified as Krissi's but also found nothing. By the time they reached the lobby, all hell was breaking out in the rear of the Intercontinental.

Krissi's hand was in her bag, firmly gripping her Glock 9 mm, expecting to have to use it at any moment. She was sure Aaron's pursuers would be watching both the main entrance to the hotel and the rear and side exits. "After that truck, we'll have a break in traffic," Aaron said, glancing at her over his shoulder, only to catch a glimpse of her foot sweeping under his leg and throwing him to the ground as she steadied her weapon. Two bullets, from an assassin he still did not see, slammed with successive *plap*s into the tree near where he had been standing. Dropping to one knee, Krissi fired three times, hitting the would-be killer in the stomach and chest, and sending him reeling backward into the thick shrubs from which he had emerged.

The sounds of gunfire reverberated on the north side of the hotel, leaving no mistake in the minds of the assassins staking out that side of the hotel that their colleague in the gardens had engaged his prey and was taking fire in return. It also alerted the two CIA agents who had just arrived at the main entrance. They weren't sure the distinctive sound of 9 mm rounds popping had anything to do with Aaron Korda, but according to the information they had been given by their boss, the Istanbul chief of station, Korda had a knack for finding trouble. The DDO had told the chief that he was to question Aaron about the cell phone conversations in Farsi picked up by the NSA over the Caspian Sea. The two CIA agents ran in the direction of the gunfire.

Aaron recovered quickly, fear-induced adrenaline pulsing in every muscle. He realized instantly what Krissi had done. She had saved his life, and had dropped the assailant from more than forty meters in the dimmest of light. He was impressed with her skill and grateful for it. Without discussion, Krissi covered Aaron as he sprinted to the assailant, confirmed that the man was dead, and took his Beretta and ammunition. He searched the man's pockets for identification, found an Iranian passport, discarded it and ran back to Krissi. They grabbed their bags, and with an exchange of glances darted across the street toward the park. Sprinting as fast as they could, they cut in front of a truck, reaching the far side of the road as a hail of bullets ricocheted off the pavement around them, the loud *pop, pop, pop* of automatic weapons filling the night air.

Lukas Kerschner shifted into first gear as he stopped at the intersection, Michelle Bäcker sitting next to him in the passenger's seat, her window partially open to take in the cool autumn air. "Did you hear that?" Bäcker asked excitedly.

"I sure did. Nine millimeter." The light turned green and he stomped on the gas pedal, shooting ahead of the car to his right, maneuvering the Mercedes to the inside lane, pulling to the curb on the opposite side of the intersection.

Bäcker was out of the car, weapon drawn, before her fellow BND agent turned off the ignition. She caught a glimpse of Krissi and a man she could not recognize running across the street into the park. From the bushes behind the Intercontinental, two men were shooting at them. "Krissi's in trouble. Call for backup," she instructed as she ran toward Luna Park.

Aaron and Krissi took refuge behind a large tree just inside the park. The Iraqi agents tried to follow, but were held up by traffic on the other side of the busy street. As Aaron and Krissi watched, two other men also rushed to the intersection. Were it not for the fact that the newcomers were dressed in business suits, it would have looked like the two teams of gunmen were acting in concert, conducting a classic pincer movement to cut them off. "Those two at the corner look like CIA . . . or BND. The guy you shot was carrying an Iranian passport. I don't know who is on whose side, but let's get the hell out of here," Aaron said as they considered their options, their eyes now accustomed to the darkness and searching for signs of danger in every direction.

"We'll never make it to the Swissôtel," Krissi said, not looking at him but at the assailants closing in on them. "It's clear across Luna Park. The Hyatt is just a couple hundred meters that way." She pointed into the night. "I think it's our only option. Maybe we can lose them inside the lobby. . . . There must be fifteen to twenty shops and probably a big crowd. If not, we'll grab a taxi."

"Did you get a good look at them?" The CIA agents had reached the intersection just in time to see the two men run across the street about a hundred meters to their west, dangerously close to where Aaron and Krissi had just made their dash across the road.

"Only the girl. Tall, trim. She might be the BND agent the boss told us about. But who the fuck's shooting at them?"

"Maybe the drug dealers. I don't really give a damn. They're armed and dangerous, and we can't let them screw up our assignment. We gotta find out if the guy's Korda. If he is, he'll run for one of the hotels. My guess is the Hyatt. Let's head straight up the sidewalk and then into the park to cut him off before he and the girl

can get there. Come on." He broke into a run, his
weapon brandished, its safety button off, ready to fire.

Aaron and Krissi inserted themselves deeper into the
park, making no noise as they proceeded. Behind them,
their pursuers closed in, as their unwitting accomplices
from the CIA cut off Aaron and Krissi's right flank and
Michelle Bäcker closed on them between the Americans
and the assassins. Aaron caught a glimpse of the CIA
agents. "Four men. Two behind us at our six o'clock,
another pair at our one o'clock," he whispered to Krissi.
Neither Aaron nor Krissi was aware that agent Bäcker
was in the park at their four o'clock. "We can't outrun
them. Let's turn and ambush the assholes behind us."
She nodded, having also concluded that it was time to
counterattack. He set his suitcase quietly on the ground.
Aaron touched his nose and gestured to the ground, indicating that he would stand and fight where he knelt.
He then tapped her chest and pointed to an outcropping
of rocks about ten meters to the right of their position.
She understood and began to move when he tugged at
her elbow and whispered, "I love you."

For a precious moment, the fox and the rabbit lay still.
Alima's men were skillful. Sensing the lack of movement
ahead of them, each lay prone on the ground, taking
stock of the battlefield. Near total darkness. The faint
din of road noise off to the right. Unnaturally quiet.
Very little wind. No shadows moving against the shapes
of the trees, bushes and rocks. The pursuers were prepared to wait out the planned ambush.

Behind Aaron and Krissi, the two CIA agents began
their stealthy approach, black shapes inching their way
toward Aaron and Krissi. Unaware that they had company, Alima's assassins mistook them for Aaron and
Krissi, who were actually midway between the two pairs
of gunmen. Nodding in silent agreement, Alima's men
were on the move again, crouching, running, kneeling
for momentary pauses, and then repeating the maneu-

ver, leading them straight into the jaws of death. When they were no more than five meters away, Krissi and Aaron opened fire. They aimed at their torsos, not risking head shots in the darkness. To Krissi's left, a figure appeared from behind a tree approximately fifteen meters away, crouched in a shooting position. Krissi reflexively fired, dropping her target with two rounds to the chest. When the reverberation of the gunfire passed, Krissi and Aaron heard the crash of bodies falling on twigs and branches, and the gurgling and spitting sounds of life ebbing away. Aaron waited for thirty seconds, looking for any signs of life. Seeing and hearing nothing, he inched forward on the damp earth and verified that the two men were, in fact, dead.

"The others are closing in," Krissi warned in German, the language she instinctively reverted to in a crisis. "Disperse. They know our position."

Aaron needed no coaching. It was a classic opportunity to flank, circle and come from behind as their pursuers closed on them. He rounded a small rock formation and surrounding shrubs and leaned his back against a thick sycamore, easing himself down the trunk into a seated position on his heels, the Beretta poised in both hands, his eyes searching in all directions for the enemy.

Aaron heard footsteps approaching cautiously; soft rubber soles on moist earth and mushy leaves. The shadowy figure moved past Aaron's position and stopped. After a few seconds, he inched closer toward Krissi, unaware that Aaron was only a few meters behind him. "Throw the weapon to your side and lie flat on the ground," Aaron ordered. The CIA agent ignored the command and began to swivel in the direction of the voice behind him. It was a fatal mistake.

Aaron's Beretta belched fire twice, hitting the man in the back, blowing holes the size of golf balls where his chest had been. Aaron's stalker dropped to the ground without so much as a whimper.

The other CIA agent fired blindly in Aaron's direction, giving Krissi the target she needed. She spun on one knee and gently squeezed the trigger of her Glock. The bullet entered the man's stomach and exited the other side. He fell to the ground, the shock momentarily masking the pain. Krissi and Aaron were on him instantly. She could see that he still held his weapon. She kicked it from his hand, sending it flying into nearby bushes, and pointed her 9 mm at his face lest he have any illusions of continuing the fight. "Who are you? Why are you trying to kill us?" Aaron demanded, kneeling at his side and rifling the agent's coat pockets for identification.

"Fuck you, Korda," the agent sputtered in a hateful whisper, excruciating pain now making it more difficult to speak but not yet silencing him. "You're a rogue, Korda. The agency will hunt you down. . . . See you in hell." The man was losing blood rapidly and needed immediate medical attention.

While Aaron knelt over the wounded CIA agent, Krissi ran to the third figure she had shot to verify that he was dead and to check his ID, if any. As she dropped to one knee next to the body, she gasped, recognizing Michelle Bäcker and scanning the surrounding area, alert to others who might be hiding. She put her ear to Bäcker's chest, checking for vital signs, and noticed that she was still breathing; unconscious, but still alive, the result of her fiancé's having insisted that she wear her Kevlar vest while on assignment. Krissi was momentarily frozen, shocked that the BND had sent Bäcker to assassinate her.

The high-low wailing sirens of police cars grew increasingly louder. Assured that Bäcker suffered no permanent injury, Krissi ran back to Aaron.

"Hang on," she heard Aaron say to the CIA agent. "We can't help you, but we'll direct them over here. They'll get you to a hospital quickly. And I haven't gone rogue. Someone set me up. Tell that to your bosses." Aaron stood and gestured to Krissi that they had to run. He returned to his suitcase and carried it with him.

When they were about one hundred meters from the

entrance to the Hyatt, Aaron and Krissi concealed their
weapons and slowed their gait, as if they were out for a
stroll, walking arm in arm. Now on the sidewalk of the
north-south road that cut through the park, Aaron
wheeled his suitcase behind him. Krissi strapped her duffel over her shoulder. A uniformed parking attendant
from the Hyatt walked off his post, drawn by the com-
motion in the park, and approached them, eager for information. "We heard guns," Krissi explained in English
to the young man. "It sounded like someone was hurt.
Over there, near the boulders." The attendant raced
back to his station and called hotel security, requesting
an ambulance. By the time he returned to the Lexus he
had been parking when the shooting first started, it was
gone and Aaron and Krissi were driving north on Inönü
Street, trying to make sense of the last thirty minutes.

At the intersection of Inönü and Kadirgalar Streets,
Aaron took a hard right, staying within the speed limit
and carefully using his directional signal in order not to
draw the attention of any traffic cops. Krissi kept watch
on the side-view mirror. So far, no one was following
them. Going south on Kadirgalar Street, they drove
through Luna Park, where it was easier to see if they
were being tailed. Aaron abruptly turned into a circle
off the side of the road and let the cars behind them
pass. It looked as if they were in the clear, but it was
time to switch cars.

Several cars were parked on the street near the
Swissôtel. Aaron slowed and wheeled the Lexus in the
space between the last vehicle and a fire hydrant. Neither said a word and they began wiping down the car
for fingerprints. Every second counted. A new Peugeot
was parked in front of them. The risk of its having an
ignition cutoff was high, so they proceeded up the line
of cars looking for something less risky. An older Opel,
with several rust spots and chipping paint, looked perfect. Aaron walked over to the driver's side of the vehicle, bent his arm at the elbow and made a fist, and
shoved his elbow, protected by his leather jacket,

through the window, shattering crystals of glass on the driver's seat. He opened the door, tossed his suitcase in the backseat, brushed the glass aside with his handkerchief and got in. He leaned across the seat to the passenger's side and opened the door for Krissi. As she sat down, he pulled two wires from under the dashboard, started the ignition and edged out of the tight space. Krissi turned on the radio and began scanning the channels until Aaron, hearing a local news station, asked her to stop. She couldn't understand Turkish, but he translated for her. Aaron drove back into Luna Park, turned right on Spor Street and left onto Bişiktaş Boulevard, and headed north along the Bosporus.

"You seem to know where we're going," Krissi observed after they had gone a few kilometers.

"My roommate at the Point—the one I told you about—his parents live in Bebek, a suburb just north of here. If they're home, I think they'll put us up for the night. We can leave tomorrow, provided we find a way out of the country. *Shhh!*" he said suddenly, turning up the volume on the radio. He listened for a few moments, shook his head and exhaled through pursed lips. "The Corleys are dead," he said as he lowered the sound. "Tossed off their terrace. A witness says she saw a Western-looking couple running from the Corleys' suite right before they found the bodies in the garden. Sandy-haired white man, Caucasian woman with light brown hair . . . shit, the Corleys are dead, and we're being set up. The police suspect us. Christ, what a fucking waste. And we're on the lam," Aaron said, slamming his palms on the steering wheel.

"The terrorists—whoever they are—know that you know what they're up to, and that they couldn't stop you tonight. The Istanbul police and Turkish national police will scour the countryside looking for you. For us. And for whatever reason, the CIA thinks you've gone rogue and wants you dead. They've written you off. You know how it is."

"You could go in. . . . Tell the BND about the

Iranians . . . Arabs, or whoever they are, and tell them about me. Tell 'em that I'm straight."

"No. That's impossible now. You couldn't see from where you were in the park, but I shot a BND agent, Michelle Bäcker. I recognized her when I went to see if the person I shot was dead." Aaron took his eyes off the wheel and stared at her in disbelief. "She wasn't. She was wearing body armor and was only knocked out. Bäcker was there to kill me. There's no other explanation. They must have found out about Wiesbaden—about us—and realize that I deceived them."

"They don't know about Wiesbaden?"

"Of course not. I couldn't tell them about that. They wouldn't have trusted me. They would have assigned someone else, and I would never have seen you again. I realized that day—when I took the assignment without telling them—that my career was probably over. But, Christ, I didn't think they'd try to kill me."

"There's more going on here than that, Krissi. They wouldn't terminate you for that. . . . At least I don't think so."

"You're probably right. But whatever's going on, let's face it. As far as the CIA and BND are concerned, we're rogue agents."

"But there must be a way out of this."

"Yes, but neither of us can go in at this point. At least not without proof of what the terrorists are plotting."

SEVENTEEN

Aaron rang the buzzer again, looking over his shoulder for any signs of danger. Krissi waited in the car, in the driver's seat, keeping the engine running and looking out for police or, worse, terrorists, CIA or BND agents, enemies that she and Aaron had to consider one and the same. Finally, the black speaker box outside the gated house crackled. "Who is it?" a voice said warily.

"General Bulot, it's Aaron Korda. May I come in? I need your help," Aaron whispered in Turkish, his lips close to the speaker. The general's house, like the others on the street and in keeping with Turkish style, was surrounded by an eight-foot-high concrete wall that abutted the street. Vines and the branches of trees overflowed at the top of the wall, in stark contrast to the harshness of the barrier.

"Aaron!" the retired general blurted out, recognizing his voice. The lock on the driveway's iron gates buzzed and the doors swung open. Krissi wheeled the stolen Opel through the opening, the thick gates closing once the vehicle cleared the entranceway.

Aaron and the general embraced in the doorway, followed by a hug and well wishes from Kemal's mother, a broken woman who would never recover from the death of her only child. Still, it gave her pleasure to see Aaron, the man who had avenged his death. Aaron had told her husband that he was in trouble, and his appearance spoke volumes: hands and blue jeans caked with mud, and the eyes, most of all the eyes, alert and watchful but deeply shadowed by sleeplessness and stress. Without a word said, she knew his predicament had to do with Kemal's death, and that she and her husband would do anything to help him.

"I have been listening to the police radio," the general said. "It's my hobby, if you will. I turned it on as soon as I heard about the English couple's death on the television. The Istanbul police suspect the two of you, Aaron. They mentioned you by name. An employee at the Intercon who saw you on the service elevator positively identified you and said that you spoke to him in Turkish. They also found your fingerprints."

"We didn't do it," Aaron said, and then translated for Krissi.

"I know that," the general responded quickly. "Now come. Clean yourselves and have some tea. Then you will tell us what we can do to help you."

An hour later, over dinner and tea, Aaron had brought the general and Mrs. Bulot up to speed, including the possibility of a plot to contaminate pharmaceutical supplies. The horrific nature of the plan and the numbers of deaths that would result shocked them. "I can go to the Turkish Army. . . . Even to the police. They will listen to a retired three-star general. We must warn the authorities. These drugs are sold everywhere. Europe, North America, here in Turkey . . . everywhere."

"I know," Aaron said somberly. "But you can't go to the authorities until we have proof. While they investigate, the terrorists will kill you—both of you," he added, his eyes gesturing to the general's wife. "Believe me, they are very good, and they will not hesitate." The general and Mrs. Bulot shook their heads gravely. "No, Krissi and I must get the evidence we need to persuade our governments, and then we'll turn ourselves in. We'll figure out a way."

"Then what can we do for you?" the general asked after a long pause.

"You can help us get out of Turkey. We can't fly out

of Atatürk Airport, not after today. We need to go to England and Holland. . . . Maybe Germany."

"I'll drive you to Edirne on this side of the border with Bulgaria. It's unlikely that the police will be looking for you at that border crossing. From there, you can take an express bus to Sofia, where you can catch a plane to anywhere in Europe. You can leave the car here. I'll throw a tarp over it. But first you need sleep."

Aaron explained to Krissi what the general had said. It seemed like a decent plan, and that was that.

"One other thing, sir, if I may," Aaron said as the general and his wife ushered them to the guest bedroom. "My brother may be at Incirlik. That's the most likely forward operating base I can think of for the raid on Aleppo. . . . Unless they're operating out of Iraq. If you could get a message to him through his wife, Helena—I'll give you her number in the States—I would appreciate it."

"Certainly, and what is the message?"

"I'm in trouble, and I need help."

"Ma'am, we have a FLASH-level message coming in from the Istanbul chief of station. I just wanted you to know that it'll be on your secure computer screen in a moment," the assistant informed his boss, Diane Felder, the CIA Deputy Director for Operations.

"Give me a preview."

"It's about Korda."

"Which one?"

"Aaron."

"Okay. Tell me," she said, annoyed that she had to ask twice.

"I'll give it to you chronologically, but the story gets worse. He killed a man at Atatürk Airport in Istanbul, and put another in a coma. The MIT says both men were carrying Iranian passports. It looks like he and his German girlfriend—turns out she's BND but you already know that—also killed a British couple, although the jury's still out on that one."

"Who were they?"

"Don't know really. A Dr. Nigel Corley, a Brit, and his wife, Iranian-born, dual citizenship." The name didn't register. The aide continued. "He was going to be the keynote speaker at the pharmaceutical conference Korda was speaking at. Witnesses claim they saw a guy who fits Korda's description, and the BND agent, running out of the Corleys' hotel suite at the Intercontinental, right after the victims were tossed off a twelve-story-high terrace. Istanbul police found their prints on shards of glass on the terrace. Apparently, Korda and the woman wiped down everything except some broken wineglasses."

"What the hell is going on?" the DDO exclaimed as she puzzled through the little she knew. Aaron Korda, rising star, who seemed to have it all, turned cold killer? "What else?"

"Korda and the woman then took out five more people near the hotel, two of them ours, ma'am. One dead, another seriously wounded. He may not make it. They killed two men carrying Iranian passports and they shot a BND agent, who would have been killed but for her vest. Korda and the woman got away, which is pretty amazing given what they were up against, but . . ." The DDO grimaced. The last thing she wanted to hear right now was the glorification of a rogue agent who was making her and the CIA look bad. The agent got the message. "The Turkish police, MIT and our people are looking, but so far they can't find them."

"When did that happen?"

"The killings outside the hotel took place about seven o'clock P.M. local time, about noon here, so . . . what, about two and a half hours ago? The incident at the airport was about five hours before that . . . or approximately two o'clock P.M. local time."

"Goddamn Korda. I never felt we had him under control, but who expected this? Does the Istanbul chief of station have a theory?"

"Well, money for one. He—and I—for what it's worth, think it's all tied to that NSA intercept from the drug runners over the Caspian, the raid on Poti, the big diamond ring he's sporting. Who knows, maybe he got in over his head on that new apartment he bought overlooking the East River, which had to go for over a mil, or maybe he developed a taste for some of the stuff they were pushing out of Poti—maybe both. Whatever caused it, it looks like he's gone bad for the money, and has recruited the BND agent."

"Or she recruited him. What does the BND have to say about this?"

"They've uncovered a bit of intel that we didn't pick up on. It turns out that the BND agent was Korda's girlfriend in high school. Despite what he indicated to Prebish in Munich, Korda's known her for years."

"I need to talk to the DCI and Kate Brind. The DCI's either still in the air or landing in Tel Aviv at this moment. I must talk to them *now*."

Ten minutes later, the director of Central Intelligence was on the line being briefed, as the DDO and the national security adviser, who had been alerted and brought up to speed, listened in. After receiving the full report, the DCI said, "What do you propose?"

"We have no choice. Take him out," Felder said regretfully. She had been over the alternatives, but that didn't make the conclusion any easier.

"Wait. Give him an opportunity to come in, for heaven's sake," Kate Brind interjected. "Think about it. He's been one of our best assets. His cover is tremendous, and he has consistently delivered in the past. Hell, we don't really know what went down in Istanbul, and we haven't debriefed Korda after his attendance at the Damascus fair. Witnesses saw him and the BND agent with the British couple before they were killed, but so what? And who are these witnesses? Fingerprints on some shards of glass? Come on. Korda wouldn't be that sloppy. It sounds like a setup."

"Right. Try telling that to the widow of the CIA agent he killed in Istanbul," the DDO countered.

"Hold on," the DCI interrupted. "I don't have time

for infighting. I'm going into a difficult session with the Israelis, and I need to jump off. I'm going to go out on a limb here. Let's do what Kate says. . . . Give Aaron an opportunity to come in. You guys figure out how to do that, but make it fast. If he resists, well, then we have no choice."

"What about the other Korda?" the DDO asked.

"What about him?" Kate Brind asked, concerned that Martin's name was coming up.

"Well, he's in Turkey. Aaron might link up with him. Hell, they might be in this together. I'm just checking Martin Korda's background on my laptop. Depending on how well the BND agent and Aaron knew each other, it's very possible that Martin knew her, too. The Korda brothers were close. Even when he was at West Point, Martin must have traveled to Germany to see his family at Thanksgiving, Christmas and the like, so he may have met her on those occasions. It may be a coincidence that he's in southern Turkey at the same time his younger brother is on a killing spree in Istanbul, but I've never been a believer in coincidences."

"And what do you propose that we do about that? Shoot him, too?" Kate asked sarcastically.

"No, but we should put him under surveillance," the DDO said. "Aaron or the German may try to contact him. We need to know if they do."

As practicing Muslims, General and Mrs. Bulot rose at 4:30 to say their morning prayers. After worshiping, the general walked to his nearby office at Bosporus University, where he taught, made the photocopies he needed, and hid the original of the list from Poti and Mrs. Corley's translation where he was sure no one would easily find them. Returning home, he knocked gently on the guest room door and was greeted by Krissi, who was folding and neatly stacking the blankets she and Aaron had used. "Aaron's in the washroom," she explained in English, her expression indicating that she was not sure he understood.

"I speak English well enough," he said with a smile. "You can't be a NATO general and not speak the language. My wife is making us a quick breakfast. We will do better if we get on the road before traffic becomes too heavy."

After a slow start on the smaller roads leading from Bebek to the 02 highway that loops the European side of Istanbul, they made good time, merging into the rapidly flowing Istanbul-to-Edirne four-lane road at 7:45 A.M. The remaining two hundred twenty kilometers took only another two and a half hours, and by 10:30, Aaron and Krissi were waiting for the 10:50 bus to Sofia, bidding their good-byes to General Bulot and thanking him for his help.

The two-lane road through the mountains from Turkey to the capital of Bulgaria was rough, but the driver kept to his schedule. At 3:45 in the afternoon, the driver pulled into the busy central bus station, and Aaron and Krissi were, they hoped, just one more couple amid the hundreds of passengers seeking connecting buses and cabs.

Two hours and fifteen minutes later, Balkan Airlines Flight 204 to Brussels, booked by Aaron over the Internet at the Bulots' home, taxied on the tarmac. The aging Airbus A300 rattled as its two General Electric CF6 turbofans powered to full speed against the plane's brakes, the roar of its jet engines growing louder within the cabin. When given the go-ahead from the control tower, the Bulgarian pilot lifted his feet off the floor pedals and the A300 shot forward, pressing the passengers' backs against the upright seats. It felt good to be in the air again.

Aaron kept several spare passports in the false bottom of his suitcase, the same concealed compartment that hid his and Krissi's 9 mm automatics, ammunition, credit cards, and a considerable amount of cash. While carry-on luggage was scanned and searched, check-in baggage, like Aaron's suitcase, was not. On this leg of the trip, Aaron traveled with a German passport, of which, like the others in his case, the CIA knew nothing. Krissi also traveled with a German passport, though not one with her real name. She, too, had more than one secret she kept from her employer.

They had considered flying directly to London for the trip to Coventry but decided that security at both airports in London was too heavy. Safer, they reasoned, to land in Belgium and take a lesser-traveled route to Midlands Chemicals. From Brussels, they would rent a car, using yet another set of credit cards, driver's licenses and passports, drive north to the Europort at Hoek van Holland near Rotterdam, then take the ferry to Harwich. Once on the east coast, they would take the winding back roads from Harwich to Coventry.

"How are you feeling?"

"Oh, I'm okay . . . now. I was pretty sick yesterday, but it was Sunday and I was able to sleep in. I think maybe I had too good a time at your brother's bar mitzvah. Thanks for inviting me. Hey, I really like your family. They're great."

"They like you, too. Who wouldn't? You're a knockout. . . . And I had no idea you could dance like that. Every guy there was jealous of me."

"Dance like what?" Saba Heshemi asked teasingly of her boss, tossing her raven hair back with a laugh and leaning her curvaceous body forward from behind her desk, revealing a good amount of cleavage. To his delight, at the same time she did that, she twisted her legs to one side of the chair, showing a shapely calf and smooth thigh, covered only by what appeared to be sheer stockings.

"That sexy slow dance . . . you know . . ." He thought about their night in bed after the bar mitzvah and felt himself getting excited again. "Now, don't tell me a nice Jewish girl like you learned to dance like that in Iran under the Imams."

"You forget that my family left Iran a long time ago, and that I studied in England and Illinois. There were plenty of occasions to learn all kinds of things," she added, rolling her tongue on her lips. She rose and closed her door, flipping the lock behind her as she turned to the head of quality control of National Pharma's Trenton production plant. She kissed her boyfriend passionately on his lips, her tongue finding its way into his mouth, her full breasts against his chest, her pelvis thrust against his groin.

"Saba, baby, we can't do it here," he said unconvincingly. He began to breathe more rapidly.

"Why not? I've taken care of the shipments, and the door is locked." She turned the light off. "If you don't make any noise, no one will know we're in here," she said as she unzipped his trousers. Fifteen minutes later, when they had satisfied themselves, he hurriedly pulled up his pants while she slipped into her skirt and blouse and tossed her hair.

"I think I'm totally in love with you," he said. They had been having sex almost daily since she first arrived at the Trenton facility just about two years before, shortly after Nasreen Jasbi in production had introduced them, but it seemed to Jay that it was getting better and better, and nothing they had done compared to the thrill of making love in the office. The risk of being caught added to the excitement. Saba smiled but did not stop combing her hair and applying her lipstick. "Where did you . . . oh, never mind. It's none of my business," he chuckled nervously. "But who would have thought that a Jewish girl from Tehran . . ."

Saba looked at him lovingly, he thought. *Your Jewish women are nothing compared to women in my country,* she wanted to say but did not. *We please our men in ways you would never dream of.* Saba Heshemi was her *nom de guerre.* She went by her real name, Farah Al-Jeddah, when she was growing up in Iraq. She had tolerated the sex and even began to enjoy it, but she continued to resent pretending to be a Jew. Faramaz had insisted upon the Iranian Jewish cover, and while she acknowledged that it had worked well, it was a

hard pill for her to swallow, especially with the humiliation of the American victory and occupation of her
country.

"Damn." He looked at his watch. "I'm behind on all
the batch testing. I haven't been around to the shipping
dock yet. The guys must be ready to roast my ass." Jay
straightened the knot in his tie, pulling it snug against
the collar of his white shirt.

"You're okay. When you were out on Thursday and
Friday, I took care of the testing and worked with the
others on the bills of lading, shipping manifests and
other documents. We got seven truckloads out Thursday
afternoon, and twelve on Friday. We're scheduled to get
another ten out today. The guys in shipping are probably
loading a couple of eighteen-wheelers as we speak. It's
good, no? You get your rocks off, and they get sore
backs loading boxes of insulin."

"But I have to sign off on quality control personally
before the trucks can roll," he said, wondering how shipping would have authorized the dispatch without his initials on the forms.

"I took care of it. I hope you don't mind," she answered, pecking him on the cheek. "Your initials are
easy enough. Don't worry. I won't tell if you don't."

"And you conducted all the composition tests?"

"Of course. I stayed late with Nasreen on Wednesday,
Thursday and Friday, without putting in for overtime,
mind you. She oversaw the production to make sure everything was right, and I backstopped her with the QC
checks. Everything is precisely according to plan," she
added, thinking how that statement was true on several
levels. "Look," she said, turning on the light. "We can
track the shipments on the computer within two hours
of their last location. I'll show you where they were at
six thirty this morning." He was fully familiar with the
software and watched with a growing sense of relief as
she pointed out the status of the delivery process, truck
by truck, as they fanned out over the eastern seaboard
and lower Canada.

"You are amazing," he said, putting his arms around her and feeling her warm response.

"*Bonjour,* Jacques," the trucker said on his cell phone to the man at receiving on the dock at Beauvais Médicaments Détaillés, S.A., a private wholesaler under contract with the French Ministère de la Santé, which administers France's nationalized health care program. Beauvais, whose distribution center was located in St. Denis in the suburbs north of Paris, had the concession to supply all hospitals, clinics and research centers in and around Paris with virtually every type of pharmaceutical. Charles Laval had driven for Beauvais for eleven years, motoring his eighteen-wheel Mercedes diesel mostly up and down the A1 from Nederlanden Groep's production plant in Sliedrecht, Holland, but sometimes to and from Germany, as well, the truck's immaculately clean white trailer and cab with a stylized green cross on the sides a familiar sight to French motorists.

"*Bonjour,* Charles. Where are you?"

"I made good time until a bit south of Lille. There was a big accident—two trucks as big as mine and several cars—north of Arras, and the traffic was backed up almost all the way to Lille. I'm on the A1 at Senlis and moving pretty well, considering the hour. Can you wait for me? If so, I'd be happy to spring for a glass or two of red."

Jacques looked at his watch. It was 5:45 P.M. A drizzle had set in, adding to the chill typical of Paris in early November. The wet streets would delay traffic. He knew that Charles wouldn't make it to St. Denis until after six, when he normally would close the gates to the motor pool and shutter the garages on the freight dock. He guessed his friend would pull in around 6:30. *I'll have to wait for him,* he thought. The refrigerated trailer was mostly carrying vaccines and would need to be hooked up to the dock's electricity overnight. *Anyway, better than going home to an empty apartment.* Recently divorced and split from his girlfriend, he could use the

companionship. He decided that he'd have Charles back
up the truck tight enough against the dock so that no
one could break the antitamper seals and open the rear
doors during the night and plug in the jacks. They'd
leave it like that until the morning and offload early.
Meanwhile, he and Charles could down a few drinks at
any number of bars in the working-class neighborhood.

Later, just before seven o'clock, they locked the thick
steel padlock to the tall woven-wire mesh gates that enclosed the freight dock and the motor pool and left
Beauvais's facility for the warmth of Le Relais St. Denis,
a smoke-filled pub where both the wine and the women
were coarse but inexpensive.

"How was Holland?" the freight dock attendant asked
the driver.

"Don't tell my wife, but I arrange it each time so that
the truck is loaded late enough at night so that I can't
make it home. I make it into Rotterdam and stay over
in a small hotel. You know the kind I mean," he added,
slapping Jacques's back, a caffeine-stained grin plastered
on his face as he shared his secret. "They have these
girls—Russian, Ukrainian, Yugoslav . . . some of them
can't be a day over eighteen. For two you normally pay
three hundred euros, but I slip them some downers and
uppers that the guys on the dock at Nederlanden Pharmacie Groep give me, and I get the two babes for the
cost of a bottle of Johnnie Walker. Greatest lay you
can imagine."

"I bet. Hey, why don't you take me with you next
time?"

"Why not?" Charles said with a Gallic shrug.

"Oh, before I drink too much of this," Jacques said,
pointing to his glass of red wine, "how much of your
load is vaccines? I need to know how to organize the
refrigerated fleet for tomorrow after we empty your
monster eighteen-wheeler."

"Pretty much the usual. I've got the manifest in my
bag here." Charles reached into a small leather satchel
at his feet and handed it with one hand to his friend,

while waving with the other hand to the waiter to bring another round of house wine and a pack of smokes.

"Hmmm," the shipping clerk muttered, exhaling a thick cloud of pungent smoke from his Gaulois, "you're heavy on vaccines . . . DTP and MMR. Looks like they're more than half the truckload. Those go to the hospitals and clinics, not the pharmacies. That's helpful. We deliver to the hospitals and clinics in the smaller vans, so I'll line them up first thing. Do you know where they are on the truck?"

"The back half . . . a little more than half," the driver of the big eighteen-wheeler answered. At that moment, the waiter placed two more glasses of red wine in front of them, tossed the pack of Gaulois on the table and slid a second receipt under the ashtray, a tab to be settled much later in the night. "Drink up. I'm buying. Hey, I saved three hundred euros last night," Charles said with another shrug and a throaty smoker's laugh.

"*Très bien. C'est parfait.* I'll move the vans out early. . . . Push 'em to the hospitals and clinics, get the drivers out of my hair, and I'll get you back out on the autoroute. Maybe I'll go with you." Jacques took a long drag on the stubby cigarette and held it in his lungs for a moment, then exhaled dramatically. He lifted his glass to Charles and said, "Here's to you and our trip to Rotterdam." Having freed himself of the next day's planning, he was now ready to drink.

EIGHTEEN

Aaron and Krissi spent the night in Vlarrdingen, a small harbor town along the vast wharves that form the greater port of Rotterdam. They chose the anonymity of a run-down rooming house used mostly by the lesser-paid mariners working the container ships, and it was perfect for their needs: cash on the counter, no passports checked, no questions asked. The food at the dark pub a few paces down a back street was heavy and greasy, but the ambiance was just right—it was empty save two other tables. Moreover, Vlarrdingen was only a few minutes' drive to the ferry, allowing them to get badly needed sleep and still catch the first departure in the morning.

Precisely on schedule, three hours and forty minutes after pulling away from the pier in Holland, the sleek Stena Line high-speed HSS Ferry nudged against the pilings in Harwich harbor, which gently shook the vessel and brought it to a halt. Moments later, the crew of the efficiently run ship began offloading passengers and cars alike. Having eaten onboard during the crossing, they were ready to make the dash to Coventry. With a little luck and hard driving, they could make it to Midlands' production and shipping facilities before late afternoon.

Making only one brief stop at a BP gas station near the town of Rugby, Aaron and Krissi arrived at Midlands Chemicals' Coventry production facility at 3:20. The rain sheeted heavy drops on the pavement of the parking lot as they ran for the door. Aaron approached the receptionist, first drying his face with his clean hand-kerchief. "Hi, I'm Michael Flynn, and my colleague here is Cathy Elliott. We're here for our three o'clock appointment with your chief of production. I'm afraid we're a bit late."

The receptionist looked puzzled, and double-checked the schedule in front of her. She glanced over to the security guard, but he was clearly more focused on Krissi's shapely legs than her right to be on the premises. "I'm sorry, Mr. Finn. You're with whom?"

"It's Flynn. No problem. We're from National Pharma. . . . Part of David Herder's transition team. His secretary, Barbara, made an appointment for Ms. Elliott and me—at least she was supposed to. Hasn't anyone called you?" The young woman shook her head apologetically. Aaron smiled reassuringly, pouring on his considerable charm. As he spoke, he leaned closer, as if taking the young woman into his confidence. "Look, I'm sure it's not your mistake. Barbara is overworked and, frankly, underpaid for what she does. Between you and me, we're not as good at National on this transition stuff as we pretend. We had exactly this sort of mix-up when we bought Pharma España last year." While he was never officially part of the transition team as a consultant to National, Aaron actually had worked with David Herder on the integration of the Spanish company's product lines into National's after the merger, and he had been on the phone with David's assistant, Barbara, on an almost daily basis. But that was months ago, and Aaron could only hope that if the receptionist knew Barbara, she was still working with Herder, who was known to be difficult.

At that moment, several employees of Midlands hurried into the lobby, folding their wet umbrellas and shaking off their trench coats. "The funeral lasted a long time," the receptionist said to them, addressing no one in particular.

"The mass and the funeral were very crowded. It was the saddest thing I've ever seen," a woman who appeared to be the most senior of the group responded. "It was tasteful and dignified, but still awful."

"I'm sorry to have come at what appears to be a bad time," Aaron offered. "Has there been a death of one of your . . . our colleagues?"

"Yes, but even worse. Her house caught on fire, and she and her entire family died. The firemen say that Anne's boiler failed and faulty electrical wiring sparked, causing the fire. They had two small children. She was rather senior here and well liked. She was a real pillar in our production department." The receptionist paused to collect her thoughts. "Look, Barbara is very efficient, but these things happen," she said, getting back to the point. "Let me see if Mr. Soraya can see you. No need to trouble Barbara. I know that Mr. Herder has her going in all sorts of directions." She winked at Aaron and called the head of production at the facility, speaking in hushed tones for a few minutes before she replaced the telephone in its cradle. "Mr. Soraya can meet with you."

"Great, thanks. I really appreciate it," Aaron said, continuing to charm the woman, who was obviously enjoying the attention he was giving her. "Let me ask you, what is his full name? I don't want to rub him wrong by not getting it right."

"Asher ben Soraya," she answered, looking at the company roster.

"And your head of quality control. We'd like to talk to him, or her, if we could while we're here."

"It's a she. . . . Laya Razavi."

"Both Iranians?"

"You got that right," the security guard said, speaking for the first time and waiting until those who attended the funeral left the lobby. "He's an Iranian Jew. . . . Supposedly escaped from Iran with nothing except his chemistry degrees," he said with a shrug. "Anyway, once he's in—back in '99 it was—he turns around and recruits more of his own kind a few months later." The man's tone left no doubt that he didn't like them. No one said anything for a few seconds. "Hey, I have nothing against foreigners, or even the Jews for that matter, but these people don't even talk English to each other. They stick to themselves, work all kinds of weird hours. They just don't seem to fit. I note that Soraya didn't go to Anne Carton's funeral. Says he's too busy, but what kind of crap is that?"

The receptionist looked at Aaron and rolled her eyes. "I don't think Mr. Flynn and Ms., um, Elliott want to hear all that, Mike."

"Okay, okay. Sorry."

"Forget it," Aaron said. "Ms. Elliott and I will just take a seat and wait for Mr. Soraya."

Aaron and Krissi sat at the end of two couches in the waiting area, separated only by a corner end table. He leaned forward with a photocopy of the translated list from Poti in his hand. Next to *Center Earth, Albert Breathing* were the notations *PAAH* and *QCFBN*. If the Corleys were right, *P* stood for "production" and *QC* meant "quality control." Corley had surmised that *AAH* and *FBN* corresponded with the initials of people in those departments. So far, there was no match with Asher ben Soraya or Laya Razavi, although the fact that they were Iranians was interesting. *And perhaps*, Aaron thought, *there are others in those departments of Midlands Chemicals whose initials correspond. But maybe Dr. Corley was wrong. What if* Center Earth *has nothing to do with Midlands?*

Asher ben Soraya entered the reception area smiling, but there was an edge in his voice. "Hello, Mr. Flynn . . . Ms. Elliott. Asher ben Soraya—please call me Asher." Aaron and Krissi shook hands with him and followed him down a long corridor and through a covered walkway between two buildings. From there they made a dash across an open courtyard that separated two dismal red brick buildings and entered the building on the right, which was the manufacturing facility. There Aaron and Krissi spent more than two hours with Soraya and his staff. Aaron, who was considerably more knowledgeable about the industry, did most of the talking, and Krissi took notes and observed the people. As a result of his work at Heller & Clarke, Aaron had some knowledge of the details of National's record keeping and their proprietary software systems designed to track control of formulae and quality-assurance measures, which made the afternoon considerably easier for him and Krissi. At five o'clock, Laya Razavi joined them as they made their way into the QC department's lab, taking over the lead from Soraya, who stayed on with the group and seemed to watch her approvingly. Both Aaron and Krissi noted that she wore a Star of David necklace. As the presentation progressed, they could find nothing wrong with Razavi, the processes or the facilities. Everything appeared to be in order. As six o'clock approached, Aaron began to worry that he and Krissi had wasted precious time in coming to England.

"Well, thank you very much," Aaron said as the meeting neared its end. "The integration of Midlands's production and QC departments with those of National is going to be a lot smoother than we had thought."

"We're all part of the same team now, aren't we?" Soraya responded graciously. "And we'll all get rich on National's stock options," he added with a chuckle.

"God willing," Aaron said in Farsi. "With God's blessing, we'll all be rich."

"You speak our language?" Laya asked, surprised.

"Only a few words. I have some Iranian friends in New York." With that, Aaron and Krissi were escorted back to the reception area, where they returned their visitor passes and said good-bye to the security guard and receptionist.

"Did we learn anything?" Krissi said as she pulled into the eastbound lane, heading back toward Harwich. They wouldn't get a ferry back to Holland that night, but they wanted to get as close to Harwich as possible, find a hotel, and catch the early, faster ferry in the morning.

"I don't know. Dr. Corley thought that the English-language letters following *P* and *QC* referred to the initials of someone working in the production and quality-control departments of these companies, but the initials don't match. . . . At least not those of Soraya and Razavi, assuming those are their real names."

Krissi could tell from his expression that he was hatching a plan. "So what are you thinking?"

"When we're at the ferry landing at Hoek van Holland, we're only going to be a stone's throw from Nederlanden Pharmacie Groep's factory at Sliedrecht. We could check them out, but we'll have to come up with a different cover. National Pharma isn't buying Nederlanden. Any ideas?"

"Yeah, but this time it's my turn."

As he did every day, on this morning General Bulot rose at 4:30 with his wife, spread his small prayer carpet on the floor, knelt facing south toward Mecca, placed his head on the fine wool rug and said his prayers. They then ate breakfast, each reading sections of the morning newspaper, trying to fathom the complexities of Turkish politics, keeping up with the soccer teams and looking to see what sales were on at the local stores in Bebek. After showering and shaving, the general dressed in a conservative blue suit and tan trench coat and headed out the door, walking a mile away to Bosporus University, where he taught history. At first appearance, this morning was no different from any other weekday since his retirement from the army three years earlier. However, instead of going directly to his small office in the university's administration building, he turned left, not right, on Atatürk Boulevard and went to the post office to place a phone call he did not want traced to his home or office.

"Good morning. I need to place a call to the United States," he said to the postal worker who handled overseas calls for the Turkish national telephone company. "Here is the number." He handed the bored-looking civil servant on the other side of the partition a slip of paper.

"Very well. You can take booth number three and then pay me when you're done," the man said, glancing at the large institutional clock on the wall, which read 6:55. He ran his index finger down a sheet of paper that someone forgot to laminate, frayed at the edges and dirty from too many oily hands. "But, sir, it's midnight where you're calling."

"Yes, I want to make sure my friends are home. They stay up late."

"Fine. Signal to me through the window when you're ready, and I'll place the call."

Twenty seconds later and 5,800 miles due west, Helena Korda heard the telephone ring. "Hello," she said tentatively as she fumbled for the phone on the third ring, knocking the open book that had been laid across her chest noisily to the floor. She looked at the digital clock radio on the table next to her bed. *How long have I been sleeping?* she wondered. "Martin, is that you?" She had hoped he would call earlier this evening. In the last three nights, Joey had had as many asthma attacks, including one earlier that evening, and she'd been up throughout the night administering albuterol.

"No, ma'am. I am sorry to wake you, but I needed to reach you and didn't want to leave a message on your machine."

"Who is this?" Helena asked, immediately terrified that this would be the call every soldier's wife dreaded.

"My name is Hasan Bulot. I am a retired lieutenant general in the Turkish Army. Ma'am, I am not calling about Martin, and I apologize for a call at this time. I was in the army for thirty-five years, so I understand that I startled you."

"Thank God," she said, leaning back on her pillow, wanting to believe that Martin was safe but still on edge. She could feel her heart beating in her chest, edge. blood pounding in her temples. Why in the world was a Turkish general calling her home at midnight if it had nothing to do with Martin? It didn't make sense.

"Mrs. Korda, I'm calling about Aaron Korda. He was my son's roommate at West Point and a dear friend of my son. He asked me to get in touch with Martin. Can you help me do that?"

"Is Aaron okay?" she asked, now sitting up in bed and fearing the worst.

"Well, yes and . . . no. He is having some trouble, and may need his brother's help. I must reach your husband. It is urgent."

"But if Aaron is in some kind of trouble, why didn't he call me himself?" It suddenly dawned on her that this could be a crank call or worse.

"I'm sorry, Mrs. Korda. Believe me, he would have called himself, but he couldn't."

"Is he injured? Please, I must know."

"No, no, but some people—some very dangerous people—are looking for him and he can't risk using the phone right now. He's okay, though. He's with an old friend, a woman named Krissi, and she's helping him."

It wasn't just the mention of Krissi's name, but rather the way he said it, that convinced Helena she could trust the man at the other end of the line. "Okay. I believe you, but I can't call Martin. It's against the rules. . . . And I don't know where he is. The only thing I can do is . . . well, when we talk—I don't know when that will be—I'll ask him to contact you."

General Bulot had hoped not to receive any calls traceable to him and didn't want to leave his phone numbers. But he didn't have much choice and he gave Helena both his home and office numbers in Bebek. "Mrs. Korda, my wife and I lost our only son recently. Aaron came to the memorial, and was . . . well, very helpful to us to establish closure on our boy's death. We love Aaron. . . . It's almost like he is our son. Please tell your husband that I will do anything—and I do mean *anything*—to help his brother."

"I will tell my husband to call you. I promise," she said, before they hung up.

Unable to go back to sleep, Helena sat in her bed wondering what to do. It might be days before Martin was able to call again. She wasn't supposed to call him, but decided to bend the rules. She picked up the phone and tapped in seven numbers.

"Command Center," a deep voice at the other end of the line responded instantly.

"This is Lieutenant Colonel Korda's wife. I know that I can't call him, but I need to get a message to him that he must call me—not at home . . . at my mom's house," she added, hesitating as her speech tried to keep pace with her thoughts. "Tomorrow morning after eight our time. It's about our son Joey. . . . And his asthma." She hated using Joey's illness as the pretext to reach Martin, but she knew he would understand when she explained everything.

"Yes, ma'am. We'll pass on the message," the staff sergeant pulling night duty said sympathetically before signing off. The staff sergeant looked at the first sergeant sitting at the desk facing him. "Top, we need to get a message to Lieutenant Colonel Korda. His wife called. Sounds like their boy's real sick."

"Okay," the first sergeant said. "Put it on the priority list right after official calls. And wait till I tell you we have confirmed secure commo. Some CIA types were snooping around this evening, wanting to be informed about Korda's calls. I don't know what they're up to, but I didn't give them anything and it's none of their goddamn business who he calls."

"Roger that, Top." The staff sergeant decided right then that he wouldn't enter Mrs. Korda's call into the night log.

Krissi drove from the ferry landing to a Hertz outlet in Antwerp and returned the vehicle she had taken out in the name of Cathy Elliott, paying with a credit card

bearing the same name. The account would be paid by
a BND front company operating out of Zurich and at
some point trigger the bureau's computers, alerting the
agency that she was in Belgium. But she knew the tech-
ies were having trouble keeping up, and that she and
Aaron would be long gone by the time BND agents, and
maybe CIA, too, converged on the Hertz office. She and
Aaron took a cab several blocks to Avis and rented a
Peugeot with Aaron's credit card under the name Eric
Putnam. If the card had been one provided by the CIA,
powerful computers would pick up his location within
an hour. But Eric Putnam was Aaron's own creation,
and the alias was unknown to the CIA. After a brief
stop at an office supply store, they were on the E19 back
to Holland. By midafternoon, they pulled into a parking
spot in front of Nederlanden Pharmacie Groep's plant
in Sliedrecht.

"Hi," Krissi said brightly, making eye contact with the
male security guard just inside the main entrance. "I'm
Deborah Knox, and this is my associate Eric Putnam.
We're with BeneluxPharma.com, software providers to
the pharmaceutical industry. I'm sorry. We don't have
an appointment, but I wanted to at least leave our card
with the head of your production department. We'll follow up with a formal meeting and present our brochures
when she or he has time. But we were in the neighborhood and just thought we'd stop by and get her or his
full name . . . correct spelling and all that." She flashed
a flirtatious smile as she handed him the business card
she had printed earlier at the office supply store. Aaron
handed his card to the guard, who was still smiling back
at Krissi, then resumed his task of discreetly examining
the security system's wiring on the doors and windows
and noting the lack of security cameras in the reception area.

"Well, the correct spelling isn't easy," the man said,
demonstrably eager to assist the very attractive woman
who, he thought, just might be interested in him. "Iranians. I can't even get them right. Let me get you the

phone directory from my office." He stood up and
stepped into a small room directly behind where he had
been sitting, and started pushing papers around the cluttered desk, looking for the list of names and numbers.
As soon as he turned his back, Aaron walked to the side
of the reception area, stood on an end table next to a
couch, and cut a wire that led though a hole in the wall,
using a tiny razor blade hidden within his key chain. A
moment later, he was back standing next to Krissi and,
like her, mentally recording the exact location of the
furniture, desks and other fixtures. In the corner of the
lobby there was a round table on which sat a picture of
Piet Stolten with black bunting draped over it.

"Here you go. I've underlined the names. Faramaz
ben Sarah. He's head of production. Oh, the formal title
is Director of Production. He isn't here today. Travels a
lot. The address is on the cover. Hey, take the directory
with you. I've got plenty."

"Thanks. By the way, while I'm at it, who is in charge
of quality control?"

"That would be Mr. Malek. . . . Daniel ben Malek,
another Iranian, but at least I can pronounce his first
name," the Dutchman said with a laugh.

"Great. I really appreciate it," Krissi said, laughing
along with the guard's effort to be humorous. "Before
we take off, do you mind if I use the ladies' room?"

"Of course not. It's down the hall to your right," he
said, pointing to one of the two corridors leading from
the lobby. "Second door on the right."

"I couldn't help but notice the photo," Aaron said,
gesturing with a nod to the corner of the room.
"Recent?"

"Yeah, just last week. It was terrible. He was the chief
of security. Worked here all his adult life . . . due to
retire in a few months. House caught on fire, and he and
his wife died in their bed. The fire department says that
their boiler leaked and faulty electrical wiring caused
sparks, setting off the fire. Funny thing is that Piet strikes
me as the kind who would have maintained his house in

perfect condition. But you never know. A real pity. He was a good man to work for."

"That's terrible. I'm sorry to hear that." Aaron paused for a moment. "Say, is the men's room down the hall, as well?" Aaron asked.

"First door on your right."

"Thanks."

The door next to the ladies' room was marked ELECTRICAL—NO ADMITTANCE. Krissi opened the door and saw the circuit breaker she was hoping to find. She quickly closed the door and entered the ladies' room.

In the men's room, Aaron opened the window, testing to see if the wire he had cut in the lobby had, in fact, shut off the alarm system and any security cameras. Provided there were no redundant silent alarms or cleverly concealed security cameras, they were in good shape. He closed the window tightly but did not lock it, used the facilities and met Krissi in the reception area. A few moments later, they were on the road. "Let's find a hotel. We need sleep," Krissi said, driving toward the port of Rotterdam.

"I opened the window in the men's room. We can enter from there tonight."

"I did the same in the ladies' room. His and her entries. Flip a coin to see whose we use tonight."

"I'm in. Your turn."

"Okay."

Coming directly from the brightly lit parking lot, Aaron and Krissi needed a moment to let their eyes adjust to the relative darkness of the ladies' room. Once their night vision was sufficient, they stepped out into the corridor and Krissi went directly to the door marked ELECTRICAL—NO ADMITTANCE, opened the door and threw the main circuit breaker. For the second time that day, the storm coming off the North Sea worked in their favor. Anyone noticing the electricity going off would blame it on the weather. They made their way silently into the reception area where they had spoken with the security guard earlier in the day, and proceeded down the hall toward the manufacturing plant, using their penlights when needed. Krissi carried her Glock, a long silencer attached, while Aaron had the Beretta 9 mm he had taken from the assassin Krissi had killed back in Istanbul. He didn't have a silencer, so Krissi would take the lead if they ran into trouble.

At the end of the hall, Krissi pushed gently against one of the double doors that separated Nederlanden's administrative offices from the plant, a steel-and-aluminum structure more than a city block square, testing whether they had successfully disabled the alarm and security cameras by cutting the electrical power. All was quiet. Inside the giant chamber was an enclosed boxlike structure with windows facing the offices that ringed the larger room.

Aaron could tell that Krissi was having trouble figuring out the inner structure. "Clean room," he whispered to her. "That's where the compounds are mixed, the pills stamped and the vials filled. Only one entry. You have to wash and put on a clean suit before you can enter. Only a few workers . . . people in production, for example, are cleared for entry." Krissi indicated that she understood. Nederlanden, like other pharmaceutical companies, had Biosafety Level-3 facilities and took every measure possible to ensure that no pollutants, not even dust particles, could contaminate the medicines.

Working their way silently in their running shoes, they reached a string of offices on the right side of the plant, each one having a clear glass window that faced the clean room. Using their penlights, they read the nameplates on each office door. The second to last office was Malek's. The last was ben Sarah's. Both were locked. Krissi removed from her pocket what would have appeared, to a casual observer, to be a Swiss Army knife, and picked Malek's lock within seconds. Aaron did the same with ben Sarah's door, using yet another device concealed in his key chain. While she looked through Malek's files, he searched ben Sarah's desk.

Suddenly, red emergency lights started flashing in the plant, one just outside ben Sarah's office. Krissi and Aaron froze, she in the doorway of one office, he inside another, afraid to trip any motion detectors that might have become activated. They could neither see nor speak to each other. At the same time, a security guard walking with a Doberman approached the manufacturing facility's double doors that Krissi and Aaron had come through only minutes earlier.

Goliath, the Doberman, became agitated, sniffing the floor and working himself into a frenzy. The dog had been taught not to bark in such situations, and remained true to its training. "What is it, boy? What is it?" The animal turned to the guard and panted excitedly, pulling on the chain in the man's hand and heading toward the plant.

From the doorway of Malek's office, Krissi saw the guard and the dog enter the plant. Krissi had a Doberman growing up in Wiesbaden and the thought of killing it didn't appeal to her. The guard bent over and unleashed the dog.

Krissi tightened the silencer to make sure it was secure and pressed the safety button on her Glock, putting it in the fire mode. She adjusted her position so that she could spring into the hallway more easily. When it became clear that the Doberman had picked up her scent, she sprang from her crouched position into Malek's doorway. Two bullets spat from the silenced weapon just as the powerful dog rushed full speed at her. Despite two shots to his wide chest, the animal still managed to leap, missing her throat with its deadly teeth only because she ducked and rolled to the ground. She turned to fire again, but the dog hit the concrete floor with a thud and a whimper and died.

Krissi pivoted toward the guard, who had pulled his weapon from his hip holster. He fumbled with the revolver, which he had only used at a pistol range, while Krissi took aim. For the first time, she noticed that the guard was the same man she had flirted with earlier in the day. At the last possible second, she adjusted her aim from his chest to his right arm and gently squeezed the trigger, sending the man to the ground with a hole in his biceps and a broken arm, his weapon *clickety-clacket*ing on the concrete floor behind him.

Aaron was out of ben Sarah's office, his Beretta ready for business, the moment he heard the silenced spits of Krissi's first two shots. As Krissi got up, he bounded past her and clubbed the guard on the head with the barrel of his 9 mm, knocking him out. "Did you find anything?" he asked Krissi.

"I got Malek's home address. Nothing else. You?"

"Nothing. Let's go."

"What about him?" she asked, motioning to the guard.

"We'll throw the motion detectors back on. When he comes to in a few minutes, he'll struggle to get up. He'll trigger the alarm and help will come." Aaron ran back to Faramaz ben Sarah's office, took a scarf he had noticed hanging on a hook and returned to the security guard and Krissi. He rapidly applied the scarf as a tourniquet to the man's upper arm. "He'll be okay," he said with a glance to Krissi.

Within minutes, Aaron and Krissi reached their car, which they parked about half a kilometer from Nederlanden's building, and drove away, she at the wheel, he studying a map they had purchased earlier that day of Sliedrecht and neighboring towns. "Go to the end of this street to a T intersection. Take a left, then a right on to what looks like a big boulevard. That road will take us to Malek's street. . . . Unless you've had enough for the night," he added, looking over to Krissi, who appeared upset. "It's three forty-five. Unless he's out of town, he's got to be home and asleep. If he wakes up, we'll see more action."

"We're here. Might as well," she said without looking at him.

"Krissi, you okay with this?"

"I think the guard back there recognized me," she

said as she slowed to turn. There were no other cars on the street, but she still used her directional signal.

"Shit. You know you could have killed him. I've seen the way you shoot. You could have put that bullet up his right nostril if you wanted to."

"I recognized him. He was just doing his job. . . . Probably working around the clock to make ends meet." She paused and glanced at Aaron, who was studying the map. "And what about you? You applied a tourniquet so he didn't bleed to death." She looked at him. With each passing day, she realized more and more that they were cut from the same cloth; trained killers yet capable of compassion, even when their own lives were at risk. For a moment, she let herself fantasize about a future together. No BND, no CIA. Just the two of them off somewhere far away, New Zealand perhaps, starting over. But it was just that—a fantasy. The reality was that she had just wounded a man, killed a dog and probably been recognized, without finding one shred of evidence related to the list from Poti, the murder of the Corleys or the connection between them. Even if they were able to break into Malek's house without being detected, the likelihood that they would find evidence of the terrorist plot was minimal, the suspect almost certainly too professional to leave clues lying around. Meanwhile, both good guys and bad guys were trying to kill them.

"It's the next street to the right," Aaron said, studying the map and reviewing the evening's events. All that risk and, unless they found something at Malek's house, they still had nothing.

"You realize we're going to have to fight our way out of this mess."

"What?" he asked, turning to her.

"We're not getting out of this without more fighting and more killing. Even if it means killing the next security guard. We may have no choice."

"Krissi, I told you I thought you did the right thing back there. I would've done the same."

"I know that. I love you for it. But we're running out

of time. When that guard comes to and gives them our description, they're going to figure it out pretty quick, and they'll be that much closer," she said as she turned off the ignition a few houses down from Malek's home.

NINETEEN

Inside Hangar C, a vast structure built during the Cold War, large enough to garage a C-17 Globemaster and hide it from Russian satellites, the Deltas and Night Stalkers lived in eleven trailers flown to Turkey four weeks earlier for Operation Shell Game. Like his troops and the two remaining Black Hawks, grounded since the fiasco at Aleppo, Martin Korda was confined to the hangar, located at the far end of the runways.

"Colonel Korda, sir. You have a call coming in on the secure line from headquarters. It's Master Sergeant Foster back in the States."

"I'll be right there." Martin pushed the chair away from his desk in the trailer he had shared with Major Kinloch.

"Sergeant, sorry to keep you waiting," Martin said, stepping into the communications van and picking up the phone.

"Sir, your wife called last night about midnight our time," Foster reported. "Wants you to give her a call at her mother's place at eight this morning, which is now, back here in the world. I'm going to patch you in through this line so you're on a secure wire." The sergeant waited a moment for the colonel to respond, but Martin said nothing as he tried to collect his thoughts. Helena never called him when he was away on a mission. Maybe it was really bad. Foster continued. "But before I do that, you should know that some CIA spooks have been around, wanting access to your phone calls

and our log, and wanting to know if your brother had
tried to contact you. I ran into your wife at Womack
Hospital's pharmacy this morning. She mentioned that
some guys had come to your home, asking pretty much
the same questions and also making inquiries about
your brother."

"My brother?" Martin asked, somewhat relieved that
Helena's call might not be about the kids but still very
concerned. "Do you know what they were asking
about him?"

"Don't know, sir . . . got no idea, really."

"Thanks, Foster. Keep me posted."

"Yes, sir. I'm gonna patch you in to your mother-in-
law's place. Wait one . . . there we have it. You both
there? Good. I'll get off, but keep the line open." Foster
hung up.

"Helena, what the heck is going on? Is everything
okay?"

"Susan is fine, but Joey's had a few bad nights. Don't
worry. Last night was actually a little better. The real
reason I left you a message is that I got a call from a
guy, says he is a retired lieutenant general in the Turkish
Army. His name is Bulot. His son, Kemal, was Aaron's
roommate at the Point. Remember the cadet we met
when Aaron brought him to your parents' place for
Christmas? Anyway, Kemal has been murdered, along
with some other Turkish special-forces soldiers Aaron
knows, and the general says that Aaron is in danger,
that he asked the general to get in touch with you. General Bulot gave me the phone numbers for his home and
office . . . somewhere near Istanbul." Martin wrote down
the numbers on a notepad as she read them.

"I remember Kemal."

"I know. I felt so badly for his parents and his
wife. . . ." Her voice trailed off and she paused for a
moment. She regained her composure. "So, a few days
ago, Aaron called. He wanted to see how you were
doing. He suspected that you might have been at
Aleppo, and he wanted to know if you were safe. He

said he had linked up with Krissi, the German girl . . .
woman—you had told me about. I invited him for
Christmas, and he said that he would bring Krissi with
him if she could make it."

"Krissi Sturm? Jesus, as far as I know he hasn't seen
her since high school. When did that happen?"

"Just a couple of weeks ago . . . I think he said they
met in California. He sounded good, although I knew
he was concerned about you. But that is part of what is
so strange. A week later, this Turkish general says that
Aaron and Krissi are in some kind of danger. . . . That
dangerous people are following them, and that Aaron
may need your help. You have to call him."

"I will. I don't like the sound of this, but I'll call him.
CIA spooks snooping around our home and Delta
Force's HQ asking about Aaron, and Kemal's father
wanting to reach me. Either Aaron's trying to get a mes-
sage to me or someone is pulling an elaborate scam.
Look, honey," he added, his mind racing, "I love you.
Tell the kids I love them, too. I'll call you in a couple
of days, but let me jump now and get Foster back on.
This is the securest line I can use to reach General
Bulot."

"Martin, wait. I love you, too."

Martin hung up and called Foster, who picked up on
the first ring. "Sergeant, please write down these numbers on a scrap of paper, not the phone log." Martin
read General Bulot's phone numbers and waited for
Foster to repeat them. "I'll stay on the horn."

Ten minutes later, Martin and General Bulot finished
their conversation. Still seated in the commo van, Martin
was deeply troubled. Bulot had accurately described
Aaron, obviously had knowledge of Krissi and knew
about Aaron's relationship with Kemal Bulot, but all
that could be an elaborate ruse. If so, the man, and
whoever he worked for, had done their homework well.
The Turk wanted to meet him in Adana, the town closest to Incirlik Air Base. No one, not even Martin's wife,
was supposed to know that he was at Incirlik, let alone

a stranger requesting a meeting. Moreover, in order to maintain operational secrecy, all the Deltas were confined to Hangar C. Even if he was convinced that the stranger was there at Aaron's behest, to meet him in Adana would be a major security breach.

"Something wrong, sir?" the communications sergeant in the commo van asked. Martin didn't hear him at first. "Everything okay, sir?" the sergeant repeated.

"Oh," Martin responded slowly, lost in thought. "I really don't know." He stood, nearly hitting his head on the door frame of the trailer, stepped out of the communications truck, and looked around the hangar. A number of the Deltas and Night Stalkers were working out in the makeshift gym they had set up. Dorne and Ryle were running on treadmills. Lieutenant Toll was working up a sweat on the Stairmaster. Several of the operators played basketball at the far end of the hangar. Galante and Cho played Ping-Pong. On the other side of the space, he saw mechanics from the 160th checking and rechecking the two remaining Black Hawks, making sure they were ready to fly on a moment's notice. In fact, despite his own inner turmoil, everything appeared normal. He cursed silently to himself, angry with the Hobson's choice he faced: Refuse to meet with the general and run the risk of not helping Aaron in what might turn out to be the struggle of his life, or if it was a hoax, meet with the man and blow security for Delta Force. And if he met Bulot and he turned out to be a terrorist or enemy agent, he'd also be putting himself in danger.

First Sergeant Trippe approached from the other side of the hangar, waving to indicate he wanted to talk to Martin. When he was close enough to him, Trippe said, "Sir, I've been talkin' to the air force security team, the guys who patrol the perimeter fences. It appears that some CIA types are very interested in your whereabouts, wanting to know if anyone has tried to contact you from the outside. The fly boys were cool. . . . Told 'em nothing. But get this. One of the suits asked the security guys if your brother had tried to reach you.

They showed the airman his picture. It's none of my business, sir, but if there's anything to talk about, or anything I can do . . . well, just let me know." Trippe and Korda went way back. Together they had been through just about every situation special-forces operators could get themselves into. The bond between them was ironclad.

"My younger brother might be in danger," Martin said to Trippe, his eyes steady on his first sergeant. "I may have to meet someone in Adana, and I may need your help to get me there."

"Going into Westfalen's facilities is crazy, Aaron. We've pushed our luck too far already, and what do we have to show for it? Nothing."

"Well, if Dr. Corley was right and the English-language capitalized letters on the list following P and QC refer to the initials of those working in those departments, then we struck out at both Midlands and Nederlanden. . . . At least with respect to the names we know. But suppose those aren't their real names. What if they are operating under false names, and the list refers to their real names?"

"Why in English and not Farsi, like the other notations on the list?"

"Because they might not be Iranians, and they might not be Jews. What about that carpet in Malek's bedroom? I'd bet money it's a Muslim prayer rug," Aaron said with more conviction than he was feeling. The break-in of Malek's home had not been easy, even though no one was home. The alarm system was very sophisticated—more so than one would expect on the home of a modestly paid, midlevel white-collar employee of Nederlanden—and could be disarmed only with the greatest of care. Still, Krissi and Aaron were able to enter and leave, rearming the system as they left. Though they were in and out without a glitch, with the exception of the rug, a dubious piece of evidence, they had come up empty-handed. No smoking guns.

"But we don't know that," Krissi said, not wanting to jump to any conclusions. "I understand that after September eleventh, a lot of Muslims in the U.S. said they were concerned about the anti-Islamic sentiment. Maybe that's why they're pretending to be Jews."

"True, but Midlands is in England, not America, and Soraya and Razavi were employed there well before 2001, just like Malek and ben Sarah at Nederlanden. If they're not Jews, then what are they hiding? And what about the two people whose families died when their houses caught on fire? Each home had faulty boilers and electrical wiring. Doesn't that seem a bit too coincidental? What if these people aren't even Iranians? Maybe the initials—if that's what they are—on the list are initials in another language? Arabic, for example."

"Okay, the two men in England claim to be Iranian Jews, and you think they're really Muslims. So they're Muslims. Try getting a conviction with that. And Malek's not Jewish, either, because there's no Jewish paraphernalia in his home, no yarmulkes, no mezuzahs, no menorah packed away for the holidays, no prayer books . . . Or at least nothing we could find. So what? Maybe he's not practicing. When's the last time you went to mass? Okay, the deaths of a person in production at Midlands and the chief of security at Nederlanden, both by fires in their homes, is suspicious but isn't conclusive of anything."

"Anyway, I'll follow my gut on this, and my gut tells me they're not Iranians and they're not Jews. . . . And I think we ought to get inside Westfalen's offices and see who is running their production and quality-control departments. It's very risky, but what else can we do?"

Krissi was silent for several minutes. "How about I call a friend of mine . . . Anna Rustiger? She and her husband live in Aachen. We used to work together at the BND. She quit when she had twins." Aaron and Krissi had just crossed the Dutch-German border at Venlo, halfway between Eindhoven, Holland, and Dusseldorf, Germany. "Aachen's not far from here . . .

about an hour. Anna still keeps up with my boss, Gerhard. I know that if I told her that I wanted to come in, she'd be willing to help. She could call Gerhard and tell him that we're at her home, unarmed, and want to talk to him in person, alone. When he gets there, we'll tell him everything, and hopefully bring the full force of the BND, and perhaps even the CIA, to bear on this investigation."

"Yeah, great," Aaron said sarcastically. "Think about what went down at the Intercontinental. What if he says he's alone but just happens to walk into your friend's house with ten agents in assault gear who have been ordered to shoot us?"

She slowed the Volvo, the third rental car they had used, to a stop at a traffic light in the small town of Venlo. They had to make a decision now. The plant where Westfalen produced the lion's share of its popular oral contraceptives was in Münster, to the northeast. Aachen was due south. "So you don't like my idea. What's yours?"

"You know the area around Aachen pretty well, don't you?" Aaron asked, apparently changing the subject. "Didn't you have a bunch of cousins from the Eifel region?"

"My aunt and uncle had a farm several miles outside Aachen, but they died. My cousins had no interest in the farm and sold it a long time ago. You would know that if you had stayed in touch," she said irritably.

He let the comment pass. They were both tense and very tired. While Krissi stopped at the traffic light, Aaron spotted a sporting goods shop across the street and watched as an elderly man cranked up the security gates and extended the awnings, getting ready for the 10:00 A.M. opening. "Pull over," he said suddenly. "Over there . . . the store with the green awnings . . . behind that blue van."

"What do you have in mind?"

"You call your friend. Tell her we'll meet her and

your boss tomorrow at nine in the morning at your aunt and uncle's old farm. We'll see if he comes alone or with the German army."

While Krissi called her friend, Aaron did his shopping. The sporting goods store had just about everything he needed, and he quickly began piling up his purchases on the counter: insulated boots; thermal underwear and socks; thick gloves; heavy flannel shirt; and green camouflage pants, jacket, and matching rain hat. "I'll also need a box of Ziploc bags." The owner, an older man who looked like someone who spent a great deal of time enjoying the outdoors, made no pretext that he was other than delighted at the quantity of high-end goods his new customer was purchasing.

"I'd like that hunting knife—the folding one—the one second to the right, closest to you," Aaron said in German, pointing to the rows of knives under the glass counter. "I need your best two-way radio set and a gun-cleaning kit. You know, rod, cloth, gunsmith's oil. Also, I'll need your best daytime binoculars and a pair of night-vision binoculars." The owner had already removed the knife from the glass case and was now listening attentively. This was by far the best sale he'd had in several months. "Zeiss, ten power if you have them . . . with recessed lenses on the daytime binoculars so the sun doesn't reflect off them. Oh yeah. I'll need batteries, too."

"Not much sun around here this time of year," the owner commented, making conversation as he pulled over a wheeled stepladder he needed to reach the radio and binoculars on the overhead shelves. "But the binoculars will last forever, if you treat them right," he added. The man took a step back from the glass counter, put his hands on his hips, pursed his lips and squinted at Aaron. "Hunter or birder?" Aaron wasn't thrilled to become the subject of the conversation, but the old man seemed harmless. "Hunter, I'd say from looking at you."

"You're right," Aaron responded warily, wondering if it was so apparent that he was a predator. "Is it so obvious?"

"Aw, I don't mean to offend. I'm a hunter myself. . . . Or rather used to be when I was younger. After all these years, I can just tell. . . . A kind of sixth sense, if you will."

Aaron studied the man, who looked eager for conversation, and decided to chat him up. "You see, a friend of mine is taking me bird-watching, so I won't be needing a weapon or ammo. She'd shoot me if she knew I killed birds." He laughed, leaning on the glass counter and closer to the elderly clerk, tapping him on the forearm to indicate that what he had just said should remain a secret between them. He had been eyeing the shotguns and rifles behind the counter and wanted one for the task he was about to undertake. But the purchase of a weapon would trigger an identity check and registration, neither of which he wanted to risk.

"Well, here you go. If you can't shoot them, at least you can look them in the eye. This is our P line in the Victory series for the daytime goggles. It's ten-power and has a range of one thousand meters. Zeiss doesn't carry a ten-power night-vision set, only five point six. But this amplifies the available light by twenty thousand times and has a range of about five hundred meters. They're the best we carry."

"Perfect. I'll take them."

"Aren't you even going to ask how much they cost?" the man asked, chuckling and curious.

"I'm trying to impress my new girlfriend. If you saw what she looks like, you'd pay any price for a pair of binoculars, believe me. Besides, I already told her I'm a birder." Aaron leaned across the counter and whispered to the old man, "To tell you the truth, I don't know shit about birds. I just want to get laid."

The elderly man laughed hard and slapped Aaron's shoulder, the male conspiracy having been sealed between them. "Well, I never heard of binoculars doing the trick," the owner said, still laughing so hard that his eyes were tearing. "Chocolates, flowers, diamonds, yes, but not binoculars. First time for everything, I guess."

"Say, perhaps you could do me a favor." Aaron leaned forward again, placing his elbows on the counter like the old man did, and lowered his voice to indicate that he had another secret. "It's not for bird-watching, and please don't tell my girlfriend, who may join us any minute, but I'm running low on ammo for my Beretta and need a couple of boxes and magazines. I target practice down in Wiesbaden, where I live. Nine millimeter."

"Do you have your permit with you?"

"No, that's the point. I lost the damn thing and have applied for a replacement, but you know the government—especially with the added security after the terrorist attacks—why, they take forever." The owner shook his head sympathetically. "Oh yeah, I'll also need a hip holster . . . right-hand, and belt."

"I'll see what I can do." He thought about it for a moment. "Just between us, right?" Aaron nodded reassuringly. "One box?"

"Two, if you can spare them . . . oh, and some empty magazines."

The old man hesitated for a moment, but then disappeared into a back room and returned with two boxes of 9 mm ammunition and four empty magazines, which he placed on the counter. "Now, listen. I'm ringing up the ammo and magazines as miscellaneous goods, so don't look for it on the receipt. If the authorities find out about this, we'd both be in trouble. Okay?" Aaron nodded somberly, holding his extended index finger to his lips. "Good. I wouldn't normally do it, but I like you. A hunter pretending to be a birder." He chuckled.

"Believe me, I can keep a secret," Aaron said, putting one box of ammo and two magazines in each jacket pocket. At that moment, a buzzer sounded behind the counter as Krissi walked in through the front door. Aaron turned to look at her and then glanced back at the owner. "That's my girlfriend. Isn't she beautiful?"

The older man watched Krissi as she approached

Aaron, who stood at the counter, planting a playful kiss on his cheek. "Damn, I wish I was young again," the owner said, mostly to himself. As Aaron and Krissi made small talk, the man rang up the purchases.

"Thanks," Aaron said as the old man handed the bags of goods across the counter. Aaron paid in cash, thanking the man again for his help with a wink as he and Krissi turned to leave.

"You're very welcome, sir," the owner said with a grin. "And I do hope the binoculars work out for you."

"What took you so long?" Aaron asked as they walked back to the rented Volvo, handing her a few bags while he toted the lion's share of his purchases.

"I decided not to use a pay phone, but to buy a new cell phone instead. There's a store down the street where you can get connected right away. We can't use our old phones. Your NSA would detect calls from those numbers instantly."

"Clever," Aaron admitted.

"I reached Anna and told her what she needed to know to set up the meeting. . . . I didn't give her all the details, of course. She put me on hold for a couple of minutes and called Gerhard. He'll meet me at nine o'clock at my aunt and uncle's old place."

"Great." The tone of Aaron's voice indicated his lack of enthusiasm for the meeting.

"And I picked up some food for later." He looked at her quizzically. "Oh, it's already in the car." He nodded approvingly as they reached the Volvo and started loading up the trunk. "But what's all this? Are you planning a camping trip?" They got into the Volvo, with Krissi back in the driver's seat. She turned on the ignition, verified that she was in first gear, and pulled away from the curb. "So what's with all the supplies?"

"I got us each a box of ammo and extra magazines. I also got us a cleaning kit so we can keep the hardware operating. The rest is for the stakeout."

"What stakeout?"

"The meeting's set for nine o'clock, right?"

"Yeah."

"Well, don't take this the wrong way, but I don't have the same level of confidence that you do in your buddy Gerhard and your long-term—no, make that short-term—prospects with the BND."

"Anna spoke directly with Gerhard. He gave her his word," she said, trying not to sound defensive. "He's coming alone and he won't be armed." She knew Aaron was right to be cautious, but on an emotional level that surprised even her, Krissi had trouble accepting that Gerhard would order her death without hearing her side of the story.

Aaron saw her ambivalence and understood. Unlike Aaron and his handler, Prebish, Krissi actually had a good relationship with her boss. "Look, the decision is probably out of his hands. He's only a division head. What happens if his superiors overrule him? I saw that happen in the army. . . . And I never did trust the people at the CIA. Now, here's the plan. If the BND is finished with you, I figure the snipers will be in place sometime during the night, which means I have to be there just after nightfall to get settled in." He looked at his watch. "In seven hours or so. I've got clothing, binoculars, two-way radios with a ten-mile range, a knife, and the Beretta we picked up back in Istanbul. I'm thinking it might be a lucky piece."

Krissi rolled her eyes. They could use some luck, but she was doubtful it would come their way. "By the way, I heard the weather report on the radio while you were shopping. The rain will continue and you can expect forty-degree weather—maybe colder—all night." Something about the plan was troubling her. She couldn't put her finger on it, but maybe the weather report would dissuade him.

"I was in the Tenth Mountain Division. I was trained for a lot worse weather than this."

"That was a long time ago. You're not in the army anymore."

"Do you know what my grandpa did at Riva Ridge in World War II? He was with F Company, Second of the Eighty-sixth Infantry, Tenth Mountain Division. Fox Company and the First of the Eighty-sixth attacked a German position in the Alps, in the cold and snow, by climbing a fifteen-hundred-foot cliff, catching the Nazi positions by surprise. A one-thousand-five-hundred-foot almost vertical ascent *in the snow! At night!* My dad was at Chau Phu on the Cambodian border during the '68 Tet Offensive. Several hundred North Vietnamese Regulars attacked seventy troops, an odd mix of Green Berets, like my dad, and Navy SEALs. The poor bastards had no chance. And by poor bastards, I mean the NVA. Within an hour of the initial attack, the special forces were counterattacking, slipping out of the razor wire perimeter behind the enemy's lines, silently slitting throats and garroting them. Those North Vietnamese who were still alive at the end of the week retreated into the jungles and abandoned the fight. I live with that tradition, Krissi. If I can't spend a night out in the cold . . . well, then I'm not worthy of being a Korda—or a Ranger."

"I repeat. You're no longer a Ranger, Aaron."

"Once a Ranger, always a Ranger. . . . And my name's still Korda. If the goons show up with snipers, I'll radio you and warn you off. And, of course, if Gerhard comes to the farmhouse without hit men, I'll let you know that, too, so you can show up for the meeting. I'm not expecting that, but hey, I've been wrong before." He reached over and gently touched her face. They had so much time to make up. He hoped she was right about Gerhard.

"But if you're right and the snipers see you? They'll have rifles with night-vision scopes, and you'll only have a handgun."

"But they won't see me. By the time they're in place, I will have burrowed into a hide site and gone deep into a field sleep. I won't be producing much heat," he added confidently.

"Field sleep? You're getting me nervous."

"Come on. This meeting was your idea. I'm just not willing to have you drive up to that farm, step out of the car and get blasted." Krissi pulled the car over to the side of the road, shifted into neutral and looked at him questioningly.

He unbuckled his seat belt and leaned over and kissed her. "This is going to be okay. We're going to get through this. Together," he added, reattaching his belt.

Krissi pressed down on the clutch, shifted into first gear and pulled back onto the road. "Anna has us set up in a house outside the village of Monschau, which is about six kilometers in the other direction from the farmhouse where I'm supposed to meet Gerhard tomorrow. The house near Monschau belongs to her cousin, who doesn't use it during the week. She promised to tell no one that we're there and I trust her."

Aaron and Krissi arrived at the remote farmhouse at a little after 1:00 P.M. They parked the vehicle in the barn to keep it out of view, just in case, and let themselves into the modest country home where they ate a hearty lunch prepared by Krissi from the food she had purchased. Immediately after lunch, Aaron fell asleep, leaving Krissi to pull guard duty.

Aaron woke at 5:30 P.M. after sleeping for nearly three hours. His feet were bare and the wooden planks of the bedroom floor felt smooth and comforting. He stepped into the living room. A light was on in the kitchen, to the rear of the house. The fireplace opened to both the living room and the kitchen. He noticed that Krissi had just put two fresh logs on the fire.

Krissi sat in the kitchen at an old oak table. She had heard him coming, and had already poured a cup of steaming coffee the way he liked it: black, no sugar. "Wow, you look ready for anything," she said in German. He was shirtless and barefoot, with a large Beretta stuffed into the waist of his jeans.

"Country living. Never know what dangerous animals might lurk around here," he joked in German and kissed her on the cheek.

"I ran our clothes through the washer and dryer. Yours are on the counter," she said, pointing to a neatly folded stack next to the refrigerator. Despite the fire, the farmhouse was chilly. He slipped on an undershirt and sweater, put on his socks and began to feel more comfortable.

"You fell asleep with your pants on. I didn't want to wake you. Change them and your undershorts, and I'll toss them in the washer." She was making a concerted effort not to discuss their plight or let her anxiety show.

Aaron looked at her. She was ravishing, her cheeks glowing in the soft, warm light of the fire. A light shone from under the wall cabinets near the sink; a pair of candles in matching brass holders flickered on the sideboard on the other side of the table. Without either of them saying a word, Krissi and Aaron knew this was the kind of weekend retreat they'd like to share someday: a cozy enclave where they could make a fire in the fireplace, read a book, watch a video, play with the kids. And make love. He wished he could spend the night with her in his arms, and her expression told him that the feeling was mutual. He would not have to convince her to call off the night's mission. But the moment was fleeting. Suddenly, the rain, driven by the storm over the North Sea, pelted heavily against the kitchen windows, bringing them both back to the harsh reality that the CIA, for whatever reason, was trying to kill Aaron, and that his task for the night was to find out if the BND really wanted Krissi dead.

"Can I make you something to eat before you go?" she asked as if he were her husband going off to his nine-to-five job at the office.

"No thanks. I won't be able to move around once I find my hide site. I shouldn't have the coffee, either, but screw it. I'll pee wherever I can."

Over coffee, the two agents on the run cleaned their weapons like a married couple polishing the family silver, she her Glock, he his Beretta. They methodically disassembled each part and wiped away every speck of dust and burnt cordite from the mechanisms, reassembling the precision-machined masterpieces of death. She finished first, sliding the barrel and letting it slam true into its receiver. A few seconds later, Aaron cocked his 9 mm briskly and let the barrel clank home. He began to fill the empty magazines with the bullets he had purchased at the sporting goods store that afternoon.

Aaron eyed Krissi's silencer resting on a hand towel on the table. "Would you consider a trade?" he asked, pointing to her Glock with his Beretta. "I wouldn't ask, but I might need the silencer," he explained matter-of-factly, sipping his coffee.

"Sure." She laughed softly. "Sharing our weapons. Kind of kinky, don't you think? What would Freud say about that?"

Aaron laughed, too, and then became more serious. He reached across the table and held her hands. "I'll see you in the morning. Promise." She slid her Glock 9 mm and silencer across the table his way, and he rapidly screwed the cylinder to the barrel. He slammed a full clip into the handle, cocked the mechanism to chamber a round and tested the weight in his hands, pointing it at the window across the kitchen. Satisfied, he verified that the weapon was in the safe mode, detached the silencer and stood. "I'd better get ready."

After dressing, Aaron strapped on his holster belt and snapped the Glock in tightly. He looked at himself in the mirror and frowned for a moment. It had been years since he was in camouflage uniform. The only thing he was missing was a helmet and greasepaint, which the sports store didn't carry. Once in the field, to make up for the greasepaint, he would have to use mud to blacken his face.

"You make a very handsome soldier," Krissi said,

standing in the passageway between the bedroom and living room. "When this is over, I want to see photos from when you were a Ranger."

"Sure. Three boxes full. When this is over, you can put them in the family album. Let's hump."

TWENTY

As Krissi drove up the narrow country road, Aaron studied the terrain and mentally noted that the lane traversed three small bridges that crossed the stream snaking its way down the valley. The stream appeared to be swollen with runoff, but it was too dark to tell. Krissi let Aaron off a little more than a kilometer northeast of the farmhouse. By reflex, they checked their watches and verified that they were in sync—6:57 P.M. It was already dark, the moon hidden by thick clouds blowing from the north. The steady but thankfully light rainfall continued.

Despite generous government subsidies, most of the small farms in this region near the Belgian border had failed, had been sold and were now being used as country retreats. It was a Wednesday night and most were vacant, their owners back in the cities, eagerly counting the days until the weekend. Aaron kissed Krissi gently on the lips, and she fought back the tears. She bade him good luck and they kissed again, more passionately this time, before he closed the passenger's-side door of the rented Volvo and disappeared silently into the darkness, carrying most of his gear in his duffel bag on his back, like a rucksack, the night-vision binoculars dangling from a strap around his neck, Krissi's Glock in his hand in a firing mode. She made a U-turn in the narrow lane and began the drive back to Anna's cousin's home, turning on the two-way radio and placing it on the seat next to her, the leather still warm from Aaron's body heat.

"Radio check," Krissi heard Aaron's voice crackle through the speaker.

She immediately picked up the apparatus. "Hear you loud and clear," she responded.

"I love you."

"I love you more."

"Prove it."

"Tomorrow. Stay in touch," she said, and heard the radio click. If things went as planned, the next time they spoke would be in the morning. By then, they would know if they were going to a meeting or continuing their lives on the run.

Aaron replaced the radio in a Ziploc bag, stuffed it back into his duffel and approached from the north through a thick briar patch and then a two-hundred-meter swath of elm, oak and spruce trees, taking time to survey the scene in front of him through his night-vision binoculars. Though unfamiliar with the terrain, with the aid of the binoculars he was able to locate a stream that ran down from the hills to the east and flowed west back toward the house where Krissi would wait for him. The undergrowth slowed his progress, but he pushed hard and made his way to the stream faster than he expected. Struggling to keep his footing, he realized too late that the last few days' rain had swollen the stream and the cold water was chest high. He reached the other side twenty meters downstream, gasping for air, and pulled himself up the slippery mud embankment, grabbing on to branches with one hand, clinging to his weapon with the other. His clothes were sopping wet and he shivered in the cold night air. He shrugged it off, with difficulty, and moved on. Finally, after traversing another thicket, he saw the outline of the farmhouse and adjoining barn. He cleaned mud off the binoculars as best he could with his wet handkerchief and focused them to the east, toward a tree line at the base of a low ridge, across what appeared to be a pasture, the animals who once grazed there long gone. He studied the tree line carefully, assuring himself that no snipers were in place.

Holding the binoculars to his chest to keep them from flopping against him, Aaron sprinted around the side of the barn, which, like the farmhouse, faced south rather than west toward the country road. The barn, which appeared to be well maintained, stood almost four stories high, with a tractor ramp leading up to the first floor, which rested on what appeared to be a firm foundation of ancient stones. Above the incline there were two levels of lofts, both closed off behind sliding wooden doors. A rope attached to a pulley hanging from a beam at the apex of the structure blew in the wind, causing the rusty mechanism to creak. Other than that, and the rope occasionally slapping the side of the barn, there was no noise or movement. The farmhouse was dark inside, the porch light off until the weekend when the owner would return.

To the east of the dwelling was a small pond, its overflow from the rain spilling over an earthen levy and down a hill toward the stream that Aaron had forded a few minutes earlier. In the optic yellow light of the night-vision binoculars, the pasture, which lay south of the house, dipped in a recession and then ascended an incline farther south, toward an abandoned barn. From that structure, a sniper would have a clear shot at the front door of the farmhouse and the short driveway leading from the country road. He calculated what snipers assigned to shoot Krissi would do when she emerged from the car at 9:00 A.M. He decided there would be a sniper in the second story of the abandoned barn south of the pasture, another in the woods on a hill east of the farmhouse just inside the tree line, and yet another, perhaps two, in the lofts of the main barn.

A trail led from the farmhouse to the abandoned barn through knee-high grass and then thick, waist-high weeds and a few taller saplings. Careful not to trample the underbrush, Aaron took the trail, crouching low, moving quickly and soundlessly. A few meters in front of the dilapidated structure, Aaron saw a rusted-out fence surrounding what appeared to be an old pigpen. Approximately thirty meters off to the side of the fenced-in area was what looked like a large compost pile of cut grass and branches, but mostly garbage. The rotting heap generated considerable heat as it decomposed, a soft glow in his night-vision binoculars. He proceeded up to the top of the ridge for a closer look. Yes, the rotting mass would provide a perfect hide site. The stench of garbage and decaying grass became stronger as he approached, which was good. Its warmth would help him preserve body heat through the night of near-freezing rain while partially masking his own thermal image. The fifteen-knot wind from the north would disperse the dangerous methane gas produced by the rot. And the location was right. The farmhouse was two hundred meters to the north. He had good visuals of the trail leading to the old barn and pigpen to his left, the front doors of the farmhouse and main barn straight ahead, and the tree line at his two o'clock. If an ambush was planned for the morning, he would know well in advance.

Aaron checked his digital watch. It was 8:06. It had taken him a little over an hour to survey the area and find his hide site. He found a bare spot in the grass off the trail and scooped a handful of mud, smearing it on his hands, face and neck, his ears covered by a wool knit cap. He emptied his bladder, mentally and physically readying himself for a long night of zero movement. He removed his gear from the duffel for use in the morning after daybreak and placed them within reach, committing their position to memory. He hoped the Ziploc bag had protected the radio from the swim in the stream and the rain, and that it still worked. He then burrowed his way in, feet first, wriggling and digging until he was almost buried in the rotting mass. Lying on his belly, with his face and arms protruding slightly from the heap, facing south, his binoculars, radio and weapon in reach, he was ready.

As a Ranger with the Tenth Mountain Division, Aaron had been trained on cross-country skis and night attacks in the frigid, unforgiving conditions at Fort Drum on the New York–Canadian border, and on training missions in Norway and Alaska. As part of his ambush training, he had been taught by an army psychologist to slow his heart rate, preserving precious warmth, lying motionless in reptilian calm, generating a minimum amount of body heat yet preserving enough to ward off hypothermia. Similarly, he had been coached in field sleep, a technique where one is half asleep, half awake, mind and body resting but alert enough to spring to action if necessary. Moreover, the field sleep would reduce his thermal image. Aaron took stock of his position. He was covered with wet, stinking garbage, but he enjoyed a commanding view of the farmhouse and its surroundings. He would be relatively warm, and he would be virtually invisible in the night-vision scopes of any enemy that might arrive during the night, unless they came up too close to him. He was grateful for the wind. If the wind were too calm, the methane gas could dull his senses and possibly kill him. At 9:25 he closed his eyes and consciously began to slow his heart rate and direct body heat inward.

Six and a half hours later, just before 4:00 A.M., Aaron saw his first sign of movement. It was not what he and Krissi had hoped for, but very much what he had expected. He retracted the two-way radio and clicked it on. Nothing happened at first. He feared that the water had ruined it. He tried again and again. On the sixth time it crackled and he heard Krissi's voice. "The meeting is off. Snipers moving into position now," he whispered into the speaker. Krissi acknowledged and told him she loved him, but he had already turned off the radio.

A Humvee-like vehicle pulled into the short gravel drive that joined the country road and the farmhouse. Five men in full combat gear jumped from the side doors, surveyed their surroundings with night-vision scopes, and moved into position, while the vehicle

backed down the drive and headed north. Two of the
soldiers walked past the main barn and the pond and
settled into the tree line, precisely where Aaron had earlier decided they would have placed one sniper, not two.
Another soldier pulled open the sliding door to the
lower level of the main barn and disappeared inside,
closing it behind him. A few moments later, the door to
the third-level loft opened a few inches, revealing one
more position that Aaron had predicted. A fourth assassin rounded the house and remained out of sight of Aaron's binoculars. Aaron guessed that the man was
guarding the northern approach on the other side of the
building, a measure of caution that told him that this
group was good, and that the BND very much wanted
Kristina Sturm dead. Finally, the fifth man trotted up
the path that Aaron had taken earlier and entered the
old barn as Aaron had anticipated. Aaron struggled hard
to control his rage. The lover in him wanted to crawl
out of his hide site and silently kill them. The Ranger
in him told him to lie low.

Aaron presumed, but was in no position to verify, that
the troops were from the Grenzschutzgruppe 9, Germany's best counterterrorism unit, its version of Delta
Force. When in the army, Aaron had been an exceptional shot with a rifle, rivaling many of the NCOs
trained as snipers. He knew that any one of the
Grenzschutzgruppe 9 operators could place a bullet in
his head from more than five hundred meters away. He
considered fleeing, but his thermal image would give him
away. He would have to wait until daylight, hopefully
after the skilled marksmen were gone. Only fifty meters
away, the fifth soldier climbed the wooden steps to the
second floor of the abandoned barn. All was silent as
the sniper settled into position. Aaron remained as still
as death, hoping that his enemy was focused on the
farmhouse and the prey rather than the compost pile.
The hit men were in place, armed and ready to take out
Krissi. It was clear to Aaron that there would be no
effort to take her alive.

Dawn filtered through the clouds, gradually turning the night into an ocean of charcoal gray, then a pale smokelike haze. A fine mist seemed to hover in the air. Aaron checked his watch—8:45.

At 8:50, a white Mercedes came down the road from the north and pulled into the gravel drive, stopping in front of the farmhouse. One man, a bodyguard, stepped out of the vehicle and stood about ten meters behind it, his jacket open. Another, the driver, stayed in the car. The vapor emissions from the exhaust told Aaron that the motor was still running.

A man wearing a suit and trench coat stepped out of the backseat and opened an umbrella, ostensibly to ward off the mist, but Aaron's experience told him it was a sign to the snipers that the kill was still on. The man appeared to be Krissi's boss. She had described him as middle-age, medium build with a paunch, with classic male-pattern balding but otherwise dark hair. The man near the Mercedes appeared to be in his midforties and was of medium height, and to Aaron looked relatively trim, the bulge of the stomach perhaps hidden by the coat. The man wore a hat, his collar raised, and Aaron could not determine the color of his hair. In all, he fit the description. *So much for Krissi's faith in her mentor,* Aaron thought bitterly.

The man with the umbrella checked his watch at 9:06, and again at 9:15. Krissi was known for her punctuality, even by German standards, but this was an extraordinary situation. They would wait for a while. At 9:40, the man spoke into a small speaker pinned to his lapel. "Come in."

The soldier in the loft of the main barn was the first to reach him, followed by the man who had been positioned on the north side of the farmhouse. The two snipers stationed in the forest appeared in the pasture. Aaron heard the creaking of the steps in the old barn to his left as the fifth would-be assassin descended and joined his comrades near the Mercedes.

The driver, a bodyguard who had remained behind

the wheel of the Mercedes, motor still running, stepped out of the vehicle and took a position at the corner of the house to provide cover while his boss and the snipers discussed the obvious. She wasn't coming. Either she had never intended to show or she had been alerted to the presence of the snipers and had left the scene.

Aaron knew that he had to act quickly. If the BND agents and the Grenzschutzgruppe 9 marksmen realized that someone had staked them out and warned Krissi away, they would fan out and search the fields and forest. He was no match for them. He had to get out of there fast. He slithered forward, struggling out of the compost pile, hidden from the view of those near the farmhouse by the waist-high weeds in front of the garbage heap. Gathering his weapon, binoculars and radio, he belly-crawled around to the back of the pile and continued to crawl toward a tree line a hundred meters to the south, keeping the compost pile between him and the German agents. When he reached the tree line he saw that a barbed wire fence was still intact, despite the farm's state of disrepair. He rolled on his back and shifted forward under the lowest wire, pushing with his heels. Once outside the fence and in the forest, he rose to his feet, crouched low and ran due south as fast as he could through the dense underbrush. Knowing that the Grenzschutzgruppe 9 commandos would soon be searching the pasture surrounding the farmhouse and that helicopters would most likely be brought in, he continued to put distance between himself and the farm, descending toward the road that he and Krissi had taken just hours before. Aaron had noted during the short drive that the road crossed the stream three times over small bridges. Within minutes, he heard the rotors of the Eurocopter 155B helicopter overhead and ducked underneath a large tree that was leaning over the stream. He had only a few inches between the trunk of the tree and the lip of the water-filled ravine, but the tree kept him from view of the chopper and the stream would be his route back to Krissi. He quickly removed the radio from the Ziploc bag inside his jacket and began to speak. "Stay inside. Keep the car inside."

"Where are you?"

"Just listen. There's at least one chopper looking for me. Cloud cover is thick and they'll have visibility problems, but they may have thermal-imaging equipment. I'm near the stream that runs down the valley. . . . The one we crossed last night. It runs in front of your friend's house. I'll meet you there," he concluded and clicked off the radio, not waiting for a reply.

Aaron zipped the plastic bag with the radio inside and put it, Krissi's Glock and ammo and his knife in his nylon bag. He tossed his jacket and the heavy binoculars into the fast-moving water. He slung the strap of his sack over his neck and shoulder and shifted the bag to his back. The helicopter passed overhead but continued an ever-widening circle away from the farmhouse. There was no way to inch into the water, so he jumped in feet first and was immediately swept downstream, the water chilling him to the bone but also reducing his thermal image. After ten minutes and after having gone through three culverts under the winding road leading to the house where Krissi was staying, he guessed he was pretty close to her. He struggled up a slippery embankment, and when reaching the top saw the house about four hundred meters away. So cold that he could hardly move, he nevertheless forced his legs to push forward as he half ran the distance.

Krissi had kept an eye out for him, focusing on the stream, hoping that he would reach her before the Eurocopter's ever-widening search would place it overhead. When she saw him, she ran to the barn, swung open the doors and started the car, everything that they carried already packed in the backseat. She intercepted him as he approached the gravel driveway that led from the road to the house. He shivered so violently that he had trouble opening the door, but managed to climb in. Krissi had the heater on full blast. They said nothing as they drove away, the only sound that of the gravel crunching underneath the tires and the chattering of Aaron's teeth.

"Get out of those wet clothes," Krissi said after they reached a secondary road about five minutes later. Aaron knew that his chances of avoiding hypothermia were vastly better without his water-soaked clothing, but given his state of fatigue, the idea of changing in the confines of the Volvo was daunting. His change of clothes was in the backseat within easy reach. Still, it was a painful struggle to turn and grab them, and even more arduous to strip and get dressed. Soon, though, the combination of dry clothing and the car's heater began to revive him. With the passing of another half hour, he was aware of his hunger and realized that it was a good sign, as was his awareness of his fatigue. He had not eaten since yesterday's lunch. He had taken a three-hour nap before going to the farmhouse and had rested somewhat in his field sleep, but had otherwise not slept in forty-eight hours. Krissi had dozed lightly during the night, prior to getting Aaron's radio signal shortly after 4:00 A.M. Both were exhausted and were reaching their limits.

"Where do we go from here?" Aaron asked.

"Christ, Aaron, those bastards were going to blow my head off," she said, not answering his question. A large tear welled in her eye and streamed down her cheek. She brushed it away angrily and quickly put her hand back on the gearshift knob. They were at war now on two fronts: against the terrorists, who were moving closer and closer to executing a plot that still remained a mystery; and with the so-called good guys, who were convinced that they had gone rogue. Either enemy would kill them, given the opportunity. "I called General Bulot right after I got your message over the two-way. We have to find a safe place to regroup and figure out our next move. Turkey was the only logical place. General Bulot trusts us. He says he still has influence within the Turkish military and he's willing to help."

"So what's the plan?"

"I asked him if there are Turkish flights—NATO flights—into Spangdahlem Air Base. It's primarily a U.S. Air Force base, but there are lots of NATO allies working there. It's near here. . . . Only a few miles. Obviously, we can't go back to Anna's cousin's house. The entire German Army will be combing the countryside looking for us. I suggest that we go to Koblenz, ditch the car and find some place to hide until we see what General Bulot can do for us. He's supposed to call me on my new cell phone sometime late tonight or tomorrow morning."

Krissi and Aaron left the Volvo in the parking lot of a large furniture store on the outskirts of town, took a bus to the center of Koblenz, changed buses and got off near a Hertz office. While Aaron tried to freshen up in the men's room and mask the lingering odor of garbage and storm water with deodorant and aftershave, Krissi rented a car, using yet another set of false passport and credit card, the last of her supply of bogus identities. Soon, they were back on the road, Aaron behind the wheel of a Peugeot 206. He headed east across the Rhine, just after passing the Koblenz Palace, and turned south on the E42 immediately on the other side of the bridge. Krissi watched the signs for a suitable small gasthaus in the hills. There was a renovated castle in the village of Marksburg that had become a major tourist attraction, and it was there, several miles into the hills beyond the castle and the rows of tour buses, that they found what they were looking for. The gasthaus was really a farmhouse with two guest rooms, and its seclusion in a small valley was perfect.

After engaging in light conversation with the white-haired widow who owned the inn, Krissi paid for two nights in advance and arranged for a snack of cold cuts, cheeses and bread to be brought to the room as soon as possible, and a full dinner in the kitchen at seven that evening. The snack had just been delivered when Aaron stepped out of the shower. He dressed quickly, and they ate voraciously. She had missed two meals; he had missed three. After eating, they took turns sleeping and keeping watch. At 6:45, Krissi woke Aaron and coaxed him out of bed with the promise of his first hot meal in forty-eight hours.

Krissi and Aaron returned to their room immediately after dinner, rotating their watch every two hours while the other slept. At 6:35 A.M., 7:35 Istanbul time, Krissi's cell phone rang during her shift. Aaron was up in an instant, fully alert. Krissi already had the apparatus to her ear. She said almost nothing as she listened to the brief instructions, while Aaron wondered what was being said on the other end.

"In Mannheim, the main street is the Kurpfalz-strasse," Krissi said when she finally spoke. "Just off that main avenue is a farmers market . . . about halfway between the Rhine and the Neckar Rivers. It's cold and raining throughout western Germany, so the open-air market will be closed. There's a pub—I don't remember the name, but it's on the northwest corner of the square. There's only one. We'll meet you outside." She clicked off the tiny cell phone, eager to keep the conversation short in case the NSA's speech-recognition systems were good enough to pick out her voice and locate her.

"What's happening?" Aaron asked excitedly.

"The general has pulled heavy strings and is coming in on a Turkish Air Force C130. It's a regularly scheduled flight. He says the Turks don't fly into Spangdahlem, which is used only for fighter jets, but they routinely fly to Ramstein Air Base at Kaiserslautern. He was calling from an airfield outside Istanbul and getting ready for takeoff in an hour or so. They land at Ramstein at two this afternoon and depart late tonight. He wants to meet us at six P.M. You heard my end of the conversation. I told him to meet us in Mannheim. I don't think we can risk getting any closer to Ramstein than that. The towns surrounding it, like Kaiserslautern, are small and filled with U.S. airmen."

"How do we get up the river to Mannheim? The autobahns and secondary—even tertiary—roads are likely to be blocked for ID checks."

Krissi thought for a moment, then brightened as she came up with a plan. "It's still early. We'll go back to Koblenz and get on a tourist boat. They still run this time of year. I think it's the best way. It'll take all day to get up to Mannheim, but hey, that's fine."

"You're a genius."

"Thanks. Do you have anything in that hidden compartment in your suitcase to change our appearance?"

"Yeah, I've got a few tricks left. But let's also see what the old lady has."

TWENTY-ONE

While the proprietor of the gasthaus was tending to her morning chores downstairs, Aaron and Krissi searched through her bedroom and bathroom upstairs. With a combination of a man's hairpiece and makeup that Aaron carried in the hidden compartment of his suitcase and some borrowed clothes and cosmetics from the unsuspecting host, the attractive young twosome transformed themselves into a nondescript, middle-age couple with graying hair, uneven complexions, tired eyes, a paunch in place of Aaron's flat stomach, and a dowdy, ill-fitting dress with matching hat for Krissi. Aaron shaved his three-day-old stubble; it didn't match his newly dyed salt-and-pepper hair. When the metamorphosis was complete and the elderly woman was puttering around in the back of the house, they quietly made their departure in their rented Peugeot, leaving her a thank-you note and enough cash to cover more than what they had taken.

Though there were roadblocks on the southbound lanes, the drive north on the E42 from Marksburg to Koblenz was unobstructed and traffic was relatively light, enabling the middle-age couple to catch the first daylong excursion up the Rhine past fabled medieval castles and picturesque mountains. Krissi parked the car near the Koblenz Palace, and they walked the short distance to the boat terminal, moving slowly on account of Aaron's heavy limp, the same feigned disability that had worked so well for him at Atatürk Airport. She held his arm to steady him, carrying a frayed shawl and worn leather handbag over her shoulder. Aaron wheeled his suitcase, in which he and Krissi had stuffed most of their clothes and their duffel bags.

The boat was half as crowded as in the summer months, making it all the easier for the couple to purchase breakfast at the snack bar onboard. The storm over the North Sea had moved on and the weather, a combination of sun and clouds with cool temperatures, was comfortable. The starboard side of the craft was tied to the pier. While most of the passengers headed for the bow of the long, narrow vessel, Aaron and Krissi found seats on the port side, away from any police that might stroll along the pier. Later, after the excursion boat left the dock, they moved to the stern, where they were, at least for the moment, alone.

Eight hours later, on schedule, the tour boat pulled alongside the quay at Mannheim and the passengers disembarked, some kind individuals letting Aaron cross the gangplank first, given his disability. Krissi pulled the suitcase with one hand and folded her free arm within Aaron's.

Aaron and Krissi took in their surroundings. The tour boat had left them off in front of the Mannheim Palace, now a museum, already closed for the day as a dull gray dusk settled over the city. A sign told them that the nearest taxi stand was on the other side of the palace gardens on Bismarckstrasse. The taxi stand was visible through the trees as they walked. A crowd of twenty or so tourists had preceded them and were already queued up for a cab. Another group of about the same size waited at a bus stop on the other side of the street.

As they rounded a corner in the path, Krissi suddenly squeezed Aaron's arm but made no other outward demonstration of her skyrocketing anxiety. He continued to limp along, having picked up her cue and coming to the same conclusion. There was no place to run. At the intersection of the gravel path and the concrete sidewalk lining Bismarckstrasse, two German national police officers were scanning the passengers, their green-and-white squad car off to the side where a third officer, with a submachine gun, stood ready to back them up if need be. A number of passengers greeted the officers pleasantly, but most just kept walking. As he walked past, Aaron said *"Guten abend"* to one of the men in uniform, who nodded, as did Krissi. A few critical moments later, after waiting in a short taxi line, the couple got into the rear of a cab as quickly as they dared. "The farmers market, in the square off Kurpfalzstrasse, please," Krissi instructed the driver, her pulse still racing, as he pulled away from the curb.

The farmers market was deserted; the one-half-square block of smooth asphalt, surrounded by towering sycamores, had been swept clean, the tarps of the aluminum-poled booths rolled back and fastened down by the vendors, who would return with their goods in the early morning. Aaron and Krissi got off on the main avenue and walked the short distance across the *marketplatz* to the pub, located at a T intersection, its quaint entryway facing the corner of the square, the side exit on a dark, narrow, one-way street heading west. General Bulot was there first, waiting on the passenger's side of an olive drab military sedan. He watched as a man and woman approached the vehicle, not actually recognizing them until Aaron greeted him in Turkish.

"Come quickly," he said, hoisting Aaron's suitcase into the trunk with one hand and shutting it with the other. Krissi and Aaron sat in the backseat. The general took the front passenger's seat. The Turkish Air Force sergeant who served as his driver walked around to the front end of the car and removed a plastic cover, exposing a license-plate-size plaque bearing three stars, indicating that a lieutenant general was onboard. Back behind the wheel, the sergeant stored the cover under his seat and pulled the sedan away from the curb. "Courtesy of the Turkish Air Force," Bulot explained proudly, turning to his passengers. "They still treat me like a general," he said with a laugh. It was obvious to Aaron and Krissi that Bulot was enjoying the excitement, once again the commander in charge of an important mission.

"And it will help us get to where we're going a lot faster," Aaron added, unsure how much to say in front of the driver.

The sedan headed west up a one-way street, turned right twice, then turned right again on Kurpfalzstrasse, then drove west toward the Rhine. Ramstein Air Base, the busiest NATO airfield in Europe, was located on the other side of the river in Kaiserslautern, a thirty- to forty-minute drive in light traffic from Mannheim. At the gate, two U.S. airmen saluted as the three-star general's car slowed down without coming to a stop and then snaked its way through the streets of the sprawling air base until it reached a remote section of the tarmac where a Turkish Air Force C130 waited. The matte gray plane was illuminated by the headlights of trucks and forklifts and from the bright lights inside the fuselage, shooting out from the open cargo ramp. Outside, uniformed men hurried to load pallets from the trucks onto the aircraft. They were too occupied with their own work to notice the passengers from the three-star general's sedan race up the retractable staircase to the front end of the fuselage, where several regular economy-class seats were fitted to the floor of the cargo bay. Large net-covered pallets loaded with military gear for the Turkish Air Force were fastened firmly behind the seats. A senior noncommissioned officer, the loadmaster, checked the palletized gear. Satisfied, he pressed a red button on a side panel and the rear ramp began to rise, its engine humming rhythmically until the heavy door closed, and then through his mike advised the pilots that the cargo bay was secure.

"We leave in ten minutes, at nineteen hours twenty," General Bulot informed Krissi and Aaron as they were seated and buckled themselves in. "Sorry, folks, no movies, no dinner, just coffee, although it is Turkish coffee," he added with a smile. "I am told that there may be two or three Turkish officers joining us on the flight back to

Istanbul." He gestured to the empty seats. "They won't ask questions or even talk to you. Don't take it personally. They've been told to keep to themselves. Likewise, I suggest that you not talk to them, particularly in Turkish, Aaron. There's no need to draw attention."

A few minutes before liftoff, Aaron and Krissi settled in for the flight, grateful for a chance to rest, unsure when the next opportunity would be. Three men in civvies, in their late twenties, with identical crew cuts, boarded and buckled in behind Krissi and Aaron, without so much as glancing their way. The loadmaster closed the passenger port and locked it firmly in place, while the ground crew removed the staircase. Instantly, four Allison turboprops, each with 4,600 pounds of thrust, began to rotate, filling the fuselage with the roar of 18,400 pounds of thrust, pushing the C130 forward toward the runway. Pausing briefly at the foot of the runway, the pilot revved the four engines to full power and released the brakes. The craft shot forward and 2,300 feet later lifted into German airspace, immediately retracting its landing gear. Aaron looked at Krissi and squeezed her hand gently, breathing a sigh of relief. She exhaled loudly through pursed lips. They looked over to the general, who flashed a knowing grin.

Faramaz ben Sarah, Fauad Al-Metar to his colleagues back in Iraq before they moved the laboratories to the United States and Europe, was distraught. He hadn't slept much in weeks, and the headaches had come back. The news that Aaron and Krissi had interviewed his comrades at Midlands, followed by their showing up at Nederlanden's Sliedrecht facility, where Krissi was identified by the wounded security guard, told him that the man who first appeared in Poti and then in Damascus and Istanbul was closing in on him fast. He had briefly considered shutting down the operation earlier than planned and returning to the Middle East. In truth, the bulk of the work was already done. Most of the poisoned pharmaceuticals had shipped out and were making their way to the unsuspecting public. But a careful listening of police radio traffic told him that Korda and the German woman, not him, were the ones wanted by the police, and there was still work to do.

He cut short his trip to New Jersey, where he had confirmed that Nasreen and Saba had made excellent progress at National Pharma and had given them their final instructions—shepherd the last batches of lethal pharmaceuticals out the door and into the American and Canadian stream of commerce, destroy any evidence and then head to the United Arab Emirates or Yemen, where safe houses awaited them. Like Asher and Laya at Midlands Chemicals in England, Nasreen and Saba had nearly finished; it was only a question of a few days.

Operation Lethal Agent was a costly project. From the outset, recruiting qualified operatives, executing the plan, holding the cells together, policing the network and purging it of threats had been very expensive. It had necessitated constant travel, which in turn had required multiple false passports and credit cards for Faramaz and his most trusted operatives, all of which was purchased dearly on the black market. The cost of the Biosafety Level-4 laboratories in Belleville and Mechelen, the processing of botulinum cultures and replicating them in large quantities had required several tens of millions of dollars, much more than initially budgeted.

Finally, now that the attack on the West was about to be launched, certain equipment in the labs would have to be destroyed, and tickets for the many flights, trains and boats home had to be purchased, and not with credit cards. It was always more difficult to deny involvement when there was a paper trail, and it was worth the effort to minimize it. He needed $170,000 in cash, and he needed it fast, which meant he had to return to Poti and tap into the dwindling proceeds of the heroin trade.

Aaron woke because of the whine of the C130's landing gear lowering into position, followed by a *clunk* as the wheel shafts were locked in place. Moments later, rubber touched tarmac at the Turkish air base in the northwestern suburbs of Istanbul. The plane shuddered as the pilot applied the brakes and feathered the turbo-props with a deafening *whoosh*. The plane came to a stop at one third the distance of the long runway and veered left to a taxiway that led to a cargo terminal. It was the middle of the night, and the ground crew was limited to those necessary to bring the plane safely to a stop. The C130 would be unloaded by the morning shift. An army sedan was parked near the open doors to the hangar, its driver waking from a nap behind the wheel when the aircraft approached. The Turkish officers de-planed first. General Bulot, Krissi and Aaron followed them. The general walked purposefully toward the wait-ing sedan, and the driver started the vehicle and popped open the trunk. Bulot sat up front, while Krissi slid into the backseat. Aaron tossed his suitcase into the trunk and slammed it shut before joining Krissi in the back. No one spoke except the general, who instructed the driver how to get to his home in Bebek.

It was 3:15 A.M. when they reached Bulot's home. Having slept on the plane and filled with excitement to have escaped from Germany, no one could sleep, so they sat at the kitchen table, drinking tea and eating sweet cakes that Mrs. Bulot had prepared. She had waited up and joined them in the kitchen, warmly welcoming Aaron and Krissi. Now that the greetings were over and they were finally out of earshot of strangers, it was time to talk.

The general began. "I spoke to Martin, explaining that you are in danger and asking to meet him in Adana, near Incirlik. I'm not sure he believed me. I mentioned Krissi, as you suggested, Aaron. Still, he seemed suspi-cious. I may have misread him, but my instinct tells me that even if he shows up, he may still have doubts. Aaron, I think you may have to go to Adana and talk to him."

Aaron's eyes fixed on Krissi's. There was no other way. "You have to go with General Bulot to Adana,"

Aaron said, watching for her reaction. He had thought it over during the flight, and he knew he was right. "Look, the two of you have to get to Martin. I can't go. The CIA will have him covered. They're looking for me, and if I get anywhere near him, they might kill both of us. They don't know you, sir," Aaron said, looking at General Bulot. "And if we play it right, the two of you might be able to pull it off."

Krissi and General Bulot looked at one another. What Aaron said made a certain amount of sense, but they knew there was more to the plan. "And while we're meeting with Martin, what are you going to do?" Krissi asked.

"I'm going to Poti."

"Oh, Aaron! There has to be another way," Krissi exclaimed. She couldn't bear the thought of him in Poti by himself, without any backup. "I'll go with you," she offered.

"I'm the only one who can go, and I have to do it alone." She started to object, but he cut her off as gently as he could. "Listen," he said, almost pleadingly, wanting Krissi to understand and agree with his decision. "The terrorists are up to something terrible. . . . We believe they're sabotaging our pharmaceuticals. They seem to be pretty far along. If they've gotten their hands on the right chemical or biological agents in sufficient quantities, the results will be unprecedented. And they know that you and I are on to them."

"Okay. So they know about us. What does that have to do with you going back to Poti alone?" Krissi asked.

"They've got to be in a real big hurry at this point. Depending on how far along they are, they might be pulling up stakes any day."

"But where's the proof? We still can't prove anything," Krissi said, beginning to realize that she wasn't going to change his mind.

"Exactly. We have to get some evidence. And my gut tells me it all goes back to Poti. The faster I can get there, the better. Look at what we have so far. Men

purported to be Iranians running a heroin operation. . . .
Like those who attacked us outside the hotel. But in a
crisis these men apparently revert to their native tongue,
which is Arabic. People have infiltrated two major pharmaceutical companies. . . . Men and women who say
they are Iranian Jews, but aren't Jewish and probably
aren't Iranian. They're almost certainly trying to avoid
any Arabic profiling that the western governments are
conducting. Pretending to be Iranian Jews is a good
cover. No one would think twice about hiring them.
Look, we also know that people at Midlands and Nederlanden who were probably suspicious of them ended up
dying from fires in their homes."

"But we don't have enough to go public with this, and
the CIA and the BND want to kill us, not listen to us,"
Krissi said, no longer challenging Aaron but trying to
work through the puzzle with him. She explained to
General Bulot what had happened at the farmhouse.
General Bulot translated from English to Turkish for his
wife, who simply nodded and looked at Aaron.

Aaron briefed General and Mrs. Bulot on what they
had learned in England and Holland. "Yeah, so these
so-called Iranian Jews are in key positions in production
and quality control at both Midlands and Nederlanden.
Midlands produces albuterol. Remember the list from
Poti," he said, reaching into his wallet for his copy and
putting it on the table in front of him. "Dr. Corley's
wife, a *real* Iranian Jew, translated it as Albert Breathing, perhaps a reference to albuterol. Consider Nederlanden. The Corleys knew the code had something to
do with vaccines. Nederlanden manufactures DTP and
MMR. And if we're right about the list, the terrorists
have also insinuated themselves inside the production
and quality-control arms of National and Westfalen. . . .
And, well, we don't know . . . there could be more lists."

"How does the heroin traffic fit in?" the general
asked.

"They need cash," Krissi offered, "and the drug
money finances their operations. Because it's all cash,

no paper trail leads back to the terrorists. No checks, no wire transfers, no accounts."

"And it would take a lot of money—cash—to fund a plot so large in scope," General Bulot reasoned. "I suppose, depending on how big the operations in Poti are, there might be plenty of cash to fund a terror plot."

"Which is why I've got to go to Poti. We've got to figure out what they're up to. I need to capture one of them and make him talk, or steal documents, if any, that shed light on this."

"You'll need backup. Can't you wait for Martin?"

"No."

"Why not?"

"We don't have time. They've made the connection between me and the incident at Poti, my presence in Damascus, the fight at the airport, the shoot-out at the Intercontinental, our showing up at two pharmaceutical companies where they're present. Think about it. . . . They've been planning this for who knows how long, and here we come along, threatening their operation. It's just a question of time for them, unless they kill us. But they haven't been able to get us yet. So what do they do? They step up operations and rush to unleash their plot before we can stop them. I think that's what they're doing right now." Aaron paused to let the general translate for his wife.

"Look, from what we know—the limited information we have—ben Sarah and Malek have been at Nederlanden since 1999. The two—what are their names? . . . Soraya and Razavi—at Midlands have been there for a while, as well. They've got to be ready . . . or close. How much toxic albuterol did they produce, and how much can they quickly dump in the marketplace, knowing that we're on their trail? How many prescriptions would be filled in the United States alone with one day's shipment of tainted insulin? Add the vaccines to that, the birth control pills, and whatever pharmaceuticals we don't know about. Think about it. Martin's son—my nephew, Joey—takes albuterol. Do we contact Helena and tell her to have the doctor switch to something else? Okay, we can try that. But who the hell knows what else the bastards are doing? Maybe they've poisoned the alternative products. Look," he said, pausing, choking on his words, "we lost Maggie seventeen years ago from a reaction to a contaminated medicine. As horrible as that was, it was an accident. What the terrorists are doing is deliberate, and tens of thousands—maybe hundreds of thousands—of kids and adults will die. Tell that to my brother. . . . And tell him I'll see him in Poti."

TWENTY-TWO

Helena Korda's parents' home was in Fayetteville, North Carolina. When her father retired from the army, her parents had decided to settle near Fort Bragg. Helena's mother had just put a load of laundry in the washing machine in the basement and was coming back upstairs to start breakfast when the phone rang. She hurried up the few remaining steps to get the call before the recorded message came on.

"Mrs. Wentworth, my name is Krissi Sturm. I don't have a long time to talk to you, but this is a message for your daughter, Helena. It's about her husband, Martin. I assure you this is not a prank. Please ask Helena to call Martin, and tell him to call General Bulot."

"What is this about?" Helena's mother asked, her voice revealing her alarm.

Krissi sensed the woman's hesitancy. "Please, I'm just asking that Helena call Martin from a secure line, and tell him to call General Bulot. I can't call your daughter directly, and you shouldn't discuss this with her over the phone, either. Helena's phone lines are probably being tapped. Mrs. Wentworth, just tell her to call Martin. It is a matter of life and death. Tell Helena that Aaron is in danger. He needs Martin's help. General Bulot will explain. Good-bye. I have to go."

Mrs. Wentworth knew that Helena and the kids were scheduled for an early appointment with a pediatrician at Womack Hospital on Fort Bragg. If she hurried, she could meet them there and talk to Helena without using the phones. Ten minutes later, she walked into the garage and started the car, leaving the laundry and breakfast behind.

Helena Korda sat in the crowded waiting room. Joey and Susie, like most of the other youngsters present, were engrossed in the cartoons playing on a large TV mounted to the wall. Joey had been somewhat highstrung, probably from the albuterol, and Helena was grateful for the relative calm. She picked up last week's *People* magazine, hoping to lose herself in celebrity gossip. Helena looked up to check on the children and was surprised when she saw her mother crossing the room, wearing a worried expression. "Mom, what's going on?"

Helena's mother sat down next to her and moved close enough to whisper. "Honey, a woman named Krissi Sturm called me this morning." She glanced around her to make sure no one was listening. "She said you should get in touch with Martin and have him call General Bulot. . . . Or something like that. She told me to tell you in person, that your phone may be tapped. According to her, it's a matter of life and death."

"Oh, my God," Helena said, her eyes filling with tears. She looked at her watch. It was already 5:15 P.M. in Turkey.

"Joseph Korda," the receptionist announced, indicating that the doctor was ready to see him. "Joseph Korda," she repeated louder than the first time. Helena glanced at her watch, dabbed her eyes with a tissue, and walked up quickly to the window. Her mother realized what she was doing and started to round up the kids.

"I'm sorry. Something has come up. We have to leave. I'll call to reschedule." She hurriedly put on her coat, and then seeing that her mother had the kids waiting by the door with their jackets on, ushered all of them out the door.

"Mom, leave your car here in the lot," Helena said. "Come with us so you can watch the kids in the car while I go inside."

"Okay. Okay. But where are you going?"

"To the South Post . . . to Delta Force's headquarters . . . to a secure phone."

Minutes later, Helena pulled into a lot in front of a nondescript building. Contrary to army custom, there were no signs or other markings indicating which unit was housed inside. Outside, two security guards, retired Deltas, checked Helena's ID, even though they knew who she was.

The staff sergeant on duty saw Mrs. Korda enter the room and approach him. He stood immediately, showing his respect for her as the wife of a ranking Delta Force officer. "Good morning, Mrs. Korda. What can I do for you?"

"I need to talk to the communications sergeant on duty. I have a family emergency and I need to contact my husband. It can't wait until he calls me."

"Come this way, please," he said crisply, and led her to the rear of the building.

Foster, the communications sergeant on duty, rose when Helena entered, setting aside *Soldier* magazine, which he had been reading between calls. "Hi, Mrs. Korda. I was on duty the other day when your husband called. What can I do for you?"

"I need to reach him again. Sorry for the inconvenience. I know the rules. . . ." she began to apologize, but he cut her off.

"Not a problem, ma'am." Foster sat down at his keyboard, slipped on his headset and tapped in a few numbers. Almost instantly, a voice from the communications van, parked inside Hangar C at Incirlik Air Base, responded. "I have a priority message for Lieutenant Colonel Korda."

"Roger that. Hold one," the noncommissioned officer said, dispatching a runner to summon Colonel Korda to the phone. "Hey," one sergeant asked another, "while we're waiting, let me ask you something. You guys got CIA types snooping around there?"

"Lots of 'em. Sounds like you got 'em there, too."

"Yup. All over the place. Okay, here's the colonel,"

he said, jumping off the call as Martin came bounding into the van.

"Korda here," Foster heard on the other end of the satellite uplink, so secure that even the NSA could not decipher Delta Force's conversations.

"Sir, I have your wife here. Hold one." Martin's heart started pounding wildly. He had been trained to control his emotions and generally was quite good at it, but he had recently spoken to Helena, and he knew she wouldn't be contacting him unless something was seriously wrong. "Martin, the kids are fine . . . just the usual. They're outside in the car with my mom." She then explained the message Krissi had left with her mother. "Honey, what do you make of this?"

"Christ. Okay. Let's back up. I spoke with the general after you and I talked a few days ago, and I wasn't convinced. . . . I mean, I wasn't persuaded to meet with him. It just seemed . . . well, too risky under the circumstances. He no doubt picked up on that. General Bulot may be trying to help him. I've got to call Aaron." He decided not to tell her that CIA agents were snooping around Incirlik, trying to find out about the two Korda brothers.

"Why are our phones being bugged by the CIA?"

"Who said anything about the CIA?"

"Foster and whoever is in your commo van. I heard them talking," she added, looking at the Delta operator seated in front of her. He cringed. She hoped she hadn't gotten him in trouble.

"Truth is, darling, I don't know. But I'm going to find out. I love you, honey. Tell the kids I love them. Please put Foster back on the wire."

"I will. I love you, too," she said and handed the headset to the sergeant.

Martin fumbled through his wallet, retrieving the scrap of paper on which he had written General Bulot's home and office phone numbers. "Foster, I need the following number. Patch me through now."

"That's a rog, sir." Foster tapped his keyboard. Martin heard a man's voice answer the phone. "General Bulot, I have Lieutenant Colonel Korda on the line for you," Foster announced.

"Yes, thank you. Colonel Korda, is that you?" General Bulot asked, his voice deep and resonant, his Turkish accent strong.

"General Bulot. Someone purporting to be Kristina Sturm called my mother-in-law this morning, Fort Bragg time, and said there is a life-and-death situation regarding my brother. If Kristina is there, please put her on the line."

Bulot said nothing, but handed the phone to Krissi. "Martin, this is Krissi. I know this is strange for me to resurface after so many years, but it *is* me, and Aaron *is* in danger. I can't discuss it now, but he—we—need your help."

"How do I know you're Krissi Sturm?"

Krissi took a breath and decided to go for broke. "When Maggie died . . . after the funeral, Aaron hid out in his bedroom and cried for days. He broke two fingers when he slammed his fist into his bedroom wall. Your mom told me that, since he and I didn't talk after Maggie's death, not until three weeks ago when we met again. Your mom has a scar on the palm of her left hand. She got it picking up glass from a mirror you broke with your fist. You probably still have a scar or two from that."

She sounded so credible. But what if this was part of the setup? Martin looked at the thin white lines across the knuckles on his right hand. "How did the two of you get back together after all these years?"

"Aaron was at a pharmaceutical conference for Heller and Clarke. I was there on behalf of a German company. The rest is a long story. I'll tell you about it later. Martin, Aaron and I have discovered something that affects the security of all of us. I can't talk about it on the phone, but I'll explain when we meet. Our governments

think that Aaron and I have become rogue agents and
they're trying to kill us. And the real enemy, what I
can't talk about until we meet, they're after us, too."

"Okay, I believe you. How and where?"

"I'll put the general on," she said, handing the phone
to him, nodding to Bulot, indicating that Martin was willing to meet.

"Colonel Korda, are you familiar with Adana?"

"No, not at all. I've never been there," he answered,
pointedly not disclosing that he was actually stationed
near the Turkish city.

"In the town, on the eastern bank of the Seyhan
River, there is a military hospital. You take the D-
400 . . . the big highway from Incirlik. Just before the
Girne Bridge, take the Mezbaha Street exit. . . . It runs
along the river. At the bottom of the ramp, turn left.
The military hospital is only a kilometer away, right after
you pass the civilian hospital. Turn right, and you'll
come to the freight dock. Tomorrow at seventeen hundred hours. Krissi and I will be there."

Moments later, after General Bulot had put down the
phone, Krissi said, "That went well."

"Yes, I thought so. His love for his brother is strong."
General Bulot was silent for several minutes. He poured
himself another glass of sweet tea. He picked up the pot,
which had been sitting on a trivet on the kitchen table,
and raised it in Krissi's direction to see if she wanted
some. She declined. "And now," the general said pen-
sively, "the question is that even with his help, what can
four people do if there's a firefight in Poti . . . if things
go bad?" Without any discussion, Bulot was letting her
know that to help Aaron, he was willing to go to the
place where his son had been brutally slain. She smiled
at him gratefully. "Aaron, Hasan, Yusuf and Naim took
on a much larger group, but they had the element of
surprise to their advantage," he continued. "I doubt the
terrorists will make that mistake again. They will be on
full alert and will be ready for any signs of attack. Alone,

Aaron has a chance to slip through their lines, but a larger force would most likely be detected."

"What are you thinking?"

"That I should make a phone call . . . and cash in some favors."

"We won't be able to use your home phone much longer. They must have figured out the connection between Aaron and Kemal. They don't know that you got us out of Germany or that we're here, but it's only a question of time before they come around and start asking questions."

"My wife will tell them nothing."

"I know." In the short time she had known the general's wife, Krissi had developed a tremendous respect for her. She had no doubt that Mrs. Bulot would stall the authorities convincingly, but ultimately they would figure it out. "When do we leave for the military air base?"

"In forty-five minutes."

"Good. I'm going to call a Frenchman I met recently, who has excellent political connections. I'll tell him about the list. . . . What the terrorists are up to, and what we're trying to do. Maybe he can help somehow. I'll make the call just before we leave. The NSA may pick up on my voice and locate the call, but we'll be long gone by then."

"Let's go to the post office near the university. I'll drive and wait outside while you call, then you watch the car and I'll phone my friend."

Lieutenant Colonel Korda and First Sergeant Trippe paced along the wall of Hangar C, talking in hushed tones, the officer explaining to his top the problem that faced him.

"Sir, if you want to get off this base, with the air force and CIA lookin' on, and go to a Turkish military hospital in Adana without being detected, I can think of only one way."

"Go ahead."

"Cho and Ryle are in charge of gettin' the blood we've been donatin' to the military hospital in town. The air force types come around and take it in. Of course, Cho and Ryle haven't left Incirlik, but hey, there's always a first. They can 'borrow' the fly boys' vehicle and put you in the back." He smiled expectantly, hoping his senior officer would like his plan. "You know, sir . . . like you're fond of sayin', 'Make the rules, break the rules.' "

"How long can you get away with the hijack?"

"Well, I figure that if we get enough people to line up that morning, round the time the fly boys usually arrive, then we can keep 'em busy for quite a while. How much time do you need at the hospital?"

"Don't know for sure. Maybe an hour. Perhaps more."

"Okay, so it takes thirty minutes to get from here to the hospital, assumin' there's some traffic. Two—maybe two and a half—hours round trip, tops. Like I said, if enough of us line up . . . and we go slow, it might give you enough time. That is, as long as the fly boys don't notice that their Humvees are gone."

"But what if they do? They might step outside for something. Then what?"

"I don't know. Whack 'em upside the head? Drug 'em?" Trippe chuckled for a moment, stopping himself when he realized that Martin was not laughing. "Okay, sorry, sir . . . but there has to be a way. . . ."

As Trippe stood there, rethinking his proposal, Martin paced back and forth, rubbing his index finger on his upper lip as was his habit when lost in thought. After a full minute or so, Martin stopped pacing and looked at Trippe, nodding his head up and down slowly, a smile finally breaking through his tension. "Sir?"

"I think I got it. We bring them into the plot. . . . Well, sort of. We simply tell them that we have to get off base. . . . And we need to borrow their Humvees. We can just make it up, tell them we need to make contact with Turk special-forces troops—or something like that—and that we need them to help us do it in complete secrecy. Cho and Ryle are good bullshitters. It'll work."

"Yes, sir. Out-of-the-box thinking, and between me and you, sir, it's a whole lot easier than knocking 'em out. We're scheduled to give blood tomorrow morning, but I think I can move it up to this afternoon."

"Do it. Tell everyone we're stepping it up a day. . . . Say we have a drill, or whatever, tomorrow morning. Make sure everyone's onboard with the change. I need to be on the freight dock of the hospital at seventeen hundred hours sharp today."

"Roger that, sir."

TWENTY-THREE

The Turkish Air Force plane descended rapidly over Adana airport, bounced twice on the tarmac and then glided to a near stop halfway down the runway, veering off to the taxiway at the last moment. A Turkish Army sedan was parked near a cluster of single- and twin-engine planes on the opposite side of the field from the busy commercial terminals. A senior noncommissioned officer stood at attention by the passenger's-side rear door, ready to carry out his instructions to ferry retired General Bulot to the military hospital on the other side of town.

Krissi was relieved to be on the ground, but was also anxious about the meeting with Martin. She had not seen him since he had taken emergency leave from West Point to attend Maggie's funeral. Martin had been openly skeptical of the general during their two brief phone calls. His tone with her had been cold initially, and was only barely cordial at the end of the conversation when he agreed to meet. Krissi understood his reticence. But Krissi had no doubt that Martin would show up. The ties between the two Kordas were strong. She also fully expected that he would bring with him a small cadre of fully armed Delta Force operators ready to drop her and the general upon even the suspicion of foul play. She had no choice, but she didn't feel comfortable with what might come next.

"Sir, we're good to go. I've lined up two Humvees that they normally use to take the blood donations to the hospital, except this time I'll be driving," First Sergeant Trippe said, giving his colonel the thumbs-up. "The fly boys are onboard. They know that we're going to borrow their vehicles while they're here inside the hangar takin' blood. I told 'em we had a need to go into Adana, for reasons I couldn't explain, and they had no problem with that. It'll cost me a few favors, but they're good people," he added with a smile.

"Top, how are you going to run this?" Lieutenant Colonel Korda asked respectfully, knowing that his first sergeant would have thought of everything, but wanting to be in on the plan.

"The airmen got us an empty refrigerator box from the BX. It goes in the ass end of the lead Humvee. That's for you, sir. You go in the box. I drive. Galante rides shotgun with his carbine. Cho and Metz will be watching over you in the rear, each packing a SAW. Crocker, Juarez, Ryle and McCarthy will follow in the other Humvee. The guys who normally make this run have drawn me a map of the area around the freight dock, behind the hospital. From Mezbaha Street there's a ramp leading round back. After we pull off the road, the second Humvee'll block off the entrance to the ramp, just to make sure no one tries to follow us in. If the spooks try to stop us or follow us, we'll persuade 'em that it's a damn bad idea. If they resist, it'll be at their own risk."

"I don't want to sound paranoid, Top, but CIA agents can get very serious very fast. What if they have helo-mounted snipers, or even Hellfire missiles mounted on a Predator drone? Don't forget, they have guys like us working for them."

"Got it covered, sir," Trippe said with a sly grin. "Spider One is good to go. The Night Stalkers and Deltas are ready to lift off and provide air support the moment we request backup." Martin looked at Trippe appreciatively. "Any time, sir."

Martin checked his watch. "If we're going to get there by seventeen hundred hours, we'd better get moving."

As if on cue, the doors to Hangar C began to slide open and two U.S. Air Force Humvees rolled in, driven by Master Sergeant Bob Crocker and Sergeant Jimmy Cho.

"Yes, sir," First Sergeant Trippe said, pleased with the timing of his men's arrival.

Martin opened the rear doors of the first Humvee and saw the empty carton. "Never thought I'd have to hide in a Maytag box," he said. "Kind of thing my kids love to play with."

"Don't I know. Forget about the stuff inside, just give my kids the box." Trippe smiled and shook his head. "Oh yeah, we reinforced the bottom with plywood so that when we carry the carton into the hospital, you don't fall through. That wouldn't be too cool."

Martin and Trippe shared a laugh, amused with the visual image of Martin's cover being blown by his falling out of a Maytag refrigerator box onto the freight dock, with CIA helicopters circling above.

Martin patted his .45 automatic in his hip holster, slid his carbine into the box and climbed in. Juarez and McCarthy followed Lieutenant Colonel Korda into the Humvee, one on each side in the space between the box and the side of the vehicle. At 1625 hours, the two-vehicle convoy exited Hangar C and headed out. After a short drive across the base, Trippe slowed as he approached the main gate, Crocker following him closely. Two air force security personnel, who had been alerted to the fact that army troops would be leaving the base in two air force Humvees, stepped back to let them pass, but several men in suits stepped forward, flashing their CIA ID cards.

"We are authorized to search your vehicles, by order of the Director of Central Intelligence. No members of Delta Force are allowed off base, or to establish contact with any nonmilitary persons."

Trippe slowly rolled down his window and leaned out, as if he might be ordering a burger at a drive-through restaurant. "What is that you gentlemen want?" he asked, rapidly identifying four agents near the checkpoint and three across the street just outside the compound. He turned toward Galante and nodded almost imperceptibly. The CIA agent repeated his demand word for word.

"Now, let me get this straight," First Sergeant Trippe began, exaggerating his Tennessee accent, "the las' time I checked, my commander reports to USASOC, who reports to SOCOM, who reports to the SECDEF, who reports to the President of the United States himself. Why don't I see the DCI in my chain of command?" he asked sarcastically.

"I warn you, we are authorized. . . ."

"Get lost," Trippe said, cutting him off and giving the agreed-upon code to Galante and the others. Galante repeated it softly into his mouthpiece, passing the message to those in the rear Humvee. Galante stepped out the passenger's-side door, while Juarez and McCarthy appeared from the rear. Other Deltas did the same from the second vehicle. Within seconds, the CIA agents found themselves facing three M249 machine guns and an equal number of M4A1 assault carbines and CAR-15s equipped with grenade launchers. Two of the CIA agents, both young and relatively new to the agency, had begun to draw their 9 mm automatics, while the more experienced agents knew better and kept their hands to their sides in plain view. The two novices holstered their weapons reluctantly, unsure what to do next.

"Now, let me make this clear," Trippe said. "We're goin' for a drive, and we don't expect to be followed. This here is Delta Force business." He stared at the lead agent, who glared right back, the anger palpable. "Clear?" The agent took two steps back. Across the street, another agent raised a mouthpiece that had been dangling from a wire around his neck and whispered into it. Trippe couldn't hear what was being said, but he would have bet serious money that they were soon going to have company.

The Deltas climbed back into the Humvees and the two vehicles disappeared around the corner, leaving the

CIA agents furious and the air force guards, who were rooting for the Deltas, quietly amused. A few minutes later, as Trippe drove up the entrance ramp to the D-400, heading west toward Adana, Juarez, who, like McCarthy, had been watching the rear, yelled, "Helo at our five o'clock . . . at about two thousand feet, three klicks behind us."

"Eulas, we have an engagement," First Sergeant Trippe said in a businesslike tone into his mouthpiece.

"Roger that," Cole responded simply from inside Hangar C.

Spider One's crew chiefs and the Delta Operators of Chalk One pushed the heavy Black Hawk, which rested on a large wooden pallet on small rubber wheels, toward the open hangar doors. Although they hadn't been briefed on the specifics of the mission, they knew that Lieutenant Colonel Korda needed help, and that was enough. Within one minute, Spider One was clear of the building and its crew and their Delta customers were boarding, the engine beginning its high-pitched whine, the main and aft rotors beginning to turn.

"Black Hawk, what do you think you're doing? You are not cleared for liftoff," the air traffic controller in the tower said excitedly.

"Training mission," Cole responded quickly. "We've got some people to train."

"Not without a recorded flight plan. You guys may think you can do whatever you want, but I've got a busy airport to run."

"Son, you whine louder than my engine."

"I'm warning you. I'm going to have to report this."

"Do that." The powerful Black Hawk lifted into the air and vanished behind a row of hangars.

Trippe found the hospital easily enough and drove down the ramp. The signs were in Turkish and English and he had studied the drawing provided by his air force buddies, and knew at once which lane led to the freight dock. At the bottom of the ramp, he immediately backed up the vehicle toward the loading platform, stopping short of the dock so that Juarez and McCarthy could jump out and open the rear doors. As soon as the doors were swung fully open and were flat against the sides of the vehicle, Trippe nudged the rear of the Humvee flush against the dock. Juarez and McCarthy lifted the Maytag box and its stowaway out of the vehicle and into the building while Trippe provided cover. Meanwhile, Crocker's Humvee blocked the top of the ramp as planned, and the Deltas in that vehicle formed a defensive perimeter outside.

Inside the hospital, Martin emerged from his hiding place, carbine in hand, face-to-face with Krissi and General Bulot. Trippe's assault rifle, shoulder high, was aimed directly at them. Juarez and McCarthy combed the receiving dock. There were no hospital workers present, having been ordered by General Bulot's friend who ran the hospital to clear the area.

"Hello, Martin," Krissi said tentatively. Although she had tried to prepare herself, she had a visceral reaction to the business end of Trippe's assault rifle and grenade launcher. "It's been a long time."

Juarez approached. "All clear on this side."

"Same here," McCarthy reported from the other side of the large storage area.

Martin gave an almost imperceptible nod and Juarez began to search Bulot for weapons. "I'm armed," Krissi volunteered, raising her hands, "with Aaron's Beretta . . . well, he took it off a dead man who I shot. It's in my shoulder holster on the left." Juarez quickly patted down Bulot and plucked the Beretta from Krissi and handed it to Martin.

"I'll hold on to this," Martin said, almost apologetically.

"I understand your hesitancy to trust me. I really do. But we have a lot to talk about, and there is very little time."

"Okay, Krissi. I know you want this back. I understand that," he said, holding the Beretta. "But first tell me what the hell is going on?"

"Aaron is in Poti, Georgia. He left yesterday. He's alone, and he is going to be up against some very heavily armed and dangerous people very soon." Krissi stopped to take a breath. She was talking too fast and was more anxious than she had realized.

The general saw her struggling and spoke up for the first time, his voice deep and resonant. "If I may."

"Go ahead," Martin said, still on alert but beginning to appear more at ease.

"Colonel Korda, your brother Aaron is a very brave man with a very good heart. When my son was killed in Poti, Aaron took it upon himself to avenge Kemal's death. Through that quest, Aaron and Krissi here, have uncovered a terrorist plot—probably Arab—to kill hundreds of thousands by sabotaging our pharmaceutical supplies."

Martin listened intently as the general spoke, as did First Sergeant Trippe and the other Deltas within earshot. Krissi, who was watching them, had no doubt that they believed the general. What she didn't yet know was that Martin was trying to put together what he had learned—and not learned—from Operation Shell Game with what he was hearing. Martin was stunned to hear that terrorists, probably Arabs, had set up operations far from Syria, where he had expected them to be.

Krissi continued. "Martin, we believe Kemal stumbled on evidence of that plot in Poti, and that is why he was killed. Aaron went back to Poti for evidence of what the terrorists are planning, before it's too late. But they know we're on to them, so there's very little time." Martin stared at her, trying to puzzle it out. "Look," she said, "we'll tell you everything we know as quickly as we can, but please put your weapon down. It's hard to concentrate with carbines and grenade launchers pointed at us, especially this close."

"Deal," Martin said. Martin took a step toward her and hugged her warmly but briefly. He was anxious to

hear more. She held on for a moment, very relieved that
he had accepted her. He then shook Bulot's hand. "Let's
talk," he said, indicating that she and the general should
sit with him on one of the nearby crates. They did, and
Krissi rapidly explained her work at the BND and how
she came across Aaron and had spied on him, her deceit
within the BND and how it had gotten her into trouble.
She told him about the farmhouse and also explained
how Aaron, too, had run afoul of the CIA: Poti, California, Atatürk Airport, the Corleys and the shoot-out in
the park near the Intercontinental. When she explained
the role General Bulot had played in giving them shelter
after the gunfight at the Intercontinental and how he
had rescued them at Ramstein Air Base, Martin turned
to the general and thanked him.

Krissi took some time to describe the list Hasan had
found in Poti and how Mrs. Corley had translated it, as
well as the infiltration of the pharmaceutical companies
by people who purported to be Iranian Jews but who
they now believed to be Arab Muslims. General Bulot,
who had learned some of the details from Aaron and
Krissi the day before, sat and listened, shaking his head
in concurrence. Martin was mesmerized.

"Where is the list that Hasan found?" Martin asked
suddenly.

Krissi reached into her pocket. "This is a copy," she
said, handing it to Martin. "As I said, Mrs. Corley translated the first and fourth columns from Farsi. . . . The
English handwriting is hers. Dr. Corley thought *Center
Earth* means 'Midlands' and that *Albert Breathing* means
'albuterol,' " she explained, pointing to the original Farsi
and then to the translation as they scanned down the
list. "To tell you the truth, as for the entries in the right-
hand column, we were all stumped. . . . And then the
Corleys were killed." Krissi's voice trailed off.

Martin studied the list for several minutes, focusing on
the right-hand column, his mouth opening in disbelief.
"Christ," he exploded. "Top, come take a look at this."

First Sergeant Trippe approached and peered over

Martin's shoulder as Martin ran his finger down the translated entries. "*Slave Boy Heat* is not a complete translation. *Slave Boy,* I think, refers to a famous eleventh-century Arabic poet named Al-Ramadi. *Heat* may be translated incorrectly. *Heet* is the ancient name of what is now Al-Ramadi, Iraq." Martin looked up at Trippe, who pursed his lips and slowly shook his head. "And look at this. *Cuneiform abba side* could also be a mistake. Translating from Farsi to English must be no small trick. Having no points of reference and very little time, I'd bet Mrs. Corley made several mistakes. I think *abba side* means 'Abbasid,' as in the Abbasid Dynasty. The most important cuneiform tablets archaeologists have about the Abbasids were uncovered in Al-Fallujah. I read it just a few days ago when I couldn't get to sleep. There were several caliph Al-Mutasims, but the most famous one was from Samarra," Martin said, looking at Krissi and General Bulot, wondering if he should divulge state secrets. He decided to break the rules.

"We suspected that the biochem labs in Al-Ramadi, Al-Fallujah, An Najaf and Samarra, Iraq, before the war were moved to Raqqa, Hassake, Deir-ez-Zur and Aleppo, Syria, respectively, sometime during or right after the invasion. Since the occupation, we haven't found anything related to biochemical weapons. We did find some documentation that indicates the Iraqis were experimenting with some neuromuscular disorders at these labs . . . Parkinson's disease, cerebral palsy, multiple sclerosis, et cetera. This type of advanced research didn't fit with Iraq's level of sophistication in the area of drug development, but we didn't know what to make of it."

"My God," Krissi gasped. "The compound thought to be a possible cure for the diseases you mention is botulinum-A. There's lots of research going on with it but it's controversial. You have to understand something about the toxin. It is *the* most lethal biological agent known to man."

Martin stood, visibly shaken, slowly pacing as he studied the sheet of paper. "Top," he said, turning to his first sergeant, "we may have been looking in the wrong country."

After a moment, Martin's eyes returned to the scrap of paper. "Valley of Peace. The most famous Valley of Peace that I'm aware of in connection with the Middle East is outside An Najaf. . . . *Wadiu's Salaam* in Arabic." He looked at Trippe and said, "Maybe there's a lab that was in An Najaf that was moved outside Iraq, and we missed it." Trippe nodded, disgusted and alarmed at the same time. "Son of a bitch," Martin said suddenly, dumbfounded, again sitting on the crate next to Krissi. "*S1187* . . . 1187 is the year Saladin took Jerusalem. My guess is that the S stands for Saladin, perhaps the Arab world's best warrior ever. Saladin was born in Tikrit, Saddam Hussein's birthplace. We can only guess what *S2004* means, but my bet would be Saddam in 2004." His eyes moved left to the handwritten notations next to Paderborn and Arvada. "Are there any pharmaceutical companies in Belleville, Illinois, and Mechelen, Belgium?"

"No," Krissi said simply. "Aaron was quite sure about Belleville, and Mrs. Corley was equally certain about Mechelen. But there could be smaller biotech companies . . . labs cloaked with legitimacy but capable of producing God knows what. We have not had the time or the resources to check out those references."

"Top, all this might explain what they were doing at Samarra, Al-Fallujah, Al-Ramadi and perhaps An Najaf before the war. It looks like the facilities that we think were moved from those cities to Syria were researching ways to poison our pharmaceutical supplies. We might still find evidence in Syria, but the labs are probably in Illinois and Belgium, where we would never have thought to look."

It was Krissi and General Bulot's turn to look surprised. Martin hesitated for a moment, but then decided to brief them fully on Delta Force's raids on the Syrian cities and the reasons why, breaking every security regulation in the process.

"When you were at Midlands and Nederlanden, did you get a sense of how much time we have before this stuff gets on the shelves?"

"No. We don't know how far along they are, but they could be ready. . . . Or very close. Some of these sleepers have been working at those companies for years. But what scares us the most in terms of timing is that the terrorists have to know that Aaron and I are tracking them. They've got to be doing everything they can to step up the pace. That's why Aaron rushed back to Poti without waiting for reinforcements, and that's why General Bulot and I are here. Aaron's going to get to the heart of this, but he's put himself in terrible danger going there alone, and I'm going to join him one way or the other."

If Martin had any lingering doubt why his brother loved this woman all these years, he lost it at that moment. "Did he take his cell phone?"

"Not his own. We trashed them," she said, explaining why. "But he took Mrs. Bulot's," Krissi added, gesturing toward General Bulot.

"We've tried to reach him twice on my wife's phone, which is identical, but we haven't been able to get through." The general pulled his phone out of his pocket.

"He probably turned it off to save the battery, and we figured he won't let it ring and divulge his position," Krissi added.

"Does it have a vibrating function instead of a ring?" Martin asked.

"It does," General Bulot said, double-checking his phone.

"Please try him now, sir."

"Certainly," Bulot said, speed dialing his wife's number and putting the phone to his ear. "Nothing. No response," he said after a pause. He waited and then tried again. Still, there was no answer.

The expression on Martin's face was that of barely contained fury. Normally ice under fire in combat, in his years as a Delta Force officer he had the ability to keep his emotions in check. But this was different. His children had taken all the prescribed vaccines and continued to be heavy users of albuterol. His wife was on the Pill. He had good friends who were diabetics. They and his brother were under siege, and he knew his control was tenuous. His heart pounded like a drum in his chest and he forced himself to take deep breaths. He knew he had to pull himself together so that he could deal with this horrific threat.

Martin stood, having made his decision and now having only the details to work out as to how he would get there. "I'm going to Poti," he said to Krissi, who nodded and also stood.

Krissi and Martin locked eyes, two warriors understanding the mission and the risks. "The last thing Aaron said to me was that he had to go. . . . He couldn't wait for you or me, because your kids are in danger."

"We have to stop them," General Bulot added as he, too, rose. "They murdered Kemal, but they are not going to take Aaron, your children or anyone else's."

First Sergeant Trippe suddenly placed his hand over his headphone, pressing it up against his ear. "We have a Huey in the air over the hospital. Metz has a pair of binoculars on it. There are two snipers. What are my instructions, sir?"

A certain inner calm returned to Martin's face as Trippe spoke. The rage that had nearly consumed him a moment ago gave way to the focused, rational decision making he was known for. "Who's in the air?"

"Spider One . . . Eulas is at the stick, side gunners ready."

"Tell them to move in closer." He made a fist with

his right hand, holding it over his head, held the palm
of his left hand out flat in front of him, and brought the
right fist down and fast, stopping a couple of inches short
of his left palm. "I want our friends in the Huey to feel
what it's like to have six barrels of a Gatling gun in their
faces at point blank range."

"Yes, sir. That should get 'em to back off."

"If not, move in closer. Stay in their faces." He moved
his fist closer to his open palm in a short, powerful
thrust. "Unless they have a death wish, they'll get the
message." He brought his arms to his sides and turned
his attention to Krissi and Bulot. "You'll have to come
with us back to Incirlik. Obviously, you won't be safe
here in this hospital." They nodded. "Okay, we'll move
the moment Eulas tells us that the Huey is gone."

Trippe repeated the orders into his mouthpiece. "Galante, you drive my Humvee. Metz, you ride shotgun
with him. I'm going with Crocker. Bob?" he said, inquiring to see if Master Sergeant Bob Crocker could hear
him. When Crocker acknowledged, Trippe said, "I need
to talk to you on the way back to base about what's
going on in here."

In the helicopter circling above at one thousand feet,
the CIA snipers readied themselves for the kills. The
Agency believed that Martin was meeting Aaron. Each
sniper was suspended on a plank hanging from wires
attached to a gyroscope, which in turn was suspended
from the ceiling inside the cabin of the chopper. The
specially designed feature allowed the marksmen to
maintain a steady aim on their target despite the choppy
movements of the helo. The pilot and copilot concentrated on keeping the Huey steady, with its right side
pointed toward the freight dock, giving the starboard
rifleman the first crack at a shot. Meanwhile, Spider One
approached the Huey from directly on top of it. When
the Black Hawk was only four hundred feet above the
unsuspecting CIA chopper, Cole slid the newer, faster
bird to his right three hundred feet and dropped precipi-
tously. In an instant, the CIA pilots and snipers were

staring at a fully armed Black Hawk three hundred feet off their starboard, Sergeant Curtis Dorne's Gatling gun pointed directly at them. Eulas Cole moved the chopper to his port, 150 feet closer to the Huey, so the snipers could get a better view. Dorne thought he could see the pilot in the CIA helicopter sweating, and was pretty sure the Huey pilot could see him grinning behind the dragonlike Gatling gun. The two opposing forces, both working for the U.S. government, remained suspended in air for a moment until the Huey banked left and retreated. Its pilot, a civilian under contract, was not willing to call the Deltas' bluff and risk death. Cole held the Black Hawk steady at one thousand feet until the other bird disappeared into the evening sky, and then gave the word to his comrades below.

On Eulas's "All clear," Martin, Krissi and General Bulot, led by First Sergeant Trippe, made a dash for the Humvee parked outside the freight dock, Galante at the wheel, the motor running, the transmission in gear. Once the passengers were secure inside, Trippe ran to Crocker's Humvee, jumping into the front passenger's seat as the vehicle started to pull away. The convoy raced north on Mezbaha Street, Galante following closely behind Crocker's lead Humvee. Spider One provided air cover.

When the two vehicles approached the main gate back at Incirlik, the air force guards stood back, despite direct orders to the contrary. The CIA had been in contact with the base commander, who had given the order to halt the Humvees if they returned, but the airmen were neither ready nor willing to take on the Delta commandos, and waved them through without incident.

As the two Humvees entered Hangar C, Eulas Cole began his descent from 1,500 feet, where he had been flying protective cover. He lowered the chopper rapidly, all eyes inside the helo looking for any signs of hostile fire from a CIA turned enemy. Suddenly, at 1,400 feet, the main valve of the fuel pump cracked and the intake hose decoupled from the mechanism, spewing aviation fuel. It was a few seconds before the pump automatically shut down and stopped the flow of highly flammable JP-8 kerosene.

Eulas Cole's many years at the stick paid off. He immediately shut down the engine. "Autorotation," he shouted to his copilot as the rotors began to slow. Faced with a total loss of power at 1,400 feet above the tarmac, he nosed the Black Hawk forward and increased the rate of descent, a maneuver that had seemed counterintuitive in flight school but now made perfect sense. As the heavy chopper gained speed, the airflow over the rotors gave it greater lift and allowed him to stabilize the craft, avoiding a crash that would have killed all on board. Landing directly below on the tarmac was no longer an option, but by angling off and landing the Black Hawk on an approach similar to that of an airplane, he was able to get the helicopter to the ground. A few moments later, the wheels hit the pavement and slid five hundred feet on the tarmac, rattling crew and passengers alike. Spider One landed in the middle of one of the two parallel runways.

When the chopper stopped, the Deltas and Night Stalkers who had been aboard deplaned and ran as fast as they could away from the aircraft, for fear of an explosion. Hearing the word *autorotation* over the speaker system, air traffic controllers immediately knew there had been engine failure on the Black Hawk and had dispatched fire trucks and rescue teams. As the ground crews approached the disabled helicopter, cautiously spraying foam on it from as far away as the powerful fire hoses would permit, Eulas Cole and the others who had been on Spider One reached the safety of Hangar C.

When Martin crawled out from the back of the Humvee, along with Krissi and General Bulot, he was surprised to see Lieutenant Pamela Toll and the entire crew of Spider Three suited and ready for departure. Turning around, he was greeted by the other Deltas and Night Stalkers, in combat gear, donning helmets, Kevlar vests and web gear weighted down with extra ammunition. All weapons were locked and loaded. "What the hell is going on here?" he asked, incredulous.

"We're going with you," Toll said matter-of-factly. "Trippe and Crocker briefed us over the mike while you were on your way back."

First Sergeant Trippe stepped forward even as he slung on his vest and tightened his ammo belt, assisted by Staff Sergeant Ryle, who was already suited up. "Sir, I heard what the lady had to say back at the freight dock . . . at the hospital. Your brother is one thing. I'd help you get him out of there if you asked. Hell, I'd do it even if you didn't ask, but this business of the damned terrorists poisonin' our drug supply is another story altogether. It *is* what Operation Shell Game was all about. . . . To find out what they're doin' with these laboratories. Look, your kids, my kids—they're all targets for these terrorists. My mom's a diabetic. Hell, everybody's on medication of some sort. And if those sons of bitches aren't stopped now, who knows how many of us they'll kill? The way I see it, we're just finishin' what we started back in Raqqa and Hassake."

"Sir, you were right about those bastards," Pam Toll said. "They're terrorists of the worst sort. The way I figure, Delta Force fights terrorists. Our job is to jockey Delta Force into battle. Night Stalkers don't quit!"

"Hooaah!" several Night Stalkers called out in a show of unwavering support. "Hooaah!" the Deltas joined in.

"Sir, you only have one helo," Eulas Cole said, joining the group. He was breathing heavily and was still visibly shaken from the near-death experience of dropping 1,400 feet without power. "Spider One blew a fuel pump. Hard to tell what else is wrong, but that bird ain't flying anytime tonight. Maybe tomorrow, but not tonight."

"Are you all right? The others?" Martin asked, knowing what a frightening experience Cole had just gone through and touched by the fact that the pilot's only apparent concern was that his chopper would not be ready to go on the mission. Cole nodded, wiping sweat from his brow.

"Okay, listen up. I appreciate what you're offering to do, but this is not an authorized mission," Martin said. "No matter how right it seems, make no mistake. Washington will have my head for this. If I make it back, I will be court-martialed. Anyone who goes with me will get the same. I'm talking about a one-way ticket to Leavenworth." He looked around the circle of Deltas and Night Stalkers to see if he was getting through to them, but their faces gave away nothing.

"Just one thing, sir," Master Sergeant Crocker said as he checked his CAR-15 and loaded a magazine. "If Lieutenant Toll doesn't fly you to Poti, how you gonna get there?"

"He's right, sir," Trippe said, as the Deltas and Night Stalkers made clear that they agreed with Crocker and Trippe.

"Has anyone tried to reach Colonel Whitman?" Martin asked. Brice Whitman commanded First Special Forces Operational Detachment—Delta, and was Lieutenant Colonel Korda's immediate superior ranking officer.

"We tried, sir," one of the communications sergeants answered. "He's out on a training exercise." Martin was disappointed, and it showed.

"Sir, I understand your problem, but do you really think you're gonna get approval from the chain of command to do this?" Trippe asked. "With all due respect, sir, they're still reeling over what happened in Aleppo. Colonel Whitman might support you. And SOCOM and CENTCOM would probably come around at some point, but I don't think we have time for that. And you gotta wonder if we'd get this raid through the Pentagon, the State Department and the White House any time before our retirement. Like the lady said"—he looked at Krissi—"we're runnin' outta time. Let's get in the air and then work on the bureaucracy."

"I want each of you to think about it. You'll all go to

jail with me, if you don't die first at Poti. This operation is unlike the others. . . . Different from any mission we've been on. We won't have air or satellite cover. We won't be able to refuel, meaning we may not be able to get out of Poti, assuming we have enough range to even get there in the first place."

Trippe and everyone else realized that Martin was coming around to his and the troops' way of thinking. "For God and country," Trippe said to Martin in a whisper, but loud enough so that most around them could hear.

"You sure about this, Top?"

"Yes, sir. I am."

Colonel Korda turned around in a 360-degree motion, studying his troops, grateful that they were truly the best of the best. "Delta Force! Night Stalkers! Mount up!"

TWENTY-FOUR

While Spider Three was prepared for liftoff, Martin and First Sergeant Trippe huddled with General Bulot and Krissi. "One chopper and squad might not be enough, Top. Also, even if we can get to Poti without refueling—Christ, we have no maps, no flight plan, no aerial-refueling capacity—we might not be able to get back to friendly territory without tanking up midair."

"Colonel," General Bulot said, "my son was First Commando, and the First Commando has a score to settle. I took the liberty to call the commander, Lieutenant Colonel Bulicet. My son's unit is available to help."

"First Commando," Martin said aloud, but speaking mostly to himself as he thought about the general's proposal. "They're headquartered at Kayseri. . . . Due north of here. But they'll need your government's authority. It'll take too long."

"If I know Bulicet, he's already figured out a way." He reached into his vest pocket and removed a small address book. "And you have the best communications equipment in the world," he added, glancing at the commo van.

"I'll talk to him," Martin said, appreciating the general's help. He looked at Trippe, who nodded as if to say that it sounded right and there was no other choice. While Martin and General Bulot ran to the commo van, Trippe took over, beginning with the selection of Deltas who would go on the mission. All of them volunteered, but given the distance to be covered, Spider Three could take only nine Deltas and five Night Stalkers.

"Shafter," Trippe shouted, "get me everything you can about Poti, Georgia. . . . Maps, nautical charts, everything on the laptop. Bring it and get your weapon. Ryle, mount up with your sniper rifle. Galante, get onboard with your SAW. Metz, you're on the list. Grab a SAW. You and Burns load a rubber duck. We may have to helo-cast and attack from the water. Crocker, you're the radio/telephone operator. Gonzales, we need a medic. You're it."

As Trippe picked his team, side gunners Dorne and Cho loaded their Gatling guns, mechanics from the 160th ensured all equipment was in order, and Kopinsky, the copilot, went through the paces with every gauge and indicator on the instrument panel. Burns would be the fast-rope master, and if the "rubber duck," a Zodiac with an outboard motor, was to be dropped into the water for an amphibious assault, he would be the helo-cast master, too. He and Metz set about checking and rechecking insertion ropes, exfiltration ladders and the Zodiac.

Martin and General Bulot called Lieutenant Colonel Yusuf Bulicet from the commo van. "Colonel Bulicet, this is Lieutenant Colonel Martin Korda. I'm with U.S. Special Forces. . . ."

"I know who you are, Colonel Korda," the Turk broke in, his English nearly perfect. "General Bulot has told me about your brother. Before their murders, Lieutenant Ertugrul and Sergeant Ciller also spoke very highly of him. Master Sergeant Naim Sukur is eager to help. I have one helicopter—a Black Hawk—with a full squad ready, if you need us."

"I am honored, sir. But what about your government? Can you do this?"

"First Commando is a counterterrorism force that trains all the time. . . . Like Delta Force. I've informed my chain of command that a small squad will be training on the Black Sea beaches east of Trabzon. That is quite

true, by the way; I just didn't tell them how far east."
He laughed. "My flight plans are cleared with those who
need to know, and a KC/MC-130 will refuel on the way
and on the return trip. We are a crack unit, Colonel
Korda. I believe we can be of assistance."

"I have trained with the Second Commando at Bolu,
but never had the privilege of seeing your unit in action.
But I know of the First Commando Brigade, sir. I have
studied your operations," Martin said respectfully. "And
I can imagine no greater honor than going into battle
side by side with the Turk First Commando."

"Thank you, Colonel." Bulicit was impressed with the
heartfelt compliment. "We are proud to serve alongside
Delta Force."

"I will instruct my communications sergeants to link up
with yours to determine which radio frequencies to use."

"We will rendezvous over the town of Erzincan, where
our direct routes meet. *Allah Akbar!*" Lieutenant Colonel Bulicet said, his voice rising.

"Allah Akbar," Martin responded, overwhelmed with
relief that Delta Force had more than just one helicopter
squad going into battle and that aerial refueling had
been arranged. He bolted out of the communications
van and ran to Spider Three, General Bulot on his heels.
"We have a Black Hawk squad from the Turk First
Commando joining us," Martin shouted over the noise
of men and women preparing Spider Three, tossing gear
inside for the long flight. "Shafter, we're going to refuel
over the Turkish city of Erzincan, wherever the hell that
is. Find it and get us maps. Crocker, coordinate with
Smith in the commo van. He's in touch with the First
Commando and working out the radio frequencies we'll
use. Metz, I want you . . ."

Martin was stopped midsentence by the sight of Lieutenant Toll and Krissi running from Pamela Toll's quarters toward Spider Three. Krissi was dressed in the
lieutenant's combat fatigues, replete with Kevlar vest,
helmet, night-vision goggles, an M4A1 carbine and Aaron's Beretta in a hip holster. "Whoa! What the hell do

you think you're doing?" he shouted to Krissi as she approached. They had talked about going to Poti together, but Martin had not taken it seriously.

"I'm a fully trained BND operative, and Aaron is in grave danger. I'm not staying here."

"This is no spy operation. This is combat, for Christ's sake. You can't . . ."

She cut him off with a wave of her hand. "I was second runner-up in the BND rifle shoot, and I was first, repeat first, with any nine millimeter automatic. In bad weather, with a handgun, I can hit a man on the run at fifty meters, when *I'm* on the run. I don't want to brag, but you need me. I saved Aaron twice so far, and I'm going to find him with you. I'd rather die trying than stay here."

"Jesus. Krissi, we have women piloting choppers, so don't take this the wrong way, but do you know a damn thing about fast-rope insertions?" he asked rhetorically, expecting her to say no.

"Actually, yes. I've done it several times. Just give me a pair of gloves. And before you say anything else, I've also helo-casted, in case you're going to water insert."

The bottom line was that it was *his* mission, and he could say no. But Martin had met his match, and he was smart enough to know it. "Get in," he acquiesced. He turned to the rest of the Spider Three's squad and shouted, "Delta Force, Night Stalkers, let's go. For God and country!"

"For God and country," they cried out.

And family, Martin said to himself as they wheeled the platform on which Spider Three sat toward the open bay doors leading to the tarmac. As soon as the helicopter was outside Hangar C and all personnel were clear of the props, Pamela Toll switched on the main and aft rotors. Just shy of two minutes later, she revved the UH-60K to full power and lifted off.

"Black Hawk, where do you think you're going? Return immediately," the air force captain in the control tower screamed into his mike.

"That's a negative," Lieutenant Toll informed him in a measured tone. "We are on a vector twenty degrees, north-northeast, proceeding on our training mission, which calls for radio silence at the outset. We will provide coordinates as appropriate," she added, and without waiting for a response, switched off all communications with the tower. Within moments the Black Hawk reached the mountain range due north of Adana, skimming only a few meters over hilltops at 150 knots.

"This is General Davies. Return to base immediately. I repeat, return to base now," the Thirty-ninth Wing and Incirlik Air Base commander shouted, grabbing the microphone from the air traffic controller and not yet realizing that the mike was dead. "What the fuck!" he exclaimed when he looked at the radar screen and saw that they had lost Spider Three behind the low mountain range to the north of Adana. "Who the hell authorized this?" He spun around to the controllers almost in disbelief. "Scramble two F18s *now*."

"Sir, the auxiliary runway is down for the night for repairs. Well, sir, you can see the repair crews out there now . . . uh, smoothing out the asphalt. The main runway is blocked by the Black Hawk that went down a few minutes ago. We're working on it."

General Davies surveyed the diagram of his air base. Spider One had crash-landed in the middle of one strip, while the parallel runway was closed for repairs. Incirlik was down, at least for the thirty to forty minutes it would take to move Spider One and clear away the fire-retardant foam that covered it. "They pulled this shit deliberately," he said through clenched teeth. "They intentionally parked that chopper there." By now he was convinced of a full-scale Delta Force insurrection on his base. Spitting mad, he imagined personally shooting down the rogue helicopter. "Damn. Damn. *Damn!*" he blurted out, wishing like hell he could contain this disaster to the confines of his air force base, but knowing it was getting bigger by the moment. After a few minutes' reflection, General Davies began making phone calls back to his commanders in the United States, seeking instructions. It took close to an hour to get through to staff officers and reach a consensus on what to do, and an additional forty-five minutes to pull the commanders of USASOC, SOCOM and CENTCOM out of meetings, coordinate the flow of information, and to set up a video conference call.

Martin Korda also tried to reach the appropriate commanders, using Delta Force's ultrasecure commo links to seek approval. Colonel Brice Whitman, commander of Delta Force, was literally underwater, at the bottom of a lake in the swamps of South Carolina observing a training exercise, when the call came. By the time the diver reached him, he surfaced and entered the communications van, two hours had elapsed.

Meanwhile, at CIA headquarters, agents in touch with their comrades and General Davies on the ground at Incirlik were frantically attempting to gather information from what was happening. The name *Korda* was invoked in the same breath as the word *mutiny* by several operatives who were following the situation.

After a little more than two hours, Spider Three linked up with the First Commando helicopter over Erzincan, both choppers having made good time in clear weather, weaving in and out of mountain passes to avoid radar. Now, just south of Erzincan, they could see one another in the night sky.

"Spider Three," the Turkish copilot said into his headset. "You've come the farthest, so you refuel first. We will continue to vector north-northeast while refueling. We are going to fill to seventy-five percent capacity, so we're not too heavy over Poti. Do you copy?"

"Roger that, First Commando," copilot Kopinsky answered. "I understand that we'll be able to tank up on the way back at these same coordinates."

"That's an affirmative. There's a storm over the entire eastern bank of the Black Sea starting at about one hundred twenty-five kilometers north of our present position. Winds gusting to twenty-five knots, so brace yourself. We'll have a wild ride tonight!"

"I have your Kilo Charlie Mike Charlie one three zero on radar and I have a visual. Proceeding to connect," Kopinsky informed his First Commando counterpart as he began midair refueling with the Turkish Air Force KC/MC 130 tanker.

"Sir," the air traffic controller at Incirlik said to General Davies, who was still in the control tower. "We have radar identification of the Delta Force helicopter north of here. Coordinates indicate it's just south of Erzincan. There's another chopper—unidentified—and a large craft close in. From the looks of it, I'd say they're refueling, sir."

Suddenly, Lieutenant Toll came on the line. "Incirlik air base, this is Spider Three, requesting to talk to General Davies, please."

Davies grabbed the phone from the captain. "Put Korda on the wire. *Now!*"

"Lieutenant Colonel Korda, here."

"Now you listen to me. I order you to return to Incirlik immediately. And don't give me any crap about being outside my chain of command. I command the Thirty-ninth Wing and Incirlik. If you lift off from my tarmac, you report to me. Get your ass back to Incirlik *now*."

"No can do, sir. I've tried to reach my command chain to explain the mission, and we're trying to make that connection. But please understand, sir. We have a Ranger on the ground, and we are proceeding to rescue."

"Don't bullshit me. I don't like it. That Ranger just happens to be your brother, and I don't believe for a moment that he's anywhere other than in your helicopter. You are off on a personal adventure, and you are in very deep shit," he said, signaling to the CIA agents who had joined him in the control tower and who were listening in.

"My brother isn't onboard, sir. He *is* the Ranger on the ground, and he's in danger."

"Oh, bullshit," Davies barked.

"Sir," an air force lieutenant in the control tower interrupted, his voice trembling with fear at the prospect of interrupting the one-star in his present state of rage, but knowing that there were two four-stars and a three-star on the other line demanding to speak to the brigadier. "I've got General Owen, CENTCOM Commander, General Hall, SOCOM Commander, Lieutenant General Howe, USASOC Commander, and Colonel Whitman, Commanding Officer of Delta Force, on the wire from the States."

"Korda, hold the line," General Davies ordered. "Give that to me," he said sharply as he grabbed the phone from the lieutenant. "General Davies here."

"Luke Owen here, General Davies," the commander of CENTCOM said. "I have Generals Hall and Howe with me, as well as Colonel Brice Whitman, CO Delta Force. What's your sitrep?"

"We have a Delta Force unit gone totally berserk. Lieutenant Colonel Martin Korda, a group of his Deltas and Night Stalkers, and we believe Korda's brother, Aaron, a former Ranger, took a Black Hawk without authorization, and set off on some personal operation. CIA agents here at Incirlik have briefed me on Aaron Korda's activities and the fact that they are trying to arrest him. It looks like we have a rogue operation on our hands. The Deltas blocked our primary runway for the better part of an hour with a downed chopper. . . . And the other runway is down for repairs tonight, but we cleared the tarmac and launched two F18s to follow them. It's unbelievable, sir. We have a veritable mutiny on our hands. The remainder of the Deltas and Night Stalkers are in their hangar and won't let us in. . . . And won't even talk to us, and . . ."

"General Davies, patch Colonel Korda into this call," General Owen demanded, making no effort to conceal his impatience.

"Yes, sir," Brigadier General Davies responded, taken aback by the manner in which the four-star had spoken to him but unable to do anything about it. "Korda. You there?" Davies asked. Getting an affirmative response, he placed the phone on the speaker mode and made the connection.

Having refueled, Spider Three broke free of the KC/MC-130 and moved clear of the refueling hose to allow Lieutenant Colonel Bulicet's Black Hawk to engage. Spider Three, the First Commando helicopter and the tanker continued their path north-northeast at 150 knots, rapidly approaching the Black Sea.

"Colonel Korda, are you on the line?" the CENTCOM commander asked, his voice indicating that Korda had better have one hell of a good excuse for taking off on a mission without authorization.

"Sir, this is Lieutenant Colonel Martin Korda, First Special Forces Operational Detachment—Delta. I read you five-by-five."

"What the hell is going on?"

"General, sir, you can check the records. My younger brother, Aaron, is a contract consultant with the CIA. He was a Ranger. . . ."

"I have his dossier in front of me," the CENTCOM commander said, cutting Martin off. "Where is he now? Is he onboard your helo?"

"Negative, sir. He's on the ground in Poti, Georgia."

"Where?"

"In Georgia, sir. About two hundred fifty klicks from my present location."

"Where in the hell are you?"

"Just north of the Turkish town of Erzincan . . . it's due south of Trabzon, if you have a chart in front of you."

"Yeah, I see it," the CENTCOM commander groused as a major slid a map of the region on a large conference table in front of him and pointed to the town. "So what in the hell are you doing there? You better goddamn well say Colonel Whitman sent you there, and he better tell me that SOCOM gave him the nod. Then I can fight with General Hall as to why in the name of God I was cut out of the loop. Colonel Whitman, are you on the line?"

"Yes, sir. I did not give any such orders, but, sir, please let's hear Colonel Korda out."

"Sir, please give me a few minutes and I'll tell you everything." Martin did not wait for General Owen to respond and began to explain, as concisely as he could. Ten minutes later, Lieutenant Colonel Martin Korda finished briefing the general and the other parties on the line. "So you see, sir, that's where we were wrong on Operation Shell Game. The Iraqis—and I have no doubt that the people in Poti and the other would-be Iranians are really Iraqis—weren't using their labs to make biological or chemical weapons. They were using them to learn how to exploit our own technology against us, how to make our own pharmaceutical supplies lethal. They've figured out how to manipulate the pharmaceutical industry's commercial delivery systems and medical delivery systems to kill us. And it appears that they didn't move the labs to Syria before we invaded. They moved them to the middle of America and to Belgium. My brother happened to stumble onto their plot when he was in Poti a few weeks ago, and we're all lucky that he did. You put what he has learned together with what the military intelligence community has been picking up on, and it starts coming together. Fast. And, sir, let me say this. I know Aaron better than I know myself. Whatever the CIA is currently saying about him, it's wrong. I don't care what it looks like. He loves his country—he'd never do anything to compromise American interests. He detests illegal drugs. . . . And he's not a murderer. Sir, Aaron's been set up, probably by the terrorists themselves." There was silence on the other end of the line as the nation's top military leaders processed the news that a terrorist plot of unparalleled dimensions, simultaneously aimed at the United States, Canada and Europe, was underway. Martin continued. "So, sir, we are under attack, and my brother can't stop them by himself. He needs backup. And we're going in, sir. We have no choice."

"Why in hell didn't you clear this mission in advance?"

"There was no time, sir . . . and . . . uh, well, sir, you might have said no," Martin answered, knowing that he had probably just ended his career.

Luke Owen thought for a moment. The colonel had balls. No doubt about it. He understood Brice Whitman better now that he heard all of it. With a little more polish, Korda would be an excellent choice to head up Delta Force someday. But there was an immediate crisis to deal with, and that was his job. General Owen pressed the mute button on the speaker phone.

"Get me the secretary of defense now!" he roared to his staff standing by. *"NOW!"*

TWENTY-FIVE

Kate Brind was interrupted by her secretary while in the ladies' room. She hurried back to her desk, drying her hands with a paper towel as she ran down the hallway at full speed, knocking into a few surprised staffers who failed to get out of her way. She wondered who the Frenchman was that was holding on the line in her office and whether the matter of "life-and-death urgency" had to do with the Korda brothers. Somehow she suspected that it did. Arriving at her secretary's desk, she picked up the phone, having no time to take the call in the privacy of her own office. "Kate Brind here," she said, suddenly feeling a bit ridiculous. The caller had told Kate's secretary nothing about Martin or Aaron, and his message might have nothing to do with them. For all she knew, this Frenchman could be a crank.

"Madame Brind? My name is François Maraud. I understand that you studied at the Ecole Normale Supérior in Paris. I, too, am an ENARC. Bertrand Pierron at the Ministère des Affaires Etrangers, your former classmate, and, I believe, your friend, gave me your direct number." Kate and Bertrand had worked together closely in connection with the breakup of an Algerian-based terrorist network with cells in Marseilles and Paris. Kate trusted him implicitly. "I am the chairman of France Biologiques, a pharmaceutical company. I recently met Aaron Korda and Kristina Sturm in Vienna. I believe you know Mr. Korda. . . . Or at least know of him." *My hunch was right,* she thought. *Now maybe Maraud knows*

something that can help Aaron come in. "Anyway, I
spoke with Ms. Sturm several hours ago, and I have a
message from her that is a matter of utmost national
security to your country and mine. If Mr. Korda and Ms.
Sturm are right, America and Europe are under terrorist
attack as we speak. Listen to me, please. Hundreds of
thousands of people will die if we do not act immediately." The French businessman paused.

"Please, Monsieur Maraud, go on," Kate said in
French, her heart pounding as she sat down at her secretary's desk, listening and taking copious notes. In the
next ten minutes, Maraud explained the list from Poti
and how his friends the Corleys had interpreted it. Kate
heard for the first time how Aaron and Krissi had followed up and gone to Midlands Chemicals and Nederlanden Pharmacie Groep, and what they had concluded.
As the Frenchman spoke, Kate pieced together what she
knew of Operation Shell Game, of which Maraud was
unaware, and, like Martin, was able to connect that information with what Aaron and Krissi had learned. As
Maraud spoke, adrenaline coursed through Kate's veins.
This was it. It was terrible, but it made perfect sense.
"Oh, my God!" she exclaimed. Without saying another
word to Maraud, Kate passed the phone to her secretary,
exploded from her chair, and raced down the hallway of
the west wing of the White House, again jostling anyone
in her path. "Where's the president?" she shouted to
the president's secretary.

"The president's in with the vice president, the chief
of staff, the party leaders and several major contributors.
He cannot be interrupted."

Kate Brind said nothing but proceeded to the Oval
Office, until she was blocked by a tall, muscular Secret
Service agent. "Michael," she said urgently to the agent.
"I have to get in there. We have a nine-eleven-class
emergency. Let me in, please."

Michael hesitated, exchanging a questioning look with
his fellow agent on duty. Both had lived through the
attacks on the Pentagon and the World Trade Center,

and both had suffered the recriminations from the failures of the intelligence community. They knew that Kate was the national security adviser, but they were under instructions not to let anyone interrupt.

"Blame me!" Kate exclaimed, pushing open the three-inch-thick wooden door to the Oval Office. "Mr. President, I'm sorry to barge in like this, but we have an emergency. Mr. President, please listen . . .

"Mr. President . . . Mr. President," Kate said haltingly, breathing heavily as she began to realize the enormity of what she was about to tell the President of the United States. "A CIA operative in the field has uncovered a terrorist plot—probably Iraqis—to sabotage our pharmaceutical supplies . . . perhaps with botulinum toxin. They have infiltrated some of our pharmaceutical companies and they are producing large quantities of contaminated drugs. We don't know the full extent of it, but it looks like . . . at a minimum, that they have targeted albuterol, insulin, vaccines used for childhood immunizations . . . and . . . and oral contraceptives," she added, shuddering with the thought that she, too, had been taking the Pill. "We don't know how far along they are, but it could be any day, or it could have already started. Sir, this could be worse than nine-eleven . . . exponentially worse."

It had taken Aaron the better part of the day to work his way to the grain elevator adjacent to Building 15. The grain elevator was comprised of ten cylindrical silos, two-by-two, each cylinder six stories high, offering from the top a panoramic view of the Southern, Central and Northern Harbors. A boxy staircase that led to the roof was attached clumsily to a cylinder at the southern end, as if an architectural afterthought. Waiting until nightfall, Aaron had picked the lock of the ground-level door and, in total darkness, climbed the stairs to the roof. He carried food and water for two days, Krissi's Glock and silencer, and Mrs. Bulot's cell phone and binoculars.

The cold, driving rain made his hide site very uncomfortable, despite the relative security it afforded. After an hour's observation, Aaron, sopping wet, removed Mrs. Bulot's Motorola from a plastic bag in his satchel and powered it up, hoping that the battery was still alive and that he was within a satellite's footprint. He moved inside the stairwell and scrolled the menu until he found the general's number, pressed the SEND button and waited. When nothing happened, he pressed REDIAL and held the phone to his ear. At first there was silence, then a familiar set of beeps and ringing. "Aaron? Is that you?" a man's voice said in Turkish.

"General Bulot. Yes, it's me. Listen carefully. The terrorists are packing up, crating all their documents and equipment. They look like they're getting ready to leave Poti, which I think means they're done with their plot and are escaping. I'm on top of the grain elevator. . . . The one I described to you. It looks like a storm is picking up offshore. It's raining hard and I'm losing visibility. Have you reached Martin? It's urgent. I need to talk to him."

"He and Krissi are heading to Poti with a helicopter full of Delta Force operators. A Turkish unit from the First Commando is with them in another helicopter."

Aaron couldn't believe his ears. Deltas *and* Turk commandos on the way! His spirits soared with the prospect. "Later you'll tell me how you pulled that off, but for now just tell me when they'll get here. The men and the documents might tell us which drugs were poisoned. We can't let them get away."

"How many are there?"

"Can't tell for sure. Maybe sixty. Possibly more in the buildings. Every one of them is packing an AK-47 or a heavy machine gun, and it looks like they all have sidearms. I'm on my way down now, so I'll know more soon. . . . I've got to delay them as long as I can."

"No, Aaron, please. Don't try to stop them by yourself. Wait for Martin."

"Where are you now?"

"I'm in a hangar at Incirlik."

"Can you reach my brother? Is there a commo van nearby?"

"Yes, stay on the line. I'm going to it now," the general said, already running across Hangar C.

"Oh, shit!" Aaron exclaimed as he heard a beep and the screen of the phone flashed LOBAT.

"What's wrong?"

"The battery is low. I'm going to cut off on you any second. Just listen. Tell Martin there's a lot of activity in Building 13. It's at the tip of the Central Pier. There's another building just to the northeast, on the Northern Harbor and the Interior Basin, also with a lot of activity. I think it's number eleven, but I'm not sure. Tell Martin to check that one. There are also heavy machine guns on the Northern Pier controlling the sea channel. . . . And a freighter tied to the end of the Central Pier. It looks like the one we stole that night four weeks ago, but it's been repainted and it's heavily—" Aaron began to say when his phone went dead. "Shit," he cursed. He tried to reconnect, failed and pocketed the now useless device.

Aaron focused on steady, even breaths, and forced himself to assess his dilemma. With the imminent departure of the terrorists, he had to give up his initial plan of capturing one of them and making him talk. There was no time for that now. Instead, he had to stop them from leaving Poti with their crates of documents and computers. To do that, he would need to block the gravel road leading from Building 13, immediately north of the intersection between the building and a narrow road that emerged from the parking lot of Building 11. If he could immobilize the first truck in the convoy, at least temporarily, he could jam up those behind it. At best it was a long shot: He couldn't hold them for long, he was far too outnumbered and outgunned, and there was a good chance that Martin and Krissi and the others wouldn't get there in time. The truck, the terrorists and the evidence might be gone. On the other hand, watching the terrorists pack up and get away while he waited for reinforcements simply wasn't an option. He had come too far, and there was too much at stake.

As Aaron weighed his limited options, he quickly realized that he not only had to engage the enemy alone, but that the only way to do it was to leave the relative safety of his hide site. From his perch on the grain elevator he could not begin to delay the terrorists with the Glock. He would be out of harm's way for a while, but he had no doubt that if he fired on the terrorists from the top of the six-story building, it would not be long before they would direct mortar rounds and grenades on his position, simultaneously with an assault up the stairs. They would kill him and then escape, rendering his death meaningless.

His only chance of preventing the killers from leaving was to bottle them up in the narrow canyon between stacks of containers north of the intersection. He had to get to the ground, conceal himself in the corridors formed between the stacks and shoot directly at the lead truck's windshield. With a lot of luck, the heavy diesel would careen into a stack and be damaged badly enough so that it could only be towed or pushed out of the way, temporarily creating a traffic jam behind it in the narrow passage.

Aaron left the protection of the overhang covering the top of the stairs and traversed the short distance to the edge of the roof. The rain came down in pellets, driven by a fifteen-knot wind that frequently gusted to twenty. He identified two lights through the haze, one coming from Building 13 and one from Building 11, indicating that the structures' main doors were open. Beyond that, he could see nothing.

Aaron returned to the stairwell and removed the silencer from Krissi's Glock and put it in his pocket. In a firefight he preferred not to have the extra weight on the barrel of the automatic. He closed the door to the roof behind him, cutting off all light, and began to descend the stairs, one by one, in the total darkness, his toes sloshing uncomfortably in his waterlogged shoes with each step. When he thought he was halfway down, judging from the number of landings he had counted, Aaron heard the sound of the door opening at the ground level, and then heard the voices of men, speaking Georgian, coming up the stairs toward him. They carried large flashlights, and he presumed they were armed.

Aaron had only two choices. He could either retreat to the roof or try to hold his ground. Aware that his shoes were noisy and that the water dripping from his clothes was leaving a trail on the steps, he crouched on a step near the closest landing, his shoulder pressed against the opposite wall. Quickly screwing the silencer back on the Glock, he leaned back as far as he could so that his position would not be revealed until the enemy reached the landing. He waited, hearing the Georgians' panting as they climbed the stairs. They stopped frequently to rest. He heard matches strike, and the smell of sulfur and burning tobacco wafted up the stairs, leading Aaron to conclude they were heavy smokers and hopefully not in good shape.

When the first man's head became visible through the railing, Aaron spun out to the landing, the Glock at the ready. To his surprise, there were three men, not two, and the third man was going for his assault rifle. As the first Georgian rapidly sought to remove the strap of his Kalashnikov, the third man was rewarded with a silenced round in his forehead that sent him tumbling backward down the steps. The second Georgian reached too slowly for an automatic in his hip holster. He, too, died, the result of two rounds in his chest, fired from only two meters away. The survivor, the first man on the stairs, lunged forward, tried to grab Aaron's right hand to seize his weapon. Aaron saw it coming and swung his arm around rapidly, crashing the Glock into the top of the man's skull. The heavy Georgian went down with a thud, his life spared by his luck of being close enough to Aaron to be knocked out rather than shot. Aaron took an AK-47 and several magazines of extra ammunition from him, and then appropriated another Kalashnikov and extra ammo clips from one of his less fortunate companions. Unable to easily carry all three assault rifles, he left one behind.

Aaron descended the remaining flights of stairs as fast and as quietly as he could, reaching the ground-floor exit within a minute. He opened the door slowly, stepping into the rain and darkness, and headed toward the intersection where the real challenge would begin.

"Mr. President, the secretary of defense is on the line with CENTCOM, SOCOM and other key commanders," the president's secretary said, flustered that she was intruding on his conference. "I'm sorry, sir. I told him you were in a meeting, but he insisted it was urgent. . . . A matter of national importance, he said, and that he must speak to you now."

Kate expectantly looked at the president and the others in the room, hoping that the secretary of defense's call would not preempt what she had said.

"Put him on now," the president said, his outward demeanor calm and controlled. He turned on the speaker.

"Mr. President," the secretary of defense began, "please forgive the intrusion, sir, but this is something you must hear. I have Generals Owen and Hall on the phone with me, along with others."

"Go ahead," the president said, turning up the volume on the speaker. "The vice president and my national security adviser are with me," he added, not bothering to mention the names of the others present.

"Okay, General Owen. You have the floor," the secretary of defense said.

"Mr. President, sir. We have credible evidence of an imminent terrorist attack. Probably Iraqi exiles who left Iraq well before the invasion. Our intelligence indicates that they have either already sabotaged or are about to poison our pharmaceutical supplies with deadly chemical or biological agents. Some indicators point to the possible use of the botulinum toxin. Hundreds of thousands of North Americans and Europeans could die within days. That's just an estimate, Mr. President—it could be worse. . . . We might be talking in terms of millions."

The president sat upright, his back rigid. He began to sweat, streams of perspiration flowing under his thick black hair. He pulled a handkerchief from his pocket and wiped his brow. During the ten minutes that followed, General Owen explained what Martin Korda had reported to him and how the two Korda brothers had pieced the information together. The president listened, not yet disclosing to the general that he had heard some of this from Kate Brind moments earlier. "So, sir, we were off on Operation Shell Game. Iraq's biochemical warfare projects apparently weren't moved to Syria before or after the invasion. It now appears that they moved the facilities to the U.S. and Europe, right under our noses. While we've been looking in Syria, they set up in our own backyard. Korda's younger brother figured it out, and is pursuing the same plot from a different angle. I understand that the CIA thinks he's an agent gone bad, but it looks like he's good as gold, sir. And he and his BND girlfriend may be the only two people who can tell us which medications have been poisoned."

"Mr. President, this is exactly what Maraud told me. . . . It's what I was going to tell you," Kate Brind said. She quickly filled in the generals on the other end as to what she had learned from the Frenchman. "And, sir, the more I think about it, the more terrible it becomes. It's not only the people who may be killed directly by the terrorists' toxins, it's that all our medications will be suspect. Worst-case scenario, you'll have people dying from taking bad drugs, and others dying or suffering because they're too afraid to take the drugs that they need. We could have a complete meltdown of our health care system until confidence is restored."

"Okay," the president said, having heard enough. He stood, his lanky figure hovering over the others in the room. "How soon can we deploy to Poti? We've got to know what drugs the terrorists have poisoned. We need prisoners, documents, whatever we can get our hands on."

"Well, sir. In exactly seventeen minutes," General Gus Hall reported.

"How is it possible to get troops there that fast?" the president asked incredulously, knowing that such an operation would on a best-case basis take days, sometimes a week or more, to mount. "This sort of thing takes time to prepare."

"Aaron Korda's already somewhere in Poti," General Hall responded. "He spoke briefly with a retired Turkish general, but his cell phone went down. We have two Black Hawks speeding to Poti at present, a Delta Force unit and a Turkish squad from their First Commando Brigade. They have refueled over Turkey and are nearing the Georgian coastline."

"Who authorized that?" the vice president asked, visibly not happy that a military strike in Georgia, a friendly nation, was underway without the president's approval, despite the exigent circumstances. "And how in the hell did the Turks get involved?"

"Well, sir . . ." General Owen hesitated for the first time. "As for the Deltas, Lieutenant Colonel Korda apparently gave the go-ahead on his own. We haven't had the time to discuss exactly how this came about, but he has a group of men and women who trust him and who are completely loyal to him, so I wouldn't be surprised if he said he was going and the other Deltas and Night Stalkers simply said 'Hooaah!' and suited up. As for the Turk First Commando, from what we gather, it sounds like their commander gave the order and off they went. You have to understand something about the First Commando. The retired general, Bulot, is the one whose son was killed in Poti four weeks ago. His boy was a First Commando officer, and another First Commando officer and two NCOs were killed by the terrorists, so it doesn't sound like they needed a lot of prodding, even without official authorization. Under the circumstances, sir, it's a damn good thing the Deltas, Night Stalkers and Turk First Commando *didn't* wait."

"Do we need to get Colonel Korda on the line? Does

he need any backup support from us?" the president asked, convinced that time was running out.

"We can raise him on the wire, sir, but as for backup, by the time we mobilize any units, the fighting in Poti will probably be over."

"What do we do about the plot itself? How do we protect our people from the lethal medications without creating a panic? Any suggestions?" The president looked at Kate Brind.

"We have emergency planning for biochemical attack, but not for something like this. . . . Nothing on this scale. All of our planning centers around the possibility of a localized attack on subways, convention centers, the ventilation systems of hotels and office buildings and the like. We have to contact the Department of Homeland Security, FEMA, the CDC, all state and local health care providers, all trauma centers, all state and local first providers. . . . And, of course, the FBI and the military. We have to do the same thing in Europe. We know they've infiltrated four big pharmaceutical companies— National, Midlands, Nederlanden and Westfalen—and that at the very least albuterol, insulin, DTP, MMR and oral contraceptives are targeted," she said, wondering if she herself had already taken a deadly dose. "But there may be more. It may be even bigger than that. There may be other drugs and other companies we *don't* know about." She paused to reflect, looking at the others in the room who were with her, and went on. "I think you have to address the nation, Mr. President. . . . The whole world . . . immediately. Just get on the television networks and shut down the drug supply. No doctors can prescribe, no hospital or clinic can administer, no pharmacy can dispense any drug until we know what we're facing. There's no way to put gloss on this, Mr. President. We'll need at least a seventy-two-hour ban on *all* medications."

"Dear God in heaven. You can't do that," the vice president exclaimed, worried about the political implications and contributors from the pharmaceutical industry.

He shoved his dark-rimmed glasses up onto his fore-head. "What about people who need drugs to survive? What about anesthesia for those undergoing an operation? Think about it! Let's shut down the use of the pharmaceuticals on the list, and take our shot with the others."

"There are substitutes—good substitutes—for albut-erol," Kate said, thinking out loud. "Look, with the im-munizations and the oral contraceptives, children and women can wait. Kids with asthma and others with respi-ratory ailments taking albuterol can switch to something else. . . . But maybe the substitutes are poisoned, as well. I don't know enough about diabetes to know if there's an alternative to insulin, but the problem is we still don't know the scope of the terror plot. I say we call all the pharmaceutical companies in the United States. . . . Go straight to their CEOs and get them to test their supplies on an utmost emergency basis . . . and find out who within their companies have done this to us. When they tell us their supplies are secure, we clear the verified products for consumption. . . . Not until then. We get on the wire to the leaders of countries all over the world and ask that they do the same. We shut down the phar-maceutical industry."

"I agree with Kate," the president said, looking at his vice president and chief of staff. "I'll go on television immediately. There's no time to call the heads of state and speak to them individually. Just ask them to turn on their sets."

TWENTY-SIX

Lufthansa Flight 412 arrived at JFK on schedule. All but two of its passengers cleared customs and immigration without a hitch, the two being a Lebanese woman who had not filled out her papers correctly and a Romanian man whose name was similar to that of a person on the FBI's terrorist watch list. Both were ultimately allowed to enter the United States. Kalman Varga, a Hungarian doctor with an H-1 visa and papers to show admitting privileges at several New York City hospitals, had no such problem. He was in a cab to Republic Airport in Farmingdale, New York, well before the Lebanese woman was pulled aside for questioning. Dr. Varga paid the cabby generously in cash for the long ride to Republic. He had previously arranged on the Internet for a chartered flight from there to Trenton, and then on to MidAmerica Airport in Belleville, Illinois.

The pilot of the King Air C-90 was happy to pick up the extra cash. Varga explained to him, a man in his late thirties whom the Hungarian knew only as Gary, that he was afraid to fly commercial and that after dropping off a gift to his daughter in Trenton, he wanted to visit his son in Belleville. Gary had no interest in the man's stated motivations. He listened, but his sole concern lay in the man's having paid double the going rate. It would have shocked him to learn that his passenger was from Iraq, not Hungary, that his name was Abdullah Aziz Abu-Naid and that he was delivering $32,500 in cash for

his comrades' trips to Yemen and the United Arab
Emirates.

The holdover in Trenton lasted only thirty minutes.
At the small, private airport, Abu-Naid met with those
he needed to see, handing them their envelopes, while
Gary and an attendant refueled. Four hours later, the
King Air turboprop touched down smoothly at MidAmerica in Belleville. Gary was paid the remaining half of
his fare, and he and his passenger parted ways. Abu-
Naid walked through the almost empty terminal and
went directly to the equally deserted parking lot, where
a car was waiting for him, its keys in a magnetized box
attached to the undercarriage. While Gary was taxiing
down the runway on his return trip to New York, the
man who called himself Dr. Varga drove away in a
rented Mercury Sable.

Arriving at the St. Clair Mall, Varga went to the per-
fume counter at Famous-Barr and asked for a brand that
he said his wife preferred, engaging the lady behind the
counter, who did not notice the exchange of identical
nylon bags between him and the wife of one of the
founders of NMS Biologics, in conversation. Shari ben
Peeran took the escalator up to the ladies' room on the
upper level and closed the door to the stall behind her.
Pretending to use the facilities, she removed two thick
envelopes filled with cash from the package and put
them in her purse. She then slid the bag under the partition to Gita, her accomplice, flushed the toilet and prepared to .exit the stall. Gita took the bag, which
contained two more envelopes, and put it in a larger
canvas satchel, waited for Shari to leave and then left
the rest room, lingering in the mall, watching to see if
she was being followed, and then, satisfied that she was
not, went to her car.

Gita headed home, where her husband, Yaakov—
Faramaz ben Sarah's younger brother—and their daughter were packed, ready for the drive to Kansas City and
the flight to London, Prague, Athens and then to Dubai.

Fifteen minutes after Yaakov, Gita and their daughter headed west on I-270, Shari and her family backed out of their driveway on Old Caseyville Road and drove north to Chicago's O'Hare and connecting flights to the British Virgin Islands, Rome, Morocco and Dubai.

As the Boeing 727 raced down the runway at Lambert-St. Louis International, Dr. Varga felt the gentle G-force press his back against the comfortable first class seat and permitted himself to relax. A thin smile began to form on his lips as he thought of how foolish the FBI would look if and when they ever discovered that NMS Biologics, located in a white-bread Midwest town, was the production hub of the most deadly attack ever on America.

"Colonel Korda, sir. General Bulot is trying to reach you from the commo van back at Incirlik," Lieutenant Toll reported to Martin, who sat on the floor of the Black Hawk just behind her, on the other side of her seat.

"Thanks. Patch him into this frequency and alert Colonel Bulicet so he can hear."

"Colonel Korda. Aaron called. The terrorists are moving out of Poti in a hurry. They're packing everything onto trucks. He's going to try to slow them down by himself. I urged him to wait for you, but he said there's no time. He estimates that there are at least sixty of the enemy, and at the time we spoke a couple of minutes ago, most of them, from what he could determine, were situated in Buildings 11 and 13, where there is, or was, a lot of activity. He said there's a boat tied to the end of the Central Pier." The general relayed the rest of his brief conversation with Aaron, his voice catching as he repeated to Martin how Aaron had refused to wait for reinforcements. Calling upon his years of military training, he pulled himself together and continued with his briefing.

"Chris, get me that map on the laptop," Martin or-

dered Staff Sergeant Shafter, who immediately slid
across the floor to sit next to him, while Sergeant Ryle
shifted to make room for him.

"General, I have a chart in front of me."

"Aaron was on top of the grain elevator when I spoke
with him. Can you pick out the elevator on your map?"

"Yes, I have it."

"I don't have a map with me, so I'm just repeating
what Aaron told me. Apparently, there's an intersection
of two roads that lead from Buildings 11 and 13. Do you
have that?"

"Got it. Go ahead."

"He said he's going to try to bottle up the convoy of
trucks that are getting ready to leave by stopping them
before they get to the intersection. He said we probably
wouldn't see it on any map, but the road leading to the
intersection is very narrow, bordered on each side by
stacks of shipping containers five or six high."

"Shit," Martin said, his voice filled with concern.
"He's out of his goddamn mind. How's he going to hold
a force of sixty? He'll get himself killed. What weapons
does he have?"

"He's got my Glock with a silencer," Krissi answered,
speaking into her headset.

"Jesus," Martin said, deflated.

"Look, it's scary as hell, but I know Aaron. He'll figure out a way to arm himself better," Krissi said, trying
to convince herself as much as Martin. "And not all
sixty are soldiers, let alone Rangers. That has to improve
the odds."

"Pam, what's our speed?" Martin asked Lieutenant
Toll.

"One six five knots."

"Can we speed it up?"

"Negative, sir. We're being buffeted by side winds in
heavy rain. We're at max speed now."

"Colonel Korda," Lieutenant Colonel Bulicet, who
had been listening until now, said from the First Commando Black Hawk, "with this wind and rain, we're not

going to be able to fast-rope onto the piers. There will be too many stacks of containers and other obstacles, and we don't know where the high-tension wires are. It's too risky. The only way is to helo-cast offshore and proceed by Zodiac."

"Come on. You heard what Aaron told General Bulot. The terrorists are heavily armed on the Northern Pier and control the sea channel. They're also on that boat tied to the Central Pier. They'll chew us to pieces in the channel."

"We have to take our chances. With this storm, they won't see or hear us until we're on top of them. They won't expect small rubber rafts in the dead of this kind of night. No one would be crazy enough to be out on the water tonight," he added with a laugh. "I recommend that we go over the breakwater, sir. We drop offshore and power straight to it, immediately west of the Central Pier, lift the rubber rafts over, and surprise them."

"Okay," Martin conceded, knowing there were no viable alternatives. "Once inside the harbor, Delta Force will bypass the Central Pier and head east to what used to be Building 15, closer to the intersection. First Commando will flank north of the Central Pier and come up from behind Building 11. Everyone in the boat and Building 13 will be cut off. We'll deal with them later. Our first priority is to reach Aaron at the intersection and stop the terrorists' escape."

"For God and country . . . and your brother," Colonel Bulicet said. "The Turk First Commando is honored to be your left flank. God is great."

"And we are privileged to be your right flank. *Allah Akbar.*"

"Fauad, we're running out of room," Mohammed reported, addressing Faramaz by his Arabic name. "There are too many crates of documents, and not enough room for the men."

"Look," Fauad said impatiently, "the Georgians will

not be traveling very far with us, and we have only twenty Iraqis. Find room and make it quick."

"Can we shred and burn the remaining documents?" Mohammed asked timidly.

"No. Absolutely not. We will leave no papers behind. We want every detail of Operation Lethal Agent preserved for history. This will be our greatest victory in eight hundred years, since Saladin took Jerusalem. The Americans think they have achieved a great victory over Iraq by crushing our armies and capturing Saddam, but we are still potent if we fight our style of war, using our tactics, not theirs. The documents we keep must be taken to Yemen and maintained for posterity." He thought for a moment, his mouth curling into a grim smile. "Now, listen to me," Fauad said, lowering his voice to a whisper. "The Georgians are all from the capital. They will leave the port with us and go as far as Simoneti. Two kilometers past the village, there is a road leading to Tikibuli. We will take that road north for two more kilometers, and then stop and kill the Georgians . . . all of them."

The younger man looked surprised. "But why, sir?"

"Unlike our files, the Georgians cannot survive. A few of them may still think we're Iranians, but don't believe for a moment that we have fooled all of them. The Americans will force them to talk, and the cowards will give us away. Every one of them must die. Cram the Georgians into the trucks any way you can."

"And what about the Italians on the boat?"

"Don't worry about the Italians. The *Roman Goddess* will explode approximately one hour after leaving port tonight. There are enough explosives onboard to break apart the vessel into many little pieces that will go down far out at sea, leaving no trace."

"What if the storm delays the Italians?"

"You worry too much. The Italians prefer the bad weather. It makes it easier for them to go undetected."

"And the Georgian interior minister and his guards?"

"I'm convinced that the fool believes we are Iranians. Which is fortunate for both of us."

"When will you leave, Fauad?"

"Right after the Italians." Fauad looked at his watch. "The *Roman Goddess* is supposed to cast lines at eleven thirty tonight. As soon as our men on the Northern Pier confirm to me by radio that the vessel has left the harbor, I want them to pack up their weapons, swing by here to pick up any extra crates and follow us on the convoy. I will take the last truck out. . . . After I have made sure that we have left nothing, and no one, behind."

"Inshallah."

"Yes. Now go. May Allah be with you. Be safe, and I will see you in Yemen. . . . At the safe house." The two men embraced.

A gust of wind drove the rain against Fauad's face as he quickly walked to Building 13 to conduct his inspection. The chill and dampness invigorated him, adding to his upbeat mood. His work was nearing completion. He had been patient for so many years, thinking through every detail of Operation Lethal Agent from its inception; convincing his superiors of the beauty of the plan; recruiting the biochemists and engineers; supervising the experiments inside the secret labs in Iraq until the right formulas were decided upon; moving the labs deep into enemy territory; researching and selecting the pharmaceutical companies; recruiting the foot soldiers, computer specialists and linguists, only some of whom were aware of the ultimate objectives. It was all coming together now. His thoughts went back to the suffering and death and humiliation at the Shatila camp outside Beirut, and to the ultimate humiliation of the American occupation of his country. *Soon,* he thought, *we'll bring the infidels to their knees.*

Lieutenant Colonel Bulicet's Black Hawk slowed to a hover 1,100 meters west of the port of Poti over a roiling

Black Sea, whose waves crested five meters above the
troughs. Winds gusted to twenty-five knots, rocking the
sleek helicopter side to side as the pilots struggled to
hold it steady. The First Commando operators in the
rear inflated the Zodiac with foot pumps, while other
commandos inspected the doorways to make sure that
there were no sharp edges that could rip the rubber raft
when it was pushed out the door. When the raft was
fully inflated, the helo-cast master shouted, "Get ready."
Upon his signal, the six-man crew, led by Master Sergeant Naim Sukur, knelt on the cabin floor next to the
raft and prepared to launch themselves and the Zodiac
out to sea.

"Check equipment," the helo-cast master shouted
over the sound of the whirling rotors and the rain pelting
the fuselage, and the men began one last inspection.
"Sound off with equipment check," he shouted several
moments later. The men verified the gear, confirming
each item as the helo-cast master called it out: outboard
engine, backup paddles, all tethers, flares, life vests.

Thirty seconds later, the helo-cast master shouted,
"Go!" The First Commandos, tethered to the rubber
raft, heaved it out the starboard door, then plunged into
the water as one. No man was in the water for more
than a few seconds. Each hoisted himself over the gunwales of the small craft and climbed aboard, ready. As
soon as his five crewmates were safely onboard and in
position, Naim, the coxswain, started the forty-
horsepower outboard and the Zodiac began making its
way up a swell in the direction of the breakwater and
the harbor behind it.

Naim braced himself for battle. The official mission
was to rescue Aaron and capture prisoners who could
be made to disclose what drugs had been poisoned. He
was committed to the mission, willing to give his life if
necessary, but as he sat aft in the Zodiac, his hand on
the outboard, guiding the tiny vessel through the rough
seas, he was focused on his personal vendetta. He would
find the man in the peacoat who had stalked and mur-

dered his friends in Kayseri, and only one of them would leave Poti alive.

Two hundred meters to the west, Delta Force prepared to repeat the drill. First Sergeant Trippe had already tried to convince Martin, but he gave it one last try. "Sir, at the risk of repeating myself and becoming a real pain in the butt, we need you here in the helo in command of the operation, not down in the raft. With all due respect, sir, war's a young man's game. You and I are gettin' too old for this. Your brother's life is more at risk with you risking yours down in the rubber duck than up here runnin' the show," he added emphatically.

"He's right, sir," Lieutenant Toll said, emboldened by Trippe's candor. "But whatever you're gonna do, do it now. I can't hold this chopper this close to the water much longer."

Martin hesitated. For most of his adult life, he was the young officer leading his men into combat, putting himself as much in harm's way as they did. It was against his grain to order his troops to move forward while he remained in the relative comfort of the rear. He knew the dreaded day would come when he would be deskbound, pushing paper and fighting the bureaucracy instead of the enemy, but he wasn't prepared for such an abrupt transition, expecting to wean himself gradually from the front lines. But the decision was suddenly here and his to make, and all the more difficult because his brother was on the ground, heroically taking on an enemy with odds at least as unfavorable as those their grandfather had faced at Riva Ridge in 1945, and their dad had confronted at Chau Phu in '68. As a Delta, he was good to go, ready to pack his carbine, to launch his grenades, to breathe in the pungent smell of cordite and the coppery stench of blood in his nostrils. But as a father and brother, he knew it had to be different this time. He exhaled heavily, a fateful resignation overcoming him. And then he spoke, hardly believing the words himself. "Okay. Metz, you take my position. Right forward on the Zodiac. Mount up!"

Trippe's eyes met Martin's. The two men had been through combat together in Desert Storm and the initial stages of the invasion of Iraq and many special ops that never made the news. Martin's eyes were moist, and Trippe more than understood. Like his colonel, Trippe was rapidly approaching retirement, with less than eighteen months left, and he knew the change would be daunting. Trippe gave a quick nod to Martin, who returned it. Trippe turned to the others onboard. "Get ready," he ordered the six Deltas kneeling next to the fully inflated Zodiac. "Sound off with equipment check!"

"Hooaah!" the Deltas shouted after each item was called off.

"Delta Force, *GO!*" The men disappeared out the side door and into the blackness. Soon they were powering their way over the heavy swells toward the port, strong winds and currents from the northwest working against them but not holding them back.

Lieutenant Toll pulled back on the stick, ascended to five hundred meters and circled at approximately 1,500 meters offshore. Under clear skies, she and the First Commando's Black Hawk would have to be much farther from the harbor to avoid detection, but in the nighttime storm, there was little risk that the enemy would see or hear them.

"What's your sitrep?" Lieutenant Colonel Korda asked of the men in the Zodiac, pressing his mouthpiece closer to his lips.

"We're proceeding as scheduled, sir, but the engine's sputtering on us. It's okay for the moment, but it doesn't sound great."

"Shit!" Martin said, wondering if he would have had a better chance at fixing the motor than the younger men onboard.

"She's slowin' down, sir. The engine may conk out on us." The Deltas onboard didn't need the coxswain to tell them to start paddling. Without saying a word, they reached under the gunwales, retrieved the short aluminum paddles and began stabbing the black waters in unison, trying to reach the designated spot on the breakwater directly west of the Central Pier, before the wind and currents pushed them too far south.

"Do we risk towing your men, Colonel Korda?" Lieutenant Colonel Bulicet asked, listening in on the agreed-upon frequency and overhearing the conversation through his headset.

"Not yet, Colonel," Martin responded. "Gonzales, do you hear me?" he asked the Deltas in the Zodiac. "What's happening with that outboard?"

"She's gone, sir. I can't fix her, either. Not on these waves." As the coxswain on this mission, Gonzales manned the forty-horsepower Honda outboard. Like everyone onboard, he was a skilled mechanic, but the motor was impossible to fix under the circumstances.

"Colonel Bulicet, we can't tow her," Martin said without hesitation. "We'd risk capsizing both rafts. I suggest that the First Commando proceed as planned. Get to the breakwater as fast as you can, portage over, and stake out a position directly across from the Central Pier. My men will be pushed further south, opposite the Southern Harbor. It's impossible to row against this sea. Gonzales, listen to me. Don't fight the waves; you'll exhaust yourselves. Let the wind and the current push you south toward the Southern Harbor. At whatever landing spot you reach, climb over the rocks and get inside the harbor behind the breakwater."

"Sir," Trippe interrupted as he studied the charts on the laptop, "there are some shoals due west of the Southern Harbor. They'll slow down the waves pounding on the breakwater. That's the point where the men should cross. Otherwise, they'll slam into the wall."

"Gonzales, did you hear that?"

"Roger that, sir. Best I can tell in this soup, the wind and currents are pretty much pushing us toward the shoals. We'll paddle our way inland as much as we can and see if we can get behind 'em. I'm dumpin' the motor," he shouted into his mike as he unscrewed the clamps holding the outboard to the raft and let it sink in the swirling waters.

"Colonel Korda," Bulicet said, pausing for a moment to ensure that he had Martin's attention, "since it's going to take your men more time to portage over the breakwater than us, we'll cross over, double around to the east of the machine gun emplacement on the northern sea wall and come from behind the terrorists. After that, we'll portage over the small strip of land between the New Port Harbor and attack Building 11. We can still hit it at oh-two-thirty hours sharp. Will that give your men enough time?"

"That's right in terms of my men, but my brother is on the ground and the fight won't wait for him."

"Understand. We'll do our best to move it up fifteen minutes. Your team should do the same if they can. We'll coordinate as we go. That's all we can do. The seas are too heavy and the rain has cut visibility, even with the night-vision goggles."

"Roger that."

TWENTY-SEVEN

Aaron inched forward from behind a stack of fifty-five-gallon drums, his back pressed against the concrete wall of the northernmost silo of the grain elevator. Between the lights coming from Buildings 11 and 13 and the headlights of the trucks that were being readied for departure, he could see several men mounting the cab of the lead truck and others scrambling into the tarp-covered rear. Aaron was still more than twenty-five meters from where he needed to be in order to attack. He had to maneuver himself behind the containers that formed the southernmost end of the narrow passageway before the lights of the convoy gave away his location. Running as fast as he could, he darted across the road to another set of containers, holding a Kalashnikov in each hand. Reaching his chosen position, he wiped the rain off his forehead with his soaking wet sleeve and glanced up the road to his north. He was close enough now to see the distinctive Mercedes insignia on the hood of the diesel, and heard the engine coming to life as the driver turned the ignition key.

The truck that pulled away from Building 13 was speeding up. The sound of grinding gears to Aaron's right probably meant that more trucks were being prepared for departure from Building 11, but there was no time to verify. He peered around the edge of the container, his right shoulder pressed against the metal, prepared to swivel and fire at the oncoming truck. When the vehicle was a third of the way through the narrow passage, it shifted to second gear and accelerated. Aaron rotated and squeezed off three rounds directly at the windshield in front of the driver. He fired another three shots at the same spot, and then fired four times at the passenger's side of the windshield, instantly killing the driver and the passenger closest to the right door of the truck. He had no way of knowing that a third man was wedged between the two dead men on the front seat and had been unharmed.

The vehicle continued forward, guided by the surviving Iraqi, who had recovered the wheel and taken the gas pedal with his left foot. Aaron fired again, this time at the headlights that shone directly at him, revealing his position. The passage in front of him was now illuminated only by the lights of the vehicles behind the Mercedes. Able, but only barely, to visualize the wheels of the lead truck, Aaron took aim and fired. Blowout. The tires went flat as the rubber shredded upon the impact of multiple 7.62 mm rounds. Still, the Mercedes rolled forward, closer and closer to Aaron's position. He fired again at the partially shattered windshield, this time spraying it with the last twelve rounds in his banana clip. As the remaining glass exploded, the man who had survived the first rounds ran out of luck, falling back with three rounds in his face. The truck careened into the wall of containers a few meters from Aaron's position, its wheel rims embedded in the gravel and mud.

A frantic voice to the rear of the convoy shouted something in Arabic, which Aaron could only partially hear, and the lights of all the trucks went out. The same voice cried out again, and the driver of the second vehicle in the column, a Volvo, edged forward, trying to push the disabled Mercedes out of the way. Aaron had anticipated this response and was already climbing up the container wall, AK-47s strapped over his shoulders, bracing himself on the thin aluminum rungs used to chain the boxes together. As he reached the sixth and highest container, the Mercedes began to move from the force of the Volvo behind it, and there was no time to waste. If the Volvo succeeded in clearing the path, the terrorists would have won, fleeing with their documents. At that point, reinforcements would be useless, and there would be no way to stop the terrorist plot.

As he reached the top of the wall, Aaron removed the assault rifles, both of which had full magazines, crawled to the edge of the container and let loose a thunderstorm of lead, instantly shattering the windshield and the roof of the cab of the Volvo. He then focused on the men jumping from the rear of the Mercedes and those trying to flee from the back of the Volvo, rendering their efforts to escape futile. The instant the magazine of the first Kalashnikov was empty Aaron set down the rifle, grabbed the other and poured more hot lead on the enemy, this time strafing the third vehicle, a Citroen.

The muzzle flashes of his weapon had betrayed his location, and he began taking fire. Showering the narrow canyon below him with the remaining bullets in the magazine of the second AK-47, he slid back away from the edge of the top container and began to make a run for it. Leaping across a five-foot-wide gap to the stack of containers behind him, he heard first one, then two, then three metallic clunks on the container he had just vacated, and dove to the platform, his stomach, palms, pelvis and cheek pressed as hard to the metal as he could in a desperate effort to stabilize and shelter himself. The three grenades exploded a couple of meters behind him on the container he had just jumped from, shrapnel exploding upward and over his prone position, the concussion lifting him off the surface of the container. Stunned for a moment, he willed himself to his feet and jumped to the container immediately south of him. He rolled onto his back, reached into his belt and loaded his last magazine into one of the AK-47s, discarding the other. *Make each round count,* he told himself.

Rolling onto his belly and low-crawling to the edge of the container, Aaron surveyed the scene below him. The passage was blocked and chaotic, with men responding to contradictory orders in Arabic that seemed to be coming from more than one direction. Some of them were trying to get inside the cabs of the trucks to drive them out of the canyon, while others sought cover. Either way, they offered easy targets, and firing in a single-shot mode, he began picking them off. He fully expected that within a couple of minutes, the enemy would be climbing the containers to fire on his position from the same height as his perch and lobbing more grenades on top of him from their positions on the ground, so he wasn't surprised when the counterattack began.

At this point, he had no real plan other than to pull back and fight a delaying action as long as he could, which he did, leaping from one container to another, until he reached the southernmost stack, which was only five containers high. He vaulted across the five-foot-wide divide to the container below, slipping on the wet surface and landing hard on his left hip and elbow. He struggled to his knees, cursing and strapping the Kalashnikov on his shoulder at the same time. Then, as he descended on the narrow rungs, he lost his footing with three meters to go and landed hard on his right ankle as he hit the slippery ground.

It wasn't easy for Martin to hold himself back from the mission, and the difficulty he was experiencing was painfully obvious to First Sergeant Trippe. The Turk First Commando crew, their outboard motor working fine, had already portaged over the breakwater. They turned off the motor when they reached the outer edge of the giant stone wall, paddling quietly once inside the harbor, making their way noiselessly toward the gun emplacements set up by the terrorists on the northern perimeter of the port. A few minutes later, Lieutenant Colonel Bulicet cut in from his Black Hawk. "Colonel Korda, my men have neutralized the machine gun emplacement in the New Port Harbor. They worked silently with knives, but the Iraqis will suspect that something's wrong when they try to reach them on the radio and get no response. What's your squad's status?"

"The wind and currents have carried them south. They've managed to paddle far enough west and they are now in the surf, heading toward the breakwater. We're circling twelve hundred meters due west of them, but we're going to loop around and hover near the grain elevator to provide supporting fire if our visuals improve."

"Roger that. We will move our helo north of the New Port Harbor, near the marshes. On your command, we will move in with supporting fire if someone on the ground can direct us to the enemy and away from friendlies."

"Fauad," Mohammed shouted, "we are being attacked from the south near the intersection. The first three trucks in the convoy have been disabled. The road is blocked. Several of the men have been killed. Many wounded. I have ordered the enemy position to be flanked, but we don't know how many there are. I will stay, but you have to get out of here. Please." Two soldiers, assistants to Mohammed, stood within earshot, not daring to speak.

Fauad hesitated for a moment, unwilling to believe that his plans might be unraveling. A bull of a man with a burgeoning ego, his instinct was to order his men to plow at all costs through the barricade now blocking his exit and make their escape, and to shoot any coward in their ranks that refused. "Kill the attackers. The vehicles must be cleared from the road. Push them out of the way. Do whatever you must do to make our escape. Consolidate the most important records and burn the rest. Move now. *Now!*" he ordered. Mohammed and the two other men ran from the container that served as his and Fauad's quarters, shouting orders to the men, rallying them to attack. Fauad grabbed his jacket and hat and raced from the container toward the intersection. He would personally take charge.

Spider Three reached the airspace over the grain elevator at the very moment that Aaron had fired on the vehicle leading the convoy of departing terrorists. Through Pamela Toll's FLIR screen, she saw the thermal flashes of the muzzles of the Kalashnikov and, seconds later, the burning trucks. Then she and Kopinsky saw three distinct flashes on the screen. "Grenades exploding near the intersection," Kopinsky shouted excitedly, getting the immediate attention of Martin, Krissi and First Sergeant Trippe, all of whom were peering out the open side doors of the chopper, searching for signs of movement through their NVGs.

"Aaron's engaging the terrorists," Martin shouted, his voice filled with alarm, knowing that the Deltas and First Commandos would need seven to ten minutes to reach the Central Pier and attack. "Pam, crew chiefs, can you acquire any targets?"

"Negative. Not without risking shooting your brother. We're picking up some thermal images on the FLIR screen, but we can't engage with precision."

"We've got to go down," Krissi said as she looked for the hook to which the insertion ropes would be attached.

"I can't get you down close enough in this soup," Lieutenant Toll shouted into her headset. "I have no idea where the high-tension wires are."

"Then put us down on the roof of the grain elevator," Martin said. "You'll be above the wires."

"Are you out of your mind? With all due respect, sir, that's crazy," Lieutenant Toll argued. "You can't fast-rope onto a surface that small in these winds. You'll be blown off course on the way down and miss the roof. Sir, the Zodiac crew will be there in minutes."

"No. Aaron can't hold that long," Krissi screamed above the rotors, the wind and the rain.

Martin saw First Sergeant Trippe reach for the fast-rope to attach it. "Top, Pam is right. It's too dangerous. It's personal for me and Krissi, but you don't have to do this."

"Like hell I don't, sir," Trippe responded. "The way I see it is that we have a Ranger on the ground. A

Ranger on the ground! Even if he weren't your brother, you and I'd still insert. Now, let's get on with it."

"Okay. Lieutenant, hold this bird over the grain elevator as best you can. I'll drop an infrared marker on the roof and we'll aim for it. Krissi will follow me on my rope." Trippe pursed his lips and nodded. "Krissi, you clear with that?"

"Yes, let's go," Krissi said, her voice cracking with emotion.

"Roger that," Pamela Toll said.

Using the GPS on the instrument panel, Toll coached the helo in closer to where she thought the center of the grain elevator should be. Kopinsky flipped a toggle switch, and a powerful floodlight, used mostly for search-and-rescue missions, briefly lit up the night sky. Those on the ground who noticed mistook the three-second flash for lightning. "We're dead on. We're two hundred feet directly over the elevator," Martin said calmly, his years of experience paying off, his nerves steel.

"Good. Drop the marker when I give the word," Lieutenant Toll said with equal self-assuredness. "You've got sixty feet of rope."

"We're at one hundred and fifty feet above the building. One hundred twenty, nine-oh, six-oh, five-oh," Kopinsky sounded off as they descended.

"IFR marker away," Trippe announced as he dropped it out the side door. Through his NVGs, he watched it fall into the rain and darkness. "Bull's-eye. It's on the roof. But watch out. It's on the edge, not in the center."

"Ropes down," Trippe shouted. Dropping the three-inch-thick lines, they were both amazed by the amount of sway in the heavy rope flapping in the gusting wind. "Ropers away!" Trippe shouted again, and he and Martin disappeared out the side doors.

As he descended, Martin's eyes were fixed on the roof, focusing a few feet to the side of the IFR marker. He had never jumped in winds this strong. He flew to the side wildly, almost colliding with Trippe on the other rope. The powerful gusts rocked the Black Hawk above them, the movement transferring to the heavy coils that supported them.

When Martin reached a point just a few feet from the surface of the grain elevator, a sudden gust swung him out over the side of the structure, forcing him to hang on with all his strength until the line swung back above the building. His legs were below the edge of the parapet, and his knees hit the concrete hard as the rope pulled him back to the building, propelling him onto the tar and gravel roof. His knees throbbed from the collision, but he was otherwise safe. Trippe was not so lucky. He, too, swung wildly on the rope, but he slammed into the side of the silo with only his head and shoulders clearing the edge of the roof. The impact caused him to lose his grip on the rope and he disappeared out of view, falling six stories to the ground below.

Krissi was already on her way down, and because she weighed less than the men, the movement of the rope was even more tumultuous in the heavy winds. As she approached the roof, she, too, swung out over the edge and almost lost her hold, but she saved herself from slamming into the wall and possibly falling by raising her legs at the last moment. As it was, her shins clipped the cornice and she was sent tumbling across the roof; her roll stopped when her carbine caught between her and the surface, cracking two of her ribs.

Martin rushed to her. "Are you okay?" he shouted.

"Ja," she answered tentatively, belying the pain of two cracked ribs. She heard gunfire on the ground near the intersection and forced herself to action. Aaron was alone down there, and she had no time to waste nursing the pain in her side. As she struggled to stand, Martin extended his hand, which she took gratefully, and looked around for the first time. In an instant, her expression went from puzzled to horrified.

"Trippe didn't make it onto the roof," Martin explained to Krissi and Lieutenant Toll, who was listening in on her headset. "Pam, did you hear me? Top fell off the roof. We need a medic down here immediately once the men on the raft get on the pier. You direct them in," he ordered, already making his way to the entrance to the staircase, not allowing himself to feel the grief of the near certain loss of his good friend or the gripping fear that he was about to lose his brother, too.

"What happened?" Krissi blurted out.

"He hit the side of the building and couldn't hold on," Martin said in a hurried tone. "Let's go." He turned and ran to the door leading to the staircase, with Krissi on his heels. Once inside, Martin flipped up his NVGs, strapped his carbine/grenade launcher over his shoulder and removed his .45 automatic. It was equipped with a tactical light, which he turned on and then began descending the steps, holding the powerful weapon with two hands, ready to shoot on sight. In less than a minute, they reached the three Georgians, two dead, one still unconscious. Both she and Martin noticed immediately that two of the Georgians were without weapons and realized that Aaron had appropriated them for the fight now unfolding outside. Martin's TAC light shone briefly on Krissi's carbine. "Let me see your rifle," he said evenly. "The barrel's bent . . . from the fall. You can't use it."

Krissi, too, looked at the weapon. There was no mistake; the carbine was out of commission. She picked up the one remaining Kalashnikov. There was one magazine in place. She searched, but there were no extra ammo magazines. She strapped the AK-47 over her shoulder.

They raced down the remaining stairs, reaching the ground floor and finding the door open. Through his NVGs, Martin searched for Trippe and quickly found him. Trippe's body straddled the side of an empty Dumpster, his back bent at an angle that left no doubt that he had died a soldier's perfect death, in combat and without prolonged pain.

Now operating on raw adrenaline, Krissi broke into a

sprint, the Beretta she had traded with Aaron in her hand, safety off, trying but not fully succeeding to suppress the pain in her side as she ran.

Seventy-five meters away, Aaron had emptied the Kalashnikov and was husbanding the last few bullets of the Glock. His ankle was too swollen to run, and he knew that he could not hobble fast enough to escape his pursuers. He had made up his mind that he would hold until he ran out of ammunition, and then take down as many of the enemy as he could with his knife, for as long as he could. The enemy distinguished the sound of the handgun from the assault rifle he had been using and was emboldened by the fact that he had run out of ammunition for the more powerful weapon. From a sheath attached to his calf, he removed the razor-sharp dagger he had purchased in Germany. He was determined to put it to good use.

Krissi had her NVGs upward and out of the way, preferring to let her eyes become accustomed to the relative darkness and to have a wider field of vision. She stumbled in the darkness and fell forward, cutting her elbows and knees, but expertly protecting her shooting hand and handgun as she rolled on the ground. A flare fired by an Iraqi arched into the air and lit the sky above the battleground. She saw Aaron in the harsh white light, crouched behind a container, his back against a large forklift, his flanks exposed. She saw the glint of a knife in his hands and understood perfectly that he was fighting for his life as never before. Oblivious to her cracked ribs, she bounded forward, instantly in a full sprint, aided by the enemy flare as she stepped over debris on the ground.

Krissi was not the only witness to Aaron's predicament. An Iraqi soldier made his way slowly around the outer containers, away from the now flaming vehicles that were blocking the passageway. Aaron spotted him and shot him from less than ten meters away. Two more Iraqis charged forward on orders shouted from the rear of the stalled convoy. Aaron saw them coming and dropped them using the last of his ammunition. He got to his feet, tossing his empty 9 mm to the ground, and inched forward to get to the weapons of the enemies he had just killed. Before he could reach the enemies' assault rifles, another soldier rounded the container, lunging straight for Aaron, who defended himself with nothing but his knife. Krissi, now less than forty meters away and closing, took aim on the run and fired three times, striking the soldier in the back twice before Aaron could reach him. Another attacker jumped from the safety of a container behind Aaron. Krissi saw him just in time to send him to Allah with two shots, one in the chest and another in his throat. "Aaron, get down," she called out.

Aaron turned toward her as she appeared out of the darkness, running at him at full speed through the rain, popping off rounds from her Beretta and reloading a magazine on the run with amazing speed. He could hardly believe his eyes. He did as she commanded and dropped to the ground, prone, as she fired over him at yet more attackers.

Initially caught off guard by a second shooter, the Iraqis quickly regrouped, led personally by Fauad Al-Metar, who had grabbed an assault rifle and was rallying his men from behind. Several ventured forward, reaching the protection of a stack of containers closer to Aaron's position.

When Krissi called out to Aaron, she became a target for the enemy. She was fully exposed at that moment, running very fast across an open expanse of gravel, ignoring the puddles as she raced to save her lover. She heard a dull thump and dropped to her belly, landing in a six-inch-deep puddle an instant before Martin's grenade flew over her and exploded in the narrow passageway between stacks of containers where the terrorists had taken refuge. The enemy had no time to react. The grenade flashed in the five-foot-wide crevice, sending body parts flying through the air.

Martin ran forward, loading another grenade into the

M203 launcher attached to the underside of his carbine and fired again, this time in the direction of the rear of the stalled convoy, hoping to disrupt or kill anyone commanding the attack. Even as the 40 mm grenade was tumbling through the air, he was removing another from his belt and reloading. *Thump. Thump.* Two rounds exploded off the stacked containers, raining down shrapnel on the enemy, killing and maiming many of them, forcing those who could to retreat toward Buildings 13 and 11.

Fauad was among those who retreated. He understood that his fortunes had just turned, that instead of preserving his documents for posterity he needed to destroy them. He removed a grenade from the pocket of his peacoat and lobbed it at the first truck. The grenade landed underneath the vehicle and exploded, igniting the gas tank. A huge fireball shot into the air, rising above the narrow space between the stacks of containers. Two Georgians were sprayed with the burning diesel fuel and tried desperately to extinguish themselves by rolling in the deep puddles of water. Ignoring their screams, Fauad reached into his other pocket, pulled the pin of another grenade and set the second truck ablaze, this time killing the two Georgians instantly. Fauad had accomplished what he sought to do. Two of the trucks were on fire, along with the evidence they carried.

"Mohammed," Fauad shouted. "Destroy the other trucks. Burn all the documents, then send three of your men to the Italians' boat." Mohammed understood that this meant that the explosives had to be removed from the vessel, which also meant that he would have to kill the Italians, who would see his men removing the bricks of C4 meant to sink their vessel.

TWENTY-EIGHT

The Deltas paddled hard to the south, in the same direction as the current and winds, the seven-meter-high breakwater two hundred meters to their left. Although they wore night-vision goggles, they could hear the roar of the waves pounding the two-ton rocks better than they could see the ominous stone barrier. As the waves lifted them, pushing them closer and closer to the deadly wall, they struggled to get farther south, behind the shoals, where the force of the waves would be cut in half by the low-lying rocks and the shallow sands between the shoals and the breakwater.

Finally, they cleared the shoals, the waves crashing against the breakwater now only one meter high. "Paddle west. We don't want to drift further south," Staff Sergeant Gonzales shouted into his mouthpiece. "Forward, move aft. Rear paddlers, maintain your position," he ordered as they neared the breakwater. The three Deltas in front of the Zodiac shifted aft and the bow of the tiny raft rose, allowing it to surf the waves without capsizing forward. When they were thirty meters from the breakwater, Gonzales told the men to store all paddles and prepare to debark. Upon his instruction, all six men rolled themselves over the sides of the Zodiac and into the cold water, keeping their feet out in front of them to protect themselves against any hidden rocks as the surf pushed them toward the barrier. Ten meters from the huge boulders that formed the breakwater, they stood on Gonzales's command in the chest-deep water, hoisted the Zodiac to their shoulders, and waded to the base of the breakwater, where they began their ascent, taking care not to slip on the lichen-covered rocks.

The Delta operators reached the top of the breakwater, surprised to find that it was paved, smooth enough for a vehicle to move slowly along the surface. The descent was more difficult, forcing them to pick their way down, each searching for a firm step, each slipping at least twice before they reached the base, bruising hips, knees and elbows along the way.

Finally, the Deltas were inside the harbor. The surface was calm, as expected. They silently eased the Zodiac into the water and boarded, paddling rapidly toward what remained of Building 15, where Aaron and his companions had wreaked havoc only four weeks earlier. With their NVGs, the Deltas easily saw the *Roman Goddess* tied to the pier next to Building 13 and the heavily armed men patrolling her deck. "What's your position?" Gonzales whispered to his Turkish counterparts through his headset.

"We have taken out the machine guns guarding the sea channel. We're in the New Port Harbor, soon to come to the Northern Pier and then back into the channel," Naim Sukur responded with difficulty, in heavily accented English. "We are going as fast as we can. There is gunfire from the shore."

"We hear it, too," Gonzales whispered, hoping he had understood correctly what the Turk had said. "But listen, there's a freighter moored to the Central Pier. . . . About two hundred meters from our position. When you come around the Northern Pier, you'll be directly in front of it. . . . About three hundred meters north of it. In this darkness . . ." Gonzales was stopped midsentence by the Iraqi-fired flare that exploded above the intersection, the same flare that had permitted Krissi to see Aaron, partially illuminating the Northern and Southern Harbors, including the *Roman Goddess*. Two Italian drug runners manning the bow of the ship spotted the Turkish Zodiac racing across the Northern Harbor toward the Interior Basin. There was a pause while the danger registered, but they recovered quickly and began firing their Uzis at the rubber raft at the same time the First Commandos began strafing the front of the boat.

On the starboard side of the *Roman Goddess,* sailors hurriedly began to cast off to escape the shooting a few hundred meters to the east and make for the open seas. When the flare burst in the sky, crew on the aft deck saw the Deltas south of them paddling toward the piers and went for their weapons, but not quickly enough to escape their fate. While four Deltas in the tiny Zodiac kept paddling, the other two operators opened fire with a combination of grenades and the powerful Squad Automatic Weapon, killing two on the *Roman Goddess,* wounding others and sending the rest center deck.

"Spider Three. This is Gonzales. All hell is breaking loose down here. Request backup on the vessel at the end of the Central Pier. We're continuing to the shore. The freighter's all yours."

"Roger that," Lieutenant Toll responded immediately, jinking left and down. Shocked and angered by the death of First Sergeant Trippe, she was also frustrated with her inability to provide backup for Lieutenant Colonel Korda on the ground. In the darkness and rain, and the close quarters of the fighting among the containers, the risk of friendly fire was too great, and like the side gunners, she felt helpless. Now Pam Toll had a target, and she would vent her full fury on the moored vessel, a veritable sitting duck.

As the Deltas in the Zodiac rounded the south side of the Central Pier and neared the point of embarkation next to what used to be Building 15, Spider Three swept in from the south, two hundred meters above the water, strafing the *Roman Goddess* from stern to bow with its Gatling guns, killing everyone on deck as well as those in the wheelhouse and chart room, whose thin ceilings were easily penetrated by the 7.62 mm bullets. Several of the bullets found their way down open cargo holds and ignited the C4 plastic explosives that the Iraqis had secreted onboard. Suddenly, the fifty-meter-long freighter catapulted into the air, breaking free of its mooring lines, splitting in two amidships in a ball of fire that rose one hundred meters, buffeting the Black Hawk with shock waves and a wall of heat. The blast flattened Building 13 at the tip of the Central Pier, bending its steel posts and girders eastward and fragmenting its sheet metal siding, shooting thousands of razorlike shards in the opposite direction. The Georgians and Iraqis inside the structure never knew what happened to them.

As Lieutenant Toll was getting the go-ahead to strafe the *Roman Goddess,* six First Commandos were silently climbing onto the pier next to Building 11, fanning out as planned to surround the enemy. The explosion of the vessel provided unexpected but appreciated cover. Colonel Bulicet's orders were to take prisoners to the extent possible. He wanted prisoners and documents, evidence that would shed light on which pharmaceutical companies had been compromised and which medications poisoned. Dead men were of no use for this purpose.

There were two visible means of entering the three-story building on the wharf side: double cargo doors with a conveyor belt leading to the edge of the pier, and a door used for personnel rather than cargo that had been left open, now noisily smacking against the door frame in the wind. On signal, two commandos, weapons at the ready, rushed that door while another belly-crawled through the cargo opening, reaching a loaded pallet and crouching behind it. Outside, two First Commandos circled to the west of the warehouse while another flanked east. Moments before, men who had been loading the trucks in the lot in front of the building began to run back in, frantically trying to escape Martin's grenades in the intersection. When the *Roman Goddess* explosion blew out windows in Building 11, the concussion stunned them. Slowly, the men realized that they were being attacked from both the east and the west, and began to regroup. Several, bleeding from shrapnel and glass wounds, limped back into Building 11 with the help of their comrades.

The explosion of the *Roman Goddess* threw Fauad facedown to the ground, where he lay on the gravel and in the mud, pelted by the continuing downpour, his ears ringing, his vision temporarily blurred. Ignoring the pain, he pushed himself up and rose to his hands and knees. Mohammed ran to his aid, helping him to his feet. "Some of the men are running away. Rally them. Do not let them flee. They must destroy the documents," Fauad ordered, shaking his head in an effort to clear it. "Go!" he yelled, sensing his comrade's hesitancy. "I'm okay. I have grenades in the office. Destroy the trucks! Burn everything!"

Moments later, Mohammed and Fauad sprinted from the container that served as their office to the trucks, their pockets stuffed with grenades. The first three trucks were now ablaze, their contents rapidly being consumed by the flames. Slowing down slightly, they tossed their grenades underneath two intact vehicles left idling in front of Building 11, their occupants having fled into the warehouse. The two vehicles went up in flames. Seeing the activity to the rear of the building confirmed that his men were running away, trying to flee to the railroad tracks along the Interior Basin and from there east toward the city of Poti. He had anticipated the cowardice of some of them, but to see so many in retreat disgusted him. "We must stop the cowards," Fauad said angrily to Mohammed. "Get them back here to fight the infidels. We have a superior force and Allah will protect us."

Naim Sukur had served as the coxswain of the First Commando Zodiac and was now in charge of the ground assault. For him, the assignment was very personal. Four weeks earlier, he, Lieutenant Hasan, Staff Sergeant Ciller and Aaron had destroyed Building 15. Since then, the terrorists had tortured and killed his Turkish comrades and Ciller's family and now stood ready to kill Aaron, if they had not already done so. Although he was under orders to take prisoners, he was in no such mood. "They're moving toward the basin, coming your way through the warehouse," he whispered into his mouthpiece from outside the open cargo doors of Building 11 to three fellow commandos, well hidden behind stacked pallets in the rear of the structure. "Here they come," he said, stepping into the wide-open space and spraying with his submachine gun in the direction of those fleeing toward the back of the building. Two commandos who had circled outside Building 11 from the other side followed his lead. Inside, three commandos had positioned themselves to ambush the fleeing Iraqis and Georgians, and began picking them off with skillfully placed shots to the lower legs, enough to disable but not to kill them. Outside, Naim crouched, his short, powerful frame low to the ground, his eyes searching for the leader in the light of the burning trucks, hoping to find the one he was looking for.

Gonzales was the last to climb up the wooden ladder affixed to the pier, careful to fasten the Zodiac to the bottom rung. He was halfway up when the explosion onboard the *Roman Goddess* knocked him back into the water. Crocker, Ryle and Galante were already twenty meters inland, crouching behind a large stack of Sheetrock. The blast jolted but did not injure them. Metz and Shafter, who were closer to the explosion, were not so fortunate. Metz took multiple shrapnel wounds to the back, shoulder and neck and fell forward, convulsing for a few seconds before he died on the wet gravel and mud. Shafter, too, was hit several times, his left arm nearly severed at the elbow. The concussion brought him to his knees, the pain in his arm excruciating. Crocker and Ryle maintained their positions to keep guard while Galante ran back to help Shafter, immediately pulling off his bandana and tying it around the wounded Delta's arm as a tourniquet. Gonzales was soon back on the ladder, scrambling onto the wharf. He checked Metz for vital signs and found none. He turned to Shafter and began administering to his wounds. "Go on without us," Gonzales said to Galante. "Colonel Korda, can you hear me?" Gonzales said into his mouthpiece.

"Loud and clear. I need you to take the north side of the intersection and stop the terrorists from destroying the rest of the trucks. Move now!"

"Metz is dead. Shafter's badly wounded. I have to stay here on the pier to help him. Crocker, Ryle and Galante are on the way," he said, knowing the three were also listening through their earpieces.

Crocker, Galante and Ryle acknowledged the command, eager to go. Each man carefully stepped over scattered construction material and molten-hot shards of twisted metal debris from the explosion, and without hesitating, raced toward the center of the battle.

Krissi crawled toward Aaron, slowly narrowing the distance between them, dropping to a prone position each time she heard the thump of Martin's grenade launcher. Aaron belly-crawled to her, also flattening himself on the gravel with each discharge of the M203. After the third round was fired and the surviving enemy ranks were seen retreating up the road, Krissi's and Aaron's hands reached out and touched, but just barely. They inched their way closer to one another, ignoring the deep puddles, and finally struggled to their knees, their eyes fixed on each other's, not knowing if they would live through the night, but spirits elevated upon discovering that the other was, for the most part, uninjured. The look in his eyes told her how much he loved her, that any betrayal or deceit was a thing of the past. The look in hers told him that she had never stopped loving him and that she never would betray him again. She removed the Kalashnikov and handed it to Aaron. Together, they crawled back to the spot between the container and the forklift where he had taken his stand moments before. Before they could utter a word to each other, Martin appeared, seemingly out of nowhere.

"What took you so long?" Aaron whispered, the beginnings of a grin forming on his lips.

"Good to see you, too," Martin whispered back. "What's your situation?"

"My ankle's sprained, but I can move. Krissi and I will follow you."

"Okay, but we can't go up the road. Even if we can get past the heat of the burning trucks, they'll pick us off. They'll expect us to flank to their left. Let's cross the road and circle to their right. We can hook up with three of my men flanking from the west." He paused for a moment. "Crocker, Ryle, Galante. Do you copy?" he asked, speaking into his mouthpiece.

"Copy five-by-five. You're loud and clear."

"Are you in touch with the Turks?"

"Yes, sir. But only one of them speaks English, and his accent is hard to follow."

"I'm going to give my brother my helmet and headset. He's fluent in Turkish. He'll coordinate from here on," Martin instructed. Aaron was crouched on one knee next to Martin and heard what he had said. He reached out for the helmet as Martin took it off.

"This is Aaron Korda," he said immediately in Turkish. "What is your position?"

"Aaron, this is Naim. Allah has kept you alive. Are you okay?"

"I'm fine. Where are you?"

"I'm on the ground, with five others in and around Building eleven. We've wounded several men and are taking them prisoners. Most of them are Georgians, but there are at least three Arabs. I'm outside at the southwest corner of the building. Your grenades have pushed a group of them back up the road, and they are now heading my way. Where are the Deltas?"

Aaron translated the question into English and Crocker reported his, Galante's and Ryle's location. Aaron continued. "We have two Deltas down and one medic tending to them. Three others are near Building 15 and proceeding in your direction. They're meeting heavy resistance, but advancing. We have the enemy in a three-way pincer. We'll push them your way. Hold your position. And Naim?"

"Yes."

"I know how you feel, but we need prisoners. . . . Especially the leaders. Even if you find the bastard who we think killed Hasan and Yusuf, please don't kill him unless you absolutely have to. I mean that. We need to take him alive. With the documents on fire, we need to get as much information as we can out of the survivors, so we can undo their plans. Do you copy?"

"Yes, sir. I copy," Master Sergeant Sukur responded, understanding Aaron's directive and the reasons behind it, and hoping he could control himself long enough to comply.

"We can't proceed up the road. It's too narrow and the heat from the burning trucks is too intense. We're flanking through the stacks of containers south of the road. Make sure you tell your men not to fire on us."

"Roger."

Fauad and Mohammed rallied several of the Iraqis and Georgians in a space formed by a Dumpster and the treads of a large Komatzu bulldozer. Having gathered weapons from their fallen cohorts, each carried at least two major weapons, assault rifles or machine guns, and a sidearm. "Destroy the last two trucks with your grenades. Aim for the gas tanks," Fauad instructed his soldiers. Three of them ran forward from behind the safety offered by the thick treads of the bulldozer and were immediately detected by Naim and the other two Turks outside Building 11. It was dark and a heavy rain continued, but they were visible in the light from the burning trucks. They were not easy targets as they darted from the Komatzu to the protection of containers and pallets stacked on the area near Building 11. The Turks moved forward silently, tracking them in their sights, anticipating their attack on the two trucks in the lot in front of Building 11, and waiting for an opening.

Several of the enemy ran from behind the containers toward the vehicles, grenades in hand. Naim and his comrades began spraying the ground at knee and ankle height, trying to disable and stop them but not to kill them. Despite wounds to his lower legs, one Iraqi managed to toss his grenade at one of the vehicles. The incendiary device landed below the cab of the truck and exploded less than a meter from the forty-gallon gas tank that was filled to capacity. Naim and his fellow First Commandos saw the grenade bounce on the gravel and roll under the truck, and immediately dropped to their bellies as the thrust of the explosion whooshed over them.

In the light of the explosion, Naim caught a glimpse of Fauad behind the high treads of the Komatzu. There was no mistaking him. He was tall, broad shouldered, wearing a peacoat and a Greek seaman's cap. "The leaders are behind a very big bulldozer, maybe fifty meters southwest of Building 11's lot," he reported excitedly into his microphone. Aaron heard him and translated the message to Crocker and the other Deltas.

"Delta Force, do you have any stun grenades?" Aaron asked.

"Yes," Crocker responded immediately.

"Take their stronghold. You must take the leaders alive!"

"Roger that," Crocker answered. "Okay, we've taken two prisoners. Galante will stay with them. Ryle and I will attack. Watch where you're shooting." Galante nodded at Crocker and handed him one of his two flashbang grenades. Both Crocker and Ryle were armed with carbines/grenade launchers. They each removed the fragmentation grenades already chambered in their launchers and replaced them with stun grenades, and ran forward into the night, spraying the battlefield in front of them with their carbines to suppress enemy fire but still taking rounds as they advanced. When they reached an open spot with the bulldozer in view, Crocker let loose his grenade. It landed behind the Komatzu on the opposite side of Fauad's position. The blast was enough to knock Fauad, Mohammed and the three other men near the bulldozer to the ground, but the main impact of the explosion was deflected by the thick steel base of the heavy machinery. Ryle's grenade landed inside the Dumpster, the force of the blast deflected upward but still helping to disorient the cluster of Iraqis huddled nearby.

"Mohammed, take these two men," Fauad ordered, grabbing two Iraqis by the shoulders. "Attack the infidels. You must stop them. Go with God," he said emphatically, pointing in the direction from which Crocker and Ryle were firing. "I will destroy the trucks myself. We will die martyrs. God is great!"

"Yes, Fauad. We shall see each other in paradise. *Allah Akbar!*" Mohammed repeated several times, replacing his magazine with a fully loaded banana clip and motioning to the other two Iraqis that they should follow him. The men were, however, far less enthusiastic about Fauad's instructions than Mohammed was, and stood fast, refusing to move. Without a word, Fauad took a pistol from his belt and pointed it at the head of the man on the left, took aim and fired. The second man needed no further convincing and took off with Mohammed a second after the first man's lifeless body hit the ground.

Ryle and Crocker, positioned behind a cement mixer, looked at each other in amazement at what appeared to be two armed men running at them in the open. Their training had taught them to kill the enemy. Their instructions on this mission told them otherwise. Disciplined like no other troops in the army, they controlled their impulses and aimed for the attackers' legs, immediately dropping both of them.

Mohammed had taken two rounds from Ryle's carbine, but not before emptying his entire magazine as he ran. One of Ryle's bullets splintered Mohammed's left tibia, spraying tiny bone and lead fragments up and down what remained of his left leg and groin. Despite the pain, Mohammed managed to remove his last grenade from his web gear. He lifted himself up into a sitting position, pulled the pin, pressed the grenade tightly to his chest and then climbed on top of his comrade. Two seconds later, the explosion splattered blood and body parts in every direction.

Martin led the way through the maze of containers to the east of where the trucks burned, his carbine ready for action, the confined space rendering his grenade launcher useless. Aaron followed, clutching his assault rifle, limping on his swollen ankle. Krissi brought up the rear, holstering her 9 mm automatic and picking an AK-47 from a fallen Iraqi, pocketing two extra magazines for good measure.

Martin saw him first, but within a split second Naim Sukur and two other First Commandos, and Sergeant Ryle, spotted Fauad, too, kneeling next to the giant bulldozer with two other men. Shocked by the suddenness of the attack as he was preparing to leave Poti, but now inspired by Mohammed's act of bravery, he, too, was prepared to take his own life, confident that he had succeeded in killing hundreds of thousands of infidels and that he would find his rewards in paradise. The eyes of the two Iraqi foot soldiers huddled with him next to the bulldozer went wide with horror as he turned his automatic toward them and shot each in the forehead, the impact flinging their lifeless bodies backward into a deep pool of rainwater. Aaron raised his rifle at the same time that the three Turks and Martin began to train their weapons on Fauad. "We want him alive," Aaron roared out in Turkish. "Don't kill him," he yelled in English as the crack of Aaron's Kalashnikov resonated. The others watched in amazement as the terrorist's right hand, still gripping the 9 mm automatic, flew into the darkness, landing in the puddle where he knelt. He was staring at the stump that was now his wrist.

Naim sprang forward, his short legs moving with surprising speed, his long muscular arms swaying as he ran. In one hand he carried his assault rifle and in the other his commando dagger. Ryle also sprinted toward the fallen Iraqi, as did Martin. Aaron ran as fast as his damaged leg would allow, but he was no match for the others. Krissi ran alongside him, supporting him with her left arm, her right gripping her weapon, her eyes scanning this way and that for the signs of the enemy, not knowing that between Crocker and Ryle and the Turks inside Building 11, those terrorists and drug traffickers still alive had been taken prisoner.

Aaron saw the glint of Naim's dagger in the light from the burning trucks and yelled to him once again in Turkish to not kill the terrorist. For a moment, Aaron considered shooting Naim, but couldn't bring himself to do it and did not want to start a firefight with the other Turk commandos. Martin and Lester Ryle sprinted with all their speed to beat Naim to the wounded Iraqi, who was now fumbling with his left hand to remove a grenade from the pocket of his peacoat, somehow managing to overcome the shock setting in from the loss of blood.

When Naim was within four meters of Fauad, he threw his assault rifle at him, butt first, to try to delay his setting off the grenade. In his right hand, Naim carried his dagger, its handle squeezed tightly in his clenched fist. He slammed his fist into Fauad's nose, breaking it, both men tumbling on top of the bodies of the two Iraqis Fauad had shot a few seconds before. Aaron saw the blade come down and yelled, but it appeared to be too late to stop Naim from slicing the murderer's throat. Martin and Staff Sergeant Ryle plowed into the two men, at the same time trying to stop Naim from killing the terrorist and attempting to prevent Fauad from detonating the grenade. As they wrestled in the blood, water, gravel and mud, Martin tried to grab Naim's arm as the sharp dagger arched toward Fauad's throat, but Naim jerked his shoulder in an evasive maneuver and the blade came down. However, instead of slicing the terrorist leader's throat, as the others had feared, Naim crammed the handle horizontally between the Iraqi's teeth and pushed hard, forcing his jaws open, preventing him from breaking the cyanide capsule in his right molar. As Naim pressed down on Fauad's mouth, Martin, who had been struggling to pull him off, realized what Naim was doing and stopped.

Meanwhile, Ryle concentrated all of his efforts on the grenade. With one knee, he landed hard on the bleeding stump that was Fauad's right hand, sending excruciating waves of pain up the Iraqi's arm, at the same time using both hands to grab Fauad's left hand, which clenched the grenade, preventing him from pulling the pin.

Aaron reached the writhing, bloody men at that point and crashed forward, striking Fauad in the head with the butt of his rifle with enough force to knock him out. The terror mastermind fell back into the pool of blood and water, his face barely above the surface, Naim still pressing the handle of his dagger in Fauad's mouth and Ryle still kneeling on the man's mangled wrist. Aaron, too, collapsed to the ground, landing in a splash next to the body of an Iraqi foot soldier.

Martin stared at his enemy, momentarily stunned by the ferocity of the fight. He turned to Aaron to see if he was injured, and watched as Aaron tried to struggle to his feet, stumbled and then fell to one knee. Martin and Krissi rushed to Aaron's side and helped him into a standing position, his arms around their shoulders, his weight on his good leg. "Put out the fires," Aaron shouted frantically in English and in Turkish. "Find fire extinguishers and save the documents. . . . We've got to know what drugs have been poisoned."

Crocker and Gonzales, who at Shafter's urging had left him back at the pier, grabbed twenty-liter plastic buckets strewn around the construction area near Building 15 and immediately began scooping up water from the deep puddles and throwing it into the rear of the burning vehicles, dousing the flaming wooden crates that carried the documents. Two of the First Commandos jumped into the rear of one of the burning trucks and began throwing the heavy crates off the back of the trailer, despite the danger to themselves. After a few minutes, everyone realized that their efforts were unnecessary. The fires had burned away the tarps that had covered the cargo, and the rain, which continued in a downpour, was doing their job for them. While some of the crates had burned through, their contents destroyed, others were only charred on the outside, the documents intact. Gonzales shouted, "Most of the documents are okay, but let's get them out of the rain."

Aaron looked at Krissi and Martin and then at Naim and Lester Ryle, who continued to pin Fauad to the ground. "Did we stop them?" he asked tentatively, his lips trembling, his physical and emotional exhaustion too much to contain, but still wanting to know. "Did we get through to Washington in time?"

"They know, Aaron. They know," Martin answered, he, too, shaken. "Once we put what you and Krissi discovered together with what Delta Force was doing—I'll explain that later—it was clear that the Iraqis were planning to sabotage our pharmaceutical supplies, and that they were getting very close."

"Thank God," Aaron said as he lost his balance and collapsed to the ground. Martin and Krissi eased him into a sitting position, grabbing a sturdy crate for back support. Krissi knelt next to him and loosened the laces of his shoe. Aaron winced as she tried to remove it, the three of them simultaneously coming to the conclusion that he had been limping on a broken ankle. "I need to know what happened," Aaron pleaded, not prepared to hear the worst but expecting it.

Martin continued to explain. "Colonel Whitman, Delta Force commander, reached me on the commo system as we were coming across the Black Sea. He said that the president had immediately gone on TV and radio to announce what was happening. . . . And warned the public to not take any medications until further notice. He specifically mentioned the drugs you and the Corleys deciphered on the list, but made it clear that others could have also been sabotaged. The whole world is on alert, Aaron, because of you and Krissi. There may be some who don't get the message in time, or those who choose to ignore it, but you saved tens of thousands . . . hundreds of thousands. Possibly more, Aaron."

"And Joey and Maggie . . . are they okay?" he asked, holding back large tears that welled in his eyes and mixed with the rain, not realizing that he had called Martin's daughter Maggie.

"They're fine, Aaron," Martin answered, understanding the full meaning of Aaron's mistake but ignoring it for the moment. "I had General Bulot call Helena to warn her. He reached her just as she was getting ready to open an ampule of albuterol that might have . . . who knows." Martin felt his own eyes fill. "Anyway, the kids are fine, Aaron. Thank you. Thank you both." He hugged Krissi, unashamed of the tears running down his face. When they separated, Krissi and then Martin knelt down next to Aaron and the three of them embraced, but only very briefly. Despite the knifelike pain that was shooting from his ankle up his leg, there was still work to do.

"We've got to go through the documents," Aaron said, his face contorted from the pain in his ankle. "We've got to know the full extent of what they've done. . . . Sick people have to get back on their meds right away."

"They are flying in a team of Arabic- and Farsi-speaking translators. They'll be here in a few hours. Our job is to secure the documents and confine the prisoners."

"I can read some Arabic," Aaron said, "but first let me interrogate that son of a bitch." He stared at Fauad a few meters away, still being restrained by Ryle, his mouth held open by Naim. "I can make him talk."

Martin looked at Krissi, who smiled and shook her head. Aaron was exhausted almost to the point of delirium and he had a fractured ankle, yet he was still willing to twist the truth out of the captured terrorist. "What do you expect?" she asked. "He *is* a Korda."

Martin put his arm around Aaron affectionately. "I'm sure you could make him talk, bro, but we're going to let others do that. You've already done more—much more—than anyone could expect. We're going to get you on a chopper as soon as we can figure out where we can land one safely, and get you to a hospital in Turkey."

Epilogue

The man known to his colleagues at Midlands Chemicals as Asher ben Soraya—Ahmed Al-Hage to his friends and family in Iraq—was arrested after successfully evading Scotland Yard and making his way by ferry and train to France, then Spain, desperately trying to work his way back to the Middle East. His cohort, Laya Razavi, also known as Fadi Bin-Numair, was found dead in her flat near Coventry, an apparent suicide. Daniel ben Malek, better known in his hometown of Tikrit as Khalid Abu-Saif, was shot dead by Romanian police as he tried to evade them after having crossed all of Western Europe using a series of false passports. Saba Heshemi, who had played the role of an Iranian Jew well enough to convince her Jewish boyfriend in Trenton, was taken into custody in Calgary by the Royal Canadian Mounted Police, while the seemingly happy couple were on their way to a ski vacation. In her purse, she carried a vial of botulinum-A-laced insulin, which she had planned to use to kill the man who loved her before she flew out of Vancouver and ultimately to safety in Yemen. Her friend Nasreen was taken to Camp X-ray in Guantanamo after being arrested in Kingston, Jamaica, on the first leg of her intended journey to Yemen.

Abdullah Taif—Javeed Ghafuri on the official payroll of Westfalen Pharma Gruppe—left Germany in the dead of night. After stopovers in Italy, Bulgaria and Egypt, he arrived in Damascus, where he was arrested by the Syrian authorities and handed over to the CIA, who immediately flew him to Guantanamo, where Fauad Al-Metar, otherwise known as Faramaz ben Sarah, was already imprisoned.

In the United States, 392 people died of botulinum-A poisoning, the majority of them women on the Pill and diabetics on insulin taken earlier in the day, before the president's television appearance. Western Europe experienced horrors of approximately the same magnitude. Fifty-three Canadians died, as did a limited number of victims throughout the Middle East, South America, and Asia, where the drugs had been transshipped. Official estimates from the CDC indicated that had the terrorist plot not been detected, more than a million people would have died worldwide, mostly in the United States, Canada and Western Europe. As a result of the actions of a handful of men and women, the loss was contained to under one thousand.

Staff Sergeant Metz was buried with full military honors in his hometown of Boise, his family told only that he died in the service of his country, but taking some comfort in their belief that his final mission had something to do with stopping the terrorists. Breaking tradition, the honor guard, seven members of Delta Force, fired off live rounds from Squad Automatic Weapons, Metz's weapon of choice.

First Sergeant Trippe was laid to rest in his family plot in a small cemetery outside Murfreesboro, Tennessee, where he was born and raised. His wife and teenage children watched as he, too, received full military honors. He was buried in his uniform with all the ribbons he had received during his eighteen and a half years in the army, including the Silver Star awarded to him posthumously for the raid on Poti. At Martin's insistence and breaking with regulations, his friend was also buried with his M4A1 carbine, fully loaded, round chambered, safety off, ready for business. The Delta Force chaplain held the services, but Martin gave the eulogy and read that portion of Walter Trippe's last will and testament that, in keeping with tradition, left enough money behind for a round of drinks in his honor at the Green Beret Parachute Club at Fort Bragg.

General Bulot was quietly honored by the Turkish Government before flying to Saudi Arabia, where he was greeted by the crown prince and two of his half-brothers, both of whom were diabetics and had come within hours of taking contaminated insulin. In the Royal Kingdom, he was greeted by the officials as a hero of the Islamic world, though no mention of his name was made in the press. After a private ceremony in the crown prince's palace near Mecca, General and Mrs. Bulot traveled to the Great Mosque, fulfilling their religious duty and a lifelong wish. Tearfully, they prayed for Kemal and thanked Allah for saving the lives of so many. Mrs. Bulot also prayed for Aaron and Krissi, that they would come with many children to visit her and the general in Turkey.

Master Sergeant Naim Sukur, Lieutenant Colonel Bulicet and the other soldiers of the Turk First Commando Brigade who participated in the raid on Poti were individually decorated, and the brigade received a unit citation, at a quiet ceremony in Kayseri presided over by the president of Turkey.

Without any fanfare or even mention of his official military record, Martin Korda was awarded the Distinguished Service Cross, the second-highest medal for valor in combat. The press was not invited and only his closest family was permitted to attend, the U.S. Government careful to not single him and his family out for retaliation by terrorists.

Shortly before Christmas, the president pinned the Presidential Medal of Freedom, the nation's highest award to a civilian, on both Aaron and Krissi in a White House ceremony kept secret to protect their identities.

Aaron Korda returned to Heller & Clarke, where he kept Cold Spring Biologics and the CIA as a client, and Prebish as his handler—after Prebish, on behalf of the CIA, apologized for having tried to neutralize him. Krissi resigned from the BND and moved in with Aaron in his new apartment on Beekman Place. She started her new job with Heller & Clarke a week later.

STAN JOHNSON is a partner in a major New York and Los Angeles law firm, where he specializes in leveraged buyouts and corporate finance. Before practicing law in France and New York, he served as a captain in the U.S. Army JAG Corps with the Second Infantry Division in Korea and then with the Fourth Infantry Division (Mech) at Fort Carson, Colorado. He is married and is the father of three (two girls and a boy). Mr. Johnson is an avid student of history and military affairs.

BESTSELLING AUTHOR
MICHAEL FARMER

TIN SOLDIERS
A Novel of the Next Gulf War
0-451-20905-2
An alliance with Iran reinvigorates the Iraqi
military. To prevent a total conquest of the region, a
U.S. Army Heavy Brigade must stand against Iraq's
greater numbers and updated
technology—while the locals are bent on
grinding the small American force into the ancient
desert sand.

IRON TIGERS
A Novel of a New World War
0-451-21262-2
In the wake of the second Gulf War, the Middle East
is in turmoil and a new communist leader in Russia
has vowed to return his country to its former power.
He's allied himself with the Saudi prince and is
poised to assert military power with a sudden act of
aggression. It's time for the tanks to roll.

S788

ALLAN TOPOL

Spy Dance

0-451-41013-0

Ex-CIA agent Greg Nielsen thought he had escaped
his shadowy past. He was wrong.
Someone has found him—and is blackmailing him to
enter the dangerous game of international espionage
once again. But there's one very deadly difference: this
time, the target is his own country.

Dark Ambition

0-451-41064-5

When womanizing Secretary of State Robert Winthrop
is murdered, Washington's top brass push for a
quick conviction of Winthrop's African-American
gardener—even though many doubt his guilt.

Also available:

Conspiracy   0-451-41107-2
Enemy of my Enemy   0-451-41172-2

**Available wherever books are sold or at
www.penguin.com**